The Valley of Lost Souls

An 18th-century tale: English nobleman Otetiani faces love, grief, and redemption on the American frontier amidst the deceits of colonization.

Mason Marlowe

Visit MarcyMichael.com for FREE advanced copies of our newest Kindle ebooks.

Again, that is MarcyMichael.com

Contents

Chapter One

There's nothing like a wanderer finding comfort by a warm hearth. I've been an outcast and adventurer since boyhood, exiled from England for supporting the Pretender, stripped of my estates, and reliant on my sword to earn my bread in a foreign land. Fate flung me across the wide Atlantic to this New World, and in just a year, I found Marjory and fortune! I quickly became as settled as any Dutch merchant between Port George and the Outward's stockade. Even though I was raised in camps and schooled in forests, I discovered a passion in the complexities of mercantile life and took pride in the small tasks of a householder. I was a model husband. But Fate wasn't ready to conclude its work. Two years of happiness I had; then the fever came, brought north by the Portuguese ships from the Main to scourge New York. In a week, my joy turned to ashes. She, who had braved the wilderness with me, wilted and died.

But there's a sense of justice in Fate. Given time, it rebuilds what it has broken, as long as we, its playthings, keep our heads up and courage unshaken—easier said than done, God knows. Truly, when Fate stepped forward to restore balance, it found me with my head bowed and spirit near breaking, treading bitterly along the monotonous path of duties I lacked the will to escape. I sat at my desk in the counting-room, fumbling through a stack of papers. A breath of spring lingered in the air, and outside on Pearl Street, the bluebirds and robins squabbled merrily, while passersby seemed equally carefree. In all of New York, it seemed, only I lacked reason for joy.

John Allen, the young Dorset bondman whose freedom I had purchased when I hired him as a clerk, whistled softly as he worked his quill across the ledgers, casting wary glances my way. Upstairs, I heard Scots Elspeth crooning, accompanied by the loud objections of my son resisting her care.

Why should that tiny voice have the power to drag me back to the bitter memories of my loss? I scowled as I sanded the last sheet of a letter addressed to my London contacts.

"An early spring after an easy winter," Allen said hesitantly. "That should mean a good haul of furs coming in from the far tribes, Master Ormerod."

I grunted in agreement. The boy meant well, always trying to pull me out of my gloom. Upstairs, a door creaked open, followed by an infant's joyful squeal echoing down the hall. I jumped to my feet and dashed out.

"Elspeth!" I bellowed. Her plump figure and gracefully graying hair appeared at the top of the stairs.

"Yes, sir!" she called back.

"I can hear you just fine," I snapped, infuriated by the silly voices and babbling nonsense floating down.

"And you should be proud to hear it," she replied sharply. "It's what my dear departed would be telling you if—"

It was useless to argue with her. Swearing under my breath, I crossed the hall to my private study and slammed the door shut. But even as

I sank into the chair by the cold hearth, I knew there was no running from that sweet ghost haunting me, so real and vivid, yet so unreachable. She was everywhere in that house, right behind me, just out of sight. It was as if she sat in the chair opposite, her lap adorned with a piece of embroidery, her brown eyes lovingly fixed on me.

I rose and walked to the window, turning my back on the ghostly vision forming on the hearth-rug. Westward, across the rooftops stretching to the Hudson River, the sun was setting in a blaze of colors only the New World could conjure. It meant nothing to me. Frustrated, I turned away and retraced my steps, still unable to escape the presence that lingered, haunting my every move.

Ghosts from every corner of time and space swirled before my eyes—spirits of London, Paris, the wilderness, and beyond. Kings, queens, mighty lords, priests, soldiers, merchants, heroes and cowards, honest men and crooks, Native American warriors decked in war paint, courtiers in extravagant ruffles. Yet, regardless of the chaotic assembly, one ghost always stood out—the one I could never escape. Her lips were perpetually poised for a kiss, her brown eyes glowing with an undying affection. A shiver ran down my spine. The door behind me creaked open.

"Master Ormerod," came Allen's voice, tentatively. "I knocked, but you didn't hear me. There are some folks here who wish to see you, sir."

"I'm in no mood for company," I snapped.

"But sir, they—"

"Send them away. I won't be bothered."

Without warning, the door flew open with a resounding crash.

"What's this now, Ormerod?" boomed a blustery voice. "Is this how you treat my dignity, let alone our friendship? Must I cool my heels on your doorstep while you ponder whether to grant me an audience?

Watch yourself, lad, or I'll have you shackled in Fort George's dungeons. And know this—there's another who has a bone to pick with you. While I've trudged all the way from Bowling Green, he has just arrived from Iroquois territory, primarily to deliver you a belt, if the tales bear truth."

I leaped to my feet, jolted out of my brooding, and horrified at my rudeness to the most important man in our province—the governor himself, Master Burnet. To him, we owed more than we could ever repay for the relentless dedication with which he nurtured our community towards greater wealth and prosperity. There are dissenters, of course, especially since his move to Massachusetts where he clashed with the Puritan zealots and their sanctimonious squabbles. But I dismiss them as nothing more than fools. He was strict about the king's rights, sure, and fiercely protective of his own authority. Yet, on matters of policy, he was right ten times for every one time his critics were.

He was a stout man, his face ruddy and his features sharply defined, blunt and dogmatic yet with a curious logic all his own. He was a loyal friend and a fearless enemy. Now, he stood in the doorway, feet planted wide, punctuating his words with the thump of his cane.

"Your Excellency!" I gasped. "It was my mistake. I beg your pardon—"

"Enough!"

He waved his hand dismissively, but a twinkle of kindness shone in his prominent eyes.

"Say no more, kid. I know what's eating at you. That's why I'm here, and I've got others with me."

He stepped aside, and I was stunned to see two figures emerge silently from the shadows of the hall.

"Annalla! Marcus!"

The first was an Indian, his lean body bare above tanned deerskin leggings and a gaka, or breechcloth. Painted on his chest was the fierce image of a wolf's head, done in yellow, white, and black. A tomahawk and knife hung in sheaths at his thighs. An eagle's feather was tucked into his scalp-lock. His bronzed face, with its high nose, broad forehead, and squared jaw, was lit by a grim smile.

"Kwa, Otetiani," he said, using the Indian name given to me when I was enrolled in the Wolf Clan of the Senecas.

* "Hail, Always-ready."

He raised his right hand high in the magnificent Iroquois gesture of greeting. I responded as befitted one who was not only his Clan brother and friend but also the war chief of the Great League, the Warden of the Western Door of the Long House.

Behind him came a mountain of a man, his vast bulk almost comically exaggerated by the loose buckskin shirt and trousers he wore, topped by a coonskin cap over his straggly yellow hair. Others might be fooled by his layers of fat, the huge belly, the simple broad face with its scattered features, and the small, mild blue eyes that blinked from behind folds of loose flesh. But I knew Marcus Corlaer as the strongest, most cunning frontiersman there was.

Hidden beneath his layers of bulk were muscles like tempered steel, harboring untapped reserves of endurance.

"Man, I'm beyond glad to see you," I called out, gripping his hand with a blend of relief and astonishment as his fingers enveloped mine in a bear-like grasp.

"Yeah," he replied, a surprisingly tiny, squeaky voice emanating from his hulking frame. I caught Allen's wide-eyed stare, and for the first time in six months, an involuntary laugh bubbled up from within me.

“I’m going to be all right now, John,” I said. “They’re old friends I never expected to see so soon.”

The governor clapped the clerk on the shoulder with the kind of affection that only a weathered leader could muster.

“You’re safe to leave him with us, lad,” he said warmly. “You’re a good sort. There’s always room for people like you in New York. Here, it doesn’t matter what you were. It’s what you are that counts. But go now; we’ve got some talking to do.”

I turned back to Annalla as Allen quietly shut the door behind him.

“What brings you here, brother? Your presence is more than welcome, that goes without saying. But you two are the last people I expected to walk in from Pearl Street. Fill me in! How are our brethren of the Long House? Has anyone dared to challenge the Warders of the Door? What’s the news from beyond the Lakes? Are the French still...?”

“For mercy’s sake!” interrupted Master Burnet. “One question at a time, Ormerod, if you please. And may we sit in your house?”

I chuckled, suspecting he’d meant to lighten my mood, and gestured for all three to make themselves comfortable.

“Relax, all of you. You’re hardly strangers in need of a formal invitation.”

The governor settled himself into my armchair with a familiar ease.

Annalla exposed his white teeth in a friendly grin; like all his people, he had a sharp sense of humor. He settled himself on the bearskin rug, and after a moment of hesitation, Corlaer followed suit.

"My friend wouldn't mind if Corlaer and I ignore his chairs, would he?" Annalla asked in his smooth, musical English, which carried the rhythmic cadence of his native tongue. "We forest people aren’t used to sitting with our legs dangling off the ground. I learned a lot from the missionaries when I was a boy, Gaengwarago, but I never grew accustomed to the white man's chairs. Hawenneyu, the Great Spirit, intended the earth not just for walking, but for sitting too. It's the only chair I need."

The governor smirked. "But Corlaer seems to have learned from your people better than you did from us," he shot back.

"The white man learns faster than the Indian," the Seneca affirmed with a nod. "That's why, someday, he will drive the Indian from his path."

"From his path?" I repeated, always intrigued by the insightful musings of this learned warrior, who seamlessly fused the philosophy of the white man with the raw instincts of his own people.

"Yes, friend," he answered. "A time will come when the white man will push the Indian out of all this land."

"But where will your people go?" I asked.

"Who knows? Only Hawenneyu can say. Maybe he will lead us to some new land out there, beyond the sunset."

Annalla waved toward the glowing horizon in the west. The governor leaned forward in his chair, his interest piqued.

"Aye, that's what's been on my mind," he said. "What lies beyond that sunset? You know something of it, Annalla, but not everything. That's the knowledge I seek."

"So, in a way, that's what has brought us here together," he said, his voice trailing off into the haunting silence of the twilight.

For a moment, there was nothing but the profound quiet of dusk, and we all stood transfixed, watching him. He leaned on his cane, chin propped on clasped hands, his gaze lost in the deepening glow of the Western sky.

"Tell your story, Annalla," he said abruptly. "That's the easiest way to explain this tangled mess. And you, Ormerod, listen closely. This is more than just a whim of mine. Your future well-being might depend on it."

My eyes locked onto the Indian's face, intent and searching.

"Yes, tell your story," I urged gently. He nodded slowly, a solemn acknowledgment.

"I will speak, brother. Annalla speaks also for Corlaer. Isn't that right, Marcus?"

The large Dutchman's response sliced through the stillness with a sharp "Ja."

"First, my brother Ormerod, whom we of the Hodenosaunee call Otetiani," the Indian continued with a voice like rolling thunder, "I'll try to answer the questions you asked. I bring greetings from your foster-father, my uncle, the Royaneh Donehogaweh. He wants you to know that his heart yearns for his white son. He's always got a place ready for you in his home. Before I left the Long House, he advised me to find you. All is well with my people. The Western Door remains secure. No enemies have dared challenge it. But Annalla has been restless, and his thoughts have wandered to the emptiness in his heart, the same emptiness you remember from years past."

He rose to his feet, embodying the timeless grace of all Indian orators who found no comfort in delivering their words while seated.

With arms crossed over his bare chest, his eagle feather almost brushing the ceiling, he loomed above us—a living, breathing spirit of the Wilderness.

"You haven't forgotten, have you? My brother remembers that Annalla once loved a girl from his tribe, Ranno's daughter. She was taken from him by a French bastard, and she died so Annalla might live.

"My brother knows the old legend of our people, that the Lost Souls of the dead travel to the Land of Lost Souls, ruled by Ataentsic and her grandson Jousekeha. It's a realm beyond Dayedadogowar, the Great

Home of the Winds, and even further beyond Haniskaonogeh, the Dwelling Place of the Evil-minded, beyond the setting sun.

"My brother knows the story of a warrior from our tribe who, trusting in Hawenneyu and the Honochenokeh, braved the west after the Setting Sun. He eventually reached the Land of Lost Souls, where he found the maiden he loved, dancing among other Lost Souls before Ataentsic. And Jousekeha, moved by their love, gave him a hollowed pumpkin. They placed the Lost Soul of the maiden inside it, and the warrior brought it back to the Long House. There, his people held a feast and resurrected the maiden's soul from the pumpkin shell.

"My brother remembers that two winters ago, Annalla and Corlaer left the Long House to find the Land of Lost Souls. But trouble brewed between the Hodenosaunee and the Shawnee. While they were in the Dakota lands, across the mighty Mississippi, a message from the Hoyarnagowar called them back. Six young warriors gave their lives to deliver that message. Annalla returned and fulfilled his duties to his people. Now, he is free once more."

He stepped toward me, his eyes burning with a sharp intelligence that marked him above all others.

"Oh, my brother, I have spoken much about Annalla. Now, it's time to speak of you. Word came to Deonundagaa in the first moon of winter that the flower entwined around your heart had withered and died. Our grief was immense, but words are nothing in the face of such sorrow. I knew your loss because I too had felt it. I thought, 'Otetiani is a man. He cannot weep. He endured the torture stake. But he will suffer deeply in his mind, just as I have. What will help him?'"

"And then, my brother, I knew what must be done. I called for Corlaer and said, 'We will go to New York, find our brother Ormerod, and take him with us to search again for the Land of Lost Souls. A new path is the best cure for a troubled mind. If we find this land, perhaps the souls of the white people will be there, and he may recover who he has lost. If we find nothing, he will still have the journey, the strange trails, new places, and the ache in his heart will lessen.'"

"So, my brother, Corlaer and Annalla came to New York. And though I worried my thought might be wrong, for Annalla, as an Indian, cannot always know what is best for a white man, we went first to Gaengwarago, who is wise in the ways of all people, and consulted him. Now it is time for him to speak his judgment.

"Na-ho."

"But Annalla," I cried as he gracefully dropped to the floor, "you forget that I am a Christian! My faith tells me nothing of a land where the dead may be recovered. Think, brother, you were educated in the natural sciences by the missionaries."

"How can you believe this myth?" My words cut through the silence, loaded with both frustration and sorrow. "I know you've told this tale before, and I've held my tongue out of respect for your grief. But I can't keep quiet any longer. Forgive me if my words hurt, brother. I'm only trying to speak honestly, as brothers ought to."

From his seat on the well-worn bearskin, he lifted his calm eyes to mine. "Your words do not wound me, my brother," he said. "Honesty cannot hurt. It's natural for brothers to disagree. It's true, I learned from the missionaries as you said. I have read their Bible. The missionaries are good men. The Bible is a good book, full of wisdom. But the men who wrote it knew nothing of the Indians. They had never even heard of this land. How, then, could they understand what the Great Spirit intended for the Indian? No, Ormerod, I believe the Great Spirit who made the world, who separated salt water from the oceans for travel and fresh water from the rivers for drinking, could have very well created a different afterlife for the Indian than for the white man."

"No," I insisted, my frustration bubbling over. The unsettling mix of superstition and camaraderie was hard to bear, especially given my recent mental torment. "A soul leaves the body as something intangible, beyond touch or sight. Remember, Annalla, the Great Spirit sent His Son to dwell among men, to give His life for the salvation of humanity. Yet He never spoke of your beliefs."

Annalla gave a scornful smile. "That's exactly why I reject your religion, brother. It cannot be complete if it excludes the Indian, for we too have souls. But, as I've said before, I make no promises. I will seek. Hawenneyu, and Tharon the Sky-holder, will determine what is best for me, just as they do for you. Life is a search, brother. Religion is a struggle. I strive for what I love. I battle for truth and justice."

"I believe the Great Spirit thinks of the Indian as much as he does of the white man."

Master Burnet tapped his cane on the floor, irritation creeping into his voice.

"You're wasting time, Ormerod," he snapped. "My father was a bishop, and I've had more than enough religion in my life to know theological debates are never- ending. Let's drop it. As for me, I don't particularly care if Annalla is right or wrong. The longer I live, the less certain I am of what's real and what's not. This continent is so massive that it could hold wonders beyond our wildest imaginations. A Land of Lost Souls! Why not? There were miracles in Judea, so why not here in this mysterious land? But shh! My father, Bishop Gilbert, must be turning in his grave. Enough. I'm no theologian, endlessly dissecting salvation. No, no! I've heard many creeds, but none outshine Annalla's."

I laughed despite myself.

"You're already falling for what you mock," I pointed out. He shot me a grin.

"True, thanks for the reminder. Let's drop it."

His expression turned serious.

"For you, Ormerod, the issue isn't what Annalla believes. You know he's a trustworthy friend. That should be enough. His offer is meant to rescue you from this rut where, to be brutally honest, you can't shake the memories of that fair Mistress Marjory whom we all loved. Don't ignore it. I've watched you lately with concern. You're losing your grip on reality, lad, that's the truth."

"Don't get me wrong. I'm not blaming you. Your life has been harsh. You've faced more trials than anyone should. Your loss is even more bitter because of that. But that's why you must embrace a sharp purge of experience to clear your mind of the rot gnawing at your sanity. Annalla shows the way."

I looked at him, utterly confused.

From him to Seneca, who sat cross-legged like a bronze statue, only his eyes alive with emotion in the mask of his face. And from Annalla to Corlaer, equally stoic, his little eyes almost entirely hidden behind folds of flesh.

"But a trip like that will take ages!" I protested.

"A year," agreed Annalla. "Maybe more. Who knows?"

"Yes," echoed Corlaer when I turned to him.

"It's impossible," I said. "I have my business."

A wild laugh erupted from upstairs. I guessed it was Elspeth, letting loose since she knew I was entertaining guests.

"And the child," I added.

"Your reasons aren't valid," replied the governor. "John Allen can manage your business, and I'll provide any guidance he needs. The child's better off with Elspeth anyway. You won't mean much to him over the next year, at least. Mistress Burnet will keep an eye on him."

"But there's serious danger on such a journey," I declared openly.

"That's true," admitted Master Burnet. "It's unavoidable. But it's better you face it, Ormerod, than continue in the slump you've been in for the past six months. You've got enough money to secure your son's upbringing and start in life. Write your will and leave his guardianship to me. Rest assured about that."

"You seem unusually eager for me to go," I noted, a bit sharply.

"I am," he responded, without hesitation. "I'll even urge you officially. Things aren't right. We block the French at one point, or in one direction, and they start something else elsewhere. They're an adventurous people, with a knack for military strategies that put us to shame. And to the south, the Spaniards are building power that can only be toppled by their own incompetence. We English are pinned along the seaboard, held back by the Allegheny Mountains."

"We're packed in here like fleas on a dog's tail," I grumbled.

"We haven't even scratched the surface of settling this province," I protested.

"That's true," he conceded, "but we're just the first wave. The future will see our people spilling over into the distant wilds. Think about it. One day, we'll be pushing our boundaries, venturing into the shadowy unknown. What's out there? What's beyond the Wilderness Country, past the Sunset, like Annalla said? That's the knowledge we need, the knowledge England needs."

He jabbed his cane in my direction to emphasize his point.

"Look, Ormerod, there are three crucial questions we need to answer. First, how entrenched are the French along the Mississippi? I've heard they've established a place called Vincennes on the River Ouabache, but I don't know if they've moved further down permanently.

"Second, how much influence have the Spaniards gained beyond the Mississippi? On this, we know next to nothing.

"Third, what are the Indian tribes like beyond the Great River? What's their stance towards us? Annalla has given me some information, but it's not enough. I need more."

"You've caught me off guard," I admitted, my mind drifting to past escapades. I recalled the stealthy step of moccasins, the earthy scent of the forest, the whisper of arrows slicing the air, the electrifying call of the war-whoop, and the thrill of a near-perfect shot. Master Burnet wasn't about to let me off the hook.

"Of course, I've surprised you," he pressed on. "But listen, lad, I've spent the whole winter trying to find something to pull you out of this house, which is weighed down with too many memories for your own good. Annalla brought me the very thing I couldn't even dream up myself. But see, this is more than just an escape from discomfort and ill health. No Englishman has ventured across the Mississippi yet. French soldiers and Jesuits have seen parts of it, but never an Englishman."

The man who spots it first and shares a true tale will be a hero to his people. He'll contribute to the lives of generations yet to come.

I glanced one last time at the empty armchair by the fireplace. As always, the delicate shade that once occupied it lifted her head, as if in wordless affection. It seemed she nodded, her brown eyes shimmering with unshed tears.

"I'll go," I declared. Annalla sprang to his feet with the grace of a predator.

"Yo-hay!" he roared.

"Good," Corlaer pronounced solemnly.

"It's settled," the governor affirmed. "You won't regret it, Ormerod. There's much to be done. Let's get to it."

Chapter Two

The sun was already high in the sky, but its light struggled to break through the gloom in the Council House. From my seat of honor opposite the doorway, I could barely make out the shadowy figures of the Royanehs and chieftains, who sat silently in concentric circles around the pit where the Seneca Council Fire smoldered. Gradually, the sun's direct rays crept over the earthen threshold. Donehogaweh, sitting to my left, extended his sinewy arm and dropped a handful of tobacco leaves onto the coals. A single, hazy blue column of smoke rose, and the acrid scent of burning tobacco filled the room.

"Oh, Great Spirit," began the Guardian of the Western Door in a sonorous voice, "and you, Tharon, Sky-holder, and Heno, Master of Thunder, and Gaoh, Lord of Winds, you too, oh Three Sisters of the Deohako, Our Supporters, and the Honochenokeh, Aids of the Great Spirit and Ministers of His Mercy, hear our plea! Listen to the words we send you through the smoke that rises from our Council Fire!"

He cast aside his ceremonial skin robe and stood tall, wearing only a breechclout and moccasins. Despite his age, his gaunt body was as straight as a young man's, and his voice resonated with a youthful strength. With arms folded across his chest, he raised his face to the smoke hole in the roof.

"We are sending three of our young men on a journey. They have far to travel. They may trespass on forbidden ground. We implore you to be merciful. If they must turn back, guide their steps to another path. They are not driven by idle curiosity. They seek to right a wrong and uncover what the future holds for our people."

"That's all," he said, voice steady but firm. "We show these to you now, before everyone."

He motioned for me to stand, and I slung my ration bag over my shoulder, rifle steady in my grip.

"This is Otetiani, my white son," he announced to the assembly. "He is a brave warrior, oh Hawenneyu. His mind is heavy with sorrow. Lift it from him, and let him live his life in peace."

Corlaer got to his feet next.

"This is Corlaer, my white brother," he declared. "A big man, oh Hawenneyu, with an even bigger appetite. But if his strength is great, he can control his hunger. He's a loyal friend and a formidable enemy."

Annalla rose, the flickering fire casting long shadows on his face.

"This is Annalla, from the Clan of the Wolf, Keeper of the Gate. He is the son of my sister, carrying what little remains of my bloodline. He seeks to fill a void in his heart. If it is wise, oh Hawenneyu, give him what he longs for."

"Na-ho!" he finished.

And from the circle of shadowy figures came a muttered chorus, "Yo-hay!"

Donehogaweh turned to us as we stood beside the fire pit, its flames now just glowing embers.

"You're about to embark on a long journey," he said solemnly. "Many enemies might confront you. You may face great danger, even death. But I charge you, show no fear. If you return with the scalps of all who oppose you, we will be proud. We will dance the War Dance for you. If you don't return, we will remember you, and the women will teach the children to honor your memory. But do not come back unless you can stand proud of all your deeds, with nothing to be ashamed of."

"Na-ho!"

He wrapped his skin-robe around his shoulders and led us out of the Council House, the assembly of Royanehs and chiefs trailing behind through the narrow doorway. Outside, in the hard-packed Dancing Place, the heart of the sprawling Seneca village of Deonundagaa, hundreds of warriors, women, and scrambling, eager children waited.

They stretched from the door to the gaondote, the war-post, its charred stump rising defiantly in the center of the clearing. Surrounding it were the ganasotes, the Long Houses where the people lived, bearing the very essence of their community. Many of them gathered out of idle curiosity, friendly but detached. However, some who knew us well pressed forward, seeking a final word before our departure. Guanaea, the wife of Donehogaweh—how I loathed the crude term "squaw," which hardly fit a people like the Iroquois, who honored their women far more than we did—grabbed my hand, her experienced eyes inspecting my gear. The deerskin garments I wore were her handiwork. She had prepared the dried meat and the mix of charred corn and maple sugar that filled my food bags. She had even made my barken box of coarse salt. And she had done the same for Annalla and Corlaer.

"Goodbye, Otetiani, my white son," she said, tears shimmering in her eyes. "May Hawenneyu protect you! I have no son of my own to tell me brave tales, so you are doubly dear to me. You must do what Annalla and Corlaer do when the snow flies: rub yourself with bear's grease. It's good always, and you should learn to like it. And don't bathe so often. Hanegoategeh, the Evil Spirit, watches those who do."

She handed me a small deerskin pouch and hung it around my neck by a strip of rawhide.

"That will protect you against all evils. Keep it with you always."

"What is it?" I asked, tucking it inside my leather shirt.

"A powerful Orenda," she whispered mysteriously. "Hineogetah, the Medicine Man, made it. It's proof against spirits and bullets. It'll turn a scalping knife and resist a tomahawk."

"But what is it?" I pressed. She looked around to ensure no one was within earshot.

Donehogaweh and Annalla were engaged in what seemed like their final conversation, capturing the crowd's intense focus.

"A fang of a bull rattlesnake," she enumerated, her fingers flicking with each item. "That's the spirit to ward off evil. The eyetooth of a wolf killed by Sonosowa of the Turtle Clan—because, naturally, no Wolf could slay another wolf in an honorable duel. That's the spirit to channel courage. A coal from the Ever-burning Fire at Onondago. That's the spirit to fight off disease. It's the most potent Orenda Hineogetah has ever crafted. I pray it keeps you safe, Otetiani. You'll need it, venturing into the Land of Lost Souls, where Tharon's wrath could strike at any moment."

"What about Corlaer?" I asked, amused yet touched by her focus on such details.

"Oh, he's different!" she responded.

I would have said more, but Annalla turned from his uncle, slinging his furled buckskin shirt over his bare shoulders.

"Come on, brother," he called to me. "We have to go."

I quickly stooped and kissed Guanaea on her wrinkled cheek. She recoiled, startled, raising her hand to where my lips had touched.

"What was that, Otetiani?" she asked, bewildered.

"It's how a white son greets his mother," I explained.

"Do it again," she ordered. I did, much to the stern amusement of Donehogaweh and his attendant warriors.

"I like it," she murmured. "A good son gives his mother such pleasure. Surely, Hawenneyu will send you back to me."

"If his Orenda is strong and his bravery true, he will return," said Donehogaweh, his tone final. "But now, enough of farewells. A warrior's strength should not be drained by sorrow before the journey begins. Goodbye, Otetiani, my son. Goodbye, Corlaer, my brother. Goodbye, Annalla, my sister's son. We await your return with honor."

He raised his right arm in farewell, a silent but powerful gesture that held the weight of their hope and the gravity of their journey.

A tangle of arms shot up in the Dancing Place, and we returned the gesture just as silently. Without a word, Annalla turned on his heel and started making his way south through the village. I followed him, with Corlaer trailing behind. No one called out after us, not a single shout from the shadows of the surrounding houses. I glanced back—a move no Native would dare—and saw the crowd frozen in place. Donehogaweh stood draped in his robe, his gaze locked on us, his face a mask of stone. Even Guanaea was still, like a carved figure.

As we reached the edge of the forest, Deonundagaa vanished into a blur of rooftops, receding behind a thickening curtain of green. The path we followed was the typical Indian trail, a narrow, well-worn groove just wide enough for a single man, carved through the heart of the wilderness. We walked in silence, each of us lost in our own thoughts. I found myself fixated on the smooth, rhythmic motion of Annalla's back, his muscles gliding effortlessly under his oiled skin, his steady, almost hypnotic pace leading us forward.

Behind me, I could hear Corlaer grunting, the snap of branches against his broad shoulders—a reassurance of our safety. The big Dutchman could move with surprising stealth and grace for a man of his size, a silent wraith in the woods just like Annalla. My mind drifted back to three weeks ago when these two men had re-entered my life after years apart. They'd pulled me from the muck of my grief with the sheer force of their presence. So much had changed since then.

The last-minute rush to settle my business dealings—conference calls with the governor and a few merchants from his council who graciously agreed to take over my affairs, drilling John Allen on the intricacies of the situation. A voyage up the Hudson River by sloop to Albany, nestled under Fort Orange's protective shadow at the Mohawk's mouth, our main outpost on the frontier. Two weeks on the Great Trail of the Long House: fleeting meetings with old friends, the intoxicating aroma of the forest, increasingly longer hours of sleep, Deonundagaa, and now this. I tossed my head back, breathed in the wild grapevine's scent curling around a giant oak, my eyes soaking up the dappled sunlight filtering through the canopy a hundred feet overhead, and a rabbit's swift dash across the trail. We passed a beaver pond—an unspoken lesson in relentless perseverance from these creatures who build tirelessly, undeterred by the toughest tasks.

Three weeks in, and I already glimpsed the prospect of being whole again. I stood a little taller, taking pride in how quickly I adjusted to the pace of the Indian trail. Annalla cast a quick smile over his shoulder.

"My brother's heart is light," he observed. "I can see it in his step."

"I feel better than I ever thought I could," I replied. "Who would choose the confines of a town over the freedom to roam the forest at will? And what a beautiful day it is."

"Oof!" grunted Corlaer from behind. "It's getting hot."

We covered thirty miles that day, camping with some Seneca hunters who generously shared their fresh venison. The next morning, we pressed on, still heading south toward the Alleghany River's headwaters.

"For the route we take," said Annalla, as we discussed the journey, "the word of my brother Otetiani shall be law. He has a mission for Gaengwarago."

"But hear me out. Head south towards the Alleghany, follow it to the Ohio, and then to the Great River, which my people call the Father of Waters. This way, brother, we'll steer clear of the French post at Detroit and get close enough to Vincennes if you want a look at it. But it'd be best if the French neither see you nor catch wind of your mission."

I nodded. "You're right. But for your plan, we'll need a canoe."

"I've got one," he said, a flicker of readiness in his eyes. "I stashed it on the Alleghany the last time I was on a mission to the Creeks."

We decided to follow Annalla's advice. Traveling by water, as he pointed out, meant faster progress than trekking overland, and it kept us clear of many tribal territories. Annalla, as a war chief of the Iroquois, expected respectful treatment from most tribes north of the Ohio and east of the Mississippi. But many of these tribes had fallen under French influence, and their reactions to my presence were unpredictable. It was safest for all involved to pass through this territory quietly and quickly. We had nothing to gain by lingering and perhaps everything to lose.

On the second day, the trail vanished, and a cold rain lashed at us from the east. The land was scarred with shallow ravines and gullies, and dense belts of undergrowth, bristling with thorns and tangled with vines, blocked our path. Sometimes we circled these patches; other times, we hacked a way through with our war-hatchets. Exhaustion had us in its grip by nightfall, and we gladly accepted the shelter offered by a group of wandering Mohicans. But come morning, rain or no rain, we resumed our march. Slippery rocks and ankle-deep mud were constant impediments.

Everything felt relentless, the country's unforgiving terrain reflecting the inner turmoil that gnawed at us. Each step, a reminder of the precariousness of our mission. And through it all, Annalla's calm determination gave me the resolve to push forward, even as the sky poured its cold dismay upon us.

The tangles of coarse grass in the swampy patches were treacherous underfoot, but we pressed on. Surprisingly, the weather did nothing to dampen my spirits. I found a strange pleasure in the raw, untamed elements—the sodden foliage, the relentless drip-drip of rain, and the fatigue that gnawed at my muscles. Most of all, I relished our third camp beneath a hastily constructed bark lean-to. The roof leaked, the fire barely managed to cook the wild turkey our Mohican guides had provided, and I was soaked to the bone. Yet I slept through the night and woke up refreshed and alert as the bright dawn greeted the new day.

By mid-morning, Annalla guided us to the headwaters of the Allegheny, landing at a diminutive creek. We reached the main stream by mid-afternoon. Annalla scanned our surroundings briefly before striding toward a grassy indentation at the riverbank.

"Here's the canoe, brothers," he said, almost nonchalantly.

"Nein," Corlaer replied, his small eyes fixed on the supposed hiding place without moving an inch. Annalla stepped back from the edge, his usually impassive face showing a hint of shock.

"This is where I left it, well-hidden," he insisted.

"Smoke, downriver," the Dutchman observed calmly. Both Annalla and I turned our heads. The Seneca warrior's eyes flashed briefly with irritation; he should have been the first to notice.

"We'll approach it," Annalla declared with finality. "This is Long House territory. Let's see who dares to steal a chief's canoe from the Western Doorstep."

He spoke figuratively, of course, as we were still a solid three days' trek from Deonundagaa. But Annalla's words were a telling display of Iroquois pride. True to his heritage, he marched directly toward the encampment without bothering with the usual scouting protocols. A half-grown boy spotted us through the trees and let out a shrill alarm, his cries piercing the air.

As we stepped from the shadows of the forest, a dozen men were clustered in front of four rough bark shelters just beyond the riverbank. Beyond them, I caught sight of a handful of women and children. They were a short, dark-skinned people with brutish, furrowed faces. Annalla frowned, pointing to a canoe dragged up onto the bank.

"Those are Andastes," he sneered. "Dogs and thieves who don't belong here. The Hoyarnagowar has ordered them to stay in the Susquehanna Valley."

Annalla, musket cradled in the crook of his arm, strode confidently into the middle of the grim-faced group, each of them gripping a musket or a bow.

"Andastes," he declared, "you've taken my canoe."

"We have only our own canoe," replied a burly warrior, stepping forward from the ragged bunch.

"I say it's mine," Annalla snapped, with an air of disdain.

"You're welcome to camp with us if you like; we'll share our food," said the Andaste, evasive.

Annalla's eyes blazed with anger. "Dog of an Andaste! Who are you to act like a master to the Hodenosaunee? You crawl when the word comes to you from Onondaga! You eat dirt if a warrior of the Long House commands it! You are the fathers of all lice!"

The Andastes scowled, drawing closer together and readying their weapons. Annalla pulled out his tomahawk, raising it high.

"I am Annalla, Warden of the Western Door," he said slowly. "I've just come from Deonundagaa. Choose now, Andastes, peace or war?"

They shrank back from him. All but two or three retreated into the lodges or the forest. Yet, there was no intention of violence; their spirit was broken. Annalla was more than just himself. He was the embodiment of that fearsome power that these lesser savages knew could bring destruction in any direction, to any distance north, south or west. He stood there, ax raised, the very spirit of the Long House, which even the white men feared.

The Andaste chief lowered his eyes, his voice a hushed plea.

"We don't want trouble," he said. "Take the canoe. We found it. We didn't know—"

"You know you have no rights here," Annalla cut in sharply, his eyes cold and unyielding. "This is the hunting ground of the Long House. The Mohicans, the Eries, and the People of the Cat can come here. But you, the Andastes, belong in the Susquehanna valley. Get back there. If I find you here again, I will bring fire and tomahawks against you and your entire tribe."

Annalla turned on his heel, motioning for us to follow. He strode down to the shore and pushed the canoe into the water.

"Let's move on, brothers," he urged. "The air here stinks."

He took the bow paddle, and I crouched in the middle. Corlaer, gentle as a girl despite his bulk, settled carefully into the stern. Their paddles carved through the shallow water, and under their steady, sure strokes, the light canoe danced downstream, picking up speed with the current. We rounded a bend, and the Andaste encampment vanished from sight.

"Will they obey you?" I asked Annalla. He let out a short, humorless laugh.

"They'll be gone before the sun rises again, brother Otetiani. They know they have no right there, but the place is remote, far from the Door, and they thought they would be safe. They're a nation of women. We don't even let them fight for us."

Paddling was a different beast from trekking through the woods, and we covered ten miles before darkness forced us ashore. We camped on a tiny island, finding shelter by a large rock. Our fire was small, its glow hidden from prying eyes on either shore, and we slept beside it under the stars. At dawn, we were up and moving again, snacking on burnt corn and maple sugar from our food sacks. That day, I noticed Annalla's vigilance had only intensified.

From his spot at the bow, he constantly scanned the shoreline, and by mid- afternoon we pulled ashore, taking advantage of the last bit of daylight to set up camp on yet another island.

"Why are you so cautious?" I complained. "Do you think the Andastes are might be tracking us?"

He shook his head, offering a wary smile.

"No, brother. We're moving into territories where the Long House's grip is feared, but no longer holds sway. Any moment, we could run into bands of young warriors from a dozen different tribes, each one hungry for their first scalps. To them, we'd look like three easy targets."

Yet, despite or maybe because of our heightened vigilance, we saw no sign of other men. That is, until we had to portage around some rapids. Just as we were relaunching our canoe, three more canoes, each carrying three red-skinned warriors, appeared from around the bend downstream. We stood ready, weapons at our sides. But they raised their hands in peace as they neared, and we held our fire. They were Cherokees—impressive, tall men who bore a striking resemblance to the Iroquois. They openly told us they were on a diplomatic mission to Detroit. Evidently, their people were having issues with the settlers in the Carolinas and wanted to form an alliance with the French.

"The French are no better than the English, brothers," Annalla replied. "They're both Asseroni. They're both white. We are red. There are white men who understand the Indian—like my two brothers here—but those are rare. You're on a fool's quest. The French will promise you the moon. They'll give you weapons and use you for their own ends. But when they've no more need for you, they'll leave you to burn."

The Cherokees, crouched in a half-circle by the shore, exchanged uneasy glances. Behind them, their beached canoes sat like abandoned ghosts.

"What would our brother from the Hodenosaunee suggest?" asked the eldest chief, his voice a gravelly whisper. "How do your people keep their strength, caught between the French and the English? Is there no help from either? What does the Indian do then?"

"The Hodenosaunee hold their place through power," Annalla replied, his voice steady as steel. "We have made our aid valuable to the English. But brothers, the time will come when the English won't need us anymore, when their firewater has corrupted our young men, when their numbers swell so much that we are but shadows to them. Then the Indian must go."

"Go where?" one of the Cherokees demanded, his eyes dark with urgency. Annalla swept his arm downstream, a gesture that hinted at endless possibility and despair.

"Brothers," Annalla said, "I am journeying to discover what lies between here and the sunset and beyond. Maybe, just maybe, Hawenneyu has reserved a land for the red man, a place the white man cannot take."

"If the red man keeps stepping back, surely the white man will drive him out completely," said the Cherokee, his voice heavy with grim prophecy.

"That's true," Annalla agreed with a nod. "But if all red men united, the white man could never push them out. Your brothers, the Tuscaroras, came north in my father's time, driven from their homes by the same white men who now trouble you. We of the Hodenosaunee welcomed them into our League. Now they are safe. The walls of the Long House protect them. Perhaps the Hoyarnagowar would consider extending those walls if the Cherokees wished to join the League."

"Yes, but as younger brothers with no voice in the Council of Roy-anehs. That's what happened to the Tuscaroras," the Cherokee spat, his words laced with passionate defiance. "They've become dependents of the Hodenosaunee. We Cherokees are a great people."

"Shall we lose ourselves in the fabric of the Long House?"

Annalla knocked the ashes from his pipe and stood up slowly, like a man rising from a heavy dream.

"My brother, you have pointed out why the red man cannot stand against the white man," he said quietly, his voice like an ancient wind through the forest. "Outside the Long House, the powerful tribes won't stick together. The Hodenosaunee can conquer people like the Eries or the Mohicans, but we see no reason to take on the Cherokees. And if we did not conquer you, you would not join us."

"Because we might not join you as equals!" spat the Cherokee, his eyes burning with a fierce light.

"There is no question of equality or inequality," Annalla responded, his tone steady as the beating drum. "The Founders of the Great League created just so many Royanehs, and we can't change their work. Go to Onondaga with your belts, and Tododaho, the greatest of our Royanehs, who warms himself by the Everlasting Fire, will strengthen your hearts with wise talk. Let him explain, better than I can, how to unite for strength."

The Cherokee stood, his face a mask of stern resentment.

"We're going to Detroit," he said, each word a drop of venom. "Better to be allies of the Frenchman, playing one race of white man against the other, than be slaves of the Hodenosaunee."

Annalla didn't respond, and silence stretched between us as we paddled on for an hour or more.

"What did you think of our talk, brother Otetiani?" he asked suddenly, his voice slicing through the quiet.

"I think you were right," I answered, feeling the weight of his conviction.

"I'm so sure I'm right that I can see the whole future of the red man," he declared, his voice rising like a storm. "He will perish because he can't break down his tribal barriers."

"Der Frenchman, too," spoke up Corlaer from behind me, a rare string of words from a man who usually spoke with his eyes more than his mouth. I turned, amused and surprised.

"Ja," he continued, his accent thick, every word a blunt instrument. "Der Englishman, he takes in all—Dutch, Swede, German, Frenchman. But der Frenchman, he is der Frenchman. Der Englishman comes out on top. He mixes. Ja."

Chapter Three

Day after day, we drifted down the widening river, our journey unrelenting. One day, a submerged log tore through the bottom of our canoe, and we had to swim to the shore, pushing the waterlogged vessel ahead of us. Annalla, resourceful as ever, cut strips of bark and melted some pitch I gathered from the pine trees. He even salvaged sinews from a deer he'd shot with his bow and arrow. With these, he patched the canoe's wound, sealing it watertight. After two days of painstaking repairs, we were back on course, breathing a sigh of relief that we hadn't been attacked during our vulnerable pause, especially with our spare gunpowder ruined by the river.

The journey was far from easy. Treacherous channels and difficult portages plagued us, but each day brought us a little closer to our goal. Finally, we reached the place Annalla called the Meeting of the Waters. As the sun dipped below the horizon, the river's current whisked us around a bend, revealing a confluence of streams. To our left, the Monongahela joined forces with the Allegheny, and together they formed the mighty Ohio River.

It was a breathtaking sight, a place of undeniable strategic value. North, south, and west stretched the three rivers, natural highways ready to unlock the resources of the surrounding wilderness. At their meeting point lay the perfect location for a fortress, one that could command the waterways and dominate the untamed land for miles. I would remember this place for years to come. I recall, in 1760, young Colonel Washington of Virginia—whom I met in New York while he was attending General Amherst—spoke of this site with a kind of solemn reverence. He mentioned that the famed French General Montcalm had chosen this very spot to build Fort Duquesne, a catalyst in the struggle for control of the wilderness. Washington, in his simple yet authoritative manner, also predicted that a prosperous town would one day rise here.

That night, we set up camp on the point, the soothing yet insistent murmurs of the spring freshet in our ears. Come morning, we let our canoe be swept into the spirited current of the Ohio, ready for whatever lay ahead.

The river rushed ahead so swiftly, we barely needed to touch our paddles. Just a nudge here and there to steer clear of rocks and keep us in the smoothest part of the current. In one day, we covered what normally took us two on the Allegheny's winding stretches. But then came the tricky days. Days when we had to dodge hidden dangers lurking beneath the foamy water, rocks and submerged sandbars ready to flip us if we weren't careful. Enormous trees crashed downstream like nature's own battering rams, ready to swamp anyone foolish enough to challenge them. Sometimes, the water was too wild, and we'd have to haul the canoe up onto our shoulders and stumble along the shoreline in the shallows.

What puzzled me was the lack of human presence. Now and again, we'd spot a lone canoe that'd slip into the bank as soon as they caught sight of us, the paddler disappearing into the thick underbrush. A couple times, other canoes tried to chase us down, but with my strength now added to Annalla and Marcus's, we left them in our wake. Near the Scioto's mouth, where it merges with the Ohio, we ran into a group of Miamis heading south, hunting for scalps and buffalo hides. They knew Annalla, so they passed by with nods and respect. Most of the time, though, the river just rolled on quietly, majestic and undisturbed, on its great journey to join the Mississippi. Days went by with no signs of other people. Not even a wisp of smoke from the dense forests that marched right up to the riverbanks, bluffs, and hills boxing in the channel.

Then, suddenly, chaos. The river had squeezed between low banks, rocks riffled on the north side forcing us to the southern edge. A gunshot rang out from the southern bank, the bullet slicing the air right past my head. More shots followed, each one answered by cracking echoes. I spun around to see smoke rising from the underbrush. The warwhoop's eerie cry pierced above the river's babbling. Painted warriors erupted from cover, feathers flying from their half- shaven heads as they ran along the bank, yelling and firing at us.

Two long canoes launched from the riverbank, slicing through the water with four paddles each. In the bow of each canoe crouched a warrior, hell-bent on shooting us down. Bullets ripped through the flimsy bark of the canoe, sending up splashes all around us.

"Shawnees!" Annalla shouted, panic threading through his voice. "For your lives, brothers!"

We plunged our paddles into the churning water, but we were trapped by the treacherous rocks blocking the northern bank. Still some distance from clearing the rocky barrier, a jagged chunk of lead blasted into the canoe between Annalla and me, bounced off a hickory thwart, and tore a long, curving slit below the waterline. I dropped my paddle and clenched the tear with both hands, trying to hold the gaping wound shut. Water trickled in, of course, and as the canoe sank under its growing weight, controlling the leak became an increasingly desperate task. But it gave us a fighting chance to keep moving.

"Good job, brother!" gasped Annalla, noticing my effort. "Just a few feet more!"

The Shawnees howled in triumph, sensing our predicament. Their canoes shot toward us at double our speed, and some of the warriors on the southern shore plunged into the river at its narrowest point, swimming for the rock ledge to cross over to the other side. Annalla and Corlaer strained to keep us afloat until we were almost past the rocks. I was the first to see the wavelet that would swamp us, and I shouted a warning.

We held our powder-horns and rifles high and made a desperate leap for the nearest rocks. I went under, barely saving my powder from another soaking. Annalla and Marcus found footholds immediately, and the hulking Dutchman dragged me up beside them.

We splashed through the water as fast as the jagged rocks would allow, zigzagging and crouching low to throw off the enemies firing from the opposite bank and the two canoes racing downstream to find a better landing spot. The Shawnees, who had braved the river, were already ashore several hundred yards upstream, sprinting toward us along the bank. As soon as we reached the first trees of the forest, we fired at them. Gasping for breath, Annalla hit a man in the leg. Corlaer drilled his target through the chest. I missed. But our shots created enough confusion to stall their advance. Instead of charging openly, they melted into the forest, trying to flank us from behind. We sensed their plan and only paused long enough to reload.

With Annalla leading, we sprinted northward, leaving a blatant trail behind us—no time for subtlety. The shouts of the river swimmers echoed from our rear- right, with responding calls from the warriors who had debarked from the canoes on our left. Through the trees, we could see a group of ten or twelve more slipping into the water from the south bank. Thankfully, the forest was an ancient, majestic sprawl of towering, widely-spaced trunks. There was minimal underbrush, and the ground was layered with a thick, springy carpet of decomposed leaves and earth, perfect for running. Light filtered down from high above through the interwoven branches, making it hard to see clearly over any distance. Despite the relentless whoops closing in on us, the odds felt vaguely in our favor. That's why it surprised me when Annalla came to an abrupt stop after we had been running for barely half an hour.

"They will be scattered," he said, reading the confusion on my face. "We'll show them they are not up against naive hunters like themselves. Run ahead about twenty strides, Otetiani, and Corlaer another twenty more."

"I'll fire when I see a target, then retreat. You each shoot in turn and then bail. That way, the ones at the back can reload. Come on, brothers, let's show these young idiots our scalps aren't as easy to take as deer antlers."

Corlaer grunted in agreement, and we pushed ahead. I ducked behind a massive oak, straining to make out Annalla's figure hiding behind an uprooted elm. Five minutes crawled by. The howling of our enemies faded into the distance. They might be greenhorns, but they knew to save their breath once they got a scent. Suddenly, I saw a flash in the gloom, and Annalla dashed toward me, musket ready. The crash of his shot was followed by a cry of agony, and the eerie silence of the forest echoed with a haunting war-whoop.

"Keep sharp, brother," whispered the Seneca as he sprinted past. I raised my musket, my eyes scanning left and right, trying to penetrate the shadowy abyss untouched by sunlight. I stared so long my eyes began to ache, forcing me to blink. When I opened them again, I saw it: a shadow darker than the rest, slipping between two tree trunks on my left. He was so close, I thought I must be imagining it, but then he appeared again—a feather atop a crouching form. I aimed a good foot below the feather and squeezed the trigger. The Shawnee leaped into the air with a strangled cry and crumpled forward. I took off running.

"Good," murmured Corlaer, crouched behind a moss-covered boulder. I kept going, stopping only when Annalla's low voice reached me.

"Reload," he said curtly. "We'll move again when Corlaer catches up. These dogs are faster than I thought."

"Listen!"

He tilted his head to the left and I caught it - the exchange of signal cries, even the distant crashing of branches. The Shawnees were maneuvering, trying to cut us off. Relief washed over me when Corlaer's musket roared and the Dutchman's bulky frame burst into view. Despite his size, he moved with a surprising grace, sprinting like a man possessed. Only a few could match his speed.

"Push on, brothers," urged Annalla. "This is our final effort."

We ran like never before, giving everything we had. The cries of the Shawnees faded behind us, and soon it seemed we had left them in our dust as we broke from the forest's shadow into a sunlit expanse. A fearsome windstorm had torn through, leveling everything in its path as if struck by a massive blade. The once proud forest now lay in chaotic, interwoven heaps of splintered timber. We had no choice but to traverse this natural barricade in the open, scrambling over the debris, rarely able to move faster than a crawl.

We were barely a musket-shot away from the forest's edge when the Shawnees reappeared, howling in triumph. Although they couldn't catch up, they were uncomfortably close as we stumbled into the standing timber on the far side of the clearing. We knew our legs would give out soon. My vision blurred with exertion as we dropped into a shallow glade sliced by a narrow, rocky stream. Boulders punctuated its flow, and an immense tulip tree loomed ten yards away.

I threw myself down for a quick, desperate gulp of water, planning to push on immediately. As I rose, I saw Annalla deep in conversation with Corlaer. The Dutchman nodded, and without a word, waded into the stream, which came up to his waist.

I started to follow him, but Annalla signaled me to stay put, his eyes scanning our trail for any sign of danger. I looked back and forth between him and Corlaer, confusion growing. The Dutchman climbed up the opposite bank, tramping heavily to a cluster of stones and boulders. He planted his wet, muddy moccasins on the first stone, then carefully walked backward in his own footprints into the river and back to our side.

"Come on," Annalla said, dropping into the riverbed beside Corlaer. Reluctantly, I followed, trying to figure out what crazy plan they had in mind. The Seneca led us downstream into the shadow of a towering tulip tree. Here, the creek spilled over a flat stone that was just at water level. Annalla stepped onto it, handed me his musket, grabbed a low tree branch, and in a blink, swung himself up onto the limb.

I passed him our three guns while he moved toward the trunk, holding them under one arm. I scrambled up beside him. Corlaer came next, his weight bending the limb so close to the water's surface that for a moment, I thought it might snap. But the resilient wood held, and the three of us made it to the crotch of the fifteen-foot bole. There was plenty of room and the dense foliage provided cover as we settled in to see what the Shawnees would do with the trap we'd set.

Time stretched on without any signs of movement, and I began to worry they had seen through our trick and were planning to catch us off-guard. But eventually, a feathered head poked out from the low-hanging foliage on the bank, examining the footprints Corlaer had left on the other side. A fierce, painted face turned in our direction for a split second before the lean body, clad only in a breechclout and moccasins, slipped into the water without making a sound and waded across. The Shawnee crept up the bank, reaching the spot where the Dutchman's wet feet had left their marks on the stones.

As he spun around with a commanding flick of his wrist, a group of menacing figures darted after him. We counted thirty-one, most clutching muskets. They vanished into the woods on the opposite bank, moving at a swift, unforgiving pace. Annalla silently dropped from the tulip tree.

"Where to now?" I asked. He grinned. Never let anyone tell you that the Indian has no sense of humor.

"Well, we're in need of a new canoe, brother. And it just so happens the Shawnees have generously left a couple waiting for us on the riverbank."

Behind us, Corlaer let out a wheeze of a laugh.

"Ja, we sure fooled those deer-hunters! Haw!"

We made our way back as fast as we had come, and now that we knew the terrain, we crossed the fallen timber in half the time. But we hadn't gone far before the war-whoop split the air behind us, and a dozen Shawnees emerged from the trees.

"They're skilled warriors," Annalla admitted. "When they couldn't find our trail beyond the boulders, they doubled back."

"Shall we give them a warm welcome?" I suggested.

"No, brother. We gain nothing from their deaths. We need a canoe, not scalps."

So we bolted toward the river, though how Annalla navigated so flawlessly, I'll never understand. It wasn't just knowing where the river lay; I could have done that much. It was as if he had an innate sense for the shortest, most direct path. We broke through the forest's edge, just a musket shot away from the beached Shawnee canoes.

Two guards, one of them the warrior Annalla had wounded in the leg during our first skirmish, rose to meet us, probably mistaking us for their comrades. But the moment they realized who we were, they lifted their bows and unleashed a pair of arrows straight at us.

Corlaer shot the wounded man with a casual flick of his wrist, and Annalla leaped forward, closing the distance with agile speed, and crashed his tomahawk down on the other's head with brutal finality.

"Ha-yah-yak-eeeee-eeee-eee-ee-e!"

The scalp-yell of the Iroquois echoed hauntingly across the riverbanks, a scream as piercing and wild as a catamount's cry. An equally fierce reply came from our Shawnee pursuers, not far behind. Annalla tucked the bloody trophy into his waist belt, then smashed a hole in the bottom of one of the canoes with his dripping tomahawk, shoving the crippled vessel out into the current to sink.

"Ready, brothers," he commanded, launching the intact canoe into the stream. "We need to be beyond musket-shot by the time the Shawnees get here. Oh, how hearts will be heavy in their lodges tonight. But they now know a group of deer hunters is no match for three cunning warriors."

We dug our paddles into the river's surface, propelling the heavy canoe—it was bulkier than the one we had lost—into the swift current. Fortune was on our side, as we were already a good distance downstream when the first Shawnees appeared on the opposite bank. Bullets splashed perilously close, but soon they ceased firing, realizing the waste of precious ammo. Their frustrated howls echoed into the twilight as they called for their distant comrades, announcing our escape.

By nightfall, we had put many miles between us and them, yet Annalla refused to let us pause. With every muscle burning and our bodies drenched in sweat and river water, we paddled on, eyes straining against the oppressive darkness to avoid hidden rocks or floating branches. Near midnight, the moon's cold silver light illuminated the channel, a different kind of urgency pressing us on. We didn't stop until the ghostly dawn light revealed a small, brush-covered islet in the middle of the river. Exhausted, we beach the canoe, hide it out of sight, and collapse beside it, succumbing to sleep like the dead beneath the sun's emerging warmth.

Chapter Four

Summer rolled up from the South like a slow, warm breath, blanketing the Wilderness Country in a lazy haze. We paddled sluggishly, our arms heavy and tired. Often, we found ourselves leaning back against the thwarts, watching the immense flocks of birds migrating north. Among them were the pigeons, countless numbers swooping together in such vast formations that they turned the sky dark. For an hour or more, their wings flapping and their sharp cries filled the air like an eerie, distant orchestra.

The forest was lush, the trees heavy with brilliant green leaves, and the occasional meadows and savannahs were dotted with wildflowers, a riot of white, red, yellow, blue, pink, and purple. The scent of blooming vegetation reached us on the fitful breeze, intermittently gusty and calm, dense as the steamy air, unpredictable. Now and then, storm clouds would hurtle toward us, black and furious like wrathful ships of war. Thunder would rumble in the sky; lightning flashed down, striking the mighty trees; and the rain poured upon us like the falls of Niagara, a relentless deluge.

For two weeks, we navigated this Eden, finding no trace of other men. We surveyed a realm fit for kings. All of France, I might claim, could have been uprooted and transplanted into this forsaken wonderland, over which her King laid an indifferent claim. Timber stood ready for the axe; expansive grazing lands, where only deer roamed, spread out before us; endless fields of rich, black soil awaited the plow. Even the natives seemed to have forsaken it. If they watched us pass, they did so from unseen places. From one horizon to the other, there wasn't a curl of smoke to indicate human presence.

But we weren't alone on the waters of the Ohio, as we found out soon enough. We slipped past the mouth of the Wabash in the dead of night, trying to avoid any eyes from the French post at Vincennes. To tell the truth, there was no sign of such an outpost.

After a few hours of rest, we resumed paddling, driven by Annalla's claim that just a couple more days would deliver us to the Mississippi. This great river, the threshold of the uncharted Wilderness, marked where our true quest would begin. But as we rounded yet another bend in the river, we were abruptly confronted by a flotilla of canoes, spread wide from bank to bank. Fate couldn't have dealt us a crueler hand. A quick glance revealed the distinct trappings of the French Marine Infantry, the regular troops from the Canadian garrisons, an officer's shining gorget, and worst of all, the dark flapping robes of a priest. Interspersed among them were habitants in buckskin and painted Ouabaches, Miamis, and Potawatomis manning the paddles. There were fifteen, maybe twenty canoes, ranging from small, fragile crafts smaller than ours, to larger ones carrying six or eight men.

Instinctively, we all started to back-paddle, but Annalla plunged his paddle in again, driving forward without hesitation.

"It's pointless to run, brothers," he murmured. "We must stay our ground."

Several shouts rang out from the approaching fleet, and two of the smaller canoes shot forward from their disorderly formation. Annalla stopped paddling for a moment, raising his right arm, palm out, the universal signal for peace. A French officer, donned in a laced coat and cocked hat in one of the larger canoes, mirrored the gesture. The Indians in the smaller canoes veered off as soon as they saw the wolf's head marked on Annalla's chest. No common forest- dwelling tribe was eager to confront a chief of the Long House during peacetime, even with the support of French troops. They knew better, taught by the bloody history of many a savage raid.

The French flotilla floated lazily, waiting for us as we paddled slowly between the lead canoes toward the one where the officer who had acknowledged Annalla's greeting was seated.

"Who is he?" I asked, when we were close enough to take in his hefty form and stern, broad face.

"Charles Le Moyne."

"The Chevalier de Longueuil?" I exclaimed.

"Indeed, brother."

I gazed at the man with newfound curiosity. He was one of the top four figures in Canada, the firstborn and heir of Baron de Longueuil, the Lieutenant Governor. He stood just below the Governor-General, the Intendant, and his own father. Such an illustrious mission must have brought him far from home. I was about to speak again when I noticed a certain tension rippling along Annalla's spine, every muscle taut and coiled. A sudden gasp came from Corlaer, sitting behind me in the stern of the canoe.

"'Black Robe!'"

I craned my neck to peer over the Seneca's shoulder. There he was. Behind Le Moyne, sitting stone-still on the hard, narrow plank, his deathly visage turned directly toward us, was the infamous Jesuit,

Père Hyacinthe. His gnarled, tortured fingers shifted rhythmically, counting the beads of the rosary draped over his bony knees. His black cassock fell in straight, stark lines down to his sandaled feet. Though I couldn't see them, I knew the awful scars marring his body, remnants of the torture stake he'd once shown me. I also knew of his unyielding hatred for all things English, his burning ambition—fueled by iron will and fervent religious conviction—to conquer the entire continent for Louis of France and the Church of Rome.

Of all those who toiled tirelessly to replace Anglo-Saxon civilization with Latin in the New World, none pursued their aims with more relentless and selfless dedication. Up and down the Wilderness Country he roamed, always toiling, indifferent to hunger, thirst, cold, and danger. The natives, with their instinct for the fitting, had named him Black Robe.

He was known to thousands who had never laid eyes on him. An odd man, one whose mind had been a bit twisted by suffering, hardship, and an obsessive focus on ecstatic devotion. Fasting and contemplation, loneliness and self-punishment, denial of all things physical, enduring fire torment and knife torment—they had all left their marks on him. If he caused harm, he also did good. He was one of those fearless souls who brought the Christian faith to the most remote corners of the Wilderness, places our grandchildren's grandchildren might not reach until the frontier pushes a thousand miles closer to the sunset. He believed that there was no need to worry about food because God would provide when needed, and it was true that he never starved to death. An odd man! One to be judged without regard to creed or politics.

His face stayed expressionless as our canoe glided next to Le Moyne's, and a Marine corporal grabbed the gunwale. But his eyes—they blazed with a fanatical intelligence deep within their hollow sockets. He leaned forward and tapped Le Moyne's shoulder.

"The Anti-Christ is among us," he announced in a voice that seemed to come from the grave. "Here are the sons of the English whore."

Le Moyne frowned slightly. A plain soldier-statesman, he likely struggled with the priest's grandiose ways. Yet, such was Black Robe's influence that Le Moyne dared not show his irritation.

"What do you mean, Father?" he asked curtly. The Jesuit pointed an accusing finger at us.

"Do you not recognize them, my son?"

"Aye, Annalla, I know. He's the Warden of the Western Door of the Long House. And Corlaer, too, I know. But not the other one."

"That's Henry Ormerod, of the Governor of New York's Council, one of the slyest minions of the English. He's a traitor to his rightful king, James, and has even held a commission from the Regent of Orleans."

In our party, only I could understand their conversation, for Annalla and Corlaer didn't know a word of French.

It rolled off my tongue easily enough after five years of service under the Duke of Berwick in the frontiers of the Low Countries, Italy, and Spain. Without waiting to consult my comrades, I struck back.

"Yes, Chevalier," I said, "my name is Ormerod, and Governor Burnet has honored me with a seat on his Council. It's true, too, that in my youth I foolishly supported the exiled Stuarts and lived in France for a time. But that's a chapter long closed. While I served James, I was loyal, and I left him because I realized he'd always be a puppet for foreign powers. Since then, I've tried to serve my country just as you serve yours. Is there any dishonor or hostility in that?"

Le Moyne started to respond, but the priest, known as Black Robe, cut him off.

"Pay no mind to the Englishman," the priest declared. "He's a servant of evil, a heretic, and an enemy of France."

"There's peace between France and England," I retorted boldly. "What is this talk of enemies?"

The priest flung his arms up.

"They speak of peace, peace," he cried, "but there is no peace! Can there ever be peace between anti-Christ and God? No, my son. But ask the Englishman what he's doing traveling secretly through the territories of France, hundreds of leagues from English soil. Why does he travel with the Iroquois chief, known as a principal ally of the English? Why do we see him with Corlaer, the emissary seducing the savages from trading at our posts? What is his mission here? Does he have a passport from Quebec?"

Le Moyne nodded.

"Father, you are right. Monsieur Ormerod, these questions need answering. Where is your passport?"

"I have none," I said. "Nor do I admit I need one. I haven't traveled through any territory controlled by France."

Since we left Deonundagaa over a month ago, we haven't seen a trace of the French or any sign they even exist out here. I'm not here to venture into French land anyway; my goal is to reach the far Wilderness Country, beyond the Great River."

"That's still French territory," announced Black Robe with a certainty that cut through the air. "God put this whole region aside for the sons of France. No Englishman has ever set foot past the Great River."

"Well, that's exactly why I want to," I replied. "There's no harm in just trying to see what it's like."

Le Moyne's jaw tightened.

"I'm not so sure about that, Mister Ormerod. But there's no point in arguing here. I'll have to ask you to come with us to our camp. There, we can talk further and try to resolve our differences. At worst, I'll send you back to New York with an escort. No harm will come to you."

There weren't many options. We were hopelessly outnumbered—three against nearly a hundred Frenchmen and Indians. Fighting or running was out of the question. Annalla, Corlaer, and I found logic in the same grim reality; when I relayed the conversation, they nodded in reluctant agreement. We fell in line behind the French commander's canoe, trudging back the way we came. The gloom hung over us; the likelihood we'd have to redo our entire journey, wasting the summer and possibly having to hold out through the next winter, loomed large in our minds. Ahead, I saw Black Robe leaning forward occasionally to whisper to Le Moyne—a bad omen if there ever was one.

By dusk, the flotilla pulled up to the northern bank a few miles below the mouth of the Ouabache. We dragged our canoe ashore with the others. Regular infantry scurried around, gathering firewood. They didn't touch our weapons, but their presence made it clear—we were prisoners. I tried to strike up a conversation with the corporal, but he didn't give me much for my trouble.

They had left Detroit while the snow still blanketed the ground. Their journey had taken them all the way to the mouth of the Mississippi, to the French outpost in New Orleans, where the Sieur de Bienville, the Chevalier de Longueuil's brother, was stationed. Now, they were making their way back through Vincennes, Detroit, Niagara, and Fort Frontenac, heading ultimately toward Montreal.

This trek was more than a simple expedition. It demonstrated the relentless ambition of the French government, far more restless and ambitious than their English counterparts. While the English colonies seemed content with a narrow strip of seacoast or the valley of a tidal river, the French continually reached for new territories to claim, develop, and preserve as a future heritage. It was a journey spanning thousands of leagues by river and forest, enduring all extremes of heat and cold. The humble corporal may not have understood the high stakes at play, but it was clear that one of Le Moyne's goals was scouting suitable locations for a network of trading stations and military posts. These would stretch along the Ohio and Mississippi rivers, linking the New Orleans settlement with Canada, effectively locking England out of the untapped resources of the Far West beyond the Great River.

I conveyed some of these thoughts to my comrades as we sat down for our evening meal. We were still deep in our discussion about the implications of our chance encounter when an ensign came to summon us to see Le Moyne. The French Commander sat by a roaring fire in a deep glade that stretched from the river's edge toward the forest. Beside him stood Black Robe, his hot eyes glinting eerily in the firelight, distorted fingers twitching rhythmically over his rosary beads.

"Sit down," Le Moyne commanded curtly. Then, falteringly, in the Seneca dialect: "Annalla, and you, Corlaer, forgive me if I speak in French to your friend. My tongue struggles with the intricacies of the Iroquois speech."

Annalla acknowledged with the regal nod of a prince.

Corlaer squeaked, "Yes."

Le Moyne turned toward me, his demeanor icy, his accent biting through the air like a whip.

"I've been hearing disturbing things about you, Mr. Ormerod. The reverend here tells me you're an undercover agent for the English, a spy sent to stir trouble between us and the natives. He claims you're Burnet's favorite emissary, and that it's mainly due to you that the Six Nations have recently turned against us."

"But, Chevalier—"

"No buts, Mr. Ormerod. It's inconceivable that I should allow someone like you to wander freely in French territory."

"But is it really French territory?" I challenged.

"If the Peace of Utrecht means anything."

"I've heard that no two people agree on that point," I said dryly. He laughed, a sound with no real mirth.

"You're right there," he conceded. "But that's beside the point. You're a agitator, Ormerod. I have to expel you. No matter where I found you, I'd do the same."

"Are the French at war with the English?" I demanded heatedly.

"Not as far as I've heard. You've come from civilization more recently than I have, Monsieur."

"Then why—"

He dismissed my objection with a flick of his wrist.

"We're dealing with the facts, Mr. Ormerod. This isn't about war; it's about keeping peace in France. As I've mentioned, you're a trouble-maker. If I let you roam freely, the next time I pass through, you might have all the tribes riled up, allied with the English Crown. Understand me when I say: France was the first to claim this land, and France intends to keep it that way."

"But I say I have no interest in this country. I—"

Black Robe leaned forward, his eyes narrow and unforgiving.

"Do not waiver, my son," he urged Le Moyne. "This man is dangerous, as are his companions."

“You’ve heard my decision, Father,” replied Le Moyne firmly.

I regarded the priest with a mix of curiosity and irritation.

"Why do you dislike me?" I asked. "Sure, we’re on opposite sides, but I’ve always fought fair. I even saved your life once."

That was the truth. On one occasion, which isn't part of this story, the Iroquois would’ve happily burned Père Hyacinthe alive if it wasn’t for my fierce opposition. He didn’t show any gratitude then, and he certainly wasn’t showing it now as he loomed over the campfire.

"Pathetic creature, writhing on the path of destiny," he spat. "This isn’t about fair or foul fighting, nor about gratitude. You serve the forces of darkness; I serve the Heavenly Father. We don’t intersect at any point. We share no common ground. If you did something good, rest assured Saint Marcus has taken note. But who are you to boast about good deeds when your soul is drenched in heresy, and your eyes blinded by English lies? Reflect on your sins, and maybe you’ll find the light before it’s too late."

He turned to Le Moyne.

"My son, I'm leaving now. There’s a village of the Ouabaches a few miles from here where I’ve preached. I’ll visit them and meet you again in Vincennes."

Without waiting for a response, he turned and walked off into the darkness.

"Wait, Father," the officer called. "Will you not rest and eat? Surely you need an escort—"

A voice floated back from the shadows.

"I need no escort when I'm on my Father's business. I’ve rested all day and already eaten."

"Damn," muttered Le Moyne. "He's uncomfortably holy, isn’t he, Monsieur Ormerod?"

"Don’t I know it!" I shot back. "This isn’t the first time either."

The Frenchman chuckled darkly.

"I figured as much. But come now, tell me your true goal; deceiving me won't do you any good. My hands are tied, as you surely know."

Roaming these woods is a drag, and I haven't heard anything about politics since I left New Orleans. What's got Burnet all riled up?"

I shot him a desperate look. He was a solid guy, with a face that seemed honest enough, iron-willed, a bit combative but smart. He lounged by the fire, clearly bored out of his mind. The only other people around were Annalla and Corlaer, who were off to the side, sharing a smoke and idle chitchat.

"You want the truth?" I said. "Fine. But it's not something for everyone to hear. You, Chevalier, strike me as a gentleman."

He nodded politely.

"And for that reason," I continued, "I'll trust you with it. Yes, I'm keeping my eyes open for information that would help my people. If you sent me back to New York, I'd have to report that I met this expedition and what I deduced from it."

"Hah!" Le Moyne exclaimed. "I never even considered that!"

"Then you wouldn't want to be in a bind," I replied. "Remember, as Père Hyacinthe told you, I'm a member of the Provincial Council. You can't lock me up without trial, especially in peacetime."

"Get on with your story, Monsieur," he urged, impatience creeping into his voice.

"I'm hoping to gather a lot of useful info. No Englishman I know has crossed the Wilderness Country beyond the Mississippi. I want to learn how much our people and the French are known to the tribes, their attitudes toward the English, and the land's value and geography."

"My word, Monsieur, you're blunt!" the Frenchman protested.

"I'm trying to be," I said. "But believe me or not, Chevalier."

I shouldn't even be here, and neither should my friends over there.

I painted a picture for him, as simply as I could, of the tangled web that had brought Annalla, Corlaer, and me to this point. It wasn't a story you could trim into a neat package, and he kept derailing me with questions that led us down unexpected paths. He already knew some of it—the whisper of Ranno's death and Annalla's ensuing heartbreak, for instance—so it was well past midnight when I wrapped up. My companions were snoring softly, and over the crest of the shallow glen, I could see clusters of men slumbering around the dying embers. Along the shore, where the canoes were hauled up, and scattered around the perimeter of the camp, sentries stood watch. Apart from them, we were the only ones awake. My vision blurred; recounting the tale had unearthed memories better left buried. The old wounds throbbed anew. The thought of the house on Pearl Street made me shudder. Right then, I felt I could never set foot in New York again. I didn't want the Frenchman to witness my sorrow.

A sudden explosion of sparks snapped me back as he shifted a heavy log from the fire, causing the flames to shrink and dip.

"Monsieur Ormerod," he said suddenly, "you were kind enough to call me a gentleman."

I looked him in the eye, hardly daring to trust what I saw there.

"I am also," he went on, "a soldier of France. I strive to place my country's interests above my pride, above friendship, above everything. But I wouldn't be a true Frenchman if I didn't honor bravery and a love that bridges heaven and earth. Tonight, you and your comrades taught me something, Monsieur. And for that, I thank you."

"You've made me a better Frenchman, a better soldier, a better Christian."

He smirked as he said that last word.

"Though Père Hyacinthe might find it hard to believe," he admitted.

"What do you mean, Chevalier?" I asked, barely able to contain my curiosity.

"I mean, Monsieur Ormerod, that your adventure can only bring about good. It serves as an inspiration for brave men of all nations. Has it not made me a better Frenchman just hearing about it? And that sleeping savage over there, he's a better Frenchman than I am, despite probably hating my race."

He stood up.

"But I'm not quite brave enough to defy Père Hyacinthe. No, not at all. So, Monsieur Ormerod, I'm going to take a walk and check on the sentries. I'll make sure they notice something by the riverbank on the left. In the meantime, this fire is dying. This glen leads deeper into the forest. Your friends are close. I see you have your weapons. Monsieur, it has been an honor to meet you. Farewell!"

He disappeared while I was still fumbling to express my gratitude. I could hear his booming voice chiding the nearest sentries, a constant stream of comments around the periphery of the camp. I snapped back to reality. A hand over the mouth of each companion, and they woke. In the next instant, we were hunched over, creeping up the glen and into the comforting darkness of the forest. Five minutes later, we were sprinting through the trees, the leaf-strewn ground crunching beneath our boots. Our left arms flung in front of our faces to bat away low-hanging branches and clinging vines.

Chapter Five

We didn't hear the whooping of vengeful savages, which must have accompanied the discovery of our escape, but we weren't about to trust Le Moyne's mercy. So we ran through the night, guiding ourselves northwest by the stars, aiming to dodge the Ouabache villages and the French post at Vincennes. We only halted when the first light of dawn showed us nearing the edge of the forest. Beyond the thinning tree trunks, an expanse of rolling savannahs stretched out to the horizon. Not a single tree broke the monotony, the tall grass rippling under a gentle breeze like green waves on the sea.

"We've gone far enough, brothers," Annalla said, his voice barely a whisper. "Out there, a man is visible for miles. Let's rest now and make sure we're not being followed."

We swung on a hanging grapevine into the center of a thorny patch of wild berry bushes. We cleared a space to lie down, arranging the torn branches like a makeshift roof to keep our haven camouflaged, and surrendered ourselves to a deep, exhausted sleep. It was noon by the time we stirred. Annalla was already up, slipping out of our hideout as my eyes fluttered open. He was gone for about half an hour and returned with the good news—no sign of pursuit along our trail.

"That means we're safe," I said, unable to hide my excitement. "Tonight we can sneak back to the river and steal a canoe from one of the Ouabache villages."

"My brother's thinking is clouded," Annalla replied, shaking his head. "Our enemies will expect us to do just that."

"Ja," Marcus agreed, stretching and yawning. "And if we did, they would follow us."

"True talk," said the Seneca. "They'd follow and catch us. And we'd lose our scalps."

"Then what can we do?" I demanded, frustration boiling over. Annalla pointed to the wide expanse of savannahs, known to the French as prairies, just visible above the tree-tops.

"From here to the Father of Waters, brother, most of the country looks like that."

Corlaer and Annalla know this terrain well. We've traveled this path before, all the way by land from the Door of the Long House. The open plains stretch even farther to the east as you head north toward the Great Lakes. We can move just as quickly across this ground as we can in the canoe, and, brother, we can go in a straight line. The Ohio snakes to the south, and after it takes us to the Great River, we'd have to paddle upstream to go north again. My goal is to reach the Dakota lands, past the Missouri River, which flows into the Father of Waters from the west. Corlaer and Annalla spent some time with the Dakota before the summons called us back to the Long House. I believe they could assist us further on this journey, where others might try to rob us or take our scalps.

"As always, you're right, brother," I said. "If Marcus agrees, let's move out."

Marcus lumbered to his feet, grabbed his musket, and stood ready for Annalla to lead the way.

"Ja," he grunted placidly. "Let's get some buffalo-hump."

"What?" I asked as Annalla started down the hill.

"He's talking about the wild cattle of the plains, brother," explained the Seneca. "You've seen their hides in our lodges. Our forefathers tell through the Keeper of the Wampum that the buffalo once roamed up to the Doors of the Long House, but now they're hardly seen east of the Ouabache. This time of the year, their meat is sweet and tender, especially the hump of a young cow. It will be a welcome change from dried venison."

"Ja," agreed Corlaer, licking his lips. I couldn't help but smile at his vigilance as he scanned the land around us, stepping out from the safety of the forest into the open expanse of the savannahs.

The chubby Dutchman was never as clueless as he let on. He could see, hear, smell, and feel with a sharpness that rivaled the savages — and that's the highest compliment I can give. But he usually used his talents quietly. Today, though, he was just as invested in our surroundings as I was, and his frustration grew comical as the afternoon dragged on without a single sign of life. When I teased him about it, he was visibly annoyed, and his silence when we stopped for the night spoke volumes.

We camped beside a tiny stream that meandered through the rolling waves of the prairie. There was no underbrush, no trees, just the waist-high prairie grass, too green and damp to catch fire. Not that we needed it, given the oppressive heat that blanketed the savannah. The sun had beaten down on us all day, and even after it set, the earth continued to radiate heat like it was sweating. Marcus and I found ourselves envying Annalla for his bare skin, and by morning we stripped off our leather shirts and rolled them into bundles to sling over our food pouches. We allowed the Seneca to smear us with bear grease from a horn-box he carried, a precaution that took the edge off the sun's brutal rays. Without it, my unseasoned shoulders would've blistered, but with that protective layer, they slowly baked until they turned a warm brown, not unlike Annalla's dusky bronze hue.

It wasn't long into the morning when we stumbled upon a broad swath of trampled grass leading from south to north.

Hoofprints were embedded in the dusty earth, and Marcus's eyes sparkled with a childlike glee.

"Buffalo!" he shouted, his voice ringing with excitement. "We're gonna have some juicy hump for dinner!"

Fixating on the distant horizon, he set off at a brisk jog, and Annalla and I trailed behind, just as eager to add some variety to our monotonous diet. Most of our burnt corn and maple sugar was gone, leaving us with nothing but dried deer meat for the past three days.

"How does he know the buffalo went north?" I asked, puzzled. "The tracks point in both directions."

"They always move north this time of year," Annalla replied. "Come fall, they'll head south again. Marcus is right. This grass was trampled just yesterday. They're close."

A sudden yelp from the Dutchman had us on high alert, and his massive form crouched down, eyes locked ahead.

"Look!" he exclaimed. We joined him at the crest of a small rise. Several miles out, a sprawling procession of brown forms meandered across the grassy expanse, hundreds of them.

"A big herd," I noted. Marcus shot me a disdainful glance, and Annalla chuckled.

"Beyond the Mississippi, my friend," the Seneca said, "you'll see buffalo in numbers like the wild pigeons over the Ohio. Their thundering hooves will rattle the ground. They'll blanket the prairie for two days of hard marching."

Marcus plucked a blade of grass, letting it drift in the faint breeze that carried it overhead.

"Good," he grunted. "They're upwind."

"Is Corlaer planning to stalk the buffalo alone?" Annalla asked with his usual politeness.

"One shot's all I need," Marcus replied, and he lumbered away through the grass, his massive frame blending into the landscape until he vanished.

I was just about to sit down and catch my breath, ready to witness the Dutchman's escapade, when Annalla, eyes twinkling with mischief, nudged me off to the right. With a playful grin, he broke into a sprint the moment one of the prairie's deceptive swells shielded us from our companion's view.

"What's the game plan?" I panted, struggling to keep up.

"We're going to surprise Marcus," he said, laughing. "He thinks he can sneak up on the buffalo, Otetiani, but we'll have the buffalo sneak up on him instead."

We looped around in a wide semicircle to the northeast, sidling up to the herd's flank. Before closing in, Annalla stopped us, and we gathered bunches of grass, fashioning them into makeshift camouflage. With our new headgear, we blended seamlessly into the grassy backdrop. Stealthily, we moved around the herd until we were positioned at its rear, with no sign of Corlaer anywhere.

"Now, brother!" Annalla whispered. He tossed his grassy disguise aside and boldly marched toward the animals. I followed suit, and an old bull sounded a bellowing alarm. It was chaos—a cacophony of distressed mooing from cows, the frightened bleating of calves, and the thunderous roars of other bulls. The herd churned and retreated before us. Annalla waved his arms, driving them into a panicked run.

"They're going straight towards Marcus!" I exclaimed.

"They won't trample him," Annalla reassured, a sly smile playing at his lips. "If it were a larger herd, maybe. But this just makes it easier for Marcus, who said he needed no help. He'll take a shot as they approach, and the herd will split around him."

The creatures crested the first swell to the south, and then a gunshot shattered the air.

"Watch!" said Annalla. The massive, frenzied herd parted as cleanly as if a giant blade had slashed through them from the scorching sky. I chased after them, cresting the slope just in time to see the divided halves merge again a quarter of a mile away. Directly below lay the body of a fat cow, with Marcus already crouched over it, skillfully working his knife.

Annalla let out a fierce war-whoop, but Marcus just kept carving away, unphased.

"Yeah," he grunted as we approached, "you thought you had Marcus beat, didn't you? Well, you didn't. I looked back and didn't see you. Then the herd started to move, and it stampedes. 'Oh,' I said to myself. 'Funny tricks! Yeah, funny tricks.' But I still shot the best cow in the pack. We'll have some nice hump for dinner. Yeah."

Luckily for Marcus's appetite, we managed to set up camp that night in a grove of stunted trees near a small river. The broiled buffalo hump turned out to be everything he had hoped for. With a plentiful supply of firewood at hand, we seized the chance to smoke the rest of the prime cuts, about 56 pounds of it, which kept us in the grove for the entire next day. Of course, we couldn't do a perfect job, but it was enough to keep the meat from spoiling in that scorching heat for another three or four days. By then, we'd moved into different terrain where game was more abundant.

Here, lush meadows gave way to dense thickets of low timber. Swamps and bottomlands, backwaters of the river, were forested but never fully drained. The growing natural obstacles slowed us down, and it took us three days to cross this rugged land. But Annalla kept our spirits up, promising that this meant we were close to the Great River, which flooded its banks every Spring, sometimes for miles.

This new country was a far cry from the cool forests and open savannahs we had come to know. The air was thick, the heat oppressive, and we were tormented by swarms of gnats. But fresh meat was never in short supply. We'd knock down squirrels with sticks and creep up on wild turkeys to snatch them from their roosts at night. There was even a kind of partridge, so dumb it practically jumped into our hands, easily killed with a swift blow from the tomahawk.

One time, a black bear blocked our path, growling low and menacing. We let him pass; we had no need for meat, and we had to conserve our powder. On the third day, we trudged through a flooded forest, water soaking us to the knees, and suddenly found ourselves on the edge of a wide, brown river. I thought it might finally be the Mississippi, but Annalla insisted it was the Illinois—a tributary that flowed down from around the Lake of the Michigans, joining the Mississippi a short distance above where the Missouri emptied. Knowing this was crucial; it gave us a rough idea of our location. We retreated to somewhat drier ground and continued southwest, following the Illinois. Progress slowed to a crawl as the thick, wet underbrush fought back every step. Briars slashed at our skin, creepers snagged our feet, and bushes grew so dense we had to hack our way, taking turns to clear the trail.

The next day, we reached higher ground—a ridge from which we snatched brief glances of the Illinois below. By mid-afternoon, we stumbled onto a trail that led from the northeast, snaking over the ridge's saddle.

"Get down!" Annalla hissed as we crashed into the green vaulted path. On the surface, the trail seemed abandoned—a silent, leafy tunnel. But nothing was ever as it seemed in the Wilderness. We slid behind a fallen trunk, ears straining for any sign of other men. The hum of bees buzzed about us in the warm, dappled light. Somewhere nearby, water murmured gently. Birds sang above in the treetops. That was it. Minute after tense minute, we waited for an arrow's whisper, the bark of a gunshot, the chilling war-whoop. But the forest remained still. Finally, Annalla motioned for us to follow him, creeping to a spot that offered a quick escape route into the tangled lands by the river. From there, he left us to scout the area alone.

An hour slipped by as Marcus and I crouched back to back in the underbrush, our eyes scanning the dense woods, ever-alert. Another hour passed, and I started to feel the first prickles of impatience. Dusk was settling over the forest when the eerie hoot of an owl signaled Annalla's return. He crawled into our hideout and dropped a worn moccasin into Marcus's lap.

"Chippewa," he murmured. Marcus nodded, methodically turning the footgear in his chubby hands.

"A war party," Annalla continued. "They're heading toward the Father of Waters. Their tracks point straight to the river."

"The trail is fresh?" Corlaer asked, eyes narrowing.

"I found the ashes of a campfire two days old," Annalla replied, his voice barely more than a whisper carried on the evening breeze. "I advise we stay put until morning. It looks like the Chippewas plan to cross the Great River to hunt for Dakota scalps and buffalo hides. The

Dakota are our brothers. Brave warriors, but they lack muskets. The Chippewas are allied with the French; they have firearms. It's easier for them to steal furs from the Dakota than to hunt the wild creatures themselves. Let's wait until they cross the river, then we'll follow and warn the Dakota."

Morning brought a relentless downpour, and we were on our feet at first light, skirting the trail and sticking to the woods for cover. The day was a grueling mix of physical discomfort and creeping progress, but patience bore fruit. By late afternoon, we emerged from a backwater onto a gentle, grassy bluff, thickly wooded, and overlooked a vast expanse of churning yellow water under a curtain of driving rain.

"The Father of Waters," Annalla said, his voice carrying a note of reverence. I gasped. The river sprawled miles wide, a monstrous, living force, its yellow waves rolling endlessly to the horizon. It pulsed with a power that was almost sentient, sullen and menacing in its sheer immensity.

"But how do we cross it?" I stammered, the enormity of the challenge hitting me like a blow. Annalla gestured toward the cluster of saplings at the edge of the bluff.

"We have our hatchets," he said simply, a grim smile playing on his lips.

"We need to build a raft."

We set up camp where the Chippewa warriors had once stayed, a hollow beneath the bluff, carved out by the rushing waters of spring. The high water had left behind traces of their raft-building, signaling to my comrades that their group had probably been no larger than twenty or thirty young warriors—a typical raiding party. It was too late to start on the raft that night, but with the first light of morning and the cheer from the sunshine, we got to work. Hatchets in hand, we chopped down a score or two of sturdy young trees, hauling them to a spot just above the waterline before heading into the backwaters for grapevines and other creepers, which we carried back by the armload.

These were the materials Annalla had marked for use. Under his guidance, we crafted a remarkably buoyant raft. His plan was straightforward: take a bundle of saplings and bind them tightly together. Across these, he laid another layer that was tied together before being securely fastened to the base. Two more layers were added on top, fashioning a high-riding, nearly watertight vessel, sufficient to carry the three of us. We anticipated trouble crossing the current, so we fashioned crude paddles and poles for pushing through the shallow waters. When at last we wiped the sweat from our eyes after two days of toil, we beheld our creation with pride—a raft tied to a convenient stump, bobbing grandly on the water.

"She floats as regally as a frigate," I declared.

"And no snag can bring her down," Annalla added, with a confident nod. "The Father of Waters knows his power. He's jealous of those who dare to travel him, hiding knives in his depths to wreck the unwary, but we—"

"Hush!" Corlaer snapped, raising a hand. From the inland came the sound of a heavy body crashing through the underbrush, accompanied by the low mutter of a voice, unrestrained and careless.

We grabbed our rifles and darted for cover. Even thinking about escaping on the raft was pointless. Enemy fire would cut us down before we even got it into the water. No, our best bet was to hold our ground, knowing that with the river behind us, we couldn't be surrounded. Maybe, just maybe, nightfall would give us a chance to slip away with the current—if we weren't outnumbered and overrun before that. Only a bold, fearless force would charge at us so recklessly. It was the kind of brash confidence you'd expect from white men, not

Native warriors. The realization sent a jolt of fear through me. I slid closer to Annalla.

"Is it the French, brother?" I whispered.

"We'll find out soon enough," he replied, his voice tight with tension. "Look—there's someone moving between the trees to your right."

Chapter Six

Something dark appeared amidst the dappled light of the woods. Annalla raised his musket, sighting along the barrel with steady precision.

"He's alone," murmured Marcus.

"Then there'll be no one to tell his tale," Annalla remarked grimly. "But don't be too sure, Corlaer. This could be a trap."

Through the gap in the trees, bathed in sunlight, a figure emerged. I caught a glimpse of a fluttering black robe and a pale, haunting face.

"It's Black Robe!" I whispered. Annalla nestled his gun against his cheek.

"Hawenneyu has delivered him to us," he said. "If I miss, Corlaer must shoot before he escapes."

"Ja," grunted Marcus.

"No, no," I said urgently, "There must be no shooting."

"He is an enemy," Annalla replied coldly. "He hates us. Why should my brother care if he lives or dies?"

"But he's done nothing to harm us," I argued. "He doesn't even know we're here."

"Maybe he does," Annalla shot back. "Maybe he's been following us since Le Moyne refused to. Perhaps his Ouabaches and Miamis are hiding behind him."

"He's alone," Marcus repeated. "But we should still shoot him. He's no good."

"It would be murder," I insisted. "Killing him won't benefit us. What harm can he do? In a few hours, we'll have crossed the river where his Indians can't reach us."

The Jesuit came into full view, walking almost directly toward us, his eyes fixed on the horizon. He was chanting to himself in a deep, resonant voice. As he drew closer, I recognized the Vesper Hymn:

"mens gravata crimine, Vitae sit exul munere, Dum nil perenne cogitat, Seseque culpis illigat."

"I'm going to speak to him," I said. "It can't do any harm. He doesn't know we're here. Annalla, the man is fearless. He'd walk right into your musket and dare you to shoot."

Moreover, he's survived torture more than once, and I don't think he's all there mentally. Would you really feel proud of killing someone whose mind the Great Spirit has cloaked in a fog?"

Annalla was all Native, despite his flawless English and the knowledge he had gained from his missionary teachers. Corlaer, after a lifetime among the Indigenous people, had absorbed many of their beliefs. My last comment tipped the scale. A person with a touched mind was sacred to any tribe. The Seneca smirked reluctantly.

"Otetiani makes a strong case. Fine. We'll let Black Robe live. But if he plans any treachery, we must kill him, even though the Great Spirit has marked him."

"He's alone," Marcus declared for the third time. "Always travels alone. I know it. But he's not our friend. We'll keep an eye on him, right?"

“Of course,” I agreed. “He’s a Frenchman and our enemy. I won't deny that. But he can't harm us. Let’s go ask him what he’s doing here. If need be, we’ll watch him afterward.”

Black Robe had stopped about thirty yards south of our hiding place, now standing on the edge of the bluff, surveying the breathtaking view of the untamed river. Its yellow waters shimmered under the sunlight, the opposite bank a low, green wall two miles or more away. His lips moved in inaudible words before he knelt, his head bowed in prayer, his body frozen in an ecstasy of devotion. I waited until he'd risen again before stepping from our hiding place and walking toward him. Annalla and Corlaer followed close behind. He spotted us almost immediately but showed no sign of surprise.

He just stood there, facing us with his horribly mangled hands clasped together, his lean frame radiating a barely contained energy, a testament to the unyielding spirit within him.

"So, you took this route," he said, his voice rough and sharp. "I suspected as much, but no one would heed my warnings."

"And you, Père Hyacinthe?" I asked. "Where are you headed?"

"I am doing my Father's work," he said with the same phrase I'd heard him use many times before.

"Alone?"

He attempted a sarcastic smile, his pale, scarred face cracking eerily.

"Should I bring along an entourage like the Holy Father does when he rides in state? No, but I am never alone, Englishman. Host of angels guard me. The cherubim sing me forward. It's enough."

"I'm not trying to pry into your business," I said, trying to remain respectful, "but you are our enemy. We don't wish to harm you, but we have to look out for ourselves."

"You cannot harm me," he responded calmly. "Enemy? No, my misguided son, I am not your enemy—only to the evil that has taken hold of you. But rest assured, I've traveled many miles today and saw no living soul, except for the creatures of the forest."

I believed him, for I knew the priest never lied.

"Do you have any food?" I asked.

"Food?" he echoed, uncertain, as though he'd forgotten the concept. "No, but I will eat."

"If a heretic's food..." I began.

"Heaven's grace comes in many forms," he interrupted curtly. "Perhaps this moment is your chance for redemption. I will eat your food, Englishman."

Annalla and Marcus listened with sour expressions, showing neither welcome nor tolerance as the Jesuit walked back with us to the shelter under the bluff. His hollow eyes sparked with rare interest when he noticed our raft.

"You're crossing the Great River, Monsieur Ormerod?"

For a fleeting moment, his somber demeanor seemed to falter.

His voice took on a casual politeness, like one gentleman speaking to another. But it was just a fleeting glimpse, an echo from a long-forgotten past.

"Yes," I replied, "as I told the Chevalier—"

"Funny," he cut me off brusquely, his old demeanor snapping back into place, "that you, of all people, are the one chosen to assist in my mission. God's ways are truly mysterious! Yet there must be a purpose here. Blessed Virgin, guide me!"

My comrades wanted nothing to do with him. They grabbed their food and moved out of earshot, leaving me to entertain him alone, which seemed only fair since it was my fault he was with us in the first place. But it ensured a rough evening for me, as Black Robe seized the chance to probe my religious beliefs—sketchy at best after a lifetime of wandering—and lecture me on the errors of my creed. Looking back,

I find that memory fascinating. I often think he was wrong, but of all the men I've met, he was undoubtedly the most devout. He didn't know the meaning of self-interest. His life was thoroughly dedicated to serving the Word of God as he saw it. He didn't waste a moment searching for Truth, believing it was blatantly inscribed across the skies for all to see.

He talked to me for hours while the others slept, and I listened with unwavering interest till the very end. The man's stern conviction was nothing short of inspiring, whether you agreed with him or not. And if anyone considers me weak for respecting him for believing what he preached, I'd argue that he and many like him were among the most powerful forces in bringing the rule of the white man into the Wilderness Country.

If he and his companions couldn't convert the natives, they at least demonstrated the unyielding spirit of the white man. Their pioneering efforts also showed their people the value of uncharted lands that always lie just beyond the horizon.

The night brought a shift in the weather, and by morning, the sky was overcast, the wind gusty and unpredictable. We debated whether it was wise to trust ourselves to the raft under such conditions. Annalla and Marcus advised against it, but Black Robe scoffed at their fears.

"What's this?" he jeered in fluent Seneca, a tongue he had mastered during his years as a missionary. "Is the Warden of the Western Door afraid to brave the waters? Is Corlaer, whose fat belly is the terror of every squaw from Jagara to the mouth of the Mohawk, scared of getting his moccasins wet? You've faced countless dangers over hundreds of miles, and now you hesitate at a few leagues of water! Summon your courage! I am but a shadow of what once was a man, yet I am not afraid. Will you let me outdo you?"

"Black Robe speaks nonsense," Annalla replied coldly. "A foolish bird has whispered idle thoughts in his ear. He knows well that Annalla does not fear even the Master of Evil, Hanegoategeh, whom he claims Black Robe serves."

Marcus stayed silent, as was his custom, but his beady eyes squinted thoughtfully before he pulled us aside.

"If Black Robe has lost his mind, we might be safe," he suggested.

"That's ridiculous," I snapped. "What does his state of mind have to do with the wind or the rising waters? It's dangerous out there on the raft or it isn't. Black Robe has no bearing on that."

"My brother Otetiani may be right," Annalla said, "but he recalls that Black Robe has claimed the Great Spirit's protection."

"Do you think Hawenneyu would let him drown?"

"Maybe not," I admitted. "But there's a chance we'd go under while he gets away."

"Otetiani speaks true," the Seneca confirmed. "But we can't let the Black Robe disrespect us. The Father of Waters holds dangers. If we back down, Black Robe will laugh at us, and one day he might even share this tale with his people. We need to go."

I shrugged. The river now looked angrier, churning more by the minute. But Annalla's peculiar logic was hard to argue with. No man likes being called a coward.

"Fine," I relented. Annalla approached the priest.

"We're going," he said evenly. "If we die, remember it was you who pushed us."

For a fleeting moment, a rare hint of the man's true self shone through the Jesuit's stoic façade. He rested his hand on the Seneca's bare shoulder.

"There's nothing to fear," he said softly. "God watches over us on water just as on land. If it's your time, it's your time. A true warrior thinks not of death, but of his mission."

Then his demeanor shifted. His hand fell to his side and his voice took on a hard edge.

"You'd blame your sins on me? You may as well blame me for your death! Neither of us controls life! Look up! I said look up! The Power that decides everything is there. You fear, you fear what you don't understand!"

Annalla's face was a canvas of steely resolve as he walked to the raft's edge, drawing his knife. He put its sharp edge against the mooring line.

"Annalla is ready," he announced. Black Robe stepped aboard without a word. Marcus and I followed. With a single decisive stroke, the Seneca severed the line.

We heaved our rifles, powder-horns, and pouches onto a makeshift stand in the center of our creaky raft, hoping to keep them dry, and then grabbed the poles, the Jesuit joining in, and pushed off into the flowing river. The raft rode higher than expected but was so heavy that it dragged sluggishly in the slack water near the bank. We leaned into the poles with all our might, but progress was painfully slow. The raft sagged, lurched, and the trees lashed together groaned and squelched as we inched forward, barely making a foot or two at a time. We got stuck on a sandbar for an hour and, after a frustrating struggle, managed to float around it. Then the battle resumed, and even with our shirts off, sweat drenched us and our muscles screamed in agony. Black Robe, as we called him, seemed unaffected; he didn't sweat but worked tirelessly until, without warning, an incredible force gripped the raft. There was a swirl, a strange sucking noise, and the shore began to drift away. The raft teetered wildly, spun around, drifted across the current, then suddenly spun back downstream. We stood there, dumbfounded, leaning on the poles, barely grasping what had just occurred.

"Looks like the river's doing the work for us," I said. Annalla shook his head, concern darkening his eyes.

"No, brother. The worst is yet to come. The river's a wild beast today."

"Ja," squeaked Corlaer, jabbing his pole futilely in an attempt to find the bottom. Black Robe stood alone at the front of the raft, staring into the murky distance as if he could see landscapes that were hidden from our mortal eyes.

"We could try to work across the current," I suggested. "It might take a while, but—"

A yellow-brown wave, its crest foamy with scum, slapped against the side of the raft and splattered our feet. Another wave came from the opposite direction and washed over the side.

The raft's frame groaned and shifted beneath us.

"It's gonna take hours," Annalla muttered. "We're just getting started."

We grabbed the makeshift paddles we'd carved and tried steering diagonally with the current. But it quickly became clear that maintaining a consistent course was a pipe dream. We'd make some headway, only to get swept up by an eddy and tossed back, or worse, be toyed with by a capricious wind. The waves climbed higher, soaking us to the waist. Still, we fought on, and as we did, our efforts grew more coordinated. There was a trick to this, a skill far different from guiding a lightweight, nimble canoe. Our raft had its own stubborn will, a certain savage dignity. If we handled it the way it wanted, it might just cooperate enough to get us where we aimed to go. Slowly, we learned its quirks, and this helped us make some headway. But nothing we did could fully combat the fickle whims of wind and current. Sometimes they aligned, pushing us downstream with haste. Other times, the wind came at us sideways, countering the current just enough to throw off our rhythm. By mid-afternoon, we'd gained little more than a perilous mid-river course, constantly disrupted by violent lurches toward one shore or the other.

When the current hurled us toward the eastern bank, we fought back with a frantic desperation. Then, as if out of some odd sense of mercy, it would shift us in the right direction, and we'd grit our teeth and double down on our efforts, only to be spun back around and set adrift again. Night fell, and we were miles from where we'd started, yet still not halfway across the river. Sleep was out of the question. We were drenched, with scant food left. But no matter how bone-tired we were, giving up the fight against the relentless river was not an option.

Now, we had to muster all our vigilance, for the river was packed with sinister debris, half-sunken projectiles that had once been majestic trees but were now deadly instruments of the river's fury. One of these monstrous wooden hulks rammed into us under the dim starlight, partially wrecking the structure where we'd stashed our weapons and spare clothing. We almost lost our entire supply of gunpowder in that mishap. The impact had a noticeable effect, loosening the fabric of the raft, making it sluggish, more prone to lurch unpredictably. Our attempts to steer it were laughably inept. Still, we didn't give up. Despite the coolness of the night, we sweated like we had in the sweltering savannahs, tapping into unknown reservoirs of strength to maintain the fight. We rarely spoke to each other; there was little need for words except to occasionally shout a warning. Black Robe paddled and poled beside us, hour after hour. I can't recall him saying a single word that night. We were scared, openly admitting it through our silence. But he, he seemed as calm and indifferent to fate as he had been when prodding us to start. He was the only one who didn't shout in hoarse triumph when the river played its final trick on us. It happened just after sunrise. For the past hour, we'd felt an erratic swirl in the eddying current. Now, about a mile ahead of us to the right, we spotted the mouth of another river, nearly as wide as the Mississippi.

"That's the Missouri, brothers!" cried Annalla. "We've come far downstream. If we get carried past this point, we'll end up in Mandan territory. And you know the Mandans are enemies of the Dakota—they feast on human flesh. Hawenneyu has turned his face away from us!"

But just at that instant, Hawenneyu lifted the veil and smiled upon us.

It all went down when the Missouri's incoming surge collided with the Mississippi's torrent, merging into the Great River. Together, they churned up a dizzying vortex, spinning us around like a hapless toy in a child's hands. Our raft became a helpless plaything, whipped around by the currents. We fought against the whirlpools for what felt like an eternity, but it was all in vain. Frustrated and exhausted, we resigned ourselves to whatever fate awaited us, gripped by a sense of impending doom.

To our astonishment, the river's wild tantrum spat us out toward the western bank at an incredible speed. Twice we were snatched and battered by rebellious eddies, but each time our raft miraculously broke free, like some live beast shaking off a predator's grip. As dawn broke, we found ourselves unceremoniously cast into a backwater near the western bank, about half a mile above where the Missouri's mouth yawned open.

We were still marooned far from firm ground, and it took two bone-weary hours of relentless poling to fight through the sandbars to where we could finally wade ashore. But we made it, just barely. Shouldering our muskets, we stumbled onto the bank, collapsing onto the damp ground, sagging with the weight of exhaustion—all except Black Robe. Without a backward glance at us or the soggy wreckage of the raft, he scaled the bank and pressed westward. Sleep had eluded him just as it had us; he had eaten meager mouthfuls since morning and toiled as hard as any of us.

I called after him, but he brushed me off with a dismissive wave. The last I saw of him, his dark silhouette was etched against a strip of low woods, his back radiating a defiant determination that unsettled me. But I had no strength left to follow, even if my life depended on it. Annalla and Marcus lay motionless beside me, already lost to the undertow of sleep, their bodies too drained to care anymore. With a heavy sigh, I let myself sink to the ground beside them, surrendering to the fatigue that clawed at my bones.

Chapter Seven

"Wake up, bro, wake up!"

The words slipped into my ears, mingling with a strange, underlying sound. "Pop! Pop! Pop!" It echoed into the crackling noise a wood fire makes when it's burning happily. I felt a rough shaking and tried to resist, but I eventually woke up. Annalla was bent over me, gripping my shoulder. Relief washed over his face as I sat up.

"Otetiani was sleeping like he was already in the Halls of the Honochenokeh," he said. "Listen!"

Still groggy, I recognized the steady crackle of musket fire that had dragged me out of my exhausted slumber.

"Black Robe!" I blurted out. Annalla shook his head.

"Maybe, but they aren't shooting at us, bro. Come on, let's join Corlaer."

I stood up, musket in hand, and became acutely aware of the soreness in every muscle, joint, and sinew. My whole body was a map of aches and pains.

"We're in no shape to fight," I muttered grimly.

"A warrior fights when he has to," Annalla replied with a grim sense of wisdom. "Hurry up, brother. Corlaer is waiting."

I climbed after him towards the top of the bank where I could make out the large shape of the Dutchman, hunched in the tall grass. The sun was dipping low in the western sky. The wind was barely there. The Mississippi behind us was as calm as a pond, and in the clear, warm light, the opposite shore seemed deceptively close. Hard to believe we had fought to cross it just that morning. From the crest of the bank, everything looked different. Crawling into the grass beside Marcus, Annalla and I cautiously peered over the rustling tips at the wall of the low woods where Black Robe had disappeared. The woods were half a mile away. A meadow stretched open between it and the riverbank. Another half-mile to our left, scattered bushes marked the edge of the Missouri.

We were huddled on one side of a triangular patch of land where two rivers converged. The battle was moving out of the dense woods and bleeding into this open space. One group of men seemed to be driving another into the triangle's trap. Just as this dawned on me, a flash of color broke through the edge of the woods. An Indian figure sprinted into the clearing—a tall, imposing man with a feathered headdress like nothing I'd ever seen. The grand bonnet circled his head and flowed down between his shoulders, making him seem even taller. He ducked behind a tree, nocked an arrow, and shot into the forest depths. Then, he bolted. He hadn't run more than a dozen yards before a shot rang out. He jerked violently in the air and crashed face-first to the ground.

More men, dressed similarly, burst into view. They paused momentarily to take cover and fire their arrows back into the woods. About twenty of them, I guessed—all tall, lean warriors wearing nothing but breechcloths, moccasins, and elaborate headdresses. They dashed across the open space like a herd of antelope. Sporadic gunfire erupted from the woods, and another man tumbled to the earth. A piercing wail followed.

"Dakota," Annalla muttered.

"What's happening?" I asked, gripping my musket tighter.

"Hold steady, brother. Let's see how this unfolds."

A new wave of figures emerged from the woods, shouting and firing at the retreating Dakotas, who, with their bows outranged, didn't even think of fighting back. They just ran for the safety of the Missouri River bank.

"Chippewa!" Corlaer squeaked. Annalla nodded, his face darkening.

"They're the war party that crossed the Great River ahead of us," he said. "What now, brothers? The Chippewa are allied with the French. Corlaer and I have spent many months in the Dakotas' teepees."

The odds are stacked against our Dakota brothers. If we side with them, we might end up losing our own lives."

"We're in danger no matter what we do," I replied. "The Chippewa wouldn't spare us if they had the chance. I'm for helping the Dakota. If we save them, they'll be more eager to help us with our mission, just like you pointed out earlier."

"Yeah," agreed Corlaer. "And we give those Chippewa a surprise, huh?"

"We give them Death," Annalla said, his voice cold as ice. He proved his point as he spoke, taking down an enemy with a single shot. I followed suit and brought down another. Corlaer bided his time until I was almost finished reloading, then he aimed and secured two in a row, hitting one in the shoulder while the other crumpled with a shot through the chest. We were firing calmly, our guns steady; there was no missing. The Chippewa, screaming in rage, dove for cover in the tall grass.

This marked the start of the second phase of our battle. The Chippewa were sharp shooters too, and when Corlaer took his next shot, they bombarded him with bullets that tore up the earth around him, making him roll down the bank, spitting dirt from his mouth. Annalla and I scrambled after him; wisdom trumping bravado in this case.

If our barrage had shocked the Chippewa, it had confused the Dakota just as much. At first, they seemed to fear a trap, but after seeing the ferocious response from the Chippewa that sent us diving over the bank, they decided we must be allies. They changed their course, heading towards us to join forces.

We, on our part, urgently needed to join them and create a strategy that would keep the Chippewa at bay long enough to plan our next move with the Dakota.

After we hustled a bit downriver, we scrabbled up the bank and fired another round at the Chippewa, their crouched forms barely hidden by the tufts of tall grass. Before they could adjust their aim, we slid back down the embankment, racing for a new position. This cat-and-mouse game forced the Chippewa into a slow, cautious advance—they couldn't risk exposing themselves too much after the beating we'd given them at the start. This gave us the time we needed to work our way downriver to where the remnants of the Dakota band clung to the safety of the bank, arrows ready, eyes full of suspicion towards these unexpected saviors. But their doubt dissolved as we got close enough for them to recognize Annalla and the hulking figure of the Dutchman.

Their chief, a sinewy giant around forty, with a high-beaked nose and piercing, direct eyes, wore a grand headdress of golden eagle feathers. He stepped forward to greet us, a light of recognition and welcome on his face that made both my friends exclaim at the sight of him.

"Do you know him?" I panted eagerly.

"He's Chatanskah, Chief of the Wahpeton Council Fire," Annalla replied curtly. "He's hunted buffalo with Corlaer and Annalla many times."

Chatanskah, or White Hawk, exchanged a few terse words with Annalla, who nodded in agreement. Then the chief led his warriors on a dead sprint toward the junction of the two rivers—the apex of the triangle where we were fighting. The Seneca motioned for us to follow.

"Quickly, brothers!" he urged. "We must outsmart the Chippewa. Chatanskah's plan is to seek the shelter of the woods near the Missouri bank, just across from here."

But it wasn't as easy as it sounded. The Chippewa soon figured out what we were up to, and we had barely rounded the blunt promontory, with its slippery mudflats, when they tumbled down the Mississippi bluff and started raining lead on us.

They tried to cut us off by sprinting across the meadow at the heart of the triangle, but Annalla, Corlaer, and I climbed the Missouri bluff, forcing them back into cover. Through sheer determination and several desperate maneuvers, we eventually scrambled up the Missouri bank, meeting up with our allies. We dashed across a narrow strip of grassland into the green shelter of the woods. Bullets zipped by, slicing the branches around our shoulders. Once we reached safety, Annalla briefed us on the situation while the Dakota pulled meat from their pouches, and we hastily devoured our meal as the shadows of evening crept in.

"This forest stretches west and north for about a mile," he began, his voice steady. "Beyond that, it's all open buffalo grazing land where the Dakota were hunting when the Chippewa ambushed them this afternoon." Annalla's eyes scanned the treetops as he spoke. "Chatanskah suggests we hold our ground here until dark. Only then can we take the risk to cross the prairie. The Dakota villages are a long day's journey away."

Before he could finish, the Chippewa renewed their assault. They had regrouped behind the Missouri bank and were now firing into the woods as fast as they could reload. Bullets thudded into the trees, sliced through the branches, and whistled ominously in the air. The sinister tune of the musketry, one that would haunt me for years, was impossible to ignore. Despite the cacophony, it did minimal damage. One of the Dakota, in a moment of bravery, stepped out to shoot an arrow, only to drop with a bullet lodged in his lungs. Apart from that, we remained unscathed, for the most part.

The intensity of the fire increased, and the forest descended into a hellish fury. We could hear the Chippewa shouting encouragement to one another, their voices merging with the ear-splitting racket of gunfire. Smoke billowed from the bank in thick, opaque clouds. Suddenly, Chatanskah's voice cut through the chaos, a sharp warning. Through the smoke emerged low-running figures, muskets in one hand, tomahawks in the other, charging toward our hiding spot.

But this was the moment Annalla, Marcus, and I had been waiting for, and we made every shot count. Our allies were undeterred. In the smoky dusk, at such close range, the bow held its own against the musket. The Chippewa couldn't stop to reload. They had to rely on the covering fire of their comrades behind the bank, but those poor bastards found it impossible to aim through the thick smoke that the dying wind refused to disperse. The Dakota bows sang with savage joy. All around us, I could hear the taut twang of the strings, the sharp "hiss-ss-s- tsst!" of the arrows slicing through the air.

Out in the open, men flailed, arms reaching for the sky before collapsing with arrows buried in their guts. Others fell, kicking and coughing, pierced through the throat, or dropped straight backward with feathers sprouting from their chests. The attack faltered, then broke, and the Dakota warriors surged from the woods. Two fell before a ragged volley from the riverbank, but there was no stopping the rest. They swept across the field with tomahawks and scalping knives, their arrows pushing the surviving Chippewa onto the mudflats. They would have chased them further if Chatanskah hadn't called them back, wary of an ambush in the gathering darkness.

That night was a triumphant one for the Dakota band. Even the youngest warrior earned his stripes, for the Chippewa had lost two-thirds of their men. But what truly thrilled our new friends wasn't the number of scalps taken; it was the eighteen French muskets they lifted from the ground. It was the biggest haul of war booty their tribe had ever seen, priceless in its military value, as the future would soon reveal. Moreover, that obscure battle in the triangle between the rivers became legendary among the plains tribes, proving that under the right conditions, they could stand toe-to-toe with the forest tribes from the east of the Mississippi, despite the superior weaponry of their enemies.

Many leaders, who had once focused solely on stealing horses, now ventured into complex plans for acquiring muskets. Exhausted as his men were, and we just as weary, Chatanskah refused to let them camp where they'd won their fight. Laden with a considerable amount of loot—including muskets, powder-horns, shot- pouches, knives, tomahawks, and other gear—the band trotted through the woods and spilled out onto the open prairie. Under the rising moon, they headed inland from the Missouri, navigating northwesterly by the stars, maintaining a relentless pace until what I estimated to be midnight.

Only then did Chatanskah agree to make camp without fires and set guards for the rest of the night. Annalla offered to share the watch duty, but the Dakota chief adamantly refused.

"What?" Chatanskah exclaimed. "Should a guest be expected to fend for himself? Chatanskah and his warriors were as good as dead men when Annalla and his white brothers saved us. We owe you our lives. You will sit at the heart of my teepee. My women will serve you. My young men will hunt for you. Our elders will tell you tales from ages past. Stay with us, and we'll find you maidens to catch your eye. We'll make powerful medicine to turn the white brothers red, and you'll become chiefs of the Dakota. Then our tribe will thrive and become mighty in war."

His eyes sparkled as he painted that vivid picture of triumph.

"That's a plan worth pondering, my brother of the Hodenosaunee," he continued, enthusiasm undimmed. "We will raid the Chippewa, the Miami, the Potawotomi, the Illinois, the Shawnee for guns. We'll steal horses from the Spaniards and the tribes past the Missouri. We will become great, brother."

"My brother forgets," Annalla replied softly. "When I was among the Dakota before, I spoke of a quest I had undertaken."

"True," the Dakota conceded, visibly deflated. "And does Annalla still pursue that quest?"

"Yes, brother."

My white brothers are with me. We're searching for the Land of Lost Souls, which our ancient legends say lies beyond the sunset.

The Dakota warrior shrugged his powerful shoulders.

“Maybe. My people don’t know anything about it.”

Annalla hesitated. Knowing him as I did, I could see the fear in his eyes as he prepared to press the question. But his will triumphed over his dread.

"Has Chatanskah ever asked warriors from afar if they know of the Land of Lost Souls?"

"Chatanskah never forgets a promise to a friend," the Dakota replied. "I've spoken many times with the brothers of the Dakota Council fires that stretch toward the Sky Mountains. What is beyond those mountains, they do not know. That land you speak of might be there. But they don't know. No warrior has ever crossed those mountains and come back. Large groups die of hunger and thirst. A few warriors are killed by the people living in the rocky places."

"Yet Annalla and his white brothers will go there," the Seneca declared.

"If you go, you will die," Chatanskah replied. "It would be much better to stay with me and become a great chief."

"Nevertheless, Annalla must move forward," insisted Annalla. "My Dakota brother has said he owes us his life. Will he repay this debt by helping us on our way?"

The Dakota bowed his head.

"Chatanskah cannot deny what Annalla and his white brothers ask. You will come with us to our villages and rest for a while. Our women will repair your moccasins. You'll eat well and grow strong, for it's clear you've traveled hard and gone hungry. Afterward, if you still seek it, I and my young men will take you west to our brothers of the Teton Council Fire, and they will guide you to the foot of the Sky Mountains.

"But for now, let Annalla sleep in peace."

Chatanskah will be watching.

Hours later, a cold wind from the north jolted me awake. I sat up and saw Annalla with his chin resting on his knees, arms wrapped tightly around his ankles, staring at the star-streaked western sky. His face bore that unsettling look of exaltation I'd seen many times before—a mix of brooding anticipation and fearful expectancy, like someone who hopes to see something but dreads the moment it comes. It was one of those eerie moments when night teeters on the edge of dawn. The wind howled above, and the stars seemed to bow toward the Earth, whispering secrets just out of reach. I felt the silent agony of my past, the very thing I'd been running from, but even in that moment, my heart raced with an odd, inexplicable hope, as if all my sorrow had suddenly evaporated. A voice whispered out of the void:

"Alone. Alone. Alone."

But the solitude didn't scare me. Yes, I was alone, but memories surged forward to soften the sting of the word. Memory—that was the trick. Out of memory, a man could carve a new life, a weapon to shatter loneliness. I delved into the shadows of my mind, testing the theory, pulling out thoughts and recollections that once rattled my nerves. Now, they tumbled into an orderly sequence, allowing themselves to be sorted, arranged, and returned to their proper places. Some offered pleasure, others a sharp pang of pain, but I was always in control. My grief had been conquered. My mind was my own once more. I spoke softly to Annalla.

"My brother, have you not slept?"

He turned his sorrow-filled eyes toward me.

"No, Annalla thinks of the past and the bleak future. But what is this?" He leaned closer. "Otetiani's eyes are clear. The Evil Spirit no longer clouds his face."

"I've found peace, brother," I said simply. A sudden glow of inner light chased the gloom from his face.

"Otetiani has saved Annalla from himself. Hawenneyu has spoken."

Hanegoategoh had lost his touch; the future held hope, brother."

He stretched out where he stood and fell asleep in an instant.

Chapter Eight

Chatanskah's village was a cluster of buffalo-hide teepees perched along a creek that lazily poured into the Missouri River. This settlement, alongside a few others, made up the Wahpeton Council Fire, one of the seven sub-tribes of the Dakota. Their domain stretched along the north bank of the Missouri, reaching out towards the foothills of the Sky Mountains. In some ways, their political structure reminded me of the great Iroquois Confederacy, a sentiment Annalla shared. These sons of the endless plains had a sturdy self-reliance and a classic dignity, much like the People of the Long House, who thrived beneath the primeval forest canopies back east of the Mississippi.

Big men, they were — lithe, muscled, with faces cut by intelligence and boldness. Fearless warriors and skilled hunters, they were also eloquent speakers. Much like the Iroquois, they understood the benefits of unity, and this made them a force to be feared by neighboring tribes.

We had been living among them for a week, resting from our recent ordeals, when a group of young men returned with news that sent a buzz through the village. A massive herd of buffalo was approaching from the north. The tail end of summer was drawing near, and the herds that had wandered north were beginning to make their journey back south toward the Spanish lands. This migration was a pivotal event for the Dakota people. The buffalo was their lifeblood.

They thrived on its rich flesh, wrapped themselves in its warm hides, and wove rope from its coarse hair. In a land almost barren of wood, buffalo dung provided vital fuel. They crafted bowstrings from its sinews, weapons from its horns, and containers as well. For the Dakota, the buffalo meant the difference between starvation and plenty, between freezing and warmth, between nakedness and protection. This reality held true for countless other tribes across a vast land as large as Western Europe, inhabited by hundreds of thousands of free-roaming souls.

As late summer gave way to fall, the buffalo had spent months grazing on the lush savannah grasses, turning them into prime targets with their thick, silky fur ready for the harsh winter. The village buzzed with activity, teepees alive with the nervous energy of preparation. Chatanskah, without wasting a moment, gathered his hunting party, and we volunteered for the journey.

On the second day, we stumbled upon scattered groups of buffalo. Yet, the chief held back his warriors, reasoning—quite wisely—that the beasts would eventually wander close to the village, where the home-stayers could take care of them.

By the third day, vast herds, thousands strong, roamed before us, but the young scouts insisted that this was not the main migration. They were right. The dawn of the next day revealed prairies black with an unending sea of buffalo. To the north and west, they swallowed the landscape. To the east, they stretched for a mere half-mile. Chatanskah quickly steered us across the front of the densely packed columns to strike their flank, maintaining a steady, relentless drive. None of us dared to face that tsunami of muscle and hoof head-on. The ground rumbled beneath their stampede, a fine dust hazing the morning air.

To gain our position, we dipped into a small creek bed, its banks shaded by scraggly trees. We followed it for a quarter mile before emerging into a startling new scene: from the northeast, another party of warriors, just as large and fearsome, was bearing down upon the herd. Cries went up from the Dakota ranks. To my eyes, at that distance, the newcomers looked no different, but Chatanskah's men knew at a glance. Annalla turned to me with certainty.

"Cheyenne, brother," he said.

They call themselves the Striped-arrow People, named after their tradition of using turkey feathers on their arrow shafts.

"Are they friends or enemies?"

He smiled, though it was a hard smile, one devoid of warmth.

"When two tribes share a herd of buffalo, Otetiani, they can only be enemies."

"But surely there are enough buffalo here for all the tribes in the wilderness!"

"My brother forgets that once the buffalo are attacked, they start running, and no one can predict where they'll go."

"Then we must fight the Cheyenne?"

"So it seems, brother," he replied with a chilling indifference. Chatanskah and his people were convinced that there was only one way out of this, so they rushed toward the opposing party. The Cheyenne saw us at the same moment we saw them and made it their business to meet us halfway. Both groups stopped, as though commanded by some unseen force, a long bow-shot apart, standing with weapons at the ready, glaring at each other with provocative intensity.

It was a peculiar scene. Less than a mile away, the buffalo surged south like a living river of flesh. The outer edges of the herd seemed to drift away from us, but the majority paid us no attention. Their sheer numbers and relentless progress were terrifying. There must have been millions of them. And here we were, a comparatively small number, preparing to clash with another small group over the right to take a few from their seemingly endless multitudes.

The chief of the Cheyenne stepped forward, a towering figure, his arms and chest scarred by the Sun Dance's trials.

"Why do the Dakota interfere with the Cheyenne's hunt?" he demanded. "Are they preparing for war?"

"The Cheyenne should know best if there is war," Chatanskah retorted. "They are the ones interfering with the Dakota's hunt."

"There is war only if the Dakota start it," asserted the Cheyenne chief. "The Cheyenne have been tracking these buffalo for a day."

"Go back to your own land and wait for the buffalo," demanded the Dakota warrior, Chatanskah.

"And since when do the Cheyenne decide what the Dakota should do?" Chatanskah snapped back, his eyes flashing with defiance. "My young men have a response for you."

The Cheyenne leader, Nakuiman, coldly assessed the Dakota's gathering before speaking. "I see you have two white men with you," he said, his voice dripping with disdain. "One of them is a big man, but he's fat. Send him out here and we'll see if there's any strength behind that belly. Tell him to drop all his weapons except his knife, and I'll do the same. If he dares, I'll rip his heart out with my bare hands and eat it in front of the Dakota. But he won't come. He's scared."

Chatanskah translated this to Corlaer with some hesitation. "The Bear is a strong warrior," he added gravely. "He's counted more victories than anyone in his tribe."

"Yeah," Corlaer grunted, and without another word, he set down his musket, tomahawk, powder horn, and shot pouch. He pulled his leather shirt over his head, revealing his bulky frame. Chatanskah, still unsure, glanced at him warily. The Dakota knew Corlaer was a marksman and a shrewd thinker, but they mocked him behind his back for his enormous girth.

"There's no need for concern," spoke up Annalla with a confident smile. "Our brother Corlaer is the strongest warrior among his people. Tomorrow, the Cheyenne will need a new chief, those who survive the Dakota's arrows. Tell Nakuiman to lay down his weapons."

Reluctantly, Chatanskah complied. A young Cheyenne warrior stepped forward and took the bow, arrows, and tomahawk from his chief.

"Nakuiman waits," the Cheyenne leader announced with a cruel grin. "The white man isn't in a hurry to die."

But Corlaer lumbered forward, his legs wobbling comically beneath his bulk, and his vast belly quivering with each step.

Fat rolled and wrinkled over his hairy brown chest, settling into deep creases along his sides. Only those who had witnessed him in action knew that under that blubber lay muscles of inhuman strength, and that his calm exterior masked an iron will that had never bent to hardship. The Cheyenne warriors greeted him with guttural laughter, while the Dakota looked on with somber expressions. And honestly, who could blame them, comparing the two champions? The Cheyenne was the largest native I had ever seen, towering over six feet in his moccasins, with the shoulders of an ox, perfectly sculpted, narrow-waisted, and legs like bronze pillars. He crouched as Corlaer approached, drawing his knife, circling on the balls of his feet, the keen blade poised across his stomach, ready to strike or block as needed.

Corlaer, on the other hand, hadn't even bothered to draw his knife; his hands just hung loosely at his sides. He slouched forward, making no attempt to adopt a fighting stance, his whole body exposed to the Cheyenne's blade. The Cheyenne warriors transitioned from laughter to taunting, throwing out remarks which Corlaer couldn't understand. Nakuiman, the Cheyenne, apparently agreed with their assessment, for he started a kind of dance around Corlaer, never closing the distance completely but maintaining a constant threat with his knife.

Marcus, maintaining his usual facade of indifferent stoicism, turned clumsily on his flat feet as the Cheyenne circled him, making no effort to counter the quick lunges that brought his opponent closer and closer. This continued for so long that the Dakota around me began to fume with rage and humiliation, while the Cheyenne were nearly doubled over with laughter. Then Nakuiman evidently grew tired of the charade. He leaped at the Dutchman like a ball launched at a wall, and despite my previous confidence, a moment of dread coursed through me as he lunged. Compact with deadly energy, the Cheyenne's thrust was so fast that we bystanders couldn't follow it. But Marcus could.

The Dutchman woke up, almost like a spell had been broken. The dazed look in his eyes evaporated, and suddenly his massive frame surged with an energy that seemed to come from a bottomless well. The Cheyenne attacked. There was a quick glint of steel. Marcus's arms reacted in a blur. The knife flashed again, slicing through the air before it flew upwards, spinning, and stabbed into the ground twenty feet away.

Just two bodies now, heaving and straining. Marcus had a death grip on the Cheyenne, one wrist and a forearm firmly in his clutches. The Cheyenne struggled like a wild animal, desperately trying to free one arm to throttle Marcus. As I watched, he leaned in and sank his teeth into Marcus's shoulder. Blood sprayed from the wound, and a shudder ran through Marcus's gigantic frame. But he was undeterred.

Steadily, with an inevitable force, he bore down. The Cheyenne's muscles strained and finally began to give. Nakuiman's left arm was wrenched back, further and further. Then came a loud, sickening snap. The Indian let out a yelp like a wounded beast. The arm went limp. With the swiftness and ferocity of a jungle cat, Marcus lunged for the man's throat.

The teeth still clamped into Marcus's shoulder loosened under the crushing force. A single, choked cry reached our ears. The Cheyenne's head fell back. With a remarkable show of strength and coordination, Marcus lifted the man's body above his head. He held it there for a moment, his eyes locking with the Cheyenne warriors who had laughed just moments ago. Then he hurled the lifeless form like it was nothing more than a sack of potatoes.

It twisted through the air, hit the ground, and rolled into a heap of dead limbs. Marcus shook himself, turned on his heel, and walked back to us with a measured pace.

"Oof," he said, almost casually. "That made me sweat."

That offhand comment seemed to jolt the Cheyenne into understanding what had just unfolded. Their eyes, previously glued to the sight of their chief's demise, now burned with rage. Overcome by fury, they abandoned any pretense of restraint and charged at us, bowstrings taut, arrows ready to fly. But the Dakotas were ready.

Chatanskah had brought along a dozen French rifles, weapons we had taught his warriors to use with deadly precision. When the enemy charged, we unleashed a devastating volley that stopped them in their tracks. Leaderless and utterly defeated, they fled across the prairie, chased by the swiftest young men of our band. The spoils of victory left us with the task of harvesting a bounty of buffalo meat. After scalping the fallen Cheyenne and congratulating Corlaer, the remaining Dakota warriors lined up and moved down toward the herd's flank. The gunfire had panicked the herd's outer ranks, creating enough confusion to slow their pace and unsettle them further as the Dakota approached within bowshot.

Chatanskah later told us this herd must have roamed unchallenged for ages, showing little fear at our presence. He also believed that such vast herds were tougher to stampede than smaller ones. It took several moments after the bowstrings hummed before the herd began to mill and change direction. In those crucial moments, the Dakota slaughtered enough buffalo to feed their village through the winter. Aiming expertly between the ribs of the shaggy beasts, they drove their flat-headed hunting arrows deep into the fat carcasses. Rarely did it take more than one shot to bring down a buffalo. Some staggered briefly, but any buffalo struck by a Dakota hunting arrow was soon to fall.

The ease and speed of their deaths were horrifying. This wholesale slaughter was ghastly—bulls, cows, and even half-grown calves, particularly the cows, fell in scores. It was a massacre.

Yet it didn't faze the multitude of the herd one bit. As far as the eye could see, from horizon to horizon, there was nothing but buffalo. They surged over one ridgeline and dwindled behind the next. Their only sounds were the low rumbling of their countless hooves and an indescribably plaintive cry—a mix of bellow and moo—before fear gripped them.

Our hunters had killed until their arms were sore from pulling back the heavy bows, and while the thousands of buffalo closest to us had thrashed and tried to gallop either backward, forward, or deeper into their ranks, the herd itself showed no sign of realizing it was under attack. I remember thinking that if these beasts had any real intelligence, they'd turn on us en masse and trample us into the ground. Instead, they fled.

Through some obscure animal instinct, the warning finally spread from the minor hordes we had so ruthlessly harried to their farthest kin on the unseen western edge. One moment they flowed from north to south, an unyielding natural phenomenon, an endless dusty procession of shaggy brown hides. The next, they turned west, showing us their backs, and galloped away with a deafening roar of hooves. It felt like the entire world was in motion. The dust clouds grew so dense they obscured all movement.

We stood there, on the edge of the prairie. From our feet, a brown desert stretched in the wake of the fleeing herd—a desert of pulverized earth devoid of any living thing. The thunder of hooves grew faint in the distance. The dust clouds slowly settled. A little while later, I glanced in the direction the buffalo had vanished, and saw nothing. The brown desert filled the horizon.

The Dakotas moved with swift, skilled hands, their knives slicing through the buffalo hides, wrapping the best cuts of meat in the bloody skins. Chatanskah dispatched runners to rally the full tribe, for this was a bounty seldom seen by any Indian community. They couldn't afford to waste the wealth nature had gifted them. Whatever hardships might befall their brothers in neighboring villages, the Dakota of the Wahpeton Council Fire knew they'd spend this Winter snug and well-fed in their teepees.

That night, the band gathered around the campfire, the scent of burning cedar filling the air. Sentries were posted around the area littered with buffalo carcasses, keeping the wolves, wild dogs, and swooping eagles at bay. Chatanskah spoke of their deeds with pride.

"This will be remembered in the Winter Count," he declared, head held high. "The old men will say we did well. The other Council Fires will envy us. But my brothers, don't forget it was our white brother who killed Nakuiman with his bare hands, making the Cheyenne's hearts quiver like leaves. That was the greatest fight I've ever witnessed! The Cheyenne will slink back home and hide under their squaws' robes.

"And what shall we say of our white brother who shattered Nakuiman? The Cheyenne called him The Bear. Is not a warrior who kills a bear greater than a bear? Hai, my warriors, I hear you say yes! So let's give the slayer of The Bear a new name. We will call him Mahtotopah—Two Bears."

"Hai, hai," echoed the warriors sitting around the fire, the old men at the outer edges, with the eager young ones pressing closer, craving names of their own.

"But Chatanskah won't forget he promised to guide Annalla and his white brothers to the land of the Teton Dakota?" Annalla reminded, his voice cutting through the warm glow of the fire.

Chatanskah shook his head, his sadness almost a palpable force.

"Chatanskah hasn't forgotten," he said, his voice heavy with a sorrow that clung to him like fog. "But he had hoped a bird might come, whispering in the ears of his new brothers, telling them to stay with the Dakota. Up in the Sky Mountains, there's no sweet buffalo meat to sustain you. No teepees to shield you from the relentless wind. Mahtotopah will squander his strength on cold, unyielding rocks. But you are brave men, and I know you'll push on until the Great Spirit calls you home."

Chapter Nine

Chatanskah kept his word as soon as the tribe had stored away the spoils of their hunt. He assembled a small group of elite warriors and handed us powder and lead taken from the Chippewa, to replenish Corlaer's stock. Corlaer carried it all in a great ox-horn and leather pouch. We bade farewell to the cluster of teepees, now encircled by racks piled high with jerking meat and stretched hides in the process of tanning. The last breath of summer had fled the air, and we were grateful for the buffalo-skin robes the Wahpeton had gifted us. But there was an upside to the sharpness in the air too, as it spurred us on with a vigor that we couldn't muster during the sweltering months.

We followed the valley of the Missouri, heading mostly north with just a hint of west, as I figured out. We traveled this way for many days, often running into bands from the other Dakota Council Fires—Mdewakanton, Wahpekute, Sisseton, Yankton, and Yanktonai. One time, a raiding gang of Arikara warriors, fierce with buffalo horns woven into their long hair and sporting wolf-skin breechclouts, charged down on us from the north. They were hunting for an easy village to plunder for the buffalo meat fate had cruelly denied them, but they turned tail at the first crack of our muskets, hauling their dead away with them.

Every night we expected to wake up to a landscape blanketed in snow, as winter tends to grip these western plains sooner than it does the coast, but Providence was on our side. After two weeks, we ran into a roving band of Yanktonai, who informed us that the Teton bands had crossed the Missouri and were trailing another river bordered by sandhills a day's march ahead of us. These Yanktonai were the first horse Indians we had encountered. Leaner than their eastern Dakota kin, with sharp, predatory faces and a rougher dialect, they were unmatched riders.

Their stolen horses, taken from Southern tribes who had originally procured them from the Spanish or bred them from stolen stock, were lean and well-muscled. These creatures bore the unmistakable elegance of the Arab breed favored by the Spaniards. In place of tomahawks, they wielded lances, bows, and arrows. They also carried small, round shields, fashioned from the thick, durable neck-hide of buffalo.

I suspect Ormerod was referring to the Platte River. As we ventured further, his account of treks became increasingly unclear, likely due to the absence of known landmarks. Chatanskah, our guide, was deeply troubled by the news that the Teton had relocated even farther west. He knew this shift meant his journey back to his own villages would likely be delayed by the inevitable winter snows. Despite our offer to release him from his obligation, he dismissed the idea and insisted on accompanying us, as he had pledged.

And indeed, as we plunged deeper into this vast, mysterious land teeming with unforeseen perils and distant, unknown tribes, the value of Chatanskah's local knowledge and protective presence became starkly clear. The horse Indians, as we would soon experience firsthand, were innate thieves—predators whose hands were constantly curled into claws, ready to snatch and plunder. They lived for the thrill of the steal, and had little regard for the name of the Long House, a name that had scarcely reached even the Wahpeton. Without Chatanskah's escort, I'm certain the Yanktonai band would have gleefully murdered us.

The river they had described was immediately recognizable by its sheer size and the distinctive, ghostly white shimmer of sandhills lining its banks. Fortunately, the Missouri was running low, making the task of fording and swimming its bed at a point just above where it joined another river much easier than we feared. Nevertheless, the water's icy grip was relentless, chilling us to the bone. We hurried to build two blazing fires, gathering around them like moths to a flame, desperate for warmth.

For the next day and the two weeks that followed, we journeyed up the river valley. Our discomfort was heightened by the necessity to cross a succession of tributaries, both large and small. Yet, the weather remained unnervingly clear, with no sign of rain or snow to break our relentless march.

The land seemed to rise slowly, as if climbing toward the jagged peaks the tribes said marked the world's end. We came across no people, just a string of empty village sites. Chatanskah said these ghost towns were signs of the Teton moving west, probably in search of better grazing for their horses. And he was right.

We hadn't seen anyone since parting ways with the Yanktonai. Then, as we crested a hill that suddenly rose above the sprawling savannahs, we spotted the first sign of life: a teenage boy on horseback. He appeared ghostlike, his presence ethereal, as he peeked at us with wide, scared eyes. A yelp escaped his lips, and he kicked his mount in a panicked dance, unsure of where to go. Finally, shaking his fist at us defiantly, he tore down the far side of the hill.

"The Teton are vigilant," I remarked. "But why did the boy hesitate?"

"He was signaling," Annalla explained. "You'll see what he accomplished when we reach the top."

From the hill's crest, a broad expanse of grassland stretched out before us. At its center, hundreds of teepees clustered in concentric circles, their openings facing east. Smoke curled lazily between the lodges, and men, women, and children swarmed like ants, all gazing up at us. Warriors sprinted from the village toward the river, where thousands of horses were being corralled by young boys whose high-pitched calls echoed faintly to us.

Before we were even close, the herd was already on the move toward the village, and a formidable group of warriors galloped to meet us. The sunlight danced on their feathered headdresses, lance points, and the intricate beadwork of sheaths and quivers.

"Hai!" Chatanskah exclaimed. "The Teton have sharp eyes."

They wisely keep watch from the hilltop, but if it were up to me, I wouldn’t put my people’s tents where we couldn't keep eyes on all sides after dark. Still, I guess they need to shield their wind-runners from the biting north winds. And down here, they do have good grazing land and easy access to water."

Upon his advice, we stopped at the base of the hill to wait for the riders, who surged forward as if they intended to trample us. But a tiny, wizened old man at the front swung out his hand with a single command, and they yanked their horses to a sudden halt, sending clumps of dirt flying as they encircled us, cutting off any chance of escape.

"Hao," Chatanskah said calmly. "Have the Teton left the Council of the Seven Fires? Does Nadoweiswe forget the face of Chatanskah?"

The diminutive chief scrutinized us grimly from his mount, reminding me of a snake, with his bright, beady eyes and the way his tongue darted out to swipe over his lips. He spoke with a hissing, sing-song accent due to several missing front teeth. His movements were abrupt and his warriors clearly feared him, even though any one of them could have easily carried him under one arm.

"Hao," he responded. "Why did Chatanskah not send someone ahead to inform Nadoweiswe he was coming?"

"Chatanskah did not know where the Teton were camped," the Wahpeton chief shot back. "This land is unfamiliar to my warriors. Are the Wahpeton welcome, or must they turn back and tell their brothers the Teton no longer honor the Council of the Seven Fires?"

Nadoweiswe made an irritated gesture with his hand.

"Chatanskah speaks like a child. He appears suddenly, without warning, and is surprised that we did not anticipate his arrival. The Wahpeton and the Teton are brothers."

"But the Teton aren't kin to the Mazzonka. I see one with you right now," the Teton chief said, eyes narrowing with suspicion.

"Why does Nadoweiswe harbor such resentment toward the Mazzonka?" Chatanskah asked, genuinely surprised. "There are none in his land."

"There was one, just a few nights ago," the Teton retorted with a savage intensity, a bitter edge to his voice. "He turned my young men's courage to mush, let the Siksika steal away a hundred horses under the moon's watch."

He spun around in his saddle, casting a dark scowl over his warriors. Their collective fear was almost palpable, like a sharp tang in the air, making him sneer with contempt.

"Cowardly squaws!" he barked. "They didn't dare leave their teepees. The white man's medicine watered their hearts."

His glare swung back to Corlaer and me, ice-cold and unyielding.

"That's why we won't deal with any white men," he finished, finality in his tone. "They could be allies of the one who bewitched my young men."

Annalla's voice cut through the tension, ringing and melodious, a stark contrast to the chief's harsh growl.

"I am Annalla, War Chief of the People of the Long House," he declared. Nadoweiswe looked at him with a mixture of surprise and skepticism.

"Hai," he murmured, "you're far from your lodge, young warrior."

"It's further than my people have ever journeyed," Annalla acknowledged. "My duty is to guard the Western Door of the Long House. Annalla holds honor in his land."

"That may be," The Adder replied curtly, "but here, you're just another stranger."

"Annalla is also known as a friend of the white men in his country," Annalla pressed on. "These white men are my allies. They came to help me in my quest. They are my brothers."

"If they are friends of the Mazzonka who bewitched my young men, they'll leave," Nadoweiswe snapped. "Or I will take their scalps for my new medicine lance."

"What did this white man look like?" Annalla inquired, his voice steady.

"He was tall, wore a long black robe down to his moccasins. My young men found him on the prairie and galloped up, thinking to take him captive."

But then he drew a weapon from his belt and brandished it at them, and a wave of fear washed over them. There was something powerful about that weapon. It didn't make a loud noise like this one here," he indicated my gun. "Nor did he strike with it. All he did was hold it out, shouting something in a booming voice, and suddenly, their courage drained away and they scattered."

"And what did this weapon look like?" Annalla pressed. The Adder crossed two fingers, and Annalla chuckled, relaying the exchange to us.

"It was Black Robe!" I exclaimed.

"Yeah," Corlaer affirmed. Annalla turned back to the Teton chief, whose gaze had never wavered from our faces during this exchange.

"Yes, Nadoweiswe," he said, "Annalla and his white friends know the man you speak of. He is our enemy."

"Hai," cried The Adder, "is it him you seek?"

"No," Annalla denied. "We cannot touch him, for the Great Spirit has marked him."

Understanding dawned in The Adder's face, and he nodded sagely.

"That was it," he said. "The Great Spirit punished my young men for threatening someone He had chosen. I have seen it happen before. Hai, it was unfortunate! But maybe we can make amends. Chatan-skah, you and your friends are welcome. There are seats in my lodge waiting for you. Come, and tell us of your travels; for soon it will be winter, and we'll have nothing to do but sit around the fire and tell stories of the past."

And I have to admit, the old rogue treated us with a wild kind of hospitality as he led us to the village. We kept asking him for more information about Black Robe, but all he could tell us was that the Jesuit had been seen south of the river that one time. Where he came from or where he was headed, the Teton didn't know. About a quarter-mile from the teepees, we were delayed by a herd of horses moving back to graze along the river.

The young men handling the situation worked with an eerie precision, tempered by that peculiar cruelty the Native tribes often seemed to wield. They had pushed the horses out of the village ring, herding them south. But then, a magnificent stallion with a dappled brown and white coat disrupted their work. This stubborn horse had resisted every attempt to be corralled with the rest of the herd.

One of the younger men finally sprinted up beside the stallion and struck it hard across the flanks with a rawhide whip. The stallion's scream split the air, anger turning its eyes wild. It reared up on its hind legs, lashing out with its front hooves and snapping its teeth. The boy ducked just in time but the other horse caught the brunt of the stallion's fury. Blood flowed, the wounded horse panicked, throwing its rider and bolting.

For a split second, the dappled stallion stood still as a statue, panting with flaring nostrils and eyes like burning coals. Then it charged after the boy, hooves dancing, teeth still bared. Nadoweiswe and his warriors paused, watching intently. None of them moved to intervene. The love of horses, ingrained in me since my Dorset boyhood, surged through my veins. I handed my musket to Annalla and moved toward the stallion.

There was an unmistakable glimmer of interest from the Tetons. Nadoweiswe called out to me.

"The Teton says to stay put," Annalla translated. "He says Sunka-wakan-Kedeshka has never been ridden."

Spotted Horse. Those words only pushed me further. As soon as I laid eyes on those spirited, half-wild beasts, my legs yearned to grip a horse's flanks once more. The idea that the stallion was unbroken fueled my determination. I've always had a natural gift with horses, something I honed back in England and later in France, learning the subtleties of horsemanship. From what little I'd gathered about these horse Indians, I knew their approach to taming was simply breaking.

And I was ready to prove there was another way.

They had no clue about the subtle arts of taming, the kind that can turn even the most high-strung beasts into docile companions. I'd picked up these tricks from countless Gypsy farriers, adding to the natural talent I'd always had. With this particular stallion, I guessed they found themselves at their wits' end, probably considering putting him down as their only option.

I pressed on, letting out a sharp whistle, just as I expected, it caught the stallion's attention, drawing his gaze from the young Indian boy to me. He hesitated, his eyes darting between us, and the boy seized the moment to grab his own, trembling horse. That brief distraction was all the stallion needed. He zeroed in on me, galloping forward on a mission, his eyes bulging with malice, lips curled back in a snarl. I simply folded my arms and waited until he was within earshot, then spoke softly, calmly, not betraying a hint of fear or unease.

It was clear he had never heard a kind word from a man before. His masters must have lived by different rules. Confused, he slowed down, circling around me warily. I made no move to grab him, increasing his curiosity. He kept his distance, too afraid of me to act on his vicious instincts. To him, an Indian was someone who would whip, kick, or stab him with a lance. He didn't know what to expect from me.

I kept talking, using the few Dakota words I knew, but more than that, I aimed to soothe him with the tone of my voice and the calm in my eyes. Slowly, I won him over. He approached, nuzzling his soft muzzle into my face with a friendly whinny, as if I were a mare he liked. Ignoring him, I continued talking. When I draped an arm over his lowered neck, his eyes widened, but he didn't rear up or pull away.

As I tangled my fingers in his mane, he shivered slightly but remained still. Soft words escaped my lips, calming him further. I gave his broad back a firm pat and vaulted up, leaning forward to whisper in his sensitive, pricked ear. He hesitated only a moment. With a press of my knees and a tug on his mane, he trotted toward the herd. Fifty feet from the others, I slipped off his back and slapped his rump smartly. He turned his head, cast me a reproachful glance, and then ambled over to a cluster of mares, slipping into the group as if it was his natural place. As I walked away, he flung his head up once, releasing a drawn-out whinny—a farewell that echoed a human's goodbye as closely as any animal could manage.

Nadoweiswe, flanked by Chatanskah and Annalla, rode out from the gathered warriors to meet me.

"The Adder says," Annalla called out, "that he would like you to sit at his right hand in his teepee. He's not sure how great a warrior you are—" the Seneca's smile gleamed, "—but he's convinced you'd make a fine horse thief."

I chuckled. "And what did you tell The Adder?"

"I said this was a talent I'd never seen you demonstrate before, and I doubted you'd be willing."

Nadoweiswe leaned down from his saddle, speaking quickly again.

Annalla translated. "He says he wants his horses back from the Blackfeet, but with your help, he would venture south to raid the Apache and Comanche pastures."

"Tell him," I replied, "that a horse doesn't need to be beaten to be mastered. As for the Blackfeet, in my land, warriors learn to stampede enemy horses by setting the grass behind them on fire."

Nadoweiswe's eyes lit up with admiration at this piece of wisdom.

Annalla conveyed his response, "He says you must be far wiser than you appear."

He's awestruck by you. He'll do whatever you ask.

And indeed, during our brief time with the Teton, they treated me like a king. It wasn't because I was some great warrior or a master diplomat, traits many tribes respect and even revere. Nor was it my skill with words. No, what truly earned their admiration was my God-given knack for horse-stealing.

Chapter Ten

There was a heavy silence in the crowded teepee after Annalla finished his story. The air hummed with the weight of his words.

"Annalla has given strength to Nadoweiswe's heart," the old Teton chief finally said, his voice like dry leaves rustling in the breeze. "Nadoweiswe will share Annalla's quest with his young men so that their hearts may also find courage. If Nadoweiswe were a young warrior, he would join Annalla and his white brothers to search for this strange Land of Lost Souls. But Nadoweiswe is old, accustomed to riding horses; and horses cannot scale the Sky Mountains that shield the hiding-place of the sun."

He picked up his ceremonial pipe from the ground at his feet, lighting it with a coal plucked from the fire, the glow casting eerie shadows on his weathered face.

"Can Nadoweiswe tell us about the land across the Sky Mountains?" Annalla asked. The little chief bowed his wrinkled, dried-apple face, contemplating the question like an ancient oracle.

"No," he said after a long pause. "The stories our wise men tell say nothing about this land you seek. But my father was a medicine man, a wakan witshasha. He journeyed farther than any of our people, though not as far as Annalla. He told us that the tribes beyond the Sky Mountains believed the Great Spirit dwells nearby. They said He sits on the earth, very white and still, with His head in the clouds. And when He is angry, He unleashes storms, filling the sky with smoke, flame, and thunderous roars. Yet, these people never spoke of a Land of Lost Souls."

"But if the Great Spirit resides there, the Land of Lost Souls cannot be far off," Annalla exclaimed with more vitality than he had shown before. "Nadoweiswe has bolstered our courage. Now, we can move forward, without fear."

Nadoweiswe shook his head slowly. "Do not go," he urged, his voice carrying the weight of many winters. "See, the fire rages here amongst us, but without robes, we would be cold. Any day now—perhaps today—the snow will fall."

"The land's gonna turn white. Death's howlin' in the wind."

"Nadoweiswe's given us a solid reason to leave his tepee," replied Annalla. "We've got a long trek ahead. We've already wasted too much time. If we stick around the Teton fires through winter, we'll end up with nothing to show for it."

"We could swipe a lot of horses," Nadoweiswe argued, casting a cunning glance in my direction. "We'll head south, raid the Spanish tribes. There's plenty to be done in winter."

Annalla's lips curled into a knowing smile.

"If we can steal horses in winter, we can travel west," he countered. "It's gonna be just as cold heading south as it is going toward the Sky Mountains."

"But you don't understand, Annalla. The Sky Mountains are more than just cold," the Teton chief replied solemnly. "The spirit beasts of the Underworld haunt those passes. They're home to the Powers of Evil."

"Annalla doesn't doubt it," our comrade agreed. "But we expected these dangers when we left the Long House. Annalla and his white brothers will go through the land of Hanegoategeh, if we have to."

Nadoweiswe made one last attempt.

"Stay, and you'll get half the horses we steal," he offered, "and come spring, I'll head west with you, along with my young men."

"It's not an option," said Annalla. "Our hearts ache at the thought of leaving Nadoweiswe, Chatanskah, and their people, but we have no choice."

The Teton sighed, resigning himself to our decision.

"Annalla and his white brothers are walking towards their deaths," he pronounced gravely. "The spirit beasts will tear them apart. It's such a pity! But we will tell your story in the Winter Count. You shall be remembered."

And indeed, the old chief parted from us the next morning, showing as much genuine regret as any man could muster.

He handed us all the dried meat we could carry, along with three pairs of snowshoes and a new, more powerful bow and quiver of arrows for Annalla to use for hunting, allowing us to save our precious ammunition for self-defense. He and his warriors escorted us to the edge of their village. I can't forget Chatanskah and our Wahpeton friends, either. Their affection was just as touching, especially considering their stoic nature.

Our final goodbyes came after we left the village, when we were skirting the horse herds grazing along the riverbank. I heard a delighted whinny, and Sunkawakan-kedeshka, the mottled stallion, came trotting towards us with his band of mares. He stopped some distance away, neighing as if to ask why I wouldn't stop to play with him. For a moment, I thought he'd follow us and pretended to ignore him; but after we had gone on for about a mile and reached the crest of a slight ridge, he lost interest and trotted back to the herd.

The incident amused me, though I didn't think much of it and quickly forgot as Annalla pointed to the cold, gray northern sky.

"There's snow somewhere," he said.

"Yes," agreed Corlaer. "And the wind is coming this way."

The flakes began to fall in the afternoon, but we were on the edge of the storm, and they never fell thick enough to block our vision. That night, we built a shelter from brushwood and stayed fairly warm beneath our buffalo robes. Still, we knew that in a severe storm, we'd need better protection, and in the morning, we were relieved to find the snow was only about three inches deep under a clear blue sky.

Two days later, Winter came in full force.

The wind howled like a giant's cry cutting through the frigid northwest air, and the snow swirled in a dense, blinding wall hardly a foot from our faces. Each step was a laborious fight just to stay upright, and even standing a yard apart, we were lost to each other, our voices swallowed by the endless shriek of the storm and the oppressive curtain of snow. It seemed ill fate had thrown us into this barren valley between two hills, with the nearest shelter—a cluster of trees—a mile to the south. Stumbling and groping our way through the blizzard, we strained against the gale's brutal pull, its freezing grip turning our breath into icy razors. The snow crusted on our clothes and bit viciously at our exposed skin, the cold seeping into our bones.

Corlaer, with his massive frame and unyielding resolve, was our saving grace. He walked between Annalla and me, and whenever one of us stumbled, he was there, his arm a swift and unerring support.

His quiet, obstinate nature seemed to give him an uncanny sense of direction, guiding us unerringly through the disorienting storm. Despite the suffocating whiteness, Corlaer kept us on course, quartering against the wind and leading us straight to the copse we had marked before the snow erased it from the world.

Once enveloped by the trees, the cold persisted, and darkness deepened around us. Snow sifted through the branches, fluttering down like the molting feathers of some colossal bird, far larger than the flocks that had once darkened the skies above Ohio. But the trees provided some respite from the biting wind, and we found a grim comfort in the need to act. We knew that only swift, desperate labor could stave off the death Nadoweiswe had foreseen. In this brutal, white darkness, we set to work fashioning a shelter—a daunting task when every gust of wind seemed to freeze the very marrow in our bones.

Deep in the heart of the wood, we discovered a massive boulder. With grim determination and aching hands, we brought down trees with our hatchets, toppling them across the rock.

The fir trees stood tall, their branches heavy with dense foliage, creating an impermeable ceiling above us. We cut down saplings to build the end walls of our shelter and gathered countless armloads of pine boughs for bedding and firewood. As we labored, our blood pumped faster, pushing back the cold grip of the storm. The snow, falling steadily, improved our work, adding an extra layer of insulation that sealed out the chill. Once inside, we managed to coax a small blaze from the damp wood using a few pinches of gunpowder, and our spirits lifted. A meal of jerky and a night's rest under a bed of pine boughs and buffalo robes left us ready to face the storm's wrath by morning.

The snow fell for three days. The first two days, the storm showed no signs of letting up, but by the third day, the wind had calmed, though the snowfall remained relentless. It was on that third day we heard a distant, mournful howling.

"Wolves," said Corlaer.

"What are they doing?" I asked. "In this weather?"

"They're hunting," Annalla replied. "The deer and buffalo can't run away in this."

The howls grew closer, then faded into the distance.

On the morning of the fourth day, we woke to a blindingly white world, with snow reaching up to a man's chest on level ground and forming drifts as tall as young mountains in the hollows. In our shelter, we had to dig a tunnel to the surface, as the boulder and our makeshift structure had created a windbreak where the snow had piled twice my height. We cut our way out slowly, careful not to let the snow collapse on us, gathered our gear, strapped on our snowshoes, and continued our journey.

Snowshoeing is slow going in the hills, but we moved faster than the wild creatures we saw struggling around us, taking advantage of a slight thaw that had crusted the snowy drifts.

In a gully, a herd of buffalo were buried chest-deep in snow, some of the outer ones frozen solid, the others surviving on their combined warmth. A herd of great deer—bucks nearly as tall at the shoulder as a grown man—that Annalla called Wapiti were struggling through the crusted snow, stumbling and falling forward on their antlers. In a narrow valley, unusually sheltered, an enormous gathering of antelope jostled and butted each other, fighting for the scarce food available.

Bears were everywhere, something Annalla found strange, saying they must have been caught off guard by the sudden storm, having delayed their hibernation due to the extended fall. A cougar, a striped, cat-faced phantom, slinked past us on a hillside, belly brushing the snow, tracking some unseen prey. As the afternoon progressed, we heard the eerie, mournful cry of wolves more and more frequently. By dusk, their howls grew closer, sending a shiver down my spine, but my companions said nothing, so I kept my unease to myself. It wasn't until we were crossing a flat stretch of plains near sunset, when a wave of low-running gray shapes poured over the skyline, that I couldn't stay silent any longer. The haunting, heart-pounding howl of hungry wolves echoed across the snow.

"Those beasts are tracking us," I exclaimed.

"They're wolves, brother," Annalla said in his usual brief manner.

"And they seem to know that we're edible," I shot back.

"They won't harm us," he replied, with a hint of impatience. "There's plenty of game for them to hunt all around."

"Then why are they following us?" I pressed.

"They're just heading in our direction, brother. Who knows what purpose the Great Spirit has for them?"

"But..." I stammered, sometimes Annalla's deep-rooted Indian perspective left me feeling disconnected, "they're wolves. They have nothing to do with the Great Spirit."

"They're hungry," he said, his tone loaded with gravity.

He looked at me intently, tapping his chest where I knew he kept the wolf's-head insignia of his clan. "They'll respect this—they're my brothers."

"Brothers!" I gasped. As an adopted member of the Wolf Clan, I had never quite understood the notion of wolves as kin.

"Yes," Corlaer chimed in, his voice gruff yet assured. "The wolves are brothers. Why not?" He used Annalla's own words. "Don't worry, my friend. They're just running our way. That's all."

Despite his reassurance, worry gnawed at me as the shadows stretched longer. The piercing howls were filled with an almost tangible menace. They seemed closer now, as dusk replaced the fading gold of the sunset. When the early moon hung in the sky, I saw them again—the gray hunters, ghostly figures slicing through the night, their broad pads only occasionally breaking through the crusted snow. They were undeniably closer.

"Aaaah-yaaah-oooo-oouuu-wh!"

The howl rose and fell, its eerie pitch brimming with unspeakable omen.

"I don't like this," I admitted, my voice trembling despite my effort to sound composed.

"What would Otetiani do?" Annalla asked, with a serene calm that irked me.

"Shoot them. There's no cover anywhere."

He shook his head slowly. "Whatever happens, brother, do not shoot."

"So, what then? Are we supposed to let them drag us down in the open without a fight?" I snapped, sarcasm sharpening my words.

"No, brother. I've already said they'll do no harm. We have a long way to go. We can't camp here without wood or shelter. Let's keep moving."

I glanced at Corlaer, hoping for an ally. But his focus was on the trail ahead, unwavering. I felt outnumbered and dubious. There was nothing to do but press on. I had known these men for years; we had braved the Eastern Wilderness together. Yet tonight, they seemed almost maddeningly obstinate. How could they put their faith in such a ridiculous totemic tradition? It was beyond comprehension. Corlaer was, after all, a white man like me.

Annalla might have had a different hue, but he was as well-educated as I was, maybe even more so by the white man's standards, better than Corlaer, that's for sure.

"Oooow-woouuow-aarrrgh!"

That terrifying howl kept getting louder. The gray shadows were now emerging as hulking forms in the moonlit night. When I looked back, I saw eyes gleaming red or green, reflecting the silvery light, with bushy tails flicking high, and powerful shoulders and haunches driving them forward. They were massive beasts! I halted abruptly, raising my musket to my shoulder. Just as I was about to pull the trigger, I heard the faint crunch of snowshoes behind me, and Annalla placed a hand on my arm.

"What's the use, brother?" he asked softly. "If you shoot one, the others will go mad with the scent of blood. They'll overwhelm you."

"Why don't you ever mention yourself?" I snapped.

"Trust me, and they won't harm us," he said, ignoring my jab. "They don't understand. Once they realize who we are, things will change."

"Are you seriously telling me you're willing to gamble our lives on your absurd, heathen theory?" I demanded.

"I'm trying to save all our lives, which, believe me, will be forfeit if you persist, brother."

I slung the gun over my shoulder with a scowl.

"Fine, have it your way," I muttered angrily. "It's on your head."

"On my head," he agreed calmly.

"Rocks," grunted Corlaer from ahead. My gaze followed his, and I saw it too. A few hundred yards away, a massive rock jutted out from the snow, breaking the monotony of the vast plateau.

"Good," said Annalla. "We can talk to the others there. Maybe we can set up camp."

"Ja," Corlaer assented. "Andt trees."

His sharp eyes had spotted a stunted patch of timber clinging to a cleft in the rock. The moon cast its glow on snow-speckled evergreen branches, but for the most part, it was nothing more than scraggly bushes and dwarf growths. Still, it promised shelter and warmth if we could shake off the eerie procession of ghostly figures trailing us.

The chill of impending doom hung thickly in the air as we closed in on the rock, forced to pick up the pace. The howls grew more savage, more crazed. It felt like death itself was snapping at our heels.

"Don't run," Annalla's voice whispered urgently in my ear. "A man on snowshoes is a sitting duck, brother. We have time."

Time was a luxury we had precious little of. In the biting cold, the steel stung like a thousand blades if touched barehanded. When we finally reached the cleft of the rock, sweat trailed my spine—not from exertion, but from raw terror. The sound of feet pattering all around us was eerie, reminiscent of swishing skirts on a crisp winter night. A half-circle of gray wolves emerged from the shadows, red tongues flapping over gleaming white teeth, their heavy breaths forming a spectral mist in the frozen air. Their eyes burned like tiny embers in a relentless night. They didn't howl; they snapped and snarled, their growls a low rumbling threat. They waited, and so did we.

"If we start a fire..." I muttered.

"Wait, brother," Annalla cut in, his voice steady. "They fear fire."

I vented my frustration.

"Are you out to save their lives or ours?"

Annalla straightened, every inch the imposing figure, his heritage unmistakable.

"Otetiani forgets we are Wolves too. Their..." he gestured to the encircling pack, "...emblem marks my chest. It's forbidden to harm the totem beast of our Clan."

"That may mean a lot to you, but it's meaningless to me," I retorted, barely masking my irritation.

"It means everything to Otetiani," his voice grew stern. "Did Otetiani not swear allegiance to the Wolf Clan? What he does affects all his clan brothers. Be wise. Stay your hand. These gray brothers are curious and hungry, but they do not know us. We tell them, and they will leave."

I laughed derisively.

"Go ahead and try! My gun's loaded, and I'm aiming for that tree. It won't be fun, but I've got enough bullets to last a while."

"Foolishness," Corlaer commented dryly. "Watch Annalla."

"He knows."

"What?" I scoffed.

"The wolves."

As if to prove his point, Annalla handed his musket to the Dutchman and unbuttoned the leather shirt covering his chest. He walked forward a few steps, facing a semicircle of snarling, grey beasts with his arms outstretched.

"Brothers!" he called out, and I swear a curious whine rose from the pack.

"You are hungry. You have followed a scent unlike any other. You've turned away from buffalo, deer, antelope, and elk to track this new scent. For a long time, you've been on our trail. Plenty of easy meat was there for the taking, but you hungered for this different flavor."

The only sounds were the rhythmic panting of powerful lungs. Scores of eyes, so luminous and chillingly indifferent, fixated on Annalla. He stepped closer as if he were addressing a council rather than a pack of killers.

"You were mistaken, brothers. You didn't know. Look!"

He bent before them, revealing a wolf's head painted on his chest.

"I am of the Wolf Totem. These others with me are of the Wolf Totem. We are bound in brotherhood with you. We cannot kill you, eat your flesh, or wear your fur. We are your brothers."

A huge, muscular wolf threw back his head and released a mournful howl. The others joined in.

"Go back, brothers," Annalla continued. "If you harm us, Hawenneyu will punish you, just as he would punish us if we harmed you. When there is free meat on the trail, brothers do not hunt each other. You have already done wrong, but unknowingly. Go back."

He strode confidently into their midst, placing his open palm against the chest of the wolf that had howled first. The beast bent his head and licked Annalla's hand.

"Go, brothers," Annalla repeated. And just like that, they vanished. I rubbed my eyes, staring into the darkness. Yes, a dull, grey shape flitted away.

Snow crunched beneath their paws, echoing through the still night. A sharp snap of teeth. Then came the leader's call, a haunting wail drifting towards the stars. Yap-yap-yap! came the chorus. Howls and counter-howls, yelps hot on a fresh scent. Fainter and fainter they became.

I gripped Corlaer's thick arm, my fingers sinking into cold flesh. "What were they?"

He shrugged, a heavy motion I felt more than saw. "Just wolves."

"Real ones? Did I imagine that?"

"Could be spirit wolves, just like Nadoweiswe warned us about," Annalla said from my other side, his voice serious as he took his musket from the Dutchman.

"You're joking," I said.

"Why would I joke, brother? We've passed beyond the realm of men, I think."

"You touched one, didn't you?" I pressed. He considered, then held his hand to his nose and sniffed.

"True. And it left a foul wolf stench. No, they were real enough. But spirit or flesh, it wouldn't make a difference. They wouldn't have touched me."

"Why not?"

"Why did the wild horse let Otetiani ride him?"

"Because I wasn't afraid of him or planned to hurt him."

"Otetiani always speaks frankly," the Seneca said solemnly. "I had no fear of the wolf brothers, and I had no thought of harming them."

"But a wolf isn't a horse!" I argued.

"True. But he is our brother. Didn't Otetiani see me show them the Clan insignia on my chest?"

"My God!" I exclaimed. "One of us is crazy!"

"Oof," Corlaer muttered with an uncharacteristic fluency. "Nobody's mad. But the white man doesn't know everything. That's all. Now let's build a good hut and a fire, eh? It's cold. Ja, I take this tree."

Chapter Eleven

Up till now, the obstacles we faced were mostly from hostile people rather than nature itself. But that was about to change. The people we encountered were pitifully primitive, ignorant, and so superstitious that they ran at the slightest scare. Yet it was nature, with its overwhelming power, that became our true adversary. Each day tested our endurance, courage, strength, and skill in ways we couldn't have imagined. Time lost its meaning against the sheer scale of what we had to overcome.

A month dragged by after our narrow escape from the wolf pack before we even caught sight of the Sky Mountains' colossal barrier. Crossing their snowy peaks took several more months of grueling effort. But I'm getting ahead of myself. It's hard to put into words just how staggering the forces we encountered were, or to capture the supreme majesty of this uncharted land. The Godlike splendor of the winter landscape, the suffocating, silent emptiness—it all underscored our own insignificance.

One of the most striking aspects was the complete absence of other humans on the plains and in the forests between the Teton villages and the mountains. For months, our only companions were the countless animals escaping the brutal cold of the highlands for the slightly warmer, lower timberline. We saw herds of great deer Annalla called Wapiti, along with red deer, antelope, buffalo, wild goats, and wild sheep by the thousands. We hunted fresh meat with our hatchets whenever we needed it. These animals roamed the lower lands, which themselves were quite high, moving upward mile after mile in search of food from tree bark and whatever herbage lay beneath the snow. In their desperation and naive unawareness of humans, they merely stepped aside from our path and watched us pass.

We encountered many wolves, heard their howls echoing in the night, but they never came close again. Why that was, I can't exactly say—maybe it was just luck, or maybe some primal understanding had kept them at bay.

For myself, I have nothing more to add, convinced by the wonders I would soon witness that Corlaer was absolutely right when he said, "The white man doesn't know everything."

That was a winter of record-breaking cold. It came late, but when it did, it brought long stretches of biting frost, interspersed with violent storms that left the forest littered with frozen animals. Through experience, we learned the importance of seeking shelter at the first sign of the Wind Spirits plucking wild geese up north, always careful to avoid crossing open lands unless conditions were favorable. This did slow us down, but without question, it saved our lives. With a roof, four walls, and a fire, men can withstand nature's fiercest onslaughts, regardless of how makeshift the shelter may be.

It was a month before we even caught a glimpse of the Sky Mountains, and they were still miles away. We had been following a fork of a river that wound through Teton country, pushing us northwest. After several weeks, we finally saw a line of jagged peaks that we initially thought were our goal. But the river curved around the broken terrain at their base, leading us into a wide upland much like the savannahs flanking the Missouri. The jagged peaks dwindled in our rearview, and the horizon remained empty ahead until one day, under a brilliant sun and cloudless sky, we saw a serrated wonder in the west: cones, saddlebacks, hulking ridges—square, round, oblong, and eccentric rock formations, all draped in snow.

A storm delayed us another week, but we resumed our journey with lighter hearts. Each sunset became a muse for swifter progression. It was as though a giant's paint pots had been tipped over, splashing harmonious colors—soft reds, purples, yellows, and the infinite shades between—all across the mountain wall.

Or the Painter's mood would shift, throwing bold, jarring streaks of color across the canvas of the sky, colors so vivid they hurt the eyes. Incredible! Even as we stood at the base of the towering wall, searching this way and that for a gateway to the land of mystery beyond, the Painter's work persisted. The nearby peaks might lose their allure, but in the hazy distance, North or South, the Painter cast his spell at random.

When I was young, I marched with the Duke of Berwick into the Pyrenees. Child's play compared to the mission we faced now. We were clueless about the secrets hidden in this chaotic landscape. Forests draped the mountains' lower slopes, and under the canopy, the snow lay so deep we would have suffocated without our snowshoes. Above the timberline, the realm of bare rock took over, and here everything was ice and snow, sometimes a smoothly slick surface, other times loose and treacherous beneath our feet. Our first attempt to climb a height set off an avalanche that swept us into the treetops of the nearby forest. We were incapacitated for days.

Time and again, we explored ravines and valleys, hoping to find a passable route, but all we managed was to waste time. We spent weeks on arduous treks that led only to the edges of sheer cliffs or dead-ends against impassable walls. It was dangerous work, grueling, made worse by the constant threat of snow-slides. A patch of sun on a slope could trigger a devastating thaw, sending entire hillsides down in a roiling wave.

Initially, we worked north along the base of the range, following Annalla's theory that perhaps the river's northern fork might cut through the Sky Mountains. When that proved fruitless, he suggested the southern fork might do the trick. Corlaer and I had no better ideas, so we backtracked southwards and ventured into a promising valley, only to hit a ramp of cliffs. We tried again and yet again, each attempt ending in failure.

After our third failed attempt, we found ourselves holed up in a makeshift hut, nestled in a crevice of rock, blanketed under a heavy snowstorm. With nothing to occupy us but basic survival—eating, sleeping, stoking the fire—we grew silent, the weight of failure and exhaustion pressing down on us. It was on the afternoon of the second day that Corlaer shook Annalla and me awake.

"I've found the way," he declared, his voice a low rumble.

"What way?" I muttered, half-asleep.

"Over the mountains," he said, annunciating each word with deliberate calm.

Annalla's eyes sparked with interest, but a wave of irritation washed over me at the interruption.

"Oh, it starts right here in the hut?" I scoffed, sarcasm dripping from my tone.

"Maybe," he replied, unbothered by my skepticism.

The Seneca leaned forward, his curiosity piqued. "What is going on in Corlaer's mind?" he asked eagerly. Marcus took his time adding wood to the fire before he spoke, each word a laborious effort.

"We follow the animals," he said finally.

"What?" I said, astonished, but Annalla merely nodded.

"He's right, Otetiani. If there's a pass, the wildlife will know it. We just have to keep an eye on them."

"But in this weather, it's likely impossible for any pass to be usable, especially for animals," I argued.

"Spring's coming soon," the Dutchman replied quietly.

"We wait and watch," Annalla added. I had to concede they had a point. Two days later, when the storm finally ceased, piling even more snow upon the mountains, we shifted our approach. Instead of battling the barrier head-on, we scoped out its foothills. For a week, we trudged southward through the lower slopes until a ridge running east forced us to stop. It seemed futile to try to go around it, so we doubled back, our confidence in Corlaer's plan waning. Despite our vigilance, we hadn't seen a single creature moving between the altitudes.

Then, a thaw set in, day by day breaking winter's grip. Tiny streams trickled down the hillsides, the packed snow beneath us grew heavy and soggy, and the avalanches—God, the avalanches—became more treacherous than ever.

Every couple of hours, there'd be a rip, a roar, and the vicious swish of shattering trees, followed by a barrage of rocks and pebbles raining down on us. It was one of these torrents that finally revealed a way across the barrier. We had ditched our planned route and stuck close to the sheltering face of a high cliff, confident that any landslide from above would overshoot us, when a mountain sheep burst out of a narrow gully we had passed without much thought. Corlaer raised his arm and pointed.

"It's the first animal we've seen this high up," I confessed.

"If we go in there, we'll need more meat," said Annalla. He quickly strung his bow, notched an arrow, and let it fly. The animal dropped just about fifty yards away, and I ran to retrieve it. But Corlaer was right behind me, hoisting the carcass onto his broad shoulders.

"Ugh," he grunted. "There's still daylight left. We shouldn't waste time cutting up the sheep now. We keep moving, ja?"

I nodded, and Annalla was on board too. We didn't even try to convince the big Dutchman to let us carry the dead sheep, knowing full well neither of us could manage it along with our gear, especially on these treacherous, snow-covered rocks with snowshoes to contend with. But for Marcus, it was like carrying a rabbit. He trotted along behind us effortlessly.

The entrance to the gully was maybe twenty feet wide. It wound back into the hills, gradually widening until it turned a sharp curve of rock and turned into a substantial ravine. The ground was littered with boulders of all sizes, and with the melting snow and trickles of water that would eventually form a decent stream, it was far from an easy path. Our only solace was that the sheer sidewalls provided some protection from the relentless avalanches, our most formidable foes.

The climb was a breeze, and by late afternoon, we'd swung around another bend and found ourselves in the heart of a stunning, secluded valley, hidden deep within the hills. Towering peaks punctured the clouds above, their lower slopes covered in lush, jade-green pine forests. The valley floor was similarly covered in trees, but now and then, the forest broke open into clearings where herds of mountain goats, sheep, and antelope rooted for food beneath the snow. At the center lay a small lake, its frozen surface shimmering like a blood-red eye under the glow of the setting sun. The silence was almost magical, like a still frame from a painting, a remote highland solitude that seemed untouched by human presence. The wildlife, surprisingly tame, milled about, drawn closer by the sounds of our axes chopping wood for a hut and the crackling of our campfire.

The valley stretched for miles, and by the time we reached the far end, it was too late to press on that day. On the morning of the second day, we dove into a ravine similar to the one we'd used to cross the eastern ridge. That night, we huddled around a meager fire, clearing a small spot amidst the rocks, fearing that the narrow gorge might trap us like so many others had over the past months. But luck was on our side, and by midday of the fourth day of our journey, we emerged into a land of rolling foothills. Behind us loomed the snowy peaks of the Sky Mountains, more impenetrable than ever.

We had accomplished what no one I'd ever met could truthfully claim. Sure, there are those who brag about crossing the Western Wilderness, spinning tales of incredible feats and sights, but let them show proof of their boasts.

Jesuit missionaries and coureurs des bois have glimpsed the Sky Mountains from afar, but Charles Le Moyne himself told me that no one has come to him or his people with a story like ours. But I digress. Patience, my friend. The relentless fury of nature lacks the emotional intensity of human hatred and struggle, but no feat of my comrades and I compares to the battles we waged against the mountain, forest, and river. With a living opponent, be it man or beast, you can touch, hurt, and visibly conquer. But what satisfaction can you draw from nature after besting her? None, I say, except the right to exist. You don't even know for sure that the victory is yours until the thrill of combat is long gone.

A day's journey from the western base of the Sky Mountains, we saw other humans for the first time in nearly five months. They were a diminutive, long-haired people, clad in rancid hides, who ambushed us with arrows as we rested in a valley. But panic swept them away at the first crack of our muskets, leaving one behind with a wounded leg. We captured him, but there was no spark of intelligence in his brutish face as Annalla grilled him with questions in the Dakota tongue. Except when Annalla asked about the seat of Wakanda, the Great Spirit. Whether he understood the word or cunningly deduced we were seeking a specific place, I can't say. But he lifted his arm and pointed northwest, his gibberish incomprehensible to us. We left him with his wound bandaged and enough meat for a day, then set off in the direction he had shown.

Detailing our subsequent wanderings would serve no useful purpose. The land beyond the Sky Mountains was wilder and more desolate than the Great Plains stretching westward from the Mississippi, and far more varied in character.

We encountered numerous smaller mountain ranges, each one a stubborn obstacle. The scalding heat of arid grasslands nearly dried us to death, while hunger gnawed at us amid a surreal landscape of sun-baked, chaotic rock formations. Yet, we trudged on, always moving northwest. Game was usually plentiful. The scattered Indigenous tribes eked out a sparse existence compared to those on the plains. They occasionally attacked us, but the crack of gunfire always sent them fleeing. Those we captured offered no intelligence at the mention of Wakanda, convincing us that our first captive had feigned recognition just to rid himself of our questioning. Despite our frustration, we pressed northwestward until we reached a wide river flowing due north, with hazy hills looming far to the west.

We decided to exploit the river, hoping it might ease our tired bodies and save us time. Mimicking our earlier crossing of the Mississippi, we cobbled together a raft from tree trunks bound with rope, but it shattered in the first rough patch of water, leaving us no choice but to continue on foot. Eventually, we stumbled upon a village of fishing Indigenous people who owned canoes carved from logs using fire and stone hatchets. Following my suggestion, we traded an extra knife for a small canoe that barely fit all of us. That night, we barely escaped an attempt by the villagers to capture us in our sleep, forcing us once again to take to the river.

As we had anticipated, the river—which was likely the Snake River, marking the boundary between Idaho and Oregon—continued northward for several hundred miles. Then it veered west, skirting the base of the distant mountain range we had glimpsed earlier.

A week later, the river joined a larger stream flowing down from the north, which, after a day's journey south, also veered westward. But what really captured our interest were the towering, snow-covered peaks, rising far higher than the Sky Mountains, their icy crowns glowing in the early morning or late afternoon light on the western horizon.

Two more days downstream, and we found ourselves passing an Indian village that made Annalla gasp with excitement. These were long, wooden structures, smoke curling lazily from numerous fires inside. They looked just like the longhouses that had given the Iroquois their unique identity. A fleet of canoes pushed off the shore, paddling swiftly to intercept us. With such overwhelming odds, it seemed foolish to fight unless absolutely necessary, so we set down our paddles and waited, muskets at the ready, for whatever might come next.

But our fears were immediately dispelled. These Indians were the most handsome and straightforward people we had encountered since leaving the Dakota. Their gestures were filled with friendly intent, eagerly signaling for us to come ashore.

"Should we go?" I asked, doubt gnawing at the edges of my mind.

"Why not?" Annalla replied with a shrug. "We've traveled far with little to show. If these people are generous, perhaps they can set us on the right path."

"If they are kind," I echoed. Marcus, seated at the stern, curved his paddle and guided us toward the riverbank.

"Ja," he grunted. "And maybe we finally get something different to eat."

We had no reason to regret our choice. The people, who called themselves Tsutpeli, were both kind and considerate, genuinely fascinated by the pale skin Corlaer and I still had, despite layers of dirt and sunburn. They were also impressively intelligent.

After we were led to the chief's house, where all his sons' families lived, the evening unfolded with a feast. We sampled various dishes, one of which I'm convinced was some sort of salmon. There were also berries and a root, leaf, and twig stew that Marcus seemed to particularly relish. It wasn't long before our hosts tried to initiate a humorous attempt to bridge the language gap between us.

They were Nez Percés, though how they ended up this far west remains a mystery. They pointed at different objects, offering their names for each, and then eagerly awaited our responses. Annalla, acting as our spokesman, responded with the Seneca terms. Over the ensuing weeks in the village, we managed to build a basic vocabulary, relying on signs and guesswork for the rest. Simple conversations became possible. The locals shared that they hadn't always ruled the river where they now resided. They had conquered it from the Chinook tribe, known for their superb seafaring skills and control over the lower river's rich fishing grounds. Annalla struggled to communicate the true purpose of our journey, but the principal men all denied any knowledge of a Land of Lost Souls.

Their reaction was vastly different when they heard the legend Nadoweiswe had shared about the abode of the Great Spirit. They perked up instantly, and Apaiopa, their leading chief, gestured for us to follow him out of the lodge. By then, the sun was setting, casting an otherworldly glow over the northern mountain wall. A procession of isolated peaks stretched across the landscape, with three or four of them towering in magnificent splendor above the hazy blue silhouettes of the lesser ridges. The most distant peak was the grandest of them all, a colossal figure on the horizon, brilliant white, and piercing through the clouds. At that range, it seemed to float in the heavens, detached from the earthly realm.

"Tamanoas," Apaiopa said, pointing. "The Great Spirit!"

The locals, the Chinook, warned us about Him when we first arrived. "Sometimes He gets angry, just like this," said Annalla, tapping my musket. "Sometimes He vanishes into the sky. He is the Great Spirit!"

Obviously, they were referring to Mt. Rainier. A.D.H.S. Annalla exhaled a contented sigh, and I jumped in quickly, trying to stave off the inevitable letdown he was setting himself up for.

"Nonsense, it's just a mountain, bigger than the others," I blurted. "Think, brother! You'll—"

"It may well be a mountain," Annalla replied calmly. "But does that mean it can't also be the Great Spirit?"

"Yes," Corlaer added, "if the Great Spirit came to earth, it would make sense for Him to come as something mighty, like a mountain, right? Yes, that fits."

I thought about the wolf brothers and abandoned my futile argument. The rest of the evening, Annalla busied himself gathering details about the path to Tamanoas's base. The next morning, our hosts loaded us up with provisions and sent us on our way. They didn't try to hold us back. Actually, they seemed to believe we could achieve anything. Their reasoning was that the Great Spirit, whom they thought was white, would be delighted to see two white men. They assumed Annalla would be welcomed on our recommendation. We parted with a touch of sadness. They were the noblest tribe we encountered beyond the Sky Mountains.

Chapter Twelve

We set up our final camp in a glade sprinkled with wildflowers, encircled by one of those dirty glaciers hanging like skeletal arms along the mountain's flanks. High above, miles up in the still sky, the summit's blunted cone loomed, silver-white at the peak, gradually darkening where black rocks jutted through the snowy cloak, turning steel-gray below where the glacial rivers crawled under loads of rock dust and boulders, gouged from the earth's fabric by their relentless march. Beneath the glaciers lay the zone of wildflowers, mile after mile of them, their pollen drifting through the air amidst the icy desolation, encircling the heights with a belt of fragrant beauty. Then, closer to the earth's level, stood the timberline; first, twisted, wind-scarred dwarf trees, and behind them, the massive bulwark of the primeval forest—stout cedars and sturdy firs, the smallest among them a king's ship's mainmast in stature. A verdant frame for the multicolored miracle of the flower-fields and the white splendor above.

"Do you intend to climb any higher, brother?" I asked Annalla, who stood with folded arms, his gaze fixed on the summit that seemed so near in that radiant air. He nodded.

"It's just a mountain," I continued softly. "Don't you see?"

He turned somber eyes on me.

"It looks like no other mountain Annalla has ever seen, Otetiani."

I gestured from south to north, where a dozen peaks shimmered, barely inferior to the giant upon whose flanks we rested.

"They are not the same," he burst out with sudden passion. "Did not all the people we met tell us that this was the Great Spirit? Tamanoas!" He repeated the name with a kind of ecstasy. "Has Otetiani ever seen anything more like what the Great Spirit must be? Is He, then, a man like us with feet and hands and a belly? No, He is Power and Strength and Beauty and Stillness!"

"Ja," agreed Corlaer shrilly. "And if we go up high, we see all the land around. That saves trouble."

Ja!"

I pulled out my tomahawk.

"Alright," I said. "It's decided. We're going for the summit. Listen up. A mountain is a ruthless enemy—strong and treacherous, as you said. In France, there's a mountain like this one called Mont Blanc. People climb it for the thrill of danger, but they do it in groups, tied together, so if one falls, the others can save him. We need to cut up our buffalo robes and braid the strips into ropes. We'll also need sticks to help us on the ice. And we have to climb during the day. In the darkness, we'd slip to our deaths, assuming we don't die anyway, which is likely."

The Seneca's face showed worry.

"Annalla is selfish," he said quickly. "He thinks only of himself. There's no need for Otetiani and Marcus to go with me. Let them stay here while I go up and pray to Tamanoas."

I laughed, and Corlaer's flat face twisted into a ridiculous grin—the Dutchman's idea of mockery.

"We've traveled thousands of leagues together," I replied, "without anyone venturing alone. Why start now? No, we go together."

"Ja," Corlaer said. "But we go in the morning, right? Tonight, we eat."

In the morning, we stashed our muskets and spare gear in a hollow tree and set off, carrying only our food pouches, tomahawks, about fifty feet of strong hide- rope, and the staves we'd carved from cedar saplings. The path was pretty clear. We passed through a belt of wild-flowers, skirted a glacier that melted into a spouting, ice-cold stream of brown water, and found solid footing on a rock ledge for about half a mile. Beyond that, there was a snowfield, frozen almost solid, where we had to cut our steps foot by foot.

The glare blazed fiercely as the bright sunlight bounced off the sleek, sloping surface. We pressed on, reaching another jagged rock face, only to find it too steep to climb. Reluctantly, we had to trust ourselves to the glacier that coiled around it. This was a test of our endurance. The dull, dirty-hued ice river was split by cracks and crevices—some just a few inches wide, others vast chasms—echoing with faint tinklings and gusts of bone-chilling cold that instantly numbed the life out of you.

But up on the glacier's surface, it wasn't cold at all. The blazing sun made us sweat as we trudged uphill, probing the ice ahead with our sticks at every step. We scrutinized each gap, figuring out ways to dodge the widest and helping each other leap those narrow enough to offer solid footing on either side.

Then the moment came—a giant, gaping crevice cut across our path, making it impossible to continue on the glacier. We painstakingly clambered over the sidewalls of boulders, molded over eons of the glacier's descent, and tackled another snowfield. Our goal was a series of rock ledges rising one above the other towards the summit. The air was intoxicating, heady yet eerily thin, leaving us gasping for breath disproportionate to our efforts. Annalla and Marcus, stronger than I, seemed to feel it more; I was alarmed when the sturdy Dutchman suddenly dropped to his knees.

"I'm bleeding," he gasped. "What hit us?"

Annalla wiped a stream of blood from his nose and collapsed on the snow.

"Tamanoas is displeased," he muttered as I crouched beside him. "Otetiani was right! We're doomed."

His bronze face had turned a ghostly pallor, and for a moment, I feared he would pass out. But he gathered himself when I shook his arm. I was more worried for him than for Marcus, which turned out to be a mistake.

"It's not Tamanoas," I insisted. "At least, brother, it's nothing more than ordinary mountain sickness I've heard about. Up here, this far above the world, the air is thinner than we're used to breathing."

"We've pushed ourselves too fast. Let's take a break and acclimate," I said.

He accepted my suggestion with a strange mix of modern logic and ancient instinct, a blend that defined his peculiar nature.

"Marcus," he muttered, pointing weakly. I turned to see the Dutchman passed out cold, blood trickling from his nose and mouth, looking like he was on death's door. But, after I used some snow to bathe his temples, he eventually groaned, eyes fluttering open before he managed to sit up.

"Who's shooting at us?" he stammered. I explained it to him as simply as I could—physics wasn't exactly his strong suit, even less so than it was for the Seneca. Once he understood, he wanted to push on immediately. But I convinced him to let his body adjust to the strain first. During this necessary break, we took in the view we'd fought so hard to reach: endless forests, icy peaks, and, off in the distance to the west, a winding stretch of water too wide to be a river and too irregular to be a lake. But nowhere was there any sign of habitation, human or otherwise, to enjoy this untouched wilderness. It was as if the surrounding tribes shunned this place, viewing the snow-capped peak of the mountain, Tamanoas, as the home of some divine entity.

Annalla was the first to rise, determination etched on his face.

"The sun's high, brothers," he said. "If Corlaer's pain is gone—"

"Oof!" grunted the Dutchman, hating to admit any weakness. "We go to the top now. If the air is thin, I've got fat, right? That's enough. Ja."

It seemed like the summit was just an hour's climb away, but we soon realized the hardest part was yet to come. That grueling afternoon, we pushed ourselves up the climb, navigating sheer cliffs and hidden crevices, stopping frequently to rest and avoid the dizziness that threatened to overtake us.

Once, we slid and scrambled down a half-mile toward death, forced to drive our staffs through the ice to halt our descent. It took us another grueling hour to retrace our steps, but we gritted our teeth and pushed through. Our moccasins tore open on the knife-edged rocks and jagged ice. The sun-glare blistered our faces, and our hands, raw from relentless ice contact, throbbed with pain. Waves of nausea gripped us. But still, we climbed. I was leading, head down, eyes scanning the treacherous ground for the safest footholds, when Annalla tapped my shoulder.

"Look, brother," he whispered, a strange excitement in his voice. "Tamanoas breathes."

Startled, I looked up. The rim loomed a few hundred yards away, and above it, what I had initially mistaken for a low-hanging cloud floated eerily. But the sky was a clear, cloudless expanse. The mist above the rim was endlessly disintegrating, only to be replenished anew, like steam from a boiling kettle.

"We'll find out soon enough what it means," I said, trying to mask my unease. "There's an opening here. Stick to the snow; the rocks are unstable."

We crossed a gentle snow ramp leading into a gaping chasm at the crest. What a sight it revealed! No, not the panoramic view surrounding the mountain's base—we didn't even glance at that. Our eyes were riveted to the enormous bowl, a mile wide, carved out at the mountain's peak. Snow blanketed the expanse, in some places deep enough to pour over the rim, forming the origins of the glaciers that snaked downward into the flower-zone like colossal, silver-tailed serpents with grime-gray, scale-covered coils. Amid this snowy abyss, peculiar black rocks jutted out, sending up the steamy clouds Annalla had noticed.

"Whose fires?" Corlaer squeaked, his voice a fragile thread in the chilling air.

The Seneca's eyes darted in every direction, searching for... who knows what exactly? His thoughts were like shadows in the twilight, hard to pin down.

"The Great Spirit made them," I said. "Yes, and still tends to them."

Annalla cast a doubtful glance at me.

"It's true," I affirmed. "Remember in the missionary's school, the talk about mountains called volcanoes?"

"But they said those are only in hot countries," the Seneca replied.

"Then they taught you wrong. I've seen a volcano in Italy, which is in Europe. And we're standing on one right now."

Corlaer visibly flinched.

"Volcanoes have fires?" he protested.

"Yeah," I nodded. "Didn't our Indian friends tell us that sometimes Tamanoas exploded with a loud noise? That's what they meant. Deep below this ice and snow, in the belly of these rocks, burns the eternal fire of the world. And I guess it's not too far off to say the Great Spirit tends to that. From it flows all life, and isn't He the Giver of Life?"

"Ja," said the Dutchman thoughtfully. "So, we go down pretty quick now, eh?"

But I pointed to the sun sinking in the West, swallowed by a sea of clouds, then to the miles of icy rocks between us and the timberline.

"What chance do we have of getting down in one piece in the dark?" I asked. Annalla spoke up before anyone could respond.

"Tamanoas is Tamanoas," he declared in his resonant voice. "As Otetiani has said, beneath us burns the fire of the Life-giver of the world. Brothers, Annalla goes to make his prayer to the Great Spirit. Surely, here in His own domain, He will listen!"

He strode to the nearest rock pile, where steam seeped from the earth-fires, and he raised his arms in the noble gesture of prayer. I believe it's far more dignified for a man to approach the Great Spirit, in whatever form, not as a beggar on bended knee, but as one who seeks favor from a worthy master.

His voice rose again, this time echoing with the rhythmic cadence of the Hodenosaunee. He laid bare his soul, his hunger, and his despair. We couldn't catch his words—they weren't meant for us. Instead, we welcomed the soft wind that breezed into the crater, wrapping his figure in the mist of the fumaroles, carrying his stirring appeals over the snowbanks. Yet, we remained captivated, as shadows deepened on the mountain's lower slopes and a pink glow bathed the peak, casting a tiny rainbow through the steam clouds. Annalla extended his arms in a final, proud plea, as if he had every right to ask, then turned back to us, a triumphant light in his eyes.

"I think Hawenneyu heard me," he said simply. "My heart, once sorrowful, now sings with courage. It grows strong. All fear is gone."

As night drew near, the gentle breeze morphed into a gale that howled through the rocks. The air, losing the sun's warmth, turned deathly cold. Winter's frost gripped us, and without shelter, we would've perished by dawn. Thankfully, I found a steam-chamber among the black rocks. It was damp and unwelcoming, but the warmth allowed us some rest.

We awoke to a world transformed. The peak was cloaked in a thick, moist fog. The brisk cold air had turned clammy, and water condensed on our foreheads. Our hide garments stiffened from the moisture. We shivered as if plagued by marsh fever; our teeth clattered as we ate our last meager meal, mistakenly having expected to ascend and return within a day. Even Annalla, buoyed by his belief that he had secured otherworldly aid for his quest, felt the weight of despair in this grim outlook.

After finishing our meager meal, we clumsily made our way back to the gap in the crater wall where we had stumbled in the night before. Fog hung thick around us, teasing our every move.

"We have two choices," I finally broke the oppressive silence, my voice a mere breath in the mist. "We can either stay here, cold and starving, waiting for the clouds to lift and risk dying here. Or, we can take our chances and navigate through this fog, with the very real possibility that one wrong step will send us plummeting to our deaths."

Just then, the fog parted momentarily, long enough for us to glimpse the flower- fields and majestic trees a few miles away, a vision of a world that seemed dreamlike from this place of dread.

"Let's go down," said Annalla, his voice resolute.

"Ja, let's," Corlaer added with a shiver in his tone. "This fog chills me to the bone."

I had led the ascent, but as we roped ourselves together, Annalla insisted on taking the lead.

"Annalla brought you into this danger," he said with a grim sense of responsibility. "It's Annalla's job to lead you out."

So, Annalla went first as we began our precarious descent along the outer edge of the crater rim. I followed close behind, and Corlaer, huffing and puffing, came last. Initially, our task was straightforward. We retraced our steps in the snow-ramp we had meticulously chopped out before. This part was a quick and relatively easy stage.

Once past the snow-ramp, we navigated swiftly over a rock ledge, but the swirling gray fog disoriented Annalla. He lost track of the faint line of footprints that led from the lower edge of the rocks across the next snow-bank. For a harrowing while, we staggered blindly around, searching for those elusive prints. Desperation growing, we finally plunged onto the white expanse of the snow-field. Here, the ground was so level we didn't need to chop foot-holds.

When we started, visibility was limited to a scant dozen feet. Annalla's form ahead shimmered like a ghost in my vision; for Corlaer, he was no more than a disembodied voice in the mist.

In the midst of the snow-covered plain, the fog thickened into a dense, soupy veil, swallowing us whole. Suddenly, we were like ghosts, each stranded in our own private hell of white mist. I couldn't see my own outstretched hand, and the oppressive clouds seemed ready to choke the life out of us.

"What do we do now?" Annalla called out, her voice sounding muffled and distant, as if it were trapped in a soundproof box.

"Oh man, we're going to suffocate here," Corlaer grumbled from behind me.

"Hold tight and give it some time," I suggested. We sat there, letting the moisture soak into our clothes until they felt like lead weights dragging us down, our teeth chattering a cold warning of impending danger. Abruptly, Seneca stood up, breaking the eerie stillness.

"Annalla made a mistake bringing us down here," he said, his voice tinged with frustration. "But sitting here, freezing and wet, will kill us just as fast. Climbing back up is as perilous as heading down. We've got no choice but to move forward. If the Great Spirit is watching over us, we'll make it through."

Ten steps later, I nearly tripped over him as he crouched low to the ground.

"Stop!" he shouted sharply. "Death is right here!"

I peered past his feet and glimpsed a blue-green abyss, briefly revealed by an eddy in the mist, then swallowed up again by the thick fog. We'd stumbled onto a glacier, and this crevasse was one of those endless abysses that bit deep into the mountain's icy heart. Inch by agonizing inch, on hands and knees, we followed the edge of the chasm to a snow bridge - a natural but terrifying arch of ice. Annalla struck it with his staff to test its strength. It held firm, and he ventured onto it as Corlaer and I dug our heels into the snow, ready to catch him if it gave way. The fog engulfed him, and his voice soon echoed back, confirming he had made it across. I quickly followed, then called out for Corlaer to make his move.

The outline of the Dutchman's shadow, misshapen by the swirling mists, emerged eerily into view. He stepped gingerly across the ice bridge, and without any warning, the sound of cracking ice shattered the frozen silence. Marcus sprang into the air, landing right on the edge of the precipice, his heels digging into the snow as the treacherous arch gave way beneath his weight. Annalla and I gasped in horror, readying ourselves for the sickening plunge, but Marcus balanced precariously for a heartbeat, then two, on the lip of eternity, before righting himself and stepping towards us.

"Oof," he murmured with a high-pitched grimace. "That time, Marcus heard the angels sing. Ja!"

We maneuvered off the glacier's peak onto a narrow rock ledge, unsure of our direction but fixated on fleeing the deadly labyrinth of crevasses. Navigating the glaciers spread across the mountainside would have been a Herculean task even with bright sunlight. In the fog, our fate felt sealed, as if these ice monsters lay in wait for us at the lower fringes of this rock island we had cautiously reached. For a brief spell, we were heartened as the mist seemed to be lifting, giving us a fighting chance to traverse the treacherously yawning expanse of this lower glacier. It could have been another deceptive loop of the one that nearly claimed us earlier. We were beginning to congratulate ourselves and cling to the hope of breaking free from the oppressive cloud bank when the wind changed abruptly, and the dense, gray shroud swallowed us once more. We pressed on, now numb to fear — or perhaps our greatest dread was the paralyzing grip of inertia. Annalla led our advance like a blind man, probing the ground ahead with his staff and calling back to us with updates on the terrain.

The descent remained consistent, and for a quarter-mile or so the ice provided solid footing, maybe too solid, breeding a deceptive sense of confidence in Annalla.

The mist thinned again, and I could see his figure, a shadow moving ahead about twelve feet away.

"The ice is broken! Watch out, there's a boulder on the right—"

He was gone! Suddenly, a violent pull on the rope tied around my waist yanked me off my feet. I scrambled madly, trying to grab onto anything to stop my fall. Small stones and chunks of ice tumbled down as I slid forward. One of my legs slipped over a ledge, and my right arm flailed into empty air. Then, some unknown force gripped me from behind, halting my descent. I sprawled halfway over the precipice but didn't fall any further, as I should have.

"Who's there?" Corlaer gasped through the fog.

"It's me! Ormerod!" I called out. "Annalla went over the edge."

"Is he dead?"

With considerable courage, I peered into the swirling blue-green mist.

"Annalla!" I shouted, my voice oddly strained.

"Yes, brother," he responded calmly, and startlingly close. "I'm here."

"Are you hurt?"

"No. I'm holding onto the rope. I've got one foot on an ice-shelf."

"I hear you," Corlaer panted from behind me. "Follow my instructions. I pull first, Ormerod. You let out the rope as you come up. Once you're safe, we pull together for Annalla. Ready? Now, up!"

The Dutchman's breath came in heavy, ragged gasps, like a dozen oxen straining at the rope. Annalla's cry warned me that the pull might drag him off his icy foothold, adding more strain on Corlaer. I wriggled sideways as Marcus dragged me up, managing to release a spare coil of the hide-rope.

The moment I had all four limbs on the ice, I shouted to Marcus to hold on, lifted myself shakily to my knees, and crawled over to where he sat. His feet were propped on the boulder Annalla had warned us about, taking in the slack of the line, hand over hand.

"Now, we pull Annalla out," he huffed. I grabbed the line beside him, but my effort paled in comparison. His massive shoulders bent forward, his muscles bulging under his hide shirt. His legs were braced like steel pillars against the boulder, now frozen solid to the icy ground. Inch by inch, we drew in slack. The heavy rope chafed against the dull edge of the precipice, but it held where no hempen cable could. Annalla's arms appeared above the brink, searching for a grip. Moments later, his face emerged, and Marcus's breath came in steady, explosive puffs. Annalla found leverage with one hand, then the other.

"Corlaer has done enough," he panted. "Hold tight! Annalla can pull himself up the rest of the way."

We held the line taut as Annalla gave a mighty heave, swung one leg over the edge, and crawled out of danger, inch by cautious inch to avoid the treacherous ice. Marcus straightened up, exhaling in a mighty blast.

"Oof!" he grunted. "That was no joke."

"No joke!" I echoed. "You saved our lives!"

"Corlaer has added more to the debt Annalla can never repay," said the Seneca. "He is stronger than the buffalo bull, like the Great Tree that holds up the sky. Annalla will not forget."

"Ja," mumbled Marcus. "And now, we go down, eh? It is not good here. I have shivers in my back."

We brushed the moisture from our lashes and pushed onward with renewed caution. The mist had thinned a bit, but the wind was fiercer, and the clouds swirled in a way that made everything more treacherous.

We managed to scramble off the glacier and onto a jagged rock edge, which led us to a steep snowfield. It was so steep that we had to pull out our hatchets again and carve steps for the descent. Funny enough, I think the blinding mist actually helped; it kept us from getting dizzy looking down those sheer drops. I had just taken the lead from Annalla to give him a break from the grueling task of hacking footholds when the entire surface of the snowfield started to slip.

Corlaer lost his footing first, tumbling head over heels down the slope, dragging Annalla and me along with him. The snow picked up speed fast, but a short way down, a terrace on the mountainside arrested its wild rush, scattering chunks of ice all around us.

Somehow, perhaps because of our weight, we bounced off that terrace, tumbling further down a slope. We got tossed around like rag dolls—sometimes crashing into each other, sometimes separated by the lengths of our ropes, and every so often, one of us would land a kidney punch or a headbutt that made the whole experience that much more painful.

How long we slid, I couldn't say, but it felt like forever. Suddenly, the clouds around us seemed to thin, and we rolled out of the darkness into the dull light of an overcast day. As I turned head over heels, I caught a glimpse of the sky's brooding complexion, then looked down just in time to see the wildflower zone almost within our grasp. The next moment, we cascaded over a bluff and dropped into a snowdrift, landing less than a quarter-mile from the glade where we had begun our ascent.

Battered and bruised, our clothes shredded, yet miraculously unbroken, we picked ourselves up from the snow, chuckling feebly at the sorry sight we made. Limping through the flowers to our hut, we lit a fire, broiled a haunch of green venison, and collapsed into a bed of sweet-smelling cedar boughs. We slept like the dead until well after sunrise the next morning.

Chapter Thirteen

The sun was burning off the fog that had hung over the landscape since we left the base of the Ice Mountain. A westerly breeze brought to our ears a peculiar, muffled booming we'd heard only once earlier that day. As the fog began to lift, the noise intensified. It sounded like powerful water cascading over a cliff, but the air wasn't thick with mist like it was at Jagara. We were completely baffled until we fought our way through the thorny forest and reached an open bluff at sunset.

The booming noise was the surf pounding against a rugged shoreline. To the west, and as far as we could see to the north and south, the waters spread out, blue- green in the distance, close in an eruption of foam. The waves came charging in, one after the other, never ending, smashing into the cliffs, sending up fine spray and spume. The bluff where we stood was drenched by it, the breeze casting a fine mist over the nearby forest leaves.

"Brothers, take a look at this sea, as vast as Lake Cadaraqui," remarked Annalla, his eyes fixed on the churning waters. I chuckled involuntarily as a drop of spray landed on my lips.

"Cadaraqui, and all this wonderful land we've traversed, could be swallowed by this sea and still not fill it," I said. "This is the South Sea, the Pacific Ocean, stretching from this western edge of our continent to the distant shores of the Indies, just like the geographers said."

"How can Otetiani be so sure?" Annalla asked skeptically.

"Taste it. It's salt, like the water of any open sea."

Both Annalla and Marcus bent down, scooping handfuls from the rock pools, quickly spitting it out.

"Ja," Corlaer agreed. "Sea water. We've reached the end of the land."

Annalla nodded, his spirits dimming.

"We've traveled as far as men can go," he admitted, "and we've failed."

"Hawenneyu has turned his face away from us," Annalla muttered under his breath.

"We haven't seen everything yet," I reminded him.

"Ja," the Dutchman interjected. "We go south down the shore, eh?"

But Annalla said nothing more. He trailed behind us, defeated and disheartened, as we traced the jagged shoreline, searching for a spot to set up camp. When we finally found a suitable place, he helped with the usual evening chores, ate his share of our scant meal, and then walked alone to a solitary rock jutting into the turbulent waters. An hour later, he returned to our circle around the fire.

“Annalla forgot that he was a grown warrior,” he confessed with a mixture of shame and pride. “His heart turned to water. He felt lost and afraid. But now, he has driven the fear from his heart. Anything worth having, the Great Spirit makes hard to find. We’ve journeyed far, my brothers, but we may still have a long way to go. Annalla will not weep if the thorns tear his feet. Shall we continue?”

“Until you’re satisfied, brother,” I said. Marcus merely nodded his massive head in agreement.

"Good," declared the Seneca. "In the morning, we head south. Annalla will take the first watch. A spirit bird whispers tales of the past in his ear."

And that was that. When my eyes finally gave in to sleep, he was sitting just beyond the firelight's reach, his back pressed against a tree, musket resting across his knees, eyes locked on the dancing shadows. His disappointment must have been abyssal. To have journeyed so far, beyond the wildest dreams of his people, facing both mythical and real dangers, only to find they had to start over—it was no common setback. And he, who had so recently felt he had conversed with the very essence of Tamanoas, who had breathed in the spirit of the Life-giver, was all the more crushed.

He steadied himself, refusing to bow to disappointment's cruel grip. Drawing on reserves of sheer willpower, he found the strength to march on into the daunting unknown, though he'd been certain the end was near. After two days heading south, we hit the estuary of a massive river. Forced inland, we trailed along its northern edge, seeking a way across. We stumbled upon several empty villages, almost ghost towns, and on the third day, a tribe of eerie, tall, gaunt figures ambushed us. Their heads sloped back from their brows to sharp peaks. They scattered at the sound of our muskets.

Chasing them to their village—an eerie collection of long, sturdy log houses—we claimed a dug-out canoe as compensation for the ammo wasted in the skirmish. From a distance, the tribe watched us, silent, eyes wide with apprehension, fearful we might torch their homes. But that wasn't our way; we took only what necessity dictated.

Crossing the river, buoyed by a stash of smoked fish and dried meat from the savages' huts, we ventured through a stretch of astonishingly lush woods nestled between the rugged sea and towering mountains, just shy of the snow-capped behemoths we'd left behind at Ice Mountain. Encounters with indigenous people were common, but these natives were less ferocious than the fisher folk by the river, usually scattering at the crack of a single gunshot. It was a palpable difference; since passing the Sky Mountains, we'd rarely faced warriors as fierce as those on the vast central plains.

For the initial weeks, our path was aimless. We had trekked as far west as possible, yet hadn't mapped a new direction. But the persistent damp winds and clinging sea fogs coursing through this land forced us to contemplate a strategy for the encroaching winter—a season we knew would test us brutally. Our clothes had worn to ragged remnants, scarcely enough to fend off the biting cold.

At this point, Annalla and I were skeletal shadows of our former selves, worn thin from endless toil, gnawing hunger, and a grueling journey that had sapped our strength. Even Corlaer, with his usual layers of blubber, bore the signs of our ordeal; fatigue had etched deep lines into his once-flabby face. The fiery tenacity that had driven us to challenge the granite peaks of the Sky Mountains had been extinguished. What we craved now was rest, abundant food, and the chance to stitch together new clothes. For nearly eighteen months, we had roamed across the vast expanse of the continent, undertaking exploits that no one else would dare try. Master Cadwallader Golden, the Surveyor General of New York, had assured me of this, given his extensive study of America's geography.

So, on a bitter night, we huddled close to a meager fire beneath a makeshift brush shelter, debating what came next.

"When the snow hits, this won't be enough," I muttered, pulling at the frayed edges of my moccasins. "I wish we still had those buffalo robes we sacrificed back on Ice Mountain."

"Otetiani speaks wisely," Annalla agreed, the firelight casting haunting shadows on his face. "We don't know what the winter here will bring, but it's far from a warm land. Snow crowns the mountain peaks year-round. The valleys will surely feel the chill."

Corlaer, gnawing at the last scraps of meat from a bone, growled his agreement through a mouthful of sinew.

"We need shelter," I continued. "We need enough food to last, meat and pelts in good supply."

"What about the fisher tribes?" Annalla suggested. "Maybe they'd give us some sort of hospitality."

"Yeah, and slit our throats while we sleep," I snapped back. "I don't trust them. They've got the kind of eyes that don't look you in the face. They won't fight fair, and we can't speak their language, and they can't speak ours."

With a disgusted grunt, Corlaer tossed the bone aside.

"Go to the mountains," he squeaked, his voice raspy. "In the valleys there's cover, wood, and game to hunt. And no other men."

I couldn't argue with that. He was right.

We had tested it during our travels; the valleys at the base of the high ranges were the favorite hangouts of all the animals. The areas were lush with trees and streams, and the savages of these regions avoided the mountains, preferring the tidal rivers. In the right valley, we might find the closest thing to paradise. So, we took Marcus's advice and, the next morning, headed southeast into the foothills.

The first valley we encountered was quickly dismissed due to its lack of trees. The second had forests but showed no signs of abundant wildlife. The third was too remote. But after two weeks of zigzagging through the terrain, we stumbled upon a valley that promised everything we were looking for. It reminded us of that hidden vale in the Sky Mountains that we had crossed earlier. Like that one, this valley was a stunning blend of forest and savannah, with a small river winding through its middle. Snowy peaks framed its borders and, remarkably, its wildlife seemed utterly unbothered by human presence—they had never been hunted by man.

We set up camp at the mouth of a narrow pass that linked the valley to the outside world, finally feeling at peace. Here, we could hope to forget, at least for a while, the frenetic urges that had driven us so far from what we each called home. That night, as we shivered in the cold wind blowing off the glaciers, we found comfort in dreaming about the cozy cabin we'd build—a snug hideaway somewhere on the hillside, complete with a fireplace made from riverbed stones and mud.

The next morning, we drew lots using blades of grass to decide the day's work. Annalla drew the short straw, which meant he'd be hunting. This was crucial, not just to provide us with ample food but also to start gathering the hides we'd need. We were all relieved at this outcome, as Annalla was our best bowman, and we couldn't afford to squander our dwindling supply of powder and lead just to fill our stomachs.

Marcus and I set out to explore the length of the valley, primarily to scout a good spot for the cabin. The day was splendid, with the sun beaming warmly and a brisk, invigorating wind brushing against our skin. Even though our feet were sore and our muscles strained, we started our journey with a steady pace. Annalla waved us off with a cheerful whoop before disappearing into the dense timber below the small pass. Meanwhile, Marcus and I began our ascent to a narrow shelf of level ground that formed a natural platform halfway up the valley's gently sloping southern side. From there, we hoped to get a sweeping view of our domain and gauge the opposite wall of the valley, which we planned to examine on our return trip.

Marcus and I were left alone, with only the crackling branches underfoot and the rustling of deer, antelope, and wild sheep in the thickets to break the silence. The valley spread out before us in a broad ellipse, the surrounding hills terraced with shelves like the one we now walked upon. Rather than sticking strictly to the path, we often climbed up or down the slopes to check out specific features of the landscape. Mostly, though, we stayed on the hillside since the thick forest in the valley floor obscured everything beyond twenty feet, except for the occasional clearings or parks by the riverbanks.

We had covered a distance of at least two French leagues when the shelf on the hillside morphed into a rocky ledge, strewn with pebbles and overshadowed by a raw outcrop of rock. Leading the way, Marcus paused, his rifle at the ready, sniffing the air.

"Come on, let's pick up the pace," I urged, growing impatient. "It's almost noon, and we need to circle the valley before nightfall."

"Hold on," Marcus replied, his tone serious. "I smell something."

"Smell something?" I chuckled. "You could pick up a dozen different forest scents out here."

"It's not just any smell," Marcus said gravely, "I smell a beast."

This made me laugh harder, and I pushed past the Dutchman, breaking into a dogtrot along the barely-visible trail.

"Wait!" he shouted after me as I rounded a shoulder of rock jutting across the path. I waved him off and continued, feeling invincible. Then a snarl—like a thousand sheets of torn canvas ripping—froze me in my tracks. Not twenty feet ahead stood the largest bear I'd ever seen. We had approached from downwind, so it hadn't caught our scent. Its small, beady eyes blinked menacingly at me as it hunched over the half-eaten carcass of a mountain sheep.

In my initial shock, I lost all sense. Forgetting the terrain, I stumbled backward while raising my musket, intent on firing before the bear could react. But my foot slipped on the loose gravel of the cliff-side. Pain shot through my twisted ankle, and my musket went skittering out of reach downhill, leaving me hobbled and terrified that the slightest movement could send me falling after it. The glint of the musket barrel caught the bear's attention. It knew I wished it harm; it saw me sprawled out, my fingers desperately grappling for the tomahawk at my waist. With a snarl that erupted into a furious roar, it rose onto its hind legs and lumbered toward me.

The beast towered over me, its thick brown fur bristling, saliva dripping from its gaping maw, and its huge forepaws raised like a boxer's, poised to strike. Long, razor-sharp claws jutted from its massive pads, quivering with menace. I was certain my end had come. Then Marcus appeared, trotting around the rock shoulder, his face slack with worry. For a fleeting moment, the Dutchman froze, one foot suspended in the air. The next, his heavy musket was at his shoulder, and a blaze of flame burst from the muzzle.

But the bear moved just as quickly. It lunged forward and to the side, disregarding me with the erratic fury of its kind, all its murderous focus now locked onto this new intruder.

The shot hit the creature's shoulder instead of its brain, and that only seemed to make it madder. The beast roared with an almost demonic fury, rearing up on its hind legs and charging forward in a lurching, bloody waddle.

"Marcus, the gun!" I yelled. "Downhill! Forget about me!"

But Marcus ignored me. He whipped out a knife and tomahawk, vaulted over my sprawled body, and met the bear halfway in a blur of steel. What a fight it was! Marcus, big as he was, seemed puny next to the massive beast. The bear's head loomed over him, and for a split second, I thought it might chomp his neck clean off. Its cavernous mouth gaped open, its eyes glinted red, jaws snapping shut with a chilling click. But Marcus wasn't there. With a swift, unexpected grace so at odds with his usually awkward bulk, he ducked, dodged the bear's colossal paws, and slashed down its ribs with both weapons. The bear howled in pain and fury, dropping to all fours as it circled Marcus.

Now Marcus was in a tight spot. He wouldn't leave me unprotected, limiting his space to move. The bear seemed to grasp this, making a quick rush at me. Marcus nimbly stepped between us, and the bear rose on its hind legs yet again, rushing at him with forepaws wide open, ready to crush him in a deadly embrace.

Marcus braced himself. I expected to see him knocked down, but he didn't budge. The bear's huge, man-like paws wrapped around Marcus, claws tearing at his shirt and pants. But Marcus was relentless, chopping away with everything he had. His knife stabbed in and out, while the tomahawk in his left hand hacked mercilessly at the bear's groin and legs.

The bear's deranged growls—low, tense, and rasping with pure rage—took on a new tone of agony. It yelped and its grip weakened, giving Marcus the chance to pull away. But my horror-stricken eyes were glued to the Dutchman's disheveled figure. He had nimbly dodged the beast's snapping jaws, but no quick movement could shield him from the relentless assault of those fore-paws flailing with desperate vigor. His back, flanks, and thighs were a gory mess, his clothes shredded to tatters. Despite it all, he stayed crouched, unflinching, his gaze locked on the bear.

"Get out of here, Marcus!" I shouted again. "Run while you can. I'll roll down the hill."

"Stay put," he croaked at me, his eyes never leaving the bear. "This time, I finish it."

The bear seemed to share his resolve and crept forward on all fours, its roars reverberating between the hillsides. Sensing its move, Marcus leaped so swiftly that his tomahawk smashed down on the bear's lowered skull, slicing out one of its little red eyes. That drove the beast into a frenzy. It had fought up to this point with the cautious intelligence of a man-beast that knew it was outmatched in wits. Now, it threw itself at Marcus with blind fury. They collided in a desperate embrace, the bear towering upright, clawing at Marcus with all four limbs, rolling over and over until Marcus managed to slip free, wiping the blood from his eyes. Yet there was no time to rest. The bear was on him again, roaring madly, its hide a torn and bloody ruin. They collided once more, chest to chest, Marcus hacking and slashing, the bear chomping its teeth and flailing with its claws.

I found myself crawling towards them, dragging my injured ankle, inching over the rocky ground in a desperate bid to help. But before I could reach them, it happened. The bear seemed to throw itself with desperate force, and Marcus reeled back, his throat exposed. The bear lunged, its jaws aiming for the kill, but Marcus twisted violently. Instead of his throat, the savage teeth clamped down on his collarbone.

Its focus on this new struggle must have loosened the beast's grip on him. In that precise moment, Marcus managed to lodge his knife deep through a gash in the creature's ribs and straight to its heart. The bear wobbled, its eyes slowly glazing over, all while Marcus frantically hacked at its organs. Blood gushed from the wound in its side, and its dying claws raked him with a last burst of energy. Finally, it collapsed backward, dragging Marcus down with it. When I reached them, both bodies lay in a tangled mess—the bear's jaws still clamped onto the man's shoulder, Marcus's knife buried deep in the beast's side. I pried the bear's teeth free with my knife before the final rigor mortis set in and gently dragged Marcus away. I was almost certain his life was spilling out with every pulse of crimson. But then, he opened his eyes and flashed me a faint grin.

"I'll make a fine robe out of this pelt, ja," he croaked feebly.

Chapter Fourteen

I did all I could to tend to Marcus's gruesome wounds, but it wasn't much. We didn't have any medicine or proper bandages, just a few scraps of tow-wadding we usually used to clean our guns. I packed the deepest gashes with this stuff and patched the rest with strips of my shirt, wrapping them around his body. Then I scrambled to his musket, loading and firing it twice, hoping Annalla would hear. With that done, I gathered a heap of twigs and damp leaves, sparking a fire with my flint and steel. The smoke plume would catch the Seneca's eye if the gunshots hadn't. It would lead him to us faster.

I tried to make Marcus as comfortable as possible, stacking a pillow of leaves under his head and scouring his limp body for hidden wounds I might have missed in my initial frantic search. He was slashed everywhere—from his feet to his scalp, barely a patch of skin left untouched. Yet, he still breathed. I confirmed it by holding my knife-blade to his lips, feeling the faint flutter of his pulse. His heartbeat was too faint to hear, and his eyes were shut tight. He hadn't made a sound since his last weak breath when he talked about a "fine robe of dot pelt." I was certain he was dying. My only thought was to ease his suffering as much as I could. But Annalla refused to accept it when he climbed up the hillside an hour later.

"Corlaer will not die today," he declared, looking up from Marcus's scarred body. "Otetiani stopped the bleeding in time."

"That's impossible," I argued. "You haven't seen how terribly he's hurt."

And the bleeding hasn't stopped."

Annalla removed the makeshift bandage I had pressed into one of the most horrific wounds on Marcus's belly.

"See?" he said, peeling back the gory flaps of flesh. "It's a clean wound—or it will be once I draw the poison out. No ordinary man could have survived this, but Marcus isn't ordinary. His fat saved him. None of these cuts go deep enough to kill."

I joined the Seneca and used a knife blade we had seared in the flames to probe the gashes. Annalla was right. None of the bear's claws had ripped through the thick layer of fat to reach vital organs. For Annalla or me, such wounds would have spelled a grim end, slicing through our intestines. But for Marcus, they had merely drained some of the copious blood that surged through his giant frame. His shoulder was savagely torn where the beast had bitten him, and we couldn't be sure if the bone was broken. Still, aside from blood loss and the risk of infection, it was just a flesh wound—gruesome, but as Annalla said, not impossible to cure.

"There's a chance he'll die," he admitted, "Not today, but tonight, tomorrow, maybe the day after. If we're to save him, we need to get him under cover. We need herbs to dress his wounds and warmth to kindle his life-spark anew.

"Otetiani must skin the bear here. We'll need the hide and meat; the fat will make a healing salve. In the meantime, Annalla will find shelter. We must hurry, brother. Before nightfall, we need him settled quietly. We should move him before his mind escapes from the haze it's in."

When Annalla came back, he brought two young saplings tied together with vines to form a makeshift stretcher. We rolled Marcus onto it carefully; my swollen ankle wouldn't let me give it my all.

He had crafted a stick for me to use, enabling me to hobble alongside him and offer some help with the litter.

"We owe much to that bear," remarked Annalla grimly. "He had a cozy den at the base of this slope. We'll lower Marcus into it, and then you'll clean it out while I gather herbs to mix with the bear's grease. If Hawenneyu smiles upon us, Corlaer will be whole again before the winter's snow blankets us."

It was a grueling task to maneuver downhill with that dead weight, most of the struggle falling on Annalla. But we managed, slowly dragging the litter into the mouth of a shallow cave, tucked under the shadow of a jagged rock pinnacle. The bear had left evidence of its stay: a litter of bones and filth. I grabbed a makeshift broom crafted from pine boughs and swept out the rocky chamber, later scorching the floor and walls with torches made of lightwood. A fire in a corner by the entrance banished the dampness and the beastly stench, and long before Annalla returned, I had fetched water from a nearby brook that flowed into our little river.

All that time, Marcus hadn't stirred a muscle. He lay there like a slab of wax, pallid and lifeless, as if already a corpse. The jostling descent had reopened several of his wounds, but I managed to staunch the bleeding with bunches of leaves Annalla had pointed out for their healing properties. I even washed the blood from his head, arms, and torso. I met Annalla as I limped back from the brook with another potful of water. He took it from me, instructing me to cut pine boughs for our bedding.

Neither of us got much sleep that night. He had too much work to do, and I couldn't find rest due to a combination of wanting to help and the relentless throbbing in my ankle. Annalla had brewed a heavy grease from the thick slabs of fat I had hacked off the bear's belly. When it was reduced to a paste-like consistency, he mixed in handfuls of shredded leaves, roots, and bits of bark, stirring it constantly to keep it from catching fire. The concoction had a surprisingly savory smell.

When the mixture was thick enough that the stirring stick could stand upright in it, Annalla took it off the fire. Together, we laid bare Marcus's mangled body. Annalla started by washing the parts I hadn't tended to, meticulously cleaning each wound before spreading the salve over them. He applied the mixture to the injuries, one by one, with a careful precision.

Next, we boiled the meager scraps of tow I had used to pack the wounds and reused them for fresh dressings. We cut up pieces of our own clothing to create bandages. Marcus's torn shirt and breeches were discarded, and we redressed him in our own garments— I gave him my shirt, while Annalla offered his pants, cutting them to fit Marcus's broader frame. To protect him from the night's chill, we covered him with aromatic pine branches and stoked the fire until it roared, filling the cave with warmth.

After attending to Marcus, Annalla turned his focus on my ankle. He prepared a poultice of leaves soaked in boiling water and wrapped the whole thing in mud, urging me to sleep. When I insisted on taking my watch, he promised to wake me in due time. But exhaustion and pain conspired against me. In those pre-dawn hours, I collapsed into unconsciousness, and did not stir until Annalla gently shook my shoulder as the noon sun poured into the cave's entrance.

He smiled, waving off my protests, and handed me a bowl made from bark, brimming with steaming bear broth.

“Drink,” Marcus’s voice croaked weakly from nearby. “The bear makes good soup.”

"Ja!"

Across the cave, the big Dutchman lay there, eyes wide open, a twisted grin etched on his scarred face.

"Is he... alive?" I asked, stunned. Annalla nodded, still smiling, while Marcus’s grin spread even wider.

"This time Marcus gets the last laugh, eh?" He shook a weak fist at me, still audacious.

"You thought I’d die, didn’t you? No, we just need some bear grease for the Winter, that’s all."

But many long weeks dragged on before Marcus was able to join us for our daily chores in the valley. Most of his wounds healed quickly, thanks to Annålla’s magical salve and the healing balsam pitch from the fir trees. But his mangled shoulder was stubborn, so we forced him to give it the necessary time. After the first month, there were plenty of small tasks that kept him busy around the cave, and in his calm manner, he entertained himself well enough. Yet, no other man I ever knew could have endured the torment Marcus did while regaining his health, nor survived the physical battle with the bear, emerging both alive and sane.

We never built the cabin we had planned because moving Marcus would have been too risky a second time. Instead, Annalla and I sealed the cave’s entrance with boulders and mud from the river, leaving a recess for a fireplace and smoke- hole. It was a snug, weatherproof home, the coziest we had throughout our travels. But Annalla and I were rarely inside except to eat and sleep, for the work was never-ending, especially as Winter began.

Naked as we had been before Marcus’s encounter with the bear, we were even less clothed afterward; the urgency for furs to protect us from the cold was dire. If not for the hardiness we'd developed, we would have died from exposure within the first week, while we tanned the skins of deer and sheep and dried sinews to use as thread.

To tell the truth, that first foray into tanning wasn't exactly our finest hour. We were too hungry to care much about the quality. But Annalla, driven by the pride of his heritage, honed his skills and turned those pelts into something soft as woven cloth. He couldn't use the superior Iroquois method—didn't have the right materials—but with some tricks from the Plains tribes, he crafted robes and garments unmatched by any white man. Instead of cornmeal, he cooked up a paste from brains and liver for the dressing process. After soaking, scraping, and dressing, he'd rub the skins over the rounded top of a tree stump. He'd laugh and call it squaw's work, but it made the leather as flexible as a wool shirt and much warmer.

That winter, we lacked nothing. We killed only what we needed, and the animals in the valley stayed close, unafraid. Firewood was abundant, just twenty steps from our door. Our cabin was snug and dry. We reveled in crafting little tools we'd long done without during our travels—crude clay vessels Marcus would tinker with for hours; bowls and containers from bark; cups, knives, and spoons carved from horn. We decorated our home with the care of dedicated housewives, laboring over intricate devices we didn't even need, just to surprise each other. But eventually, we grew tired of it. The call of the uncharted country beyond the valley's eastern edge wove its spell around us. The hunger for untrodden trails stirred once more in our hearts.

One evening, as we sat by the open doorway, listening to the drip of melting snow on the lower hillsides, I broke the long silence. It was a silence filled with three men's unspoken thoughts.

"Marcus," I asked, "how far did you hike today?"

He shrugged.

"Around the valley, who knows how many miles."

"Does your shoulder still hurt?"

He flexed his arm and shoulder in response. I turned my gaze to Annalla.

"It's been a long rest, brother. Time to get back to our quest."

His face lit up, much like it had when we first set out from the Long House.

"Annalla is ready," he said. Corlaer yawned sleepily.

"Yeah," he mumbled. "We should go. If we stay, we'll gather moss. Better we move on."

We gathered our gear and left the valley at dawn, uncertain of our direction yet committed to moving forward. After wandering aimlessly through the mountains for a week, we decided to head due east, at least until something compelled us to change course. In this godforsaken land, there was no real reason to head anywhere else. As we pushed beyond the snow-capped mountains encircling our once-contented valley, we encountered a high plateau, well-watered but deceptive. A few days' trek eastward revealed a stark change in landscape.

Between low mountain ranges or hills, we found barren plateaus or basins. Some were covered with rough grass; scattered along the sparse streams were patches of dwarf timber. More often, we trudged over bare, blistered rock or desolate sand deserts. When the wind blew, it scorched us like the fiery breath of an oven. We would have perished had it not been for Annalla's foresight. During the winter, he had sewn two sheepskins into water-bags. These saved our lives as we crossed the desert.

Initially, the heat wasn't unbearable. But as spring turned to summer, it grew severe. The dust from these high deserts had a strange chemical reaction on our skin, leaving our faces cracked and creased with dried blood.

Food had become scarce, and whenever we managed to bring down an antelope or deer, we meticulously preserved every scrap of meat. Twice, we pondered turning back, but the sense that we had to traverse this unforgiving land before reaching a more bountiful territory drove us forward. Reluctant to tarnish our streak of overcoming every hardship, we pressed on. Yet, the farther we ventured, the more severe our suffering grew. Our resolve shifted; what once pushed us forward now felt more like a dread of the hell we'd left behind than any hope for what lay ahead.

Three months after abandoning our idyllic valley, a sliver of hope emerged. We were navigating a barren expanse of rocks when Annalla's sharp eyes caught the glint of sunlight reflecting off water in the distance. Our spirits soared as we imagined drinking our fill and soothing our parched bodies. As we hurried closer, our excitement mounted. The water extended beyond the horizon, seemingly boundless. We believed it to be a vast lake. But when we reached the shore and plunged our faces into the nearest pool, the water burned our throats with its bitter salt.

"The sea again!" Marcus exclaimed, bewildered.

"We've circled back," Annalla muttered, crestfallen.

"We've walked with the setting sun at our backs for three months," I argued. "We couldn't have circled."

"This is another sea," Annalla insisted.

"Ja," Corlaer agreed. "The Spanish Sea, maybe?"

But I knew that couldn't be right. Having diligently studied Master Golden's maps, I was convinced we hadn't reached the Mexican Gulf. We were thousands of miles to the north and west of it. Besides, we had encountered no signs of Spanish presence, not even glimpsed any native tribes for months. And lastly, the water was far saltier than the spray of the Western Ocean.

"Let's follow the saltwater south," I had suggested. And I was right. Three days in, the vast expanse revealed itself to be no more than a great lake. We pivoted southeast, drawn toward the mountains etched against the horizon. At last, our spirits lifted; we'd found enough water to sustain us. But then we saw it: smoke signals billowing on the horizon. The sight chilled us. Clearly, the Indians were watching us, and our ammunition was perilously low. We couldn't afford a confrontation unless it was absolutely necessary.

It's curious how trivial choices shape our destiny. We could've just as easily turned north along the Salt Lake's edge. And had it not been for those smoke signals, we would've certainly headed eastward. Either of those paths would have spun this tale in an entirely different direction. Strange indeed! But if we ponder oddities in our insignificant lives, how much more astonishing is it that this lonely Salt Lake sits a thousand miles from the sea that must've birthed it? What, after all, is truly strange?

In these mountains, we found that the easiest route was to follow the streams carving their way through the landscape. They funnelled us south of east, leading us into a world more terrifying than the nightmarish deserts and craggy ranges we'd recently endured. It was a realm sculpted by monstrous plateaus, dissected by chasms so deep that daylight seemed a distant memory. We trudged along the rivers' courses, the sky a mere sliver above, confronting rocks painted in wild, vivid hues, as if some cosmic artist had unleashed every color in his palette here.

The land was devoid of trees or true grass, just stunted bushes clinging to life in pulverized soil. Did I say the previous was a nightmare?

This was far worse—an abyss of emptiness and desolation that clawed at your very soul.

We were picking our way among the boulders at the bottom of a daunting ravine when an arrow splintered against a rock near Annalla's arm. Marcus didn't hesitate; he raised his gun and fired. A squat savage tumbled through the air, landing almost at our feet in a twisted heap. What remained of him showed that he had been naked, with long, scraggly hair, armed only with primitive weapons. As we looked over him, his comrades launched another wave of arrows, the air whistling with their menace.

We hurried on, hoping to appease them by retreating. It was a false hope. They hounded us all day, and we spent most of the night wide-eyed, fearful of a sneak attack. But morning brought no reprieve; they were right behind us again. Day after relentless day, they stuck to us like shadows. Though they never attempted a head-on assault again, their numbers and persistence were unnerving. They excelled at using the rocks for cover, forcing us to waste precious bullets to keep them at bay. Each shot drained our ammo, pushing us to the point where we had to cut bullets in half and reduce the powder charge.

A week of this torment, and we were lost, our sense of direction obliterated. The sun's course, once our trusty guide, became an unpredictable phantom. Occasionally, we'd stumble out of the oppressive gloom of the ravines into broad, rocky valleys. These were dotted with bizarre, square rock formations rising abruptly from the valley floor. But no matter how many of them we gunned down, the squat bowmen would swarm over the valley behind us and on both flanks, herding us into yet another ravine.

Two things kept us from utter despair: we had enough water—for now—and they never attacked at night. We grew so accustomed to this nocturnal truce that we forsook our watch and slept, all three of us, from dusk till dawn, exhausted beyond measure. But then we hit a ravine devoid of water. One of our water skins had been punctured by an arrow and was useless. The other was rapidly depleting.

As the days stretched on, the oppressive weight of our situation buried us deeper into despair. The rocks watched us like spectral sentinels, silent witnesses to our slow march towards a desperate end.

Our supplies were dwindling fast. Thirst and hunger gnawed at us. We were in a tight spot, and our relentless pursuers knew it. They crept closer and closer. If we were to avoid an arrow to the chest, we'd need to move carefully, matching their stealth. Each charge we made, burning through powder and lead, only drove them back temporarily. They'd always catch up when we found another bend in the ravine. Lately, they seemed unusually excited. We could hear their guttural calls echoing from cliff to cliff, see them darting between the boulders and along the ledges. Their confidence grew as they closed in, and we darted under their arrows, pushing forward around the next elbow of the cliff. Annalla, leading us, stopped dead, frozen at the sight ahead.

But it wasn't the valley below that gripped him. Not at all. His gaze was locked on the figure of a shepherdess standing defiantly before her feathered flock. Bow raised, arrow nocked, she dared us to come closer.

Chapter Fifteen

She was a striking figure—slender, with ruddy skin that glowed under the sun and hair as dark as a moonless night, fine like spun silk, not coarse like most native hair. It was bound with a strip of serpent's skin. She wore a white cotton robe, edged with crimson, draped over her right shoulder, under her left arm, and belted at the waist with another band of serpent's skin. The robe stopped just short of her bare knees. Her sandals were crafted cleverly from some kind of plant fibers. All around her strutted hundreds of turkeys, their iridescent feathers a vibrant contrast to her bronze beauty.

Her arrow was aimed right at Annalla's chest, and she called out with an air of disdain in a throaty dialect none of us could understand. But mid-sentence, she noticed Corlaer and me, and her deep brown eyes widened in surprised shock.

"Espanya!" she exclaimed.

Now, during my youth, among many other experiences of varying worth, I had campaigned in Spain with the Duke of Berwick—a good lord and an honorable man, even if he was a bastard. So I had picked up some Spanish. I called back to her.

"Not Spaniards, but Englishmen!"

Her arrow wavered, shifting between us nervously.

"Espanya," she repeated uncertainly. I stepped forward, but her arrow steadied again, and for a fleeting moment, I thought she would release it.

"We are friends," I said.

"Stop," she commanded in broken Spanish, with an accent unlike any I'd ever heard. "What are English? You are Spanish! Leave!"

Just then, a yelp echoed from the squat bowmen on our trail, and a volley of arrows rained down on us from the cliffs above. She looked up, more startled than ever.

"We are friends," I insisted. "The bowmen chased us here."

"Awataba," she murmured, almost to herself.

In one swift, fluid motion, she snatched a turkey-bone whistle from her robe and blew a piercing note that sliced through the crisp air like a razor. As she half-turned, I stole a glance at the valley spread out behind her. It was a bowl-like formation nestled in the plateau country, about three miles wide and twice as long. A respectable stream flowed through it, emerging from a ravine to our right. The valley floor was a patchwork of green fields, punctuated by stunted trees, the only flora this arid land begrudgingly supported.

The whistle's sharp call summoned dozens of men from the riverbank. Looking closer, I realized they had been toiling in the cultivated fields. The entire surface of the valley seemed to be devoted to agriculture. Beyond the river, against the right-hand wall of the valley, a rounded rock formation jutted out from the cliffs, resembling a woman's breast. Atop this natural monument sprawled a complex of walls and towers. As the whistle's shrill warning reverberated, tiny figures appeared on the roofs and battlements, like a swarm of ants disturbed from their nest.

"What place is that?" I asked, my curiosity piqued. The girl with the turkey whistle responded with a practiced, almost robotic tone.

"Homolobi."

The name meant nothing to me then, but later, its significance struck me. It was aptly named The Place of the Breast.

I moved forward to get a better look, and the girl with the turkey feathers promptly re-notched her arrow.

"You have to wait for Micki," she announced.

"But we're friends," I insisted. "If we stay here—"

"Who's that?" she interrupted, her curiosity piqued as she gestured with her arrow toward Annalla. He hadn't moved a muscle since he'd first seen her, his eyes drinking in her face with an intensity that was unusual for the normally reserved Seneca warrior.

"He's an Indian warrior who traveled with us from the country by the Atlantic Ocean, where we English live. He's from the People of the Long House."

She shook her head, dismissing my explanation.

"You're talking nonsense. What are English? People of the Long House! Aren't we of Homolobi also dwellers in long houses? Micki says our people all live this way, except the Awataba, who were cursed by Massi to wander naked among the rocks. And what's an ocean?"

How I would've answered those bewildering questions eluded me, but fortunately—or unfortunately—at that moment, the Awataba, as the turkey-girl called them, gathered the courage to launch a final charge. They started by sending a storm of arrows in a high arc, aiming to land behind the boulders we used for cover. One arrow killed a turkey, and the girl looked ready to cry. Another arrow lodged in Marcus's sleeve, and he squealed indignantly.

"Let's teach these naked men a lesson, eh? Then we'll deal with the girl's friends."

There was no choice left. Our attackers were darting in and out between the rocks at the mouth of the ravine. If we tried to flee, we'd become perfect targets on the valley floor. Marcus tackled one of the nearest attackers, and I knocked another poor soul from his perch on a cliff. Annalla, snapping out of his dazed stupor, proved equally effective in the skirmish.

A bowstring thrummed beside me, and the turkey-girl pointed proudly at a savage who staggered away with her arrow buried in his arm. But the Awataba refused to back down this time; they hadn't caved like in previous assaults. Within ten minutes of relentless firing, we were out of ammo. Just as I discharged my last shot, I glanced back, relieved to see hundreds of men charging up from the valley. The stark-naked bowmen were now dangerously close, their grotesque faces flashing between the rocks, dropping from ledge to ledge as they tried to flank us. They reached Marcus first, and he shocked them by flipping his rifle and using the butt like a hammer. I followed his lead, but Annalla opted for knife and tomahawk, his weapons of choice. Between swings, I caught glimpses of the turkey-girl, still standing her ground, loosing arrows with icy precision.

Then the tide of reeking bodies overwhelmed me. I was knocked down but scrambled back to my feet. Gap-toothed maws snapped at my throat. Squat demons wielded stone mauls and flint knives. I hammered left and right with the musket-butt, maintaining my ground until Corlaer came to my aid, swinging his clubbed musket in one hand and brandishing a knife in the other, a savage grin lighting up his piggy eyes.

"Annalla!" he grunted, exultant. Side by side, we hacked our way through the fetid horde to where the Seneca stood, his back to a boulder, the turkey-girl crouched beside him. Her turkeys had finally scattered, and she was wielding a stone maul dropped by one of the natives, giggling as she bashed at men who tried to strike Annalla from behind. She even waved the weapon at us, as if questioning why we dared to interrupt. But the battle was over—the reinforcements surged into the defile, their arrows clattering against the rocks, and the squat savages fled in disarray.

The turkey-girl flung aside the stone-maul, her eyes blazing with a fierce light.

"Whoever you are," she said, her voice laced with a strange respect, "you're good fighters. Better than Simba, I think."

"Who's Simba?" I asked, curiosity piqued. But she dismissed my question as if I hadn't spoken, her eyes now burning into Annalla.

"What's his name?" she demanded, nodding toward Annalla. I relayed the name, and at the sound of it, Annalla paused in cleaning his knife, giving her a slow, intense look.

"Ask the maiden who she is, brother," he said. I did as instructed, and she replied without a moment's hesitation.

"I am Trisha. Is Annalla a priest, too, or just a warrior?"

"He's a great chief, a war-captain," I explained. "He guards the Western Door of the Long House where his people live."

She pursed her lips in disdain. "Anyone can be a warrior," she scoffed. "But warriors need priests to pray for them and ensure their victory."

I couldn't help but smile at her naivety. "In my brother's country, the warrior is honored above the priest."

"Then they must be very ignorant," she declared. "Like the Awataba. Are you a priest?"

"I am a trader. I buy and sell."

Her disdain for me was even sharper than her contempt for Annalla. "And the fat one?"

"He's a warrior, too."

"I'm disappointed," she said with an air of royalty. "I thought perhaps you were great ones, priests from faraway lands come to sit at Micki's feet and hear Simba cast spells for Yoki, or maybe to watch me dance."

"Are you a priestess?" I asked, treading carefully on her pride.

"I am Trisha," she replied, her words carrying an unmistakable rebuke. I wanted to ask more, but a young man with eyes full of anger and wearing a kilt of serpent-skins shoved himself between us, gesticulating wildly as he spoke to her. She answered him as serenely as she had spoken to me and then turned away, beckoning to an older man who was leading back the men from the fields who had chased the squat bowmen. The older man barked a quick order to his followers and strode over to where we stood.

Just like the talkative young guy, he sported a kilt made of snake skins. Both of them had long, black hair tied back with the same kind of material. They looked strikingly similar, with muddy reddish skin and slender, under-sized figures. In fact, everyone in Homolobi bore the same general resemblance to the squat savages who had driven us into their midst—except these people were less muscular and had faces that hinted at a higher intelligence. They were notably shorter than the Plains tribes, yet seemed far ahead in terms of domestic life.

Trisha, the turkey-shepherdess, stood out starkly from the people of Homolobi. Her bronze skin had a warm, tawny glow. Her figure was beautifully sculpted, with delicate hands and feet, and her features were sharp and aquiline, a striking contrast to the flat faces of the others around us. From all these details, along with other clues we picked up, I couldn't shake the suspicion that she had a decent bit of Spanish blood in her. But Micki, the only one who knew the full story, never gave up anything concrete about her origins.

The older man, after giving us a quick once-over, launched into what seemed like an intense conversation with Trisha, often interrupted by his impatient younger companion. As they talked, a crowd of curious townspeople slowly gathered around us. They were dressed in cotton kilts of various colors and wore sandals made of vegetable fibers. Many were armed with bows and arrows, spears, hatchets, and knives. Their demeanor was cautious—neither openly hostile nor friendly. The conversation came to a sudden halt when the younger man, after giving Annalla a fierce glare, barked a sharp retort at Trisha and stormed out of the circle, nearly half the onlookers trailing behind him.

The old man and the girl turned to us as if nothing had happened.

"This is Micki," said the girl. "He's the High Priest of Massi."

I bowed.

"Tell him," I began, but Micki interrupted me, speaking in halting but understandable Spanish.

"You're not Spanish?"

"No."

"Say after me: 'Vaya con Dios, most excellent señor,'" he instructed. I repeated it, not making any extra effort with my accent—a sloppiness that didn't seem to matter. Micki seemed satisfied.

"You're French?"

I was taken aback. This man knew something of the world outside.

"No."

"English?"

"Yes."

He nodded thoughtfully.

"Why are you here?" he demanded.

"We were chased by the squat bowmen Trisha calls Awataba."

"Were you searching for Homolobi?"

He studied me closely as he spoke.

"We'd never heard of it."

"Then what are Englishmen doing here, so many months away from their homeland? And why do you have this red man with you?"

"We've been traveling, trying to forget the sorrows the Great Spirit has placed upon us, and to see new lands."

"Have you traveled far?"

"To the coast of the Western Ocean."

He nodded again.

"What the Spaniards call the Pacifico?"

"Yes."

"And this red man?"

"He's a chief of the Hodenosaunee, a great nation of the Eastern Indians allied with the English. He is my brother."

Micki nodded a third time. He was clearly an unusually intelligent man. His face was pensive, with a high forehead and deep-set, inscrutable eyes. There was none of the trickster or charlatan typical of most Indian priests or medicine men about him. He was clearly well-informed, with an air of knowing more than he let on.

"All we ask," I continued, "is permission to rest in your valley before we continue our journey."

An enigmatic smile flickered across Micki's face. He gestured toward the smoke puffs beginning to rise from the rocks bordering the defile.

"The Awataba wouldn't let you go that easily," he replied.

After a pause, he said, "If you went, you might lead the Spaniards to Homolobi."

"We've got nothing to do with the Spaniards," I argued.

"You speak their language," he noted.

"So do you. I picked it up when I was in the French army in Spain."

He shrugged.

"You seem to be everything. An Englishman, yet you served as a French soldier in Spain."

I laughed. "That's true enough, but don't worry about us coming back. We've been through too much. All we want is to get home and our chances of that are slim; we're out of powder and lead."

He tipped my powder-horn to confirm my words.

"Huh!" he grunted. "We talk too much. Come with me to Homolobi."

"And the Awataba?" I asked. "Won't they cause trouble if we go?"

"I don't think so," he answered calmly. "They're like children. They can't hurt us, and if they mess with our gardens, they'll know I'll curse them, leaving them to starve when winter comes."

"But if we go with you, can you guarantee we won't be betrayed?" My eyes shifted from him to Trisha, intently following our conversation, then to Corlaer, who was impassively gazing at the valley, and finally to Annalla, whose eyes were still locked on the girl's face.

"Everything happens according to Massi's will," he replied.

"That may be," I snarled, trying to summon all the fierceness I had left, "but if we're going to die, we'll die here in the open, taking as many of you with us as we can."

The girl interrupted, her voice urgent.

"What is this talk of betrayal and killing? Micki only said that everything is Massi's will. Do you think Massi wants your deaths when you fought to protect the sacred turkeys?"

Micki's smile was enigmatic and shadowy.

"Stay here and risk the Awataba if you like," he offered.

I didn't quite know what to say, but Annalla tugged at my sleeve, distracting me.

"Ask the chief where the girl came from," he pressed. I hesitated, skeptical of prying into such personal matters.

"Ask!" he insisted. "Annalla has a reason."

Micki, curious about our exchange, asked what we were discussing. I responded reluctantly, but Micki didn't seem offended.

"Tell your red brother," he said, remarkably polite, "that the maiden is Trisha, the Sacred Dancer. She tends the sacred turkeys at Massi's shrine. She brought me a message from Massi once, when I was fasting in the desert, seeking visions of the future."

I relayed this to Annalla, who sighed, tearing his gaze from the girl's face with visible effort.

"Annalla thought... But Hanegoategeh bewitches me!"

"Be careful he doesn't bewitch us all to death," I snapped. "Must you, of all people, risk our lives out of curiosity for a woman from another tribe?"

"What is death, brother?" the Seneca replied mournfully. "There were times when we both prayed for it. Shall we fear it now?"

Marcus leaned in, his lips brushing my ear as he spoke.

"She looks like Ranno," he whispered. "Say no more. It's just a passing fancy. He'll forget."

He was right. Though they were different in many ways, this girl Trisha bore a haunting resemblance to the long-dead priestess from a renegade Iroquois rite, the one Annalla had mourned for years. Her memory was the driving force behind our bizarre quest, the Lost Soul he believed awaited him in some shadowy realm between worlds, ruled by Ataentsic and Jouskeha, demigods of his heathen beliefs.

"Forgive me, brother," I softened my tone. "I spoke harshly. My nerves are frayed. But what should I tell these people? They offer us sanctuary or leave us to be slaughtered by the savages who chased us here. And if we go with them—"

"Let's go with them!" Annalla interrupted eagerly. "Yes, let's go!"

"Marcus?"

The Dutchman yawned.

"Yeah, we better go."

"I've got a hole in my stomach," he said, his voice low and cracked like an old vinyl record left too long in the sun. The twilight hours loomed outside the dusty windows, painting the room in ghostly blue hues. Shadows danced on the peeling wallpaper, making it seem alive, as if the room itself breathed along with him.

He lifted his shirt, revealing the jagged, inky dark wound that looked less like a puncture and more like some gaping maw. The edges of the wound puckered with dry, angry skin, and the darkness seemed to crawl—inky black tendrils pulsing slowly, reaching out as though seeking something to devour. His breath hitched, echoing off the barren walls, filling the space like a dirge.

In the silence that followed, time seemed to stretch out, elongating every minute detail; the rusty radiator ticking, the distant hum of the refrigerator, the muted sound of branches scratching against the window like the bony fingers of long-forgotten specters.

He met my eyes—those once temperate pools of brown, now clouded with pain and something else, something ineffable. Desperation, maybe. Or the gnawing edge of madness.

Chapter Sixteen

Micki didn't say a word when I confirmed we'd accept his offer of hospitality—or whatever it was. He just turned on his heel and started walking, forcing me to hustle to catch up. Trisha decided to stick with Annalla and Marcus, while the remaining men in white kilts drifted back to their interrupted tasks. No one seemed to care about the Awataba anymore. Their bonfires flickered along the northern cliffs as if nothing had happened. A group of young girls chased the sacred turkeys back into line, and the riverbank was dotted with women scrubbing clothes. Farm work continued in the fields, undisturbed. Both sides of the river for miles were lined with open gardens, and just below the Breast where Homolobi stood were fenced gardens and stone storehouses, fortified and ready for defense. The closer we got to the village, the more impressive it became. You could only access it by ladders and a narrow trail where one man could fend off an army.

The houses, built from sturdy stone blocks, reached three and four stories high, connected and encased by a wall fortified with round and square towers. Overcrowding the tip of the Breast, the village was safe from an attack from above due to a bulging outcrop in the cliff above.

"How long have your people lived here?" I asked Micki.

"Since the beginning of time," he replied, his voice dripping with gravity.

"Do you have many other villages?"

He gave me a sideways glance before answering, "The Spaniards and others before them destroyed all but ours. Some of our kin live under the rule of Christian priests in the South, but they build their homes on open rocks. We are the last of the Clifftop Dwellers."

This statement, astonishing as it was, has been confirmed by scientists from the Smithsonian Institution, who acknowledge that some cliff dwellings were possibly inhabited in recent historical times.

"That's why you hate the Spaniards," I said.

"Yes, Englishman."

Wherever they went, they left a trail of death. If it hadn't been for what you told Trisha and the stand you took to protect her and the sacred turkeys, we would have killed you on sight. The Awataba chased after you, despite the losses you dealt them, because they thought you were Spaniards. And they knew if the Spaniards escaped, they'd return with more, eventually killing or enslaving everyone not like them.

"The Spaniards have always been enemies of the English," I said, trying to placate him. "The English were the first to deny the Spaniards' right to exploit your land."

Did I mention that Micki had green eyes, sometimes sparkling, other times blazing? They pierced me like daggers as he responded, "The English are white; we are red."

I dropped that line of defense. Micki was sharper than I had imagined, cunning, with a depth of knowledge unexpected in such a remote community in the heart of the vast rock desert.

"We're friends," I insisted, returning to my original point. "We came to you nearly unarmed."

"You shouldn't have come any other way," he shot back.

We crossed an irrigation ditch, and I praised its craftsmanship. He nodded, silent but his expression screamed, "Foolish white man! Do you think your people are the only ones who can work in stone?"

I tried a different approach. "How come you're not afraid of the Awataba?" I asked.

"They're children," he said, dismissively.

"But they outnumber you so greatly."

"They fear us."

We had reached the walled enclosures at the base of the Breast, and he gestured to the overflowing storehouses.

"When they starve, they come to us for food. If we have extra, we give them some."

"They know that if they ever tried to stand against us, we would never lift a finger to help them out. They're too clueless to fend for themselves."

We didn't get a chance to chat any longer because we had reached the first of several ladders. Each one was wide enough for two people to climb side by side, leaning against narrow ledges carved into the cliffside. Micki scrambled up them with the nimble ease of a seasoned sailor. I had just put my foot on the lowest rung when I heard a laugh behind me. Trisha, with a mischievous grin, shoved her way in front, dragging Annalla along. She'd found a new game, it seemed—pointing at things and naming them in her own language, while Annalla followed up with their names in the Seneca dialect.

She was going into all sorts of details about the ladder and the trail, her eyes bright with excitement while Annalla looked both thrilled and embarrassed, when Micki's curt command snapped through the air. Trisha instantly grew serious, racing up the ladders after him. The people of Homolobi watched our climb with amused grins. It seemed easy from the ground, but it was tough, in its own way, as scaling the Ice Mountain of Tamanoas. The ladders were the simplest part.

After them came a series of rock trails that snaked over the Breast as far as a nipple-like projection, where another ladder led to the topmost section. This part angled up to the village's entrance—a doorway so narrow Marcus had to twist sideways to squeeze through. Inside, we were plunged into total darkness, an oppressive black that gnawed at my nerves with the cold sharp talons of fear.

I dreaded betrayal, expecting the worst, but we only ended up banging our heads and shins on hidden stairs, corners, and doorposts as we were shuffled along through a maze of grimy passages. Micki guided me, while strangers led Annalla and Marcus, each of us stumbling through the darkness like blind men groping for the way home.

Trisha must have gone on ahead, because she was the first person we saw as we emerged from the dim vestibule, stepping abruptly into the glaring, sun-drenched plaza at the heart of the village. The space was vast enough to hold the entire village's population, which had to be upwards of fifteen hundred people. The plaza was ringed with communal houses that made the Long Houses of the Iroquois seem as primitive as the Dakota's skin teepees.

These structures towered above us, each floor set back from the one below it, creating a series of open-air porches or verandas. The rooftops teemed with onlookers, and several hundred men lounged in the central plaza, their eyes following our every move. Directly opposite us, set into a niche in the cliffside, was a building that stood out from the rest. It shared the same stepped design, but instead of four floors, it had only three, with the first story being twice as tall as those of the neighboring houses. Its windowless facade was dominated by a massive doorway, flanked by monstrous stone figures—grotesque creatures with human bodies and the heads of mythical beasts, entwined with snakes.

In front of this looming doorway stood three figures, and Trisha was the least remarkable among them. At the center of the trio was a very fat old woman, her gray hair framing a face with dull, snaky eyes. She wore a white robe trimmed in garish red, and she held herself with a certain conscious majesty that was hard to ignore, regardless of what you thought about her character or hygiene.

To her left was the young man who had been so vocally disapproving after the fight. He had added to his serpent-skin kilt by draping a live rattlesnake around his neck, its head arrogantly poised next to his left ear. As soon as we appeared in the plaza, he took a step forward, his voice rising in a harsh declamation, the serpent at his ear hissing in eerie harmony.

Occasionally, he would pause his speech and act like he was listening to the snake's whispers. The crowd watched in awe, but I thought I caught a hint of mild cynicism on Micki's face. As for Trisha, she didn't even try to hide her feelings. After the chatty young man and the snake had carried on long enough for you to hear a blade of grass rustle, Trisha ruthlessly interrupted, just as she had interrupted me. And she didn't stop at just talking. She danced her opinions. Literally.

She would say something, lift her eyes to the sky, raise her arms in a pleading gesture, and then glide into a slow, stately dance, or whirl into a fast, spirited one. Between dances, she argued with an unseen force inside the temple, sparred with the fat old woman, or exchanged barbs with Micki. When she finally stopped, the chatty young man tried to resume his sermon, but Micki stepped forward and cut him off. What ensued was a four-sided debate, with the fat old woman joining in. Eventually, she lifted her arms in a gesture of invocation, squeezed her eyes shut, and waited while everyone, including us, grew tense and chanted a single sentence. Then, she reopened her eyes and waddled into the shadowy depths of the temple, the young man trailing behind, no longer talkative but very sullen, dragging the snake from its perch.

Micki's face remained emotionless, but Trisha's expression was pure delight, a sharp contrast to her earlier disapproval of the young man's words. She danced away toward a narrow door in the corner of the temple's main block. Micki crooked his finger at us.

"Come," he commanded, leading us through another door to a staircase that took us up to the terrace atop the front part of the temple. We crossed the roof, under the wary eyes of several men in serpent-skin kilts, to a doorway opening into a room roughly twelve feet square.

The room had no windows, and the walls and floor were starkly empty.

"You can sleep here," Micki said abruptly. "Food will be brought later."

"Can we go out if we want?" I asked as he was about to leave.

"Why not?" he shrugged. "But be careful. Your faces will stand out to our people."

We were left to ponder his words until our doubts were put to rest by a visit from a group of temple priests, dressed in serpent-skin kilts. Leading them was the talkative young man we had encountered earlier. They barged in while I was tending an arrow wound on Annalla's shoulder, their faces grim and hostile. They gathered up our guns, powder-horns, and shot-pouches without a word and walked out. Marcus started to get up but sank back down to his haunches at a quick signal from me.

"We should break that bastard's head," he grumbled.

"That's exactly what they want," I said.

"Otetiani is right," agreed Annalla. "The guns are useless. If we had resisted, they would have used it as an excuse to kill us."

"Yeah, maybe you're right," Marcus admitted thoughtfully. "So, what do we do now?"

"Nothing," I replied. "It's wise to bide our time. The situation is still unfolding. I don't know what other powers might be at play here, but of the four leaders we've seen, I think Micki is still on the fence about us. The serpent priest despises us for reasons of his own. The old woman hasn't given any sign. The girl, Trisha, has a fancy for Annalla, but that's a double-edged sword. Your path is a perilous one, my friend."

Annalla smiled—a smile I hadn't seen in him for years—filled with a kind of hopeful anticipation.

"There's a name echoing in my heart, brother," he said. "I don't know yet what it's saying, but it calls louder and louder. Maybe—"

Just then, Trisha slipped through the doorway like a ghost.

"Ignore what Simba does or says to you," she ordered curtly. "He's jealous, poor, crawling ant! And he thinks he can ruin my plans."

"Who is Simba?" I asked.

She looked at me with a frown, baffled that anyone could be so clueless.

"The guy who just left."

"Oh, the dude with the snake?"

"Yes, you idiot," she spat at me.

"And why is he jealous?"

A knowing smile crossed her face, and she scuffed her sandal in the dirt.

"Because of me, obviously."

"Obviously," I parroted back. "But he's not jealous of me, is he?"

"Oh no," she replied frankly. "He's jealous of Annalla."

She said the name with a charming little lisp.

"Is he your boyfriend?"

"He wants to be." Her voice dropped to a conspiratorial whisper. "Ever since he took over from his dad as the Priest of Yoki and Voice of Chua. He's been doing rain dances for two years now, and everyone says he's some powerful priest and spellcaster. But Micki says I have to serve him first as the Sacred Dancer, since Massi sent me directly to him and not to Simba. Besides, I don't even like Simba. He might be a good warrior and a clever priest, but I don't trust him."

"So, Simba's not the Chief Priest?"

"You are so ignorant, Englishman! No, Micki is the Chief Priest, and Runsi is the Priestess of Tawa, the Sun, the Giver-of-Life. Simba's just the priest of Yoki. But when a priest of Yoki is as successful as he is, he basically becomes as important as the Chief Priest and Priestess. And Simba's been telling the young men how much better things would be if he were the Chief Priest or had more influence in the Council."

"And what does your chief think of all this?" I asked.

"Chief? What chief?"

"The village chief! And the war-chiefs."

She laughed a soft, mocking laugh.

"You are like one of the Awataba, Englishman! We don't have chiefs like that. We look down on warriors. When we need to fight, we all do, but we don't glorify war. The priests and the council run the village."

"Who's on the council?" I pressed.

"Oh, the priests and the elders the priests choose," she said, now sounding bored. "But I'm tired of talking to you, Englishman."

I came here to learn Annalla's language, I told Micki I needed to. He warned me against it, and I replied that if I couldn't, I'd marry Simba tonight. Micki doesn't want me to marry Simba.

She slumped down between the Seneca and me, pointing a finger at Marcus.

"What's that bear's name?"

"Wait, hold on!" I pleaded. "Tell me why you left us on the ladder and went ahead into the village."

"No, I'm done with all that," she said defiantly. "I'll talk with Annalla now."

"But he wants to know," I lied. "And he has to learn through me."

Her face lit up.

"Oh! You really are clueless, Englishman! Why didn't you say so before?"

"I didn't get the chance," I chuckled.

"You're an Awataba," she insisted. "You must have killed a Spaniard and taken his clothes. But you asked why Micki called me. It was because I talked with Annalla and I'm going to talk to him whenever I want. So I just told fat old Runsi! Micki said Simba would stir up trouble and that I should go ahead and tell Runsi he was bringing you to the village because you saved me and the sacred turkeys and weren't Spaniards."

"And then?" I prompted her.

"Then I went to the kiva, and Simba was talking to Runsi against Micki. I told him I'd dance against him if he kept being foolish. He said Chua the Snake advised him that you three were to be the doom of Homolobi and must be sacrificed to Chua."

"So that was what he was talking about when Micki brought us in?"

"Yes, he told the people what Chua had said, and that you would probably bring heavy rain to ruin the harvest or a drought next summer."

Chua's voice rang out ominously as he prophesied again, his words heavy with accusation. "You came here with evil intentions, especially the red one named Annalla."

"I danced for Massi," she continued, her eyes wide with the memory, "and in my dance, I called upon all the Gods. And as I moved, they spoke to me. They said that Chua's voice had been mistaken, that men who saved the Sacred Dancer and the revered turkeys of Massi's shrine couldn't possibly be Massi's enemies. Simba denied it, claimed you were indeed Chua's foes. But I cried out in the temple, and Massi responded, saying that such claims should remain unsaid, for they implied a rift between Chua and Massi."

She let out a soft, nostalgic laugh as she recalled the scene. "Simba was left speechless." A mischievous glint flickered in her eyes. "So Micki consulted Runsi, who offered a prayer to Tawa for enlightenment."

I leaned in, tension knotting my stomach. "And what did Tawa say?" I urged, watching as her attention shifted back to Annalla.

"Tawa said it was too early to decide."

Her words hit me like a punch. In the razor-thin margin between life and death, it all hinged on an old woman's divine conversation with the sun.

"Is it left at that?" I asked, feeling the unease gnaw at me.

"How else?" she snapped, her patience fraying. "I didn't come here to chat with you."

"But how long does it stay like this?"

"Until the festival at the end of this moon—the one just before the harvest. But if you keep pressing me, Englishman, I'll go to Runsi and have her ask Tawa to save the others and throw you off the cliff."

CHAPTER SEVENTEEN

For all practical purposes, we were prisoners during the weeks we spent in Homolobi. However, I can't say that we were exactly shackled or chained. The entire village, with its labyrinthine passages, massive stone structures, towering walls and spires, and scattered rock gardens—all patched up in the cliffside nooks—was ours to wander freely. Accompanied by Trisha, we even ventured into the shadowy depths of the temple and gazed at the wooden effigy of Massi. It was a sinister figure, part-human in its features, overseeing a stone tank filled with writhing rattlesnakes. Our guide reassured us that the snakes still had their fangs. But the creepy priests of that grim place handled them fearlessly, and none of them ever seemed to get bitten. Explain that if you can.

After another one of these unsettling visits, a knife fell from the air, landing just in front of Annalla's feet. It missed the gap between her collar-bone and shoulder by mere inches. If it had fallen by accident, no one came forward to claim it, nor did we see anyone who could be its owner. We couldn't shake the feeling that it had been hurled at Annalla. But we decided it was best to keep this incident to ourselves, confiding only in Trisha. She had become a steadfast friend and ally, more out of a whimsical curiosity about new faces, especially Annalla's, than anything else. Or perhaps she saw it as a chance to torment Simba and needle the stern Micki. But here I am rushing ahead. Trisha approved of our decision to stay silent.

"It was definitely that ant Simba," she spat out, eyes blazing. "He'll pay for it! I'll dance until his heart bursts, and laugh as he suffers. But it's pointless to accuse him outright. He'd just laugh it off and turn the crowd against you, accusing you of sowing discord. And that would be bad because it hasn't rained since you arrived. People are already murmuring that you've brought us good luck and the promise of a bountiful harvest."

"You have to be cautious, avoiding dark passages."

At her suggestion, we started walking on the valley floor every day, where it was safer. One day, as Annalla broke through a thicket by the river to explain this intricate irrigation system, an arrow sliced through the air, embedding itself in a tree trunk beside him. He scanned the area for the hidden archer, but found nothing. He then hurried to rejoin us. After that, we made sure to steer clear of any copses and groves, as well as dark corners and spots overshadowed by walls. Probably the best reason Annalla hadn't been taken out was because she stayed so close to him.

"What chance does a warrior have when his enemy is a priest?" she chuckled. "It's a good thing he has me looking out for him. Do Simba and his minions think I would let them kill Annalla before I've mastered this grand language of his?"

No one stopped us from our wanderings, but there were always men nearby. When we were out in the open, a few priests in snakeskin kilts stayed within eyeshot. And now, the smokes of the Awataba encircled the valley. To the north, south, east, and west, they rose lazily into the calm air, the days still, moderately warm, free of intense heat, and marvelously dry. Twice I asked Micki, mainly to provoke him, if we could leave the valley. Each time, he smiled cryptically, raised his arm, and gestured to the surrounding cliffs.

"If you go, you go to your death," he said the first time. A week later, he added, "Shall we send you to your deaths, Englishman? That would hardly be kind."

"I sometimes think we linger here only to await death," I countered. His face was serious, but his green eyes danced with amusement.

"Can you see the future?" he asked.

"No, I'm no miracle-worker."

"Then how can you predict what Massi has in store for you?"

"Why do those naked bowmen linger so long?" I demanded, steering the conversation elsewhere.

His brow furrowed, a look of uncertainty clouding his eyes.

"Who knows?" he replied with a nonchalant shrug. "They're kids. Maybe they've hunted enough to keep them going for a while."

Sometimes, he'd open up, and we'd talk about his people's customs and their societal and religious setups. They struck me as the most cultured group of Native Americans I'd encountered, especially since we had just come across a string of wild, depraved tribes west of the Sky Mountains and along the Western Ocean coast. The remoteness of their home seemed to have shielded them, allowing them to focus on farming and raising turkeys rather than war. Some turkeys were specially bred for the sacred flock that served the shrine of Massi, providing feathers women used to weave stunning screens and robes. Their crops rivaled those of European farmers and easily surpassed what our American farmers manage to grow, all with nothing more than sharpened sticks and primitive rakes and hoes.

In a rare talkative mood, Micki shared one of their traditions. It said that long ago, this rocky wasteland had been far richer, supporting a vast population. Over centuries, though, the climate shifted, transforming the land. Rivers dried up, fertile soil blew away, vegetation perished, and the sun's fury turned most things to dust, sparing only a few lucky patches. Around the same time, hordes of northern savages attacked—low-browed, fierce people, probably related to the Awataba and, by extension, to the Homolobi themselves. These invaders, known as the Shunwi, or "Flesh Creatures," stormed many villages. Driven to insanity by hunger and bolstered by sheer numbers, they wreaked havoc, leaving devastation wherever they passed.

The other villages, crushed by their circumstances, drifted southward, chasing better prospects and gradually losing contact with those who stayed behind in their ancestral lands. Then came the Spaniards, sealing their fate. Micki, who had seen the devastation firsthand—having roamed the Spanish colonies and possibly even dabbled in the sporadic Indian rebellions aiming to resurrect a new Montezuma—felt the tragedy of his people deeply. He had witnessed one village after another on the edge of the desert fall, one by one, conquered and converted. His life's mission became clear: to shield Homolobi from the inevitable doom that seemed to consume everything in its path.

This dedication was evident in his hesitant welcome to our group. The same uncertainty lingered even after he had saved our skins. He wrestled with us as a resource—whether to let us go or to feed us to the superstitious fury and political scheming of Simba's faction. At the heart of it all were the factional politics tearing the village apart. As Trisha had informed us, the priestly hierarchy doubled as the political framework of their society. The council of the wise men was, in reality, a cabal of priests, with a sprinkling of others handpicked and controlled by these religious leaders.

These priests not only dictated the spiritual life of the village but also oversaw agriculture, industry, resolved family or clan disputes, enacted and enforced laws, interpreted traditions, and provided military leadership when war loomed. This monopolized intellect, Annalla believed, was likely the reason for the tribe's decline. His insight held weight, as he straddled both worlds, understanding the mindsets of both the red man and the white. In the end, it was this insular intellectualism, devoid of broader perspectives, that might have sealed their fate.

Despite being lost in his own tangled thoughts and his strange obsession with Trisha, he couldn't help but become deeply involved in the problem at hand. It was that infatuation with her—so full of electric intensity—that would eventually bring everything to a head. Thanks to him and the irresistible pull he had on the girl, with all her mysterious power, we got a close-up view of the unfolding drama that enveloped our lives, each of us alien in this small community.

Essentially, it was the same old tale told in every corner of every town. Micki symbolized the wisdom of age. Fifteen years ago, he'd gone out into the desert to fast and seek a vision of the future, and he came back with Trisha, a woman- child who he claimed was sent by Massi to serve in the temple and dance for the Ruler of the Dead. Micki's sharp mind, combined with Trisha's graceful presence and unique personality, cemented his authority. He ruled almost unchallenged, often brushing aside the rival authority of old Runsi, who represented the women in their hierarchy.

Homolobi's social structure was distinct, valuing women and granting them significant standing in the priesthood. They were equals, owning property and having the right to weigh in on public issues. They upheld the sanctity of monogamous marriage and could demand punishment for any husband who mistreated his wife. While they were barred from serving Chua and excluded from the priestly clan or religious dances, they had Runsi, a representative just below the chief priest in rank, who could sometimes even force his hand on policy matters.

Runsi was a shrewd priestess-stateswoman, nearly as sharp as Micki but lacking his breadth of experience.

She had played a pivotal role in boosting Simba's prestige, the young priest of Yoki and suitor for Trisha's hand. But as soon as Simba grew strong enough to challenge the chief priest, she swiftly moved to even the scales, hoping the clashing ambitions of these two men would create an opportunity for her own hidden motives. But the game got trickier with Trisha's unexpected rise. Initially viewed as nothing more than Micki's assistant, circumstances fueled by Simba's courtship and rivalry thrust her into equal prominence among the group. And Trisha wasn't one to waste such an opportunity.

I can't say how loyal she has been to Micki. Yet, knowing her later, I'd wager she would have stuck by him after ensuring her own gains, if not for Annalla's arrival. Emotions ran hot—love, hate, the magnetic lure of beauty, and the insatiable hunger for power fueled every move in this upheaval. If only we had gone north instead of south around the Salt Lake, never venturing into these mountains! Where would Micki, Trisha, Simba, and Runsi have ended up? What fate would have befallen the people of Homolobi, or Annalla, Marcus, and myself? Fifteen hundred lives would have diverged into an alternate reality. I won't even touch on the fate of the Awataba, who died for reasons they couldn't grasp. The thread of destiny that binds our lives is tenuous indeed.

All my musing is moot, though. We were destined to act as we did. It was written in the Book that our path led to Homolobi, just as Annalla's obsessive quest had to reach its own inevitable end.

How else can you explain the immediate magnetism he felt for the girl, the light sparking in his eyes when he first faced her threatening arrow, or how easily the two of them dismissed the needs, wants, and desires of the fifteen hundred others around them? It was destined to be. Even Marcus's extraordinary strength had a part to play in this grand drama we were all living. And, as the narrator, I tell you there was no accident in what happened. If chance had its way, it would have ended us long before Destiny set us on the path to fulfill our fates.

If Micki, priest of Massi, were to look over my shoulder from whatever afterlife he inhabits, I know he would nod in agreement. Some forces defy human control. We were ensnared by such a force when the Homolobi people assembled before the kiva of Massi for the pre-harvest festival. It was the end of that moon when we found ourselves in their valley. I can't be more precise about the date, having lost all track of time during more than two years of wandering.

The day was clear and cloudless, not too hot, with barely a breeze—just like every other day since we arrived. I remember the villagers making room for us in the front row around the open space in front of the temple, some even smiling, so popular had we become on account of the favorable weather we seemed to have brought. To these people, weather was everything. Afraid of a bad harvest, they always stored a year's worth of dried crops in advance. There had been times when crops failed two years in a row, and their entire existence revolved around securing enough to eat.

Religion, for them, was weather. Which is why Simba, Priest of Yoki, garnered such acclaim; twice, he had secured abundant early summer rains for them.

So here we were, the unlikely heroes of our own story, who had somehow managed to stave off the unseasonal storms that could have ruined the crops. Funny, isn't it? We'd gained popularity by doing exactly what Simba claimed was his unique talent. No wonder he glared at us with such venom as he danced out of the temple, leading his snake priests, each man draped in writhing coils of slimy serpents. This, right here, was how the ceremonies began.

Micki and Runsi sat in front of the temple's entrance on sturdy wooden blocks, while the grotesque visage of Massi leered at them from behind, dragged out of his dark shrine into the harsh daylight for this occasion. Trisha hadn't shown herself yet, but behind the idol, priest, and priestess were the masked dancers of the various clans, dressed as birds, beasts, reptiles, plants, or even insects. Looming overhead was the cliff's bulging brow, and beyond the rooftops, the distant wall of the valley stretched, its top tinged with the faint smokes of the Awataba—the persistent savages whose relentless siege belied their seemingly insignificant nature. The plaza teemed with villagers, the men clad in white kilts with red borders, a mark of the highest members of the priesthood and the Wise Men of the Council. The women wore simple white robes, elegantly falling over the right shoulder and under the left breast, snugly cinched at the waist.

Inside the temple, drums began to thud, announcing Simba and his abhorrent entourage. They pranced slowly into the light, snakes coiling around their torsos, arms, and necks, their forked tongues flickering and hissing, yet miraculously never striking. The snake priests droned a low chant, shuffling forward with a serpentine rhythm, their steps mimicking the undulating motion of their sacred beasts. The chant's mournful notes built in intensity, the rumble of the hidden drums rising to match it, as if the earth itself had begun to growl in unison.

Around the open space, the grotesque procession weaved its way, causing everyone to instinctively step back as the men, draped in snakes, drew near. Simba, with a devilish scowl etched into his face, strode past us, his eyes cold and unyielding. I could finally breathe again after the entire line had passed; the sight of those writhing, unrestricted serpents gnawing at my nerves. Any one of them could break free, slithering into the crowd, bringing death within its bite.

The drums pounded louder, reverberating through the plaza as the priests circled a second time. The snakes became increasingly agitated by the clamor, the unexpected flood of sunlight, and the rows of white-clad spectators. They squirmed above the priests' heads, striking at each other, hissing wildly into the empty air. It was a nightmare come to life, a tableau straight out of Dante's depiction of Hell's torments. Simba passed once more, and again I felt the urge to exhale sharply, tension coiling in my chest. Then it happened, just as I had feared.

The drumming turned frantic, disordered; the priests stumbled into each other, caught off guard. A sickening plop hit the sandy ground – a rattlesnake, as long as Marcus, twisted into its combat stance, just an arm's length from Annalla. But the Seneca stood utterly still, not a twitch to his face or body. A collective gasp rippled through the crowd. Women screamed, children whimpered in fear. Micki sprang up from his stool, his command sharp and immediate. One of the priests broke rank, stepping forward to grasp the snake. With a practiced hand, he slid his fingers just beneath its venomous head, stroking its belly to calm the thrashing reptile.

Everything unfolded so swiftly that most didn't even catch the incident. But Marcus's massive hand clamped down on my arm with a force that made me think he'd rip it clean off.

"If he'd moved, he was dead," Marcus gasped into my ear, his voice a harsh whisper. "Yes, if he moved, Annalla was as good as dead."

"Did he drop it?" I hissed at Annalla, my voice low and urgent. "Did you see the priest drop it?"

"Yes, brother," Annalla replied calmly, "But who could swear he was responsible?"

"And you stayed silent!" I was astonished. "How did you know the snake wouldn't strike?"

"It was nothing," Annalla shrugged, his tone indifferent. "That snake only bites if it senses your fear. The man messed up—he should have dropped it on me. Then it would have struck out of instinct. But Hawenneyu didn't allow it. My medicine is too strong for the snake-priest, Simba."

Chapter Eighteen

The last of the snake priests slithered through the temple entrance, their shadows vanishing into the darkness beyond. Old Runsi, creaking with age, rose from her stool and lumbered before Massi's image. With great effort, she lowered her bulky frame to the ground, drenched in the mid-afternoon sun, and recited her invocation. Her words were a prayer, but here and there, the masked clan dancers behind her echoed back responses, their voices a sinister harmony. At the end, the crowd erupted in unison, faces turned skyward, shouting their answer to the heavens.

Runsi shuffled back to her seat, a dying ember amidst the rapt silence. That silence broke only when Micki raised his "paho," the prayer-stick adorned with paint and feathers, a totem of his authority. As he lifted it, the drums inside the temple rumbled into life, and the masked dancers began their eerie song, bodies swaying in time with the haunting beat. Micki interjected after each verse with chants of his own, prostrating himself in the sand before Massi. Each invocation culminated in a thunderous chorus from all gathered, the drums' deep thud weaving through the roar of voices that ricocheted off the surrounding cliffs.

The singing faded, leaving a heavy stillness in its wake. Micki, now by the imposing figure of the Ruler of the Dead, lifted his paho once more. Tap-tap- tap! The drums answered, slower this time, marking a cadence more ominous than before. The masked dancers slowly divided into two lines flanking the temple doorway. The eyes of the crowd, which had wandered since the snake dance, now focused with renewed interest. A murmur swept through the gathered masses—one word passed from lip to lip. "Trisha."

I watched as Annalla's jaw muscles worked furiously beneath his skin, his usually stoic face now a canvas of confusion and intent. However, the curiosity in his eyes turned to bewilderment when instead of the Sacred Dancer, the snake priests reemerged, led by Simba. They staggered under the weight of a burden between them—a massive pumpkin, resting incongruously on a makeshift stretcher.

It was twice as thick as Marcus and half as tall, perched on a tangled bed of stalks and vine leaves. The drums pulsed slowly, their deep throb setting the rhythm for the masked dancers who launched into a new song—a haunting, minor-key melody that seemed to implore Massi for continued favor. The snake priests, carrying their burden, moved between the two lines from the temple doorway to the image of the Ruler of the Dead. They paused a moment to face it, then turned. With Micki and Runsi leading Simba, and the column of masked dancers trailing behind the hurdle-bearers, they solemnly paraded around the plaza. As they passed, the townsfolk, sitting or crouching on the ground, bowed their heads and muttered, "Trisha!" or "The Sacred Dancer comes!" Some whispered personal prayers to Massi and lesser deities like Yoki and Chua.

Annalla's excitement had reached a fever pitch. His breath whistled through his nostrils, his chest heaving as if he were sprinting. His face was drawn and haggard, his eyes glued to the gigantic pumpkin.

"How could they have grown it to such a size?" I whispered.

He didn't hear me, but Marcus, on my other side, replied with a sharp retort.

"It's not real."

"Not real?"

"Yeah, you watch."

I leaned in closer, scrutinizing it. It looked for all the world like a regular pumpkin, just blown up to monumental proportions. There were the familiar ridges, the mottled yellow with hints of pale green, and the blunt-ended stalk. But as I watched, the snake priests completed their circuit of the plaza and gently set the hurdle down in front of Massi. They then lined up behind the idol, forming a single rank, with Simba a step ahead, arms folded on their chests. The masked dancers formed a ring around the image, the giant pumpkin, and the priests. Micki and Runsi, positioned on either side of the hurdle, moved to the next phase of the elaborate ritual. Micki seemed to be delivering an oration to the god.

He included everyone in his gestures—the people in the plaza, the villagers, the priests, the valley below the cliff, and finally, the pumpkin. We later learned he had been making the tribe's case for divine assistance, speaking on behalf of the men. Runsi, who followed, detailed for the deity the efforts of the women and their special reasons for deserving aid. To cap it all, they both turned their attention to Massi, pointing out the magnificent pumpkin they planned to sacrifice.

A prolonged shout erupted from the ring of dancers. The temple drums pulsed into a frenetic, erratic beat. Masked figures pranced crazily around the idol and the pumpkin, while the priests chanted another of their eerie, staggered songs. The drums beat faster and faster, the dancers spun wildly, and the song grew more frenzied. The finale came in a crescendo of noise, color, and movement that snapped off almost physically. Priests and dancers flung themselves face down in the sand. The drums fell silent. A quiet so profound followed that I could hear everyone's breathing, Annalla's gusty pants as loud as musket fire by contrast.

For a dozen breaths, this stillness held. Then Micki rose, bowed low to the monstrous idol, and approached the vast yellow pumpkin, sitting serenely on its platform. He extended his paho before Massi's unseeing eyes, recited a brief prayer, and tapped the pumpkin once. A collective sigh of anticipation surged through the audience. The pumpkin split apart, cleanly dividing into quarters, and from its hollow shell stepped Trisha, a lithe bronze statue come to life, clad from breast to thighs in a sheath of turkey feathers that puffed out under her arms like mock wings. Her blue-black hair flowed freely beneath the serpent- skin band encircling her brow.

For a moment, she poised in the fallen shell of the pumpkin, arms spread as though ready for flight.

Then she leaped, almost as if she flew from the hurdle to the sand, swooping this way and that, her movements like a bird in flight. Her glide was graceful, her motion wavy, her presence a living tapestry of rhythm. She hovered before Micki, paused before Runsi, and knelt in a dramatic pose of reverence before Massi's gnarled face. With a sudden burst, she launched into a dance full of grace and fiery emotion, a dance no Indian could replicate, enrapturing her audience with its exotic allure, its wild passion, both demonstrative and deeply seductive.

Simba made no effort to hide its impact on him. The grim face of the young priest was now lit by the unholy fires that smoldered deep within him. Stepping away from his place among the snake priests, he stood alongside Micki and Runsi by the wooden idol. His eyes drank in every sinuous movement of the dancer. Her slender, bare feet barely kissed the sand as she leaped and shifted from one emotion to another. Her eyes, flaring through the disordered veil of her hair, her lips, pouting, smiling, luring, challenging, repulsing—all combined into a vivid dance of entangling emotions.

But I had little chance to observe the Priest of Yoki's reaction. Beside me, Annalla rose to his knees, his face painted with the look of a damned man who glimpses heaven's gates opening for him. It was a mix of doubt and trust, disbelief and paralyzing joy, all singed with fear. He started to rise, and the people behind us murmured in low protest. I seized his arm.

"Sit down," I urged him. "What's gotten into you?"

I don't think he even heard me.

"Use your head," I snapped irritably. "You'll get us all killed. You can see the girl later."

It was Marcus who whispered the key to Annalla's state.

"He thinks she's Ranno," he muttered. "That's it."

Summoning all my strength, I pulled the Seneca warrior back to his seat.

"Will you destroy us, brother?" I hissed. "This is sacred to these people."

For the first time, he seemed to grasp what I was trying to convey.

"Otetiani doesn't know," he said softly. "She is my Lost Soul."

"A mist has clouded Annalla's eyes," I replied, realizing that in this state, I had to speak in the imagery of his people.

"No, brother," he responded, still with an unsettling calm. "You haven't seen. You have forgotten. But Annalla knew... before this all happened, there was a song in his heart, a warning."

"Of what?" I asked, feeling the weight of the hostile stares from the crowd that marked my interruption. "What did this song say? Was it about one maiden disguised as another?"

"She doesn't resemble another," he said with dignity. "She is another. She is my Lost Soul."

"You're delusional, brother," I groaned. He gave me a sorrowful, almost pitying smile.

"No, my eyes have been opened. But Otetiani remains blinded. What did the ancient story of my people say? That the warrior who journeyed beyond the sunset would find the land of Lost Souls..."

"Is this land beyond the sunset?" I asked, sarcasm dripping from my words.

"It must be!" His voice resonated with unwavering conviction. "Did we not see the sun sink behind the Sky Mountains? And we crossed those mountains, so this must be that land—beyond the Sky Mountains."

"Ay, but Annalla, you know that's just a myth—"

"Yes, a tale of my people," he agreed, his gaze steady and unflinching. "If one warrior could do it, why couldn't Annalla? I always believed it. Now I know it's true. I have done it. Here we sit, in the valley of Lost Souls."

"Look, there's Ataentsic, brother."

He pointed toward the corpulent figure of Runsi, whose eyes were boring into us with a malevolence to match Simba and those ominous snake priests. The flickering firelight cast eerie shadows, but Trisha danced on, her movements a poetic defiance, graceful and unrelenting, before the wooden sneer of Massi.

"And there's Jouskeha, her grandson." He motioned to Micki. "Just like in the legend, when the warrior came to the valley, his Lost Soul was dancing with the others before Ataentsic and Jouskeha. Jouskeha, feeling pity, took the Lost Soul and locked her inside a pumpkin. The warrior carried that pumpkin back to his homeland.

"Everything is here. There's the pumpkin, there are the Lost Souls. Ataentsic doesn't want to release my Lost Soul, but Jouskeha looks sad. It's all happening as the story said. All that's left, brother, is to put the Lost Soul back in the pumpkin and take her back to my village."

Arguing was futile. He was utterly convinced by this bizarre chain of coincidences. In many ways as cultured as an English gentleman, he was wholly primitive in this belief, trusting in the nebulous myths of his people, mistaking familiar shapes and a series of parallel events for truth. I turned to Marcus in helpless frustration.

"What can we do?" I asked.

"Nothing," replied the Dutchman, his voice as flat and unyielding as a brick wall. While my back was turned for that brief exchange, the Seneca broke free from my grip and marched to the center of the plaza. He moved toward the knot of priests and masked dancers encircling Trisha's spinning figure. The ceremony screeched to a halt, every movement frozen as if Massi's grotesque effigy had roared a command. A low growl of anger rippled through our side of the plaza. The snake priests' eyes burned with homicidal intent. The masked dancers' rage was mirrored in their rigid postures and vitriolic shouts. Runsi scowled; Simba's grin curved with devilish glee. Trisha looked surprised, her elegant motions stilled, a flicker of revulsion playing on her features. Micki alone remained an enigma, his face a mask. For us, there was no choice but boldness, our only ally in this deadly theater.

We were in deep. Annalla's actions were enough to stir the wrath of any wild tribe. There were no excuses, no way out. Our only option was to charge ahead boldly. That meant we had to strike first and stay on the offensive.

"Come on," I said to Marcus. He straightened himself and lumbered next to me.

"Ja," he wheezed through his nose, "we're in for a hell of a time."

I caught up with Annalla, gripping his arm again.

"Stay quiet. Let me do the talking."

He didn't respond, didn't resist. I don't think he had any kind of plan when he stood up. He was just driven by the urge to claim this girl, believing she was the embodiment of his lost love, and that raw impulse had broken him free from all restraint, compelling him forward to take what he thought no one would deny him. But he couldn't speak coherently to anyone in the priests' circle, except maybe to Trisha herself. Whether he realized this or not, he now obeyed me as meekly as a child.

"Follow my lead," I whispered to my companions as we moved past the circle of masked dancers. Opposite Massi's statue, I paused and gave a low bow. Annalla and Marcus mimicked me precisely, which defused the first swell of anger. The priests were baffled. We had acknowledged their deity and paid him proper respect. I seized the advantage while it was still mine.

"We are strangers here," I said to Micki, speaking in Spanish. "We may have breached your customs, but let our excuse be that my red brother thinks he has just seen a powerful piece of magic."

This piqued their interest and soothed their anger. Micki was naturally pleased with the idea of an outsider affirming his close connection with his deity. He and Trisha, who had danced over to join him, quickly translated the essence of what I had said.

Simba and his serpent priests glared, eyes smoldering like the coals of a dying fire. Old Runsi watched with a flicker of curiosity, while the others seemed utterly confused. Despite whatever hidden emotions churned within them, they found themselves unable to resist hearing me out. This was crucial—it allowed me to further exploit the political schisms already fracturing the priesthood.

Trisha's reaction to my tale was almost laughable. She swelled with pride, savoring Annalla's claim that he had known her in a previous life, a revelation that placed her on a pedestal of undeniable superiority. Micki, too, found validation in my story, which echoed his own proclamations about Trisha's divine origins. However, Annalla's sudden appearance had thrown him into a loop of bewildering uncertainties. Runsi, on the other hand, dismissed the tale entirely—it did nothing for her, except perhaps solidify her association with a foreign goddess. She grew leery, calculating the boost in Trisha's position and the inevitable rise in Micki's influence.

But it was Simba who truly erupted, his fury uncontainable. The Priest of Yoki stamped his feet and gnashed his teeth, his eyes blazing hot. Sweat glistened on his forehead as he fought to keep a grip on his temper, yet his savage objections burst forth repeatedly, cutting through the tense air. He saw our story as a twin-edged sword, solidifying Micki's power and erecting a barrier between himself and Trisha.

"The stranger lies!" Simba bellowed, his voice like a hammer on an anvil. Micki translated his scornful words, each dripping with vitriol, while Trisha reveled in the attention.

"If Trisha was one of his people, why can't she speak his language?" Simba scornfully challenged.

"The Great Spirit has taken that memory from her for reasons beyond our understanding," Annalla countered, and I relayed his defense.

"I can speak Annalla's tongue," Trisha retorted sharply, pride flickering like a flame. "It feels familiar, as if it once flowed naturally from my lips." She shot a sly glance at the Seneca warrior.

"It's a fabrication!" Simba howled, spittle flying. "Didn't he say that this lost soul of his was fully grown when she died?"

"And don't we remember when Trisha was just a kid with new teeth, when Micki first brought her to Homolobi?"

"The Great Spirit's ways are beyond our understanding," Annalla replied calmly. "He might change her age, but not her face or the soul that was lost. What are years to Him?"

"Ha!" Simba growled. "Do you expect wise men to believe such tales? Does it make sense that the Ruler of Death or any other god would allow such wanderers to know Heaven's secrets?"

Micki, who'd kept mostly silent, translating the arguments back and forth, and occasionally stopping Trisha when she seemed to provoke Simba further, pursed his lips, searching for a safe middle ground.

"This isn't a matter to be judged in anger," he declared. "There's a lot that's strange in what these strangers say. But how can priests, who deal with the unreal every day, refuse to believe a tale just because it contradicts their truth? It's odd to me that Massi, whom I serve, has never seen fit to share what these strangers have said, even though he often reveals the future to me for the village's good."

At this, the crowd erupted with shouts of:

"Great is Micki!"

"Micki is favored above other priests!"

"The Chief Priest speaks wisdom!"

"But who am I," Micki continued, "to expect Massi to tell me everything? If he did, I'd be his equal, a god. Maybe Massi sent these strangers here to deliver this message instead of calling me into the desert to fast for wisdom. I don't know. But the strangers have told us a marvelous tale. If it's true, then we are indeed favored by Massi, and Trisha, the Sacred Dancer, is twice holy. If it's not—"

“How can it be true?” Simba cut in boldly. “Chua the Snake, after all, has taken Homolobi under his protection.”

"Hasn't he trusted me these past two years? Hasn’t he shared things with me that Massi, busy ruling over the dead, has long forgotten? Do you seriously think Chua would keep such an extraordinary event from me?"

"Chua's told you things that never happened," snapped Trisha. "You said these strangers would bring bad luck, but they brought good luck."

"Yeah, that goes in their favor," Micki cut in.

"But there’s been nothing but arguments since they got here," spat Runsi, her voice laced with bitterness.

"There was arguing before," Micki replied sternly. "Enough talking. We need to look into this carefully. As Massi's priest, it's my duty to serve him. Let all—"

His words were drowned out by shouts of alarm from the edge of the crowd. The villagers, who had gathered thickly around the circle of priests, turned to the commotion. A path was being cut through the throng. Villagers armed with bows and arrows pushed back the onlookers, creating space for a group of squat, naked, brown-skinned men. They moved cautiously, darting glances and jumping away to avoid touching anyone not of their kind. A murmur arose.

"The Awataba!"

People backed off even faster when they recognized the newcomers as the bowmen from the rock desert. These were men only barely above animals, their bodies caked in grime, their hair matted, their weapons rudimentary. Their bellies bulged from eating dirt when no other food could be found, their eyes glassy with stupidity but alive with a primal fear of the unknown. They advanced until they reached the open space before Massi's statue. At the sight of its terrifying visage, they collapsed, writhing on the ground until their leader managed to grasp Micki's foot.

The villagers who had attended them gave a quick report, and Trisha leaned forward between Annalla and me, her lips close to my ear.

"This is bad," she whispered. "The field guards say the Awataba have left the cliffs and descended into the valley. They've come to demand that Micki hands you over to them. They..."

But now the Awataba were speaking for themselves in awkward, guttural clicks and clucking noises, peering at us from under heavy brows and greasy mats of muddy hair. They prostrated themselves again at a mere wrinkle in Micki's face, yet their persistence, their blunt determination, reminded me of the smoke that swirled each day above the valley cliffs. Trisha inhaled sharply.

"They're asking for you," she translated. "They say they've dreamed that if they sacrifice the three of you, their wanderings will end and they'll always have food."

Micki silenced her with a command that sent the snake priests to surround us. They herded us out of the crowd and up to the temple roof, signaling us to enter the room assigned to us. In there, we could neither see nor hear anything of what was happening outside. Leaving one man to watch us from the terrace, the priests hurried back to partake in the decision about our fate.

Chapter Nineteen

Homolobi had no twilight to speak of. Nestled beneath the overhanging Western cliff, the village was swallowed whole by darkness the instant the sun dipped below the horizon. One moment I glimpsed the gaunt figure of the serpent priest, our dogged sentinel, silhouetted against the gray walls across the temple plaza; the next, he was consumed by shadows. The only light left were those few stubborn crimson rays, slicing through the Eastern cliffs, flickering bravely before snuffing out. But then, other lights sparked to life. The plaza, which had thrummed with murmurs and whispers just a moment before, now blazed with torchlight. More torches gleamed from the rooftops across the way, and from the unseen depths of the valley at the base of the Breast, a colossal bloom of fire erupted, its savage roar echoing with dissonant, untamed voices.

The voices of Homolobi, however, were silenced in an instant, as if a single wave of Feathered Paho's hand had suppressed them. The village was cloaked in a deathly hush. In that unsettling calm, we could hear the cacophony from the depths of the valley—a deranged symphony of noise, rising and falling with the flames that licked the sky, illuminating the dark beyond the village walls. Distant yet piercing, the relentless, savage chorus seemed inescapable.

"The Awataba," I muttered, almost as if to reassure myself.

"Ja," Corlaer nodded. "The bowmen have lost it. They've gone crazy, right?"

Annalla remained silent. He hadn't spoken in the hour since the serpent priests had driven us from the plaza. As the light faded, I could see him, seated motionless against the wall, eyes fixed on some unseen point. Now, I imagined him exactly the same way.

I couldn't see him anymore.

"If we just had a pound of powder and ball between us," I groaned.

"What's the point?" Corlaer replied. "Even if you kill everyone in Homolobi, we still face the Awataba."

"Yeah, you're right," I admitted. "But I really hate the thought of dying in a trap."

"We're not going to die alone," the Dutchman grunted. "Ha!"

His exclamation was caused by the soft tread of a foot in the doorway. I jumped to one side, drawing the knife and tomahawk from my belt.

"Into the open!" I whispered. But Trisha's voice answered me, a whisper in Spanish just loud enough to reach my ear.

"Quiet! It's me."

I extended my arm and felt the familiar texture of her feather garment.

"You alone?" I whispered.

"Yes. Let me in. Where is Annalla?"

The Seneca's voice came from the darkness right next to me.

"Annalla is here, Ranno."

The joy in his voice sent my heart racing up into my throat. There were tears in my eyes. She understood him.

"Tell him," she ordered me with a musical laugh, "my name is Trisha."

"She is Ranno to me," Annalla answered. I felt her press by me, and a moment later her voice reached me again, strangely muffled.

"What I'm called matters little," she said. "I think Micki lies when he says I came from Massi. I seem to remember a time, years ago, when I often saw people who looked like you. But that doesn't matter. Annalla is a man! And I'm tired of priests and their ways. Yes, a man who would travel as far as Annalla for a woman is a man!"

"We're all going on a longer journey soon," I said with a grim tone. "And you will too, if you stay here."

"Yes," she agreed, her voice still muffled. I reached out my hand and found her body in Annalla's arms.

"What!" I gasped in astonishment.

Annalla's quiet laughter echoed, a soft, contented sound, and Marcus joined in with his own low chuckle.

"That's funny," he said, his voice barely a whisper. "We come all this way, Annalla gets what she wanted, and we die quick."

"What did the fat one say?" Trisha asked, prying herself away from the Seneca's embrace. I relayed the message.

"Yes," she repeated, her voice taut. "Death is coming. That's why I'm here. The Awataba told the council they needed you for a sacrifice. They said they dreamt that your lives would appease their gods. But I think that snake Simba planted the idea in their heads. I would have said something, but Micki wouldn't let me, so I ran away."

"What will the council do?" I asked, feeling the helplessness creep into my voice. The village buzzed with a soft hum, and the distant murmurs of the bowmen at the foot of the Breast grated through the night.

"They will give you up. Simba insisted there was no room for argument. The Awataba's audacity was proof enough of your danger. And when Micki contested, the Bowmen threatened to raze the valley, even if it meant their own deaths. Runsi sided with Simba, and I spoke as I said."

"Listen!" Marcus hissed. From the plaza, a chorus of voices rose.

"The council is finished," Trisha exclaimed. "They're coming."

"Some of them will die," I said with grim resolve. "You should go."

"Old fool!" she spat back, her contempt slicing through the darkness. "You have no brains. They'll block the doorway and break in from above. You have no chance here."

"Then we'll go out into the open."

"No, you'll come with me. I know a way. It's dangerous during the day, and we might all perish, but if we reach the cliff-top, we can hold out. Come! I'll lead Annalla. The rest of you, follow him."

We slipped out softly, Trisha guiding us against the wall of the temple's upper story. The night was a deep, impenetrable black, the cliff's overhang blotting out even the faintest starlight.

We had passed two other doorways, judging by the feel of my fingers, as the chaos outside grew deafening. Suddenly, a rush of footsteps and torches flared to life on the terrace. Figures darted past us, nothing more than vague shapes in the dim light, and we pressed ourselves against the wall, praying the shifting shadows would hide us. But then came a group, a dozen strong, their torches lighting up the night like it was midday. A holler marked our discovery. They charged, and we met their advance with ready blades.

"Run! Don't stop to fight!" Trisha shouted over the din.

We carved out a brief moment of respite and she darted into a nearby doorway. We stumbled down a steep, twisting staircase that spilled us out into a vast chamber—we recognized it instantly as the temple. Men were already flooding in from the plaza, with Simba leading the charge, a torch clutched in one hand and a knife in the other. The confined stairway behind us echoed with the shouts of our immediate pursuers. Trisha ignored Simba's advance, steering us past the tank in front of Massi's deserted altar, where the temple's guardian snakes writhed in eerie patterns.

Simba, however, took the shorter route around the temple. Foam flecked his mouth, his eyes were wild. When he saw Trisha move towards a faintly lit doorway behind the altar, he screamed in rage and hurled his torch at her. It would have struck her if Annalla hadn't snatched it from the air, his reflexes honed by years of practice catching tomahawks thrown by his own warriors.

For a heartbeat, Annalla held the blazing resin torch. Then, with a blood- curdling cry—the war-whoop of the Iroquois, feared from the Great Lakes to the Ohio—he charged forward to confront the Priest of Yoki.

They met by the snake tank, a sinister arena for a showdown. Annalla, his eyes narrowed, held his ground as the priest teetered dangerously at the edge. The hissing below was a symphony of malice, each serpent a note in a chorus of rage. Above them, pursuit and escape paused, caught in the snare of this deadly ballet.

Marcus and I held the line between the other side of the tank and the temple wall. It was a gap too daunting for any, even the snake priests, to attempt a leap. Trisha stood in the doorway behind the tank, her feathers rustling rhythmically with her calm breaths. She watched the duel without a flicker of worry, her hands resting on her hips. If any fear lurked within her, she masked it with effortless poise.

Simba hurled a curse at Seneca. Annalla returned it with an easy smile, mirroring Trisha's indifference. The priest lunged, channeling all his desperation into the stab, a wild animal cornered. Annalla dodged, shifting his shoulders with a predator's grace, and struck the priest with a torch. The blow landed on Simba's thigh, sending him reeling into the pit of writhing serpents.

Without a word, Annalla flicked the torch after him, and the tank erupted. The snakes, frenzied by the sudden assault of heat and light, lashed out. I glanced over my shoulder and regretted it instantly. The Priest of Yoki was engulfed by a writhing sea of bodies, scales shimmering in the firelight. Venom-dripping fangs struck again and again, targeting the helpless form beneath the thrashing swarm.

It was a ghastly vision—triangular heads darting with deadly precision, twisting lengths coiling and recoiling in chaotic motion. Beneath this storm of terror, Simba's body convulsed, then fell still.

I turned away, horror etching itself on every nerve. Marcus was right behind me, his face a mask of dread.

I felt a gut-wrenching nausea that left me shaky as I staggered behind Annalla through the doorway where the idol of Massi once stood. Trisha flitted ahead, unseen but guiding us with the faint echo of her footsteps and whispered directions at each twist and turn in the passage. Close behind, the frenzied clamor of our pursuers echoed, a mob driven mad with hate. It was their sheer hatred that snapped me back to focus.

At a corner where a glimmer of light signaled an opening ahead, I grabbed Marcus and told him to stop. "We need to fight them off," I panted. "They won't expect us to hold our ground."

We crouched, ready to block the way, and the leaders of the frenzied mob burst around the corner, right into our waiting knives. We hurled the bodies into the chaotic mass behind them, slashing and hacking in the torchlight's dim glow. We formed a barricade of corpses, giving us a brief lead as our pursuers hesitated to cross the bloodied heap.

But we were only a dozen steps ahead when we burst from the passage into a courtyard carved deep in the cliff's cleft. Looming above was the peculiar, bulging rock formation that protected Homolobi from attacks above. The cliff-top jutted out like a mushroom, overhanging the sacred Breast. Leaning against its base was a double ladder, and Trisha and Annalla urged us onward from its rungs.

Despite the absurdity of climbing to a rock-lodge where daylight archers on the temple roof might easily pick us off, there was no time for debate. The yelping horde hot on our trail left us no choice. Marcus and I sprinted across the courtyard, our hands gripping the ladder's hidebound rungs as we scrambled skyward, racing against death itself.

The men were already down on the lower rungs when we stepped onto a narrow ledge where the girl and Annalla were waiting for us.

"Come," she said nervously in Spanish, reaching out and grabbing the Seneca's hand.

"Hold up," Marcus said solemnly. He grasped the ladder-ends with his huge hands, gave them a tentative shake, and pushed. The ladder teetered upright, ready to fall back against the cliff, and then went over backward, sending its load of priests tumbling down with a chorus of terrified screams.

"Now we've got a better chance, huh?" commented the Dutchman. Trisha chuckled, amused. She had fully joined our side. The death of these people, who had nearly worshipped her just moments ago, didn't bother her any more than the killing of the Awataba in the pass.

"That was a good move on the fat one's part," she remarked. "They'll set the ladder up again, but we'll have more time, and that means everything."

"How?" I asked, scanning for a way out from our scant foothold on the rock ledge.

"I'll show you," she replied. "This is a secret path used by the priests. Micki used it when he went into the desert to commune with Massi. But it's very dangerous, and you guys who aren't used to climbing rocks will have to go slowly. That's why I say the fat one did well to push over the ladder. By the time they dare to set it up again, we'll have climbed beyond their reach."

She took Annalla by the hand. He led me, and Marcus brought up the rear as we edged cautiously along the shelf, our ignorance blessing us because we couldn't see how close we were to an eternal fall. About twenty feet from where the ladder had rested, the ledge ended in a series of foot- and hand-holds that led up a slope. We climbed by feel in the pitch darkness; it was impossible to see the others ahead. But we moved quickly because behind us, we could hear the ladder creaking back into place.

The third stretch of the path was another ledge, guiding us into an eerie cleft in the cliff face—a natural chimney, a scar from some ancient upheaval. Inside, it was somehow darker than the outside, if that were even possible. But the footing was steadier, and the pounding footsteps of our pursuers drove us forward. They knew this terrain far better than we did, moving twice as fast.

Occasional footholds hacked by the priests and makeshift ladder rungs embedded in the rock helped, making the climb bearable. Initially, the path plunged straight into the cliff's core, then veered sharply to the right, angling upward along a vein of softer rock I could identify just by touch. In two places, the incline was so severe we had to push ourselves up by straddling. At the top of the first chute, the passage broadened into a chamber strewn with rock fragments, where a sliver of moonlight pierced the gloom, highlighting a jagged crack along the side facing the valley.

Trailing behind, Marcus grumbled that he could see one of the priests gaining on us, clambering up the slant to the path's start. In my haste to make space for him, I showered him with pebbles and fine gravel. This upper section of the crevice was treacherous, likely baked brittle by the relentless sun, and we slipped continually, losing ground with every step gained. But finally, Trisha made it to the top and helped Annalla up, and between them, they hauled up Marcus and me.

To our astonishment, we found ourselves standing on the cliff's summit. Homolobi lay obscured beneath a jutting overhang that stretched eastward from our perch. Beyond that, the valley unfolded under the moon's silvery gaze, dotted with the flickering fires of the Awataba. The river below shimmered, a ribbon of liquid silver, while the opposite cliffs loomed black and ominous.

The night was eerily bright and clear, the sky sprinkled with countless stars, the moon shining full between drapes of dark velvet.

"What now?" I asked. Trisha shook her head, her eyes reflecting the moonlight with a haunted intensity.

"We have to keep the priests from tracking us," she said. "If we stray from the path, they'll catch up in no time."

"And if we wait," I pointed out, "they'll send runners to guide the Awataba on a different trail. Maybe they already have."

"True," she agreed coolly. "I've gotten you this far. Now, it's your turn to figure out how to save yourselves."

I translated her words to the others. Marcus instantly marched over to a massive boulder lying on its side in a bed of shale.

"We're gonna plug the bottle," he announced. He braced his shoulder against the boulder, heaved, and it rolled toward the narrow pass. Another push and it teetered at the edge. With one final shove, a shower of gravel erupted, followed by a startled yelp from deep within the rocks. He turned back to us with a broad grin.

"Ja, dot's goodt," he said, the accent heavy but the satisfaction clear.

For a moment, it felt like the world was ending. Deep below, there was a heavy jolt, then a deafening, sky-splitting roar that echoed violently, pounding our ears, clouding our senses. The sound swelled into a monstrous thunder, bursting and rolling in waves. A dense cloud of dust rose around us like a shroud. The rock beneath us bucked as if struck by the hammer of a god. Slowly, the roar dwindled into a series of fading rumbles. The dust settled.

We stood at the edge of a sheer drop, staring down at what had once been Homolobi.

Marcus's boulder, hurtling down the narrow cleft in the cliff, must have hit a weak spot in the rock—perhaps that jagged crack I'd noticed above the first funnel. With the force it had gathered and the avalanche of smaller stones and gravel that followed, it triggered a chain reaction. This surge ripped away the overhanging ledge that had shielded Homolobi from attacks for generations. The massive slab plummeted, shearing off the top of the Breast, transforming it into a slope of rock fragments that stretched deep into the valley below. Beneath this crushing mass lay the people and homes of Homolobi, their storehouses, prized gardens, and most of the Awataba, who had clustered at the base of the Breast, waiting for the verdict of their demands. It was the most complete, heart-wrenching devastation I had ever witnessed. Dust clouds billowed above the wreckage like the smoke of victorious fires, yet no blaze could have achieved such total destruction. There were no ruins, no ashes. Homolobi was obliterated. Erased, with nothing left to mark where it once stood. Trisha threw herself at Annalla's feet.

"How powerful are your gods!" she cried. "I am yours. Save me from them."

Annalla lifted her gently into his arms.

"Ranno has nothing to fear," he declared, his voice brimming with pride. "Annalla's medicine is strong. All who oppose us shall perish. But Ranno is safe. Surely, Hawenneyu watches over us, for He has visited such destruction upon our enemies! He'll send the Hon-ochenokeh to protect us. Tharon, the Sky- holder, will rain down upon those who stand in our way. Gaoh will unleash the winds against them. Annalla's orenda will triumph over all!"

Chapter Twenty

We were free, but new problems quickly emerged to challenge us. Our only weapons were the knives and tomahawks tucked in our belts. Stranded, virtually defenseless, in a desolate and unknown land, the absence of our muskets made it highly doubtful that we could travel far against any real opposition. The Awataba, a tribe of archers, could easily overpower us. Furthermore, winter was fast approaching. Autumn had already arrived, bringing along the pressing concerns of finding food and shelter.

Adding to our worries, we had a fourth comrade to care for—a responsibility that could have been daunting. Yet, Trisha's superior connection to the high gods held her in good stead. Her self-reliance, courage, and intelligence rejected any notion of disadvantage because of her gender. From the very beginning of her journey with us, she demanded her place as an equal and fulfilled that role impeccably. She was no ordinary maiden to meekly accept the drudgeries often assigned to women. Annalla, to my quiet amusement, acknowledged her worth. The Seneca carried an innate chivalry, a far cry from the courteous tolerance typically shown to women by the People of the Long House.

No history I've read describes a society that honors its wives and mothers more than these forest-dwelling "barbarians." Here, women select candidates for the high rank of Royaneh, the noble leaders forming the Hoyarnagowar, the ruling body of the Great League. They arrange marriages and largely control clan politics. A Hodenosaunee warrior, when asked his name, will tell you he's the son of his mother, not his father. These people, beyond all other Indians and indeed most white men, grant significant power and position to women. However, they treat women as a distinct, separate entity. The lives the men lead remain inaccessible to the women.

In matters of love, that powerful and transcendent bond beyond mere physical attraction, they were clueless. Annalla, unique in his exposure to the Hodenosaunee and the white man's spiritual fervor, loved with his entire being. He worshipped, he reveled in a partnership of equals, all thanks to what the missionaries saw fit to instill in him. They were the architects of his inner drive. So, asserting the guardianship of his gods and the preeminence of his orenda over any force that dared oppose it, he naively yet earnestly acknowledged the truth of the aid she provided us—a crucial intervention that likely saved our lives. Never once did he treat her as just a squaw, only worthy of honor in the lodge but barred from warrior councils. This, I must confess, struck me as truly bizarre. Any other Indian maid would have naturally followed the ingrained habits and thoughts of her people. Yet Annalla never wavered in his belief about the miraculous feat he attributed to himself. So steadfast was he that he never spoke of it again.

To him, it had been a gift from Hawenneyu—an acknowledgment of human endurance and loyalty. He accepted the gift, gave his thanks, and moved on. Why dwell on the obvious? Annalla, with his unique mix of Christian and pagan beliefs, truly thought anyone who tried hard enough could achieve what he had. It had been done before, he was convinced of that. He didn't even question the fact that Jouskeha or Micki failed to seal his Lost Soul in the pumpkin-shell she initially appeared in or deliver her like that. The gods, like men, didn't need to repeat themselves in the same way each time they acted. They had dealt with him as they saw fit.

He didn't bother getting caught up in the minor details. He was content. Without Trisha, we might not have survived; I might be exaggerating, but it's true she led us from the cliff-top above Homolobi's grave down to the valley floor, which we needed to cross to get to the Eastern vents. It was Trisha who navigated around the jagged mound formed by the rock slide and solved our first problem by retrieving a pair of bows and a quiver of arrows some of the Awataba had tossed aside as they fled. These weapons were crude, hastily made, with flint-tipped arrows that were neither straight nor reliable in flight, but they were better than being unarmed.

Trisha also gathered corn and vegetables from the still-standing fields and gardens on the far side of the river, untouched by the disaster, and used them to cook us hearty stews. These meals helped us push through the hunger pangs that tormented us, accustomed as we were to eating meat. One evening, she managed to take down a turkey from one of the village flocks, providing us with a much-needed substantial meal. Moreover, she knew the best passes and ravines leading out of the valley, saving us weeks of wandering—and quite possibly saving our lives from starvation or the threat of hostile tribes—as we resumed our journey eastward.

Trisha was a quick-witted and devoted girl, as sharp-tempered as she was capable. She mocked Marcus's bulk while respecting his strength and viewed me with a sort of amused tolerance, seeing me as a relic, an old burden to endure for the sake of Annalla. At first, I think she was drawn to the Seneca because of the novelty of his story and the unusual role it cast her in, making her feel as if she were reborn, a favored child of the gods. But there's no doubt she grew to love him with a devotion that matched his own. He was a man among millions, or as she put it herself, *a Man*.

Marcus and I, seen through the playful torment and mischievous antics of a child, grew to love her like a sister, like a true companion. There was something mesmerizing about her, a mix of indigenous stoicism and flirtatious innocence. Marcus, bless his practical heart, decided it was high time to rid her of that laughable costume made of turkey feathers, which had been her only attire. She didn't mind it, really. It might have been relatively warm, even if it was anything but solid. Her sense of modesty was as sparse as her belief in her semi-divine nature was strong. Marcus, ever resourceful, crafted for her a respectable outfit from his own worn clothes: moccasins, breeches, and a coat. He spent days near-nude, nearly as exposed as the Awataba, until fortune allowed us to find more clothes.

But I digress, led astray by the old memories that awaken with fresh vigor. Let me return to where we were. With weapons and provisions secured for now, our immediate concern shifted to shelter for the impending Winter. We were all in agreement: we needed to escape this valley of death before the cold and snow made travel impossible. Annalla's quest had concluded, so there was no longer any reason to stay. Eastward was our direction. Had it just been the three of us, Marcus, Trisha, and myself, we might have followed the stream winding through the abandoned fields of Homolobi, likely taking us hundreds of miles south. But Trisha, with her keen sense, suggested we follow a ravine leading us directly east, into richer lands where game was plentiful.

We worried about running into the last of the Awataba, but if any of them remained, they kept their distance. We saw no sign of other tribes until we reached a substantial river about four days beyond the rocky desert's edge. There, we were ambushed by a small group of fierce warriors, whom Trisha identified as Navahu.

They came at us with bravado, seeing how outnumbered we were. We put on an act, pretending to retreat into a thick grove. But as they moved in, we sprang out with heavy wooden clubs Marcus had fashioned. When they caught sight of our white, bearded faces, their courage fizzled out. They bolted, screaming that we were Naakai, which seemed to mean Spaniards to them. We caught a few and looted their campsite by the riverbank, nabbing some finely woven blankets. Trisha reassured us these were highly valued by all the local tribes.

Up until then, Marcus and I had managed with just clubs alongside our knives and tomahawks. It made sense to let Annalla and Trisha keep the two bows, given they were the better shots. But now, our spoils included two more bows and nearly two quivers full of arrows. Feeling braver, we figured we could handle anything short of gunfire. We crossed the river easily and pushed east until rugged foothills halted our progress beyond a smaller stream. We had long since left Trisha's familiar territory behind. After some debate, we decided to follow the stream north.

Three days later, it took a sudden turn west, dampening our spirits. We agreed to stick to its banks for one more day, and our patience paid off. The stream flowed into a larger river, possibly the same one we had first crossed, seemingly coming down from the northeast. Instinct told us that northeast was where we should head. As fast as the rough terrain allowed, we pressed on.

Several days of harsh traveling brought us to a third stream, which joined our river from the east. Range after range of jagged peaks loomed ahead; the view to the southeast looked equally grim. We made the only choice we had left—we turned east and followed this new river upstream.

Of course, it could have taken us anywhere. In this land, the streams seemed to shoot off in every direction. But we got lucky; its headwaters sprang high from the western slopes of the Sky Mountains. We ended up spending the winter in a gorgeous valley, much like the one we called home the year before.

Ormerod's path grew harder to follow, but I'd bet he emerged somewhere in the Wasatch Mountains of Utah, crossed the Grand River, and followed it to the Gunnison. We built a cozy little cabin with two rooms and had all the food we needed. We grew plump and content. Marcus, with his skillful hands, made new clothes from deerskin. The blankets we'd taken from the Navahu kept us warm through the frosty nights. When we weren't hunting or working on pelts, we passed the time crafting arrow shafts, chipping stone heads, and attaching feathers. Our weapons were better than ever, and both Marcus and I got sharper with our shooting. Still, we couldn't hold a candle to Annalla and Trisha, who had been drawing bows since they were kids. Yet, even they paled in comparison to the master archers of the Plains tribes, who spent their entire lives perfecting their skills because they relied solely on bows and couldn't get their hands on firearms.

Spring eventually nudged us out of hibernation. We waited until we were sure the final snowstorm had cloaked the mountains, but once we set off, we moved quickly. Annalla had crafted snowshoes for all of us, and the soggy crust packed firm beneath our feet.

Two weeks of hard travel led us across a rugged ridge running north to south, pushing through valleys that guided us out of the mountains and through a monumental gate between two massive peaks stretching far apart.

We soon encountered a river flowing east, swelling with the icy melt from countless smaller streams. With no better guidance, we followed its southern bank, twice abandoning it when it veered northward, only to find it again each time after striking out east in a straight line. On this lower plateau, the snow had vanished, giving way to the tender green of new grass and budding foliage. Antelope and deer were plentiful, and we often saw buffalo herds, the vanguard of vast migrations moving from their southern winter grounds. This was the land of the horse tribes, those far-roaming warriors who would ride a hundred miles for a bit of loot or a scalp, reveling in the fight. We took great care to steer clear of them, twice lying low in the grass to let splendiferous groups ride past. Once, we huddled in a patch of timber by the river's edge, motionless, watching a band make camp.

Still, we knew it was only a matter of time before our luck ran out, especially as the terrain flattened, offering little in the way of cover as we moved east. At last, the river veered north for a third time, and we left it behind, turning our backs to the setting sun and striking out onto the open plains. Here, the grass was still sheared short, far from its summer height, and the land undulated in vast, gentle swells, offering scant chance of concealment.

We were trudging up one of those endless hills, dead tired and desperate for water, when a war party crested the ridge. Fifty warriors, smeared in paint, clad in breechcloths and moccasins, with feathers tangled in their long hair, rode down on us. Their white shields and lance tips shimmered ominously, quivers brimming with arrows that shifted like deadly promises. They screamed in wild delight as they descended, their eyes wide with the thrill of the hunt.

Two of them peeled off, riding hard toward the rear to ensure we weren't bait for a larger ambush. We huddled together, throwing up the peace sign, arms lifted, palms out. But they circled us warily, closing in tighter, arrows nocked and ready to rain death down upon us. Their bows could send an arrow flying twice as far as ours, horn-bound and lethal. When their scouts raced back with triumphant yells, they tightened the circle until we were squarely within bow range from every direction. A chief, adorned in majestic eagle feathers, called out to us, his booming voice rolling like thunder.

"They're the Nemene, or Comanche," Annalla blurted, eyes wide. "We're in real trouble, brothers. These are the fiercest raiders on the plains."

"Do we fight?" I asked, my heart pounding like a war drum.

"Yes," Trisha hissed, already notching an arrow. "Let's fight."

"What's their chief saying?" Marcus inquired, frowning. "Can you make it out?"

"Some of it. I've heard Comanche when they traded with the Dakota to the North. I'll try speaking Dakota."

Annalla shouted back, his voice steady, and the Comanche chief signaled for an interpreter.

"He wants to know who we are," Annalla relayed quickly after a rapid exchange. "I told him. He says we have to go to their camp."

Another volley of words fired back and forth.

"I told him we're just passing through, no harm intended, but he's not buying it. He insists we're on their land without permission. I'll try to spin it that we were looking for him, but—" Annalla shrugged, his face a mask of grim resolve.

Once more, the shouting questions and answers began to echo around us, this time mixed with anxious gestures and wild signs. The circle of warriors tightened around us, a living noose of hostility. The chief rode off to the side, watching us with a disinterested gaze. His interpreter barked two words.

"It's no use, brothers," Annalla said. "We have to drop our weapons, or they'll shoot."

"So it's a choice between dying now or later?" I asked, bitterness coating my words.

"Seems that way."

"Let's die here, in the open," Trisha proposed, her voice unwavering.

"No," Marcus interjected. "If we fight now, we're dead for sure. If we go with them, we might die. Maybe not. We better go and see what happens. Ja!"

Marcus was right. We let our weapons fall, and the circle of Comanches instantly closed in. We found ourselves in a whirlwind of men and horses, sweaty bodies pressing in, hostile faces glaring down at us. Rough hands yanked at our belongings; rawhide thongs bit into our waists, and we were dragged away. Each of us struggled to keep pace with the horsemen leading us, stray hooves constantly threatening to crush our skulls if we tripped.

But after the first mile, the pace relented. By evening, we entered a ring of teepees set by a small river. A grove of trees hugged the high-water mark on one side, while ponies grazed lazily in a natural meadow on the other. We were bound hand and foot and left on the grass between the easternmost teepees and the horse herd. Young guards watched over us, their bored eyes flicking between us and the grazing ponies.

The chief and his warriors paraded us before a gathered crowd of a few hundred people, including women and children. After the show, they shooed everyone away and left us, probably to decide our fate, which likely meant debating how to execute us. The shadows grew longer, but no one brought us any food. Occasionally, a man wandered over to check our bindings or peer at us with unsettling curiosity.

As the light dwindled into dusk, an uneasy hush slipped over the settlement. Women and children, initially curious, backed off under the stern glances and sharp warnings of the adolescent herd-guards. The temperature seemed to drop suddenly, and that's when I felt it—a cold muzzle gently pressing against my cheek. For a second, I didn't dare to believe it. Then came a delighted whinny that sent shivers down my spine.

Turning my head slowly, I found myself face-to-face with the quivering nostrils of a mottled stallion. His nostrils flared, emitting a puff of warm breath against my skin, and his white mane fluttered like ghostly tendrils in the growing twilight. He nuzzled me again, each whinny infused with what could only be recognition. My heart, already heavy with the weight of the journey, felt light for the first time in days.

"Hey there, boy," I murmured, my voice breaking but filled with warmth. The stallion responded eagerly, burying his muzzle into my neck, nuzzling as if to say, "I remember you." He pawed at the ground with his forehoof, creating little puffs of dust, as though beckoning me to rise and ride. His eyes, dark and rich with history, mirrored the endless skies we had once traveled beneath.

There was no mistaking him. This was Sunkawakan-kedeshka, the spotted horse I had tamed at Nadoweiswe's Teton village before we first crossed the haunting expanse of the Sky Mountains. His sudden reappearance here, in this place and time, whispered of fate and forgotten promises, of tales not yet fully unraveled.

Chapter Twenty-one

"What's happening here, brother?" Annalla whispered, her voice barely audible. I explained, and Trisha and Marcus shifted closer to listen intently.

"Wow!" gasped Trisha when I finished. "This god Hawenneyu is really something! He sent the horse to help us escape."

"How can that be?" I snapped back, frustration lacing my words. "We're stuck here, bound and helpless. Even if the whole herd came to join the stallion, we couldn't make use of them."

"Still, it's a good omen," Annalla insisted, her voice steady. "I feel hope stirring in my chest again."

"Yeah," Marcus agreed, showing more interest than usual. "We're halfway to an escape. We just need to figure out the first part."

Sunkawakan-kedeshka's silky ears twitched forward near my face. I heard the soft shuffle of moccasined feet.

"The herd-guard!" I exclaimed. "Remember, I'm going to scream like I'm terrified. The stallion's biting me."

I let out a series of blood-curdling shrieks, causing the spotted stallion to back up in confusion, his eyes wide in disbelief at the bizarre behavior of his so-called friend. The young herdsman bolted towards us, and Annalla called out to him in a mix of Dakota and Comanche:

"Hurry! Is this how you treat captives? The horse is biting my white brother!"

The Comanche laughed, squinting through the starlit gloom, and I noticed he approached the horse with noticeable wariness.

"The spotted horse will give him a quicker death than our warriors at the torture stake," he boasted. "What are a few bites and kicks compared to the knife and fire? If I leave the horse, it'll finish the Taivo soon enough. But tomorrow, that'll be a different story. He'll beg for mercy for hours."

"They say your father would dress you in women's clothes and whip you if the Taivo came to harm before the Council decides his fate," Annalla said sternly. "Get on the horse and ride it away."

"Ride the spotted horse?" the boy scoffed. "Never!"

Not one of our guys has managed to break him since we took him from the Teton."

"Of course not, they're Comanches," Annalla sneered. The boy gave him a hard kick in the ribs and chased the stallion off with quick jabs from his light lance. Sunkawakan-kedeshka, hooves thrashing and teeth bared, shot me a look of longing, let out a whimper of confused pain, and vanished into the night.

"What do you mean by 'the middle of an escape'?" I whispered, my curiosity peaking as soon as the guard was out of earshot.

"The first part," answered Marcus, the Dutchman, "is getting out of these bindings. That's something we've got to do. The second part is finding a way to leave the village. We're banking on that horse."

"How?" snapped Annalla.

"He's the king of horses," Marcus replied calmly. "Remember that little group of mares he led at Nadoweiswe's place? Where he goes, they follow."

"It's true," I agreed, excitement creeping into my voice. "With him, we could stampede the whole herd."

"But why are we even talking about this when we're tied up and powerless?" Annalla said, his voice tinged with despair.

"We're not powerless," Trisha interrupted. She rolled over and over until she was lying on her stomach, close to Annalla.

"The warrior who tied my wrists didn't do it as tight as he did yours," she explained. "I smiled at him, and I think he's hoping to ask the Comanche chief if he can take me into his teepee. If he tries, I'll kill him with his own knife. If your teeth are as sharp as mine, you can chew through the knots. Then, I'll free the rest of you."

Annalla hesitated, baffled by her suggestion.

"Hurry! The eagles are singing of victory up there," she urged. "They say we shall defy the Comanche."

"Yes, yes," I pleaded. "Move quickly, brother."

"The herd guards might come back."

Annalla rolled over, positioning himself so he could get his strong, barbarian teeth—untouched by the diseases of the white man—around the girl's knotted wrists, tied just above her hips. While he gnawed at the stubborn hide thongs, Marcus and I kept a vigilant eye out for the return of the adolescent guard. If he showed up, we planned to give a signal so that Trisha and Annalla could slip back into their usual positions. But the boy never reappeared. I figured he and his friends were taking turns sneaking into the village to eavesdrop outside the Council teepee, where the warriors were deciding our fate. This meant more work for the ones guarding the grazing horses. Twice, I heard the distant whinny of Sunkawakan-kedeshka, a sound that pulled at my attention, and I suspected it took one boy's full focus to keep the horse from wandering off entirely.

Time seemed to stretch on forever, and Annalla's lips grew slick with blood from his torn gums. I took over, and when I couldn't go on any longer, Marcus's powerful jaws picked up the task. It was he who finally pried the last knot loose, but it took several agonizing moments before Trisha could get the blood flowing back into her hands. She quickly untied her ankles and, without wasting a second to rub life back into her feet, got to work on our bindings. In ten minutes, we were all free, crawling—walking wasn't an option—toward the herd. Our plan was simple. It had to be.

We advanced until we could make out the shapes of two of the herd guards against the faint starlight. They were scruffy, naked adolescents, holding their lances like slender wands in their right hands. On this side of the village, the task was a bit easier, so most of the guards were positioned on the flanks and opposite to where we were. Beyond the two sentinels lay the restless throng of horses—hundreds of them—grazing, fighting, rolling, sleeping.

Annalla and I ditched our shirts and pants, blending seamlessly into the landscape like shadows, resembling Comanche warriors under the moonlight. We crouched and crawled back a little, before sprinting forward in the open, pretending to carry a vital message from the village. The two guards, hearing the soft thud of our moccasins, approached us without suspicion, likely mistaking us for their comrades. When they called out, we replied with grunted breaths, exhaling heavily as if we were winded. They never suspected a thing.

I was right beside my target, one hand already clutching his thigh before he realized something was wrong. As he opened his mouth to shout a warning, I clamped my hand around his throat, choking the life out of him. His scream was nothing more than a strangled gurgle in the night air. Annalla proved even quicker, disposing of his man with lethal efficiency.

To our left, we caught the faint murmur of another pair of guards in conversation, possibly alerted by the muted cries of my victim. We didn't have the luxury of time to devise a strategy for confronting them. Annalla's voice called out softly, summoning Trisha and Marcus from their hidden positions. Meanwhile, I dashed into the herd, whistling for Sunkawakan-kedeshka. The response was immediate, a long, joyous whinny piercing the night. My stallion plowed through the others, hooves thundering as he neared me. In one fluid motion, I swung from the guard's horse onto Sunkawakan-kedeshka's back and trotted over to my comrades.

"Quick, brother!" Annalla hissed urgently, pointing at two mounted figures dangerously close to us. One of them hailed, mistaking me for another guard. I growled something unintelligible, then scooped Trisha up, placing her in front of me. My fingers twisted into the stallion's mane, gripping it like reins. He remained steady under the added weight, tossing his head and neighing softly, much to my relief. I wasn't certain how he'd handle carrying two riders, and there was no way I could leave Trisha behind. She'd never been on a horse before, and neither Marcus nor the others had much more experience.

Annalla and Marcus climbed cautiously onto the horses of the fallen guards, and we plunged into the heart of the herd.

"Ha-yah-yah-yaaaa-aaa-aa-ah-hhh-yeeee-eee-ee!"

The war cry of the Long House shattered the stillness of the night. I urged Sunkawakan-kedeshka into a frenzy. Annalla and Marcus jabbed their lances left and right. The horses, barely tamed at best, fought against any control, reacting instantly to the chaos. A shrill scream from the spotted stallion triggered a chorus of responses. Mares fought to reach him, while other stallions battled to keep them away.

The herd went wild—kicking, biting, neighing, and screaming as it smashed through the attempts of the guards to contain it, charging southeast into the open prairie.

In the chaos, my comrades swayed precariously in their saddles, constantly in danger of being thrown off. Trisha and I clung desperately to the bare back of the stallion, his powerful muscles propelling him to the front of the stampede. I saw a boy go down amidst the madness, he and his horse trampled into nothing. Others dashed wide, raising the alarm. The village behind us quaked with the thunder of hooves; cries of dismay echoed up to the stars in the dimly lit sky. Then, teepees, herd-guards, warriors, trees, and river vanished into the darkness. We were alone with our loot on the prairie, surrounded by tossing heads and manes, flashing hooves, lean bodies stretched low to the ground, tails flicking the grass-tips.

Mile after mile, we pounded on, and I knew my comrades must be suffering. But stopping was impossible. There was no way to halt that wild flight. I doubt if I could have reined in the spotted stallion in the first hour. All I could do was grip him tightly with my knees, cling to Trisha, and pray the stallion and his herd mates would choose safe ground in the darkness. It was near dawn when I began to think there might be a chance to contain the herd.

I started with the stallion, calming him down, soothing his nerves. Gradually, my touch extended to the other horses, mostly his attendant mares, and a few colts. No foals could have kept up with our frantic pace. We had been pushing the horses hard for over three hours, and only the toughest were left. Their eyes were bloodshot, their flanks foamy, lungs near bursting. I finally slowed them to a canter, then a trot, with Annalla and Marcus matching my pace as best they could. Eventually, we brought them to a walk and urged them to graze.

I felt safe for the moment. We had traveled at a grueling speed, and there was no way the Comanche could keep up with us. We were exhausted, and I had plans for our spoils that made me unwilling to exhaust the herd completely. So we took refuge in a grove of trees, driving in the stallion's close followers, letting the rest graze freely while we four collapsed, sleeping through the late morning.

When we woke, we killed a colt for food, making sure to dispatch him down-wind from the rest of the horses. After eating, I set my plan into motion to cover our future trail. Annalla, Marcus, and I picked out twenty of the best ponies from the herd, driving them into the woods to join Sunkawakan-kedeshka's group, guarded by Trisha for the time being. Once that was done, we chased the rest south, terrifying them with bunches of burning grass.

If the Comanche or anyone else picked up our trail now, they'd likely follow the larger group, given the mass of hoof prints, and we might continue eastward undisturbed. We had a number of extra horses to trade for weapons or food, and enough mounts to keep our journey swift.

At sunset, we left the grove, moving at a slow pace until the stars whispered midnight. Camping near a babbling brook, with ample grass and water for the horses, we found a semblance of peace. The next day, our journey took us to another grove along a sizeable stream. We figured it must be the same river we had trailed eastward from the base of the Sky Mountains. We decided to stop there for two days, resting our herd and pondering our next move. I wanted to press on as we were, but Annalla and Marcus believed we should cross the river and head north to Dakota country. There, they argued, we'd find friends and a potential escort to the Mississippi. But fate, as it tends to, had other plans and took the decision out of our hands.

That second afternoon, our debate was interrupted by Trisha's urgent call. She'd been watching the grazing horses when she saw something. Beckoning us to the bluff above the river, she pointed.

"Strange people over there," she said, her voice tinged with unease.

The stream was narrow, only a couple hundred yards wide, and the clear air allowed us to see them distinctly. A war party, looking travel-worn and beaten, were straggling back from some grim adventure. Of the sixty or so warriors in sight, ten or twelve bore visible wounds. Their lances were splintered, buffalo- hide shields slashed and torn. But the horses—God, the horses were in the worst shape. One collapsed and died as we watched, and others seemed unable to move from where they stood.

Annalla's eyes sparkled with an unsettling gleam.

"Here's a fresh favor from Hawenneyu," he exclaimed, his voice brimming with a sinister kind of delight.

"What do you mean?" I demanded, not liking where this was headed.

"These people need horses. We need arms. A trade, simple as that," he said.

Trisha's face twisted in concern. "They look like very bad people," she objected.

Annalla shrugged. "Desperation makes for willing partners," he replied.

In truth, they were a brutal, dark-clad, cruel-eyed band of savages.

"No problem," said the Seneca, his tone cold and determined. "They're across the stream from us. We'll make sure they stay there until we finish our business. Otetiani and Annalla will ride across and talk to their chief, and Ranno and Marcus will make a show in the woods to make us look like a larger group. Lead the horses where they can be seen. Shout to each other. Move about where glimpses of you can be caught. We'll fool them. Their need is desperate."

None of us argued. If those savages were in dire need, so were we. We had only two lances for hunting and defending ourselves, not even a knife among the four of us. We needed weapons to journey across this vast open land, patrolled by the most dangerous tribes on the continent. I whistled for the spotted stallion and one of the mares, and Annalla and I mounted, riding out from the trees. We made a great show of handing our lances and other fake weapons to Marcus, who marched back into the woods. We also pretended to bark orders to various spots along the riverbank, with the Dutchman and Trisha responding with shouts and whistles.

The band on the opposite bank rose to their feet, glaring at us with sullen eyes as we splashed into the shallows, arms raised in a gesture of peace.

"They look sturdier than any tribe we've seen," I said. "They're wearing body armor, buffalo-hide cuirasses. Look, one of them still has an arrow sticking out from under his arm."

Annalla frowned. "Trisha was right about them. These are bad people. They're the Tonkawa."

"Who are they?" I asked.

We weren't close enough to hear them yet, gathered by the riverbank.

"Chatanskah used to tell Annalla about them back when I first stayed with Corlaer in his teepee years ago. They're the scourge of the plains. No home, no allies. They go where they want, hunting, killing. They're at war with everyone. No treaties, no ambassadors. One year they're slaughtering in Spanish territories in the South, clashing with Apache; the next, they descend upon the Dakota or Cheyenne. They're like a wolf pack—never leave their prey and you have to kill them all to stop an attack. And their favorite meal? Human flesh."

I shuddered, casting a wary glance at the bestial faces glowering from the bank—faces just as vile, if not more cunning, than those of the Awataba.

"And we're supposed to negotiate with them?" I blurted out.

"We have to, brother. They're fierce warriors. Show fear and they'll hunt us down. Our horses alone would lure them. No, we've come this far, there's no turning back. We have to act strong. Be bold. Glare at them. Show contempt. We have the upper hand, but it's not convenient for us to fight right now. That's our angle."

We spurred our horses up the bank's slope, halting in the center of a half- circle of Tonkawa warriors. Not a single weapon was in sight—it would have been a grave breach of Indian etiquette, and even these marauders abided by some basic tribal codes. Yet, the tension was palpable; I could feel every man there itching to drive a knife into our hearts. My lips drew back in a primal snarl as Annalla stepped forward, crossing his forefingers at right angles—the sign for wanting to trade.

When a young warrior tried to edge his horse closer, I nudged Sunkawakan- kedeshka with my heel. The spotted stallion, sensing my intent, shoved the offender off the bank. The youngster scrambled up again, his eyes burning with a murderous glare, but the Tonkawa chief—a giant of a man with broad shoulders, wearing a hide cuirass and a feathered helmet—spat out a harsh command. His voice, rough and guttural, cut through the simmering tension, holding back the tide of hatred.

"What do you want?" he demanded, his words coming out in the broken jumbles of Comanche, the makeshift trade language of the plains.

Chapter Twenty-two

"We're holding this ford," Annalla barked, the gravel in his voice echoing the harsh dialect of the tribes. They communicated in a jigsaw of languages—a bit of Comanche patched up with Dakota, Pawnee, Arikara, Cheyenne, and Blackfoot. When words fell short, they defaulted to the artful dance of sign language, effortlessly conveying even the most intricate thoughts. Occasionally, one of the lead Tonkawa warriors would inject a suggestion if his chief seemed stuck, but the showdown remained a grueling tête-à-tête.

"Who exactly are you?" the Tonkawa chief asked, scrutiny evident, though slightly taken aback by Annalla's brazen demeanor.

"We belong to no tribe," Annalla declared, defiant. "We're outlaws, fugitives. We ravage everyone we encounter."

"Not the Tonkawa," retorted the chief, a sinister hint of amusement flickering in his eyes.

"Yes, the Tonkawa, if they dare get in our way," Annalla shot back without missing a beat.

"How many of the white men are in your band?" the chief shifted gears, curiosity tinged with suspicion.

"There are many," Annalla lied as smoothly as oil on water. "The one you see with me is an Englishman. He's exiled from his people, a murderer. We have Frenchmen, Spaniards, Dakota, Shawnee—men from every tribe, even those beyond the Sky Mountains. We just raided a Comanche village and took their herd."

Annalla's statement had the intended effect. The Comanches were no enemies to be taken lightly, and the lure of rich horseflesh struck a chord with the Tonkawas' hungry aspirations.

"Good," the chief responded with a malevolent grin. "We need horses. We'll come over and take yours."

Annalla laughed, a dark, menacing sound.

"Come on, Tonkawas," he invited. "My men are waiting for you behind the trees."

"They'll shoot you in the water, and those lucky enough to reach land will be fresh meat for our women's axes."

"Liar," said the Tonkawa chief. "You've got fewer than we do."

"Thirty warriors are hidden behind those trees," Annalla declared. "How many of yours would fall before you even got their scalps or scared them off?"

"We need horses," the chief repeated. "We don't fear death. We are warriors. We are Tonkawa."

A murmur of fierce approval, like the low growl of a wolf pack, rippled through his men.

"Good to hear," said Annalla, almost flippantly. "But the Tonkawa aren't thinking straight. A cloud covers their eyes. They say their medicine is weak."

"Why?"

"The Comanche are on our trail. They'll be here soon, following our horse tracks. If we stay put, they'll fight us. If you chase us off and steal the Comanches' horses, they'll still come for you. How many Tonkawa will survive, after battling us, to face the Comanche?"

The chief paused, considering.

"We need horses," he repeated for the third time. "Give us what we need, and we'll leave you in peace."

Annalla burst into laughter.

"They say Tonkawa are men of blood," he said, wiping tears of mirth. "But you're just men who play at laughter."

A low growl of suppressed rage rose from the Tonkawa band.

"Why should two wolf packs rip each other apart when deer are plentiful on all sides?" Annalla continued. "The Tonkawa's eyes are filled with their own blood; they can't see straight. They don't understand that my people don't fear them. Do you think we would've ridden out to meet you, practically announcing our presence, if we were afraid of you?"

"Listen up, Tonkawas, you're in deeper trouble than we are!"

The Tonkawa chief, who had been silently glaring, now muttered briefly with some of his older warriors. Their eyes were cold, their faces etched with suspicion.

"So why are you here?" he demanded, trying to sound tough.

"To trade," Annalla said, unflinching.

"Trade? We ain't traders. You see our weapons? We've been on a mission of vengeance." His chest puffed up with pride. "The Kansas ambushed a small hunting party of ours months ago. Three nights back, we burned their village down and drank their blood. Their scalps hang on our lances."

He wasn't lying. The lances were adorned with tufts of human hair — varied in length, all gruesomely fresh. Annalla nodded calmly.

"Good," he said. "Our tradition demands we kill anyone who crosses our path. We would have killed you if we weren't here for something else."

The Tonkawa chief leaned forward from his pad-saddle, his jaw set in a menacing clench.

"Watch your mouth, or we might test your big talk!" he snarled.

"You wouldn't dare," Annalla replied softly. There was a quiet force in his words that brokered no argument. The Tonkawa glanced nervously at the swaying branches on the opposite bank. The dense woods could be hiding anything. Horses grazed here and there, and shadowy figures flickered among the trees, never lingering long enough to be fully seen.

"You claim you want to trade," the Tonkawa chief pressed. "But I've told you, we have nothing to trade but scalps."

He grinned a vicious smile, implying we were warriors too eager to add to our collection. Annalla ignored the barb.

"We want what you have," the Seneca leader said. He gestured to the full quivers strapped to every warrior's back.

The Tonkawa laughed harshly. "So you're out of weapons!"

"It's true," Annalla replied in that same soft, dangerous tone. "We've used most of our arrows, but we still have enough to put you down."

"Will you try us?"

"Why should we believe you?" mocked the chief. "Do the Tonkawa trade like the Comanches?"

"We're here to find ways to trade better with the Comanches," Annalla fired back, eliciting bitter chuckles from the crowd. Despite their rough habits and uncivilized manners, the Tonkawa shared that dark sense of humor common among all tribes.

"How many horses will you trade?" the chief asked, eyes darting among his warriors.

"How many do you need?" Annalla shot back. The chief scanned the hollow ranks of his people and held up his fingers, counting twice to twenty. Annalla shook his head.

"That's too many. We don't have enough arrows for that many. You'd have to empty every quiver."

"Then trade us what you can, or we'll just take them," the chief threatened. Annalla began to turn his horse back toward the river.

"Wait!" the chief called. "We'll give you other weapons."

This offer was more than Annalla had expected. Later, he admitted he was hoping to nudge them into expanding the scope of the deal. He went through the motions of consulting with me, then asked:

"Everyone knows the Tonkawa make fine weapons. What will you give for twenty horses?"

"Six quivers of arrows, two bows, and a leather cuirass for yourself."

"That's not enough," Annalla said firmly. "With six quivers, you'll have to throw in six bows, four cuirasses, and ten knives and hatchets."

The chief's face twisted in anger.

"Would you leave us weaponless too?" he roared. "We'll come and take what we need first!"

For a moment, I thought the situation was about to explode. But when Annalla played his card of walking away again, it had the same calming effect as before. In the end, we settled for six quivers, four bows, two cuirasses, and ten knives and eight hatchets. It was more than we really needed, but the inflated demand kept up the pretense of our numbers.

After we hashed out the terms of the deal, we needed to figure out how to seal it. The Tonkawa chief insisted we drive the horses across to his side of the river. At first, he suggested his crew come over and pick up their new mounts at the edge of the woods—to make it easier for us, or so he claimed. But Annalla stood firm, persuading him to settle the exchange in the middle of the river. Four people from each side would meet there, while the rest would stay out of arrow range on the banks. Once that was sorted, we headed back to our group, rounded up twenty horses, and brought them to the riverbank. Trisha and Marcus pitched in to manage the herd.

The Tonkawa stuck to the plan, keeping their main group a good distance from the bank. But the four at the water's edge, armed to the teeth, showed no intention of relaxing their grip on their weapons. Annalla rode forward, demanding they drop everything but the goods meant for us. That caused a bit of a delay, and Trisha nudged me, pointing out the western sky, which was darkening ominously. The day had been suffocatingly hot, the air thick and stifling. Now, the sun vanished behind a curtain of haze, and in the west, a wall of black clouds loomed, rolling over each other like titanic waves in a stormy sea, their jagged edges clawing at the sky with streaks of inky black. The air was heavy, as if the world was holding its breath.

"A storm's brewing," she whispered. "We need to hurry."

"Yeah," I muttered, "but we can't risk rushing this. These folks are slippery."

"The storm will be worse than the Tonkawa," she insisted, her voice steady but urgent. I didn't buy it, nor did I give her warning much thought.

My focus remained fixed on the quartet of warriors locked in a heated exchange with Annalla, paying little heed to the brewing storm on the horizon. It turns out my instincts were spot on; they were hatching a plan for a surprise attack. Their scheme? Startle our horses into a stampede over to their side of the creek, then make a break for it, assuming we had backup lurking in the woods.

Annalla's voice cut sharp through the tension as she argued with the Tonkawa chief, one of the four emissaries from their side. As Marcus and I began herding the horses back toward the trees, the chief finally relented. The four warriors, with Annalla tagging along, waded into the water, each clutching a bundle of trade weapons.

Our job was tricky—turning the horses midway—but we managed. The chief, sensing something was amiss the moment he laid eyes on Trisha, sneered, "Wah! Can't you send real warriors to meet us?"

"The women in our tribe fight alongside us," Annalla shot back, meeting his gaze coolly. "They stand with the warriors."

He scanned the woods behind us, noting the absence of hidden figures. Whatever thoughts of aggression might have crossed his mind dissolved when Marcus pulled up beside him and grabbed hold of two of the weapons bundles with his giant hands. I took the third bundle and handed it to Trisha, keeping my own hands free for whatever might erupt next. But the chief decided against rolling the dice. He and his men expertly corralled about twenty horses and nudged them toward the northern bank, while we steered our bunch southward.

Just as we reached the shore, a thunderous clatter of hooves made us whip our heads around. The rest of the Tonkawa warriors were charging down the bank, driving their exhausted horses to a frenzied gallop, lances slicing through the air.

Their leader, devoid of any weapons, didn't pause to retrieve his arms from the northern bank but immediately took the lead as his warriors plunged into the water. They splashed noisily, their war cries blending into a cacophony of chaos, driving our herd before them. The ones whose horses began to falter in the shallows dismounted swiftly, climbing onto the nearest fresh horse they could catch, bareback.

"Run, brothers!" Annalla commanded tersely. Anticipating such a desperate moment, I had chosen Sunkawakan-kedeshka and three of his fleetest mares for our mounts. The stallion had an insatiable love for running; his favorite mares would push themselves to the limit to keep pace. Like an arrow shot from a bow, the four of them dashed up the bank and streaked across the prairie. When the first of the Tonkawas finally came into view, we already had a mile's head start. They would capture the rest of the herd in the woods, but we had no capacity for remorse. Our sole objective was to place as much distance as we could between us and that demonic horde.

The sky grew increasingly sinister. Though the afternoon had advanced, summer sunsets lingered, but this darkness was unnaturally oppressive. Objects stood out starkly against the gray light, and behind us, the scene looked like a grim tableau. A strip of open grass, then our pursuers, low and hunched over their ponies, spurred on by a furious pace; beyond that, the green barrier of trees—and hovering over it all, the thick, smoky-black storm clouds, menacing and drawing closer. The sun had been swallowed completely, the last remnants of blue sky swallowed in the east's maw. A low, eerie moan drifted through the air, making me wonder if the Tonkawa shouts could carry so far.

Trisha turned in her saddle, her face pale with worry, and pointed. "Look!" she shouted.

We turned to follow her gaze. The Tonkawa had halted their pursuit abruptly, drawing their horses to a sharp stop. Some were already turning back toward the woods. The moaning sound grew louder, not just a sound but a primal rumble, a harbinger of something terrible.

The horizon to the west was swallowed by a curtain of clouds, stretching from the flat prairie all the way up to the heavens, dark and foreboding as the grim reaper himself.

"They're scared of the storm!" shouted Trisha.

"This one's going to be a soaker," Annalla agreed, looking worried. "We've got to pack up our new bows."

"Forget the bows," Trisha snapped, her voice trembling with urgency. "You've never seen a storm like this, or you'd know the kind of danger we're in. The wind will rip the grass right out of the ground and toss us around like ragdolls on our horses. Back in Homolobi, I've seen storms tear through the valley like they're alive. Out here on the open plain, it's going to be much worse!"

"So, what do we do?" I asked, feeling the cold fingers of dread tighten around my heart.

"We need to find shelter."

Annalla and I exchanged a glance, then burst out laughing at the absurdity of it.

"The only shelter was in the woods we left behind," I pointed out, trying to keep my voice steady.

"We're lucky we got out of those woods," she argued vehemently. "Trees get blown over. No, we need to find a hole, a dip in the ground, anything to shield us."

"This way," Marcus said quietly but authoritatively, steering his horse to the left. He guided us down the steep bank of a small stream that fed into the river where we had made camp. The bank offered a hidden refuge, out of sight from the prairie and somewhat shielded from the incoming tempest. At Annalla's suggestion, we wrapped our precious new bows in the scraps of clothing the Comanches had left us, finding a crevice in the bank to stow them safely. With everything that could be done, we huddled closely on the ground, gripping the horses' rawhide bridles.

The sound of the storm grew, a haunting symphony of dread, escalating from a low moan to a bone-rattling roar, vague but menacing. Lightning slashed through the sky, jagged and fierce. The air turned bitterly cold, making us shiver in the clothes we had left behind. A strange tension thickened the atmosphere, as if nature itself paused in fear. Our horses sensed it too, their hooves stamping nervously, ears twitching at every unexpected noise.

The stallion whinnied at me for reassurance. I stroked his muzzle, trying to calm him.

"It's been coming for a long time," Annalla said, her voice tight with anticipation.

"Yeah," Trisha agreed. "And when it gets here, we'll be lucky if we can even breathe."

Suddenly, the moaning roar soared into a deafening scream. Darkness cloaked the earth like a heavy shroud, and we huddled close to the ground, feeling the violent sweep of some massive force just above our heads. It was the wind. No rain fell, but a hail of debris began to pelt the opposite wall of the gulch. Shadowy shapes crashed down into the bed of the stream. The horses went wild. The stallion jerked back as something whizzed past him, pulling me to my feet. It felt like a giant's hand squeezing my neck, lifting me off the ground. I knew I was being sucked up. The stallion broke free, but I kept rising. Suddenly, I was yanked back to earth by a violent grip on my ankles. Marcus dragged me against the bank beside him.

"Stay down!" he shouted in my ear over the howling wind. "The wind will blow you away!"

"But the stallion!"

"All the horses are gone. There's nothing we can do."

Chapter Twenty-three

A lightning bolt shattered the sky, casting a cold, purple glow over our surroundings. The brief illumination revealed trees violently whipped by the storm, tufts of grass torn from the earth, and scattered clods of soil painting a scene of chaos. Across the depression, the twisted forms of a man and a horse lay crumpled against the bank—undoubtedly the ones responsible for spooking our mounts. They seemed to have been flung there by the storm's malevolent whims.

For a fleeting moment, I glimpsed the strained faces of my comrades: Marcus's wide, terrified eyes; Trisha's hair, a wild tangle around her face; and Annalla, grimly vigilant. Darkness enveloped us again, as the relentless roar of the wind filled the air—a force so powerful, so unyielding, that no living being could possibly stand against it. This was no simple gust; it was a monstrous, cunning entity, dropping pebbles and earth on us, swirling through the depression like a malevolent spirit, its whirlpools snatching at us with a malicious hunger.

Then, there was a sudden crash overhead—a crumbling of the bank—and a massive tree came tumbling down, narrowly missing

Trisha by a mere hand's breadth. But this seeming disaster turned out to be a hidden boon; as the rain began to pour, we managed to prop the fallen tree against the bank, creating a sparse yet precious shelter, denuded of leaves.

The rain that followed was a relentless torment. At first, it drove against us, propelled by the still-ferocious wind, striking like icy daggers, the droplets rebounding from the ground with force. When the wind finally began to ease, the rain fell straight down, cold and unforgiving, lashing our bare skin with icy whips. The chill invaded the air, setting our teeth chattering uncontrollably, while the rain and darkness pressed upon us, unrelenting, hour after agonizing hour.

Time seemed to stretch into infinity as we endured the storm's cruel assault. Eventually, I noticed the rain easing, slipping away towards the East, and the sky began to clear. The stars emerged, frosty and indifferent, twinkling overhead like distant, apathetic eyes.

We were too dead-tired to think of anything but rest. We huddled under the fallen tree trunk, searching for warmth, somehow managing to fall asleep despite the chaos. When we woke up, the sun was rising, the air was crisp, and the sky stretched out cloudless and pale blue above us. All around, the remnants of the storm painted a grim picture. The corpses of the man and horse that lightning had horrifyingly highlighted the night before still lay there, broken heaps of bones and flesh. Three other horses, so battered they were barely recognizable, lay scattered along the bank of the shallow ravine.

Curiosity pulled us to the top of the bank. The prairie spread out in front of us, large patches completely stripped of grass, as if a massive plow had ripped through the earth. The grove where we had sought refuge looked like it had been mauled by a monstrous hand—trees down, branches twisted, splintered. The Tonkawas had vanished without a trace. Whatever casualties the storm had inflicted on them, it was clear they'd abandoned this cursed ground. We knew they had suffered because the dead man blown into our hiding place had worn the distinct hide cuirass marking him as one of their raiders.

They probably resumed their trek south as soon as the rain let up. Our horses had disappeared just as thoroughly. The rain had obliterated any tracks, and there was no way to trace them. It struck me as oddly cruel, the way fate had thrown that spotted stallion in my path twice, only to whisk him away without warning once his role was fulfilled. I hope that Sunkawakan-kedeshka and his mares escaped the fury of the storm and lived out their days wild and free, leading their herd across the endless prairies. But that's a hope, no more. Destiny had its purpose for him. He served his silent role and moved on.

I like to believe—and maybe it's just from spending too much time around the old tales of the Native Americans—that in the shadowy world beyond, a place where both red man and white believe spirits dwell, a man will find the brave beasts that loved him back on Earth. There, I might ride through fields of asphodels again, feeling between my legs the spirit of what once was Sunkawakan-kedeshka. I would feel the powerful muscles throb and strain, just as they had under my reins, the velvet ear twitching for a kind word or drooping from a scold. But maybe that's just an old man's dream.

Now, consider our situation. We, who had been so hounded by fate, were once again at its mercy. Once we were prisoners, then free but unarmed; today we were at liberty and armed, but our horses—the ones we depended on to cross the plains—were gone. Also, we were desperate for food, having not eaten since noon the previous day. I won't emphasize our nakedness; Annalla, being Native, was used to it, and Marcus and I had grown accustomed to it through years of exposure. We managed to save enough clothing for Trisha, though she resented being singled out, as she was just as ready to endure hardship as any of us.

Marcus solved our food problem, much to our relief. He insisted, and eventually proved, that the flesh of the horses killed by the storm was still edible. We ate it without excitement—tough, stringy meat, soaked through with moisture—but it kept us going. We dug up our cache of weapons, examining them carefully. We were able to rearm ourselves, with Marcus taking it upon himself to carry the extra quivers of arrows. We discarded the two hide cuirasses—clumsy garments made from the thick neck-hide of buffalo, slowly dried by fire—as they were too hot, too confining, and reeked of their former owners.

We tossed the knives and tomahawks we couldn't use into the stream, keeping only four of each, all made from fine Spanish steel and likely acquired by the Tonkawas from the Apache or other southern tribes. We had grown tired of eating horse meat and were desperate to leave behind a land so cursed with bad luck for us. So, after testing our bows and drinking deeply from the murky water that churned through the ravine, we set out northeast, with the intention of tracing back to the river we had been following since leaving the eastern edges of the Sky Mountains.

Our decision to follow this course was fueled by the same reasons that had guided us earlier: fear of straying too far from water, a higher likelihood of finding game near a river, and having a natural guide in this untamed expanse. Sure, we knew the risk of running into hostile tribes was greater near a substantial river, but that was a gamble we had to accept. We vowed to be doubly alert after our encounters with the Comanches and Tonkawas.

For three days, we shadowed the river, maintaining a course several miles to the south of it and approaching its banks only when we needed water. During this period, we survived on hares and a small prairie-dwelling animal that lived in burrows, along with a few fish that Annalla caught using a bone hook he crafted himself and a rawhide string from Trisha's shirt. We didn't see any other humans or large animals; the land seemed to have been swept clean by the storm.

On the fourth day, we began to spot buffalo, and we feasted contentedly on the succulent hump of a young cow that Annalla managed to shoot. The change in diet was a sheer delight. But, little did we know, the buffalo would be our downfall.

The scattered herds we first saw were just the tip of a much larger swarm, grazing its way north. Not wanting to get stuck in their slow advance, we crossed the river to the north bank and rushed east, aiming to outflank the main mass. We managed to do this, and then figured we'd stay on that side of the river. After all, we knew we were far south of where we needed to hit the Mississippi, and really should be heading slightly north of east.

This decision, while wise, soon brought new troubles upon us—though, in the end, it saved us. Had we stayed on the south bank, we might've faced our enemies differently, but then this tale would've taken another twist—a testament to Destiny's relentless grip on our lives. Blinded by our hurry and the isolation left in the storm's wake, we missed the glaring bait a massive herd sets for any tribe with scouts in the area. But, guided by accident or Destiny, we pressed on north of the river, sticking to our plan to avoid its visible path and scout the terrain ahead carefully. We never considered what might be behind us, and were stunned when Trisha, lazily scanning the horizon from a gentle rise that broke the flat plain's monotony, grabbed Annalla's arm and pointed westward, speechless, terror and disbelief etched on her face.

It was mid-morning, on a warm, bright summer day—not too warm to stir the dancing heat haze that could play strange tricks on your eyes across these expansive open lands.

The next hill behind us loomed two or three miles away, and over its crest galloped a string of tiny figures—horsemen brandishing lances and blinding white shields. We were as clear to them as they were to us, and their lack of triumphant shouts confirmed they'd been tailing us for a while. Scores of them, no, hundreds, poured over the crest in a wild, barbaric rush, exuding martial vigor, and they could cover ground three times as fast as us. They must've picked up our trail when we headed to the river to meet the buffalo herd, shadowing us with the relentless curiosity and predatory instincts of their kind. All this we gathered in the first mere moment of realization. We didn't waste a breath on words. Instead, we ducked behind the next slope and sprinted toward the riverbanks, seeking shelter in its potential cover.

But the cunning savages had anticipated our move. After a grueling mile, Annalla scouted their positions and discovered they had sent a troop to cut diagonally across our path, intending to cut us off from our goal. Two hundred of them were now abreast of us, less than a mile away. Annalla halted abruptly.

"It's useless," he said, his voice edged with finality. "We'll just exhaust ourselves for nothing. All that's left is to sell our lives dearly."

He turned his face to the heavens, appealing to his gods with the dignity of a warrior confronting fate.

"Oh, Hawenneyu," he called out, "and you too, Honochenokeh, have you led Annalla through all perils to reclaim his Lost Soul, only to abandon him now to Hanegoategeh? Look, Annalla calls upon you for aid. And you, Deohako, Three Sisters of Sustenance, Our Supporters! Annalla invokes your names by right.

"Will you desert him now, after all he's toiled and suffered?"

Will you abandon your white brothers—those who've stood by you through perils no one else dared face? Will you forsake the Lost Soul who's remained true even in death, who returns from the land beyond the sunset, the one who's navigated the Halls of Haniskaonogeh, the Dwelling-place of Evil? She has passed with us through the lodge of Gaoh, lord of the winds, and defied Hanegoategeh.

"Oh, Tharon the Sky-holder, Annalla calls upon you to support him! But if death must come, then, oh, Hawenneyu, let Annalla and his Lost Soul die together! Let the white brothers accompany us to the Halls of the Honochenokeh! Let us take with us the spirits of many warriors! Grant us a good death, oh, Hawenneyu!"

I'm a Christian, yet that prayer sent a thrill down my spine. I shouted "Yo- hay!" just like the People of the Long House. Trisha notched an arrow and sent it soaring into the sky.

"Whatever the gods decide, we fight," she declared. "We fight where the arrow lands."

It thudded into the ground a hundred yards ahead, right below the crest of the rise.

"Yeah, that's as good a spot as any," Marcus said calmly. "And now, we fight, right?"

We jogged over to the arrow and gathered around it just as the attacking flank burst over the crest between us and the river. Their triumphant whoops filled the air as they realized they had boxed us in. One warrior spurred his pony into frantic circles, signaling the main group that they had us trapped, while the rest charged to engage us. Within minutes, they had formed a tightening ring, drawing closer and closer, into bowshot range. Of all the tribes we had encountered, these men were the most striking—tall, broad-shouldered, their bronze skin gleaming with grease. They sat on their pad-saddles without stirrups as if they were extensions of the horses beneath them.

Their heads were shaved clean, except for a narrow strip from forehead to scalplock, stiffened with paint and grease until it stood upright like a devilish horn. Their faces were both fierce and intelligent, and they showcased their reckless bravery by how effortlessly they overpowered us. As archers, they were unparalleled. We began shooting as soon as we thought we had the slightest chance of hitting them, but they clung to their horses, shooting not only from the opposite sides but sometimes even from under their bellies. Laden with lances and shields, they still managed to send back arrow for arrow, and we avoided their deadly aim only by darting around like desperate ghosts. It was clear in an instant—against these demons, any hope of winning an archery duel was a fool's delusion. When they appeared in no hurry to press the attack, Annalla suggested we hold our fire. Mirroring our move, they ceased their attack, circling us like vultures around a dying animal, poised to snuff out any attempt at escape.

"Why are they waiting?" Trisha cried out, her voice a blend of anger and fear. "They can't be afraid of us!"

"They're not," snapped Annalla. "These warriors are formidable."

"Who are they?" I demanded.

"Annalla has never seen them before, brother."

"Here comes their chief," said Marcus, his voice low but carrying the weight of dread.

With a thunderous chant echoing through the air, a massive cavalcade crested the rise, row upon row of horsemen, the sun gleaming off their white or painted shields, a forest of feathered lances crowning their horned headdresses. Leading them was a warrior taller than any we'd ever seen, his chest broad like a barrel, the muscles rippling across his shoulders as he controlled the fiery white horse beneath him. His face held the same striking handsomeness as Annalla, with a high forehead and a prominent, hooked nose, but his eyes—they were the eyes of a predator, fierce and vigilant, and his mouth was a thin line of cruelty.

"A thousand! A thousand warriors!" gasped Marcus, his disbelief hanging heavy in the air. The warriors encircling us drew their horses to a halt, tossed their lances skyward, and joined their voices in the resonating chant of their comrades.

Two warriors broke from the line and galloped up to the chief on the white horse, urgent whispers turned shouts, wild gestures slicing through the air like knives. You could almost feel the weight of their fear. The chief lifted his hand, and the chant died away. He spurred his horse forward, flanked by the two messengers, and stopped within shouting distance of us. Annalla stepped up to confront him, confidence radiating from his every move. It was clear that the power of the keepers of the Western Door stood behind him.

"Who are you?" he demanded, his voice thick with authority, speaking a blend of Comanche and Dakota, the same jumbled language he'd used with the Tonkawas. The chief on the white horse seemed taken aback by Annalla's boldness, but he answered calmly in the same tongue.

"They call me Awa, war-chief of the Chahiksichahiks. Who are you, who walks with white men?"

"They call me Annalla, warden of the Western Door of the Long House, war-chief of the Hodenosaunee," Annalla shot back, his tone sharp as a blade.

"Annalla is many moons' journey from his home," Awa retorted, his voice laden with suspicion. "He did not come to our village and seek permission to cross our land."

"Why should a chief of the Long House ask permission to carry out the Great Spirit's will?" Annalla's voice cut through the heavy air. "We have done your people no harm."

"If that's true," said Awa, "then hand over the maiden with you, and you may go free."

"Why?" Annalla's voice wavered with confusion.

"Each summer, Tirawa, the Old One in the Sky, sends a maiden for sacrifice," Awa said, his voice almost reverent. "They say the girl with you is destined to die on the scaffold under the morning star."

"They speak falsehoods," Annalla's voice rose with fervor. "You shall not have her. She is sacred."

Awa's reply was a sharp gesture and a barked order in his native tongue.

A hundred warriors dismounted from their horses, dropping lances, shields, and bows as they charged toward us. Annalla, his face twisted with rage, yanked an arrow from his quiver and aimed it at Awa's chest. But the chief on the white horse deflected it effortlessly with his shield. The flood of warriors on foot forced the Seneca to retreat back to us. We had barely understood anything of the earlier conversation and were left bewildered, unable to comprehend the situation. Annalla himself seemed equally puzzled.

"Fight!" he barked hoarsely. "We must not be captured!"

We unleashed arrows as quickly as we could draw and notch them. At that close range, it was impossible to miss, and we took down a dozen men before they reached us. Then the fight turned brutal, hand-to-hand, knives and hatchets against bare hands. Trisha, as relentless as the rest of us, fought fiercely while our assailants, evidently following Awa's orders, avoided drawing weapons for fear of harming the girl meant for sacrifice.

Back to back, we shielded Trisha, fighting like starving wolves. Our arms burned from the constant slaughter, yet the Pawnee refused to relent. They darted between the legs of their comrades grappling with us barehanded, pulling us down bit by bit. Marcus was the last to fall, a dozen men clinging to his limbs. Trisha, biting and struggling, was dragged from a heap of writhing bodies. The rest of us were hauled to our feet, arms bound, and dragged along.

The Pawnee horsemen surrounded us, their eyes cold as they stared at the dead men we had felled. The chief on the white horse gazed with satisfaction at Trisha's slender body, barely covered by the remnants of her clothes. He grinned as she spat at him, trying to sink her teeth into the arm of one of her captors. He turned his attention from her to the exhausted, bleeding warriors holding us, then to the pile of corpses around the arrow Trisha had once shot into the sky.

It stood there still, an ominous relic at the center of a grim circle of bodies, its feathers rustling in the wind. It had a strange hold on him. His grin twisted into a frown.

"You've made me pay for the girl," he said to Annalla. "Fine. The Pawnee aren't afraid to pay what Tirawa demands. But now, you'll pay your price to me."

He pulled his bow from its case, selected an arrow from the quiver at his side, notched it, and aimed right at my chest.

"Awa will shoot you, one by one," he declared. "After that, we'll cut out your hearts and make strong medicine with them. This white man will die first."

I barely had time to exchange a glance with Annalla and Marcus before he drew the bowstring taut and released it. I'd braced for impact, certain the arrow would pierce me clean through at such close range. And, indeed, the hit was everything I'd dreaded. I staggered from the force. If it weren't for the warriors gripping my arms, I would've toppled over. Instinctively, my eyes shut tight. Opening them, I was ready for a different world, surprised that the pain felt no more severe than a hard blow to the chest. Around me, I heard a collective gasp as people exhaled sharply.

Looking down, I expected to see blood, a wound, something. But there was nothing. No arrow, no blood, no mark. The savage holding my left arm suddenly slumped, and I turned to him. His face had gone gray, his eyes glazing over. The arrow meant for me was buried in his side, halfway to the fletching. He collapsed as I watched him.

There was a stunned gasp from the gathered horsemen. I found Awa's face in the crowd, and saw it had turned almost as pale as the dying man next to me.

The chief gripped the bow tight in his left hand, right arm still raised as if frozen in that moment of release. Annalla's laugh cut through the tense air like a blade.

"Quite the magic your Awa has!" he sneered. "He fired at my white brother from point-blank range, only for the arrow to turn back on the great chief's own warrior. Shall Awa try his medicine again? Do we brew him a fresh batch?"

Awa's arm shook as he stowed the bow back in its case.

"Your white brother wields strong magic," he conceded. "We'll take you to our village, where our medicine-men will work their spells on you. Awa leads in battle; he's no magic-maker."

"We're both warriors and shamans!" Annalla taunted. "Want to see whose magic is stronger?"

Without a word, Awa wheeled his horse around, barked an order, and galloped to the front of his procession. Our guards bound our arms loosely behind us and tied strips of rawhide to our wrists, securing us to their sides before hoisting us onto ponies. Each of us was tethered to a pair of Pawnee warriors. As Annalla was dragged past me, I called out.

"What happened? My eyes were shut. I—"

"Your Orenda is powerful, brother," he replied solemnly. "It has shielded us, a divine answer from Hawenneyu to Annalla's prayer."

I was mystified but Marcus let out a sharp cackle.

"Look at your chest," he squeaked. I glanced down. My chest was bare, untouched. The only thing on it was the small deerskin pouch Guanaea had placed around my neck on the day we left Deonundagaa. It had stayed with me through every ordeal. No Indian would dare take it; they understood that to meddle with another man's medicine could unleash untold evils.

I stared at the pouch, lost in thought—until something caught my eye. There, on its front, was a slit. I peered closer.

Yes, there it was, a jagged slit, like one an arrowhead might leave behind. What had Annalla said?

"Your Orenda is strong, brother."

And Guanaea, what had she pronounced when she hung it there?

"That will shield you against all evils! A most potent Orenda! I had it crafted by Hineogetah, the Medicine Man."

But this was absurd, I told myself! I wore it to honor Guanaea, to acknowledge her thoughtfulness. But was that a reason to succumb to such blatant superstition? Still, the fact remained—the bag had stopped an arrow. How? I racked my brain, delving into the murky waters of my memory. What had it held?

"The fangs of a bull rattlesnake. The spirit to defy evil. The eye-tooth of a wolf. The spirit to resist fear."

The eye-tooth of a wolf! That was it. I flexed my chest muscles, feeling the small bulge beneath the drawstring and the accompanying tenderness. The arrow had struck the tooth dead-on and then veered off into the warrior beside me. How mysterious were the tricks of Providence or Destiny, or perhaps the craft of an Iroquois medicine man?

Chapter Twenty-Four

On the afternoon of our fifth grueling day on horseback, our guards moved us up from the middle of the column to ride next to Awa. The chief had gradually emerged from his dazed wonder; he'd half-expected me to keep working miracles. Now, he eyed us with a dark satisfaction.

"Soon, we'll enter the villages of my people," he announced, sweeping his arm toward the endless prairie ahead. "The medicine men of the Chahiksichahiks will test the white man's medicine, and we'll build a scaffold where the red maiden will lie when she weds the morning star."

"That remains to be seen," Annalla replied, her arrogance unwavering. "A voice whispered to me that the Great Spirit has other plans. It says the Horn-wearers will face misfortune if they sacrifice the red maiden."

Awa's expression turned grim.

"We shall see," he muttered, spurring his horse forward.

Feathered lances bobbed overhead as our retinue of fierce horsemen trotted out of a shallow gully onto the banks of a substantial river.

About a mile east, sitting back from the high-water mark, a series of low, humpbacked mounds stood. At first, I thought they were natural features of the land, but as we neared, people emerged from them. They were homes, partially dug from the earth, roofed and walled with sod. These were roomy dwellings, larger than the biggest teepees and always round in shape.

The people who greeted us were the elderly, with the occasional young child just learning to walk. Awa barked a question to the first group, and one of the old men gave a trembling reply, pointing downriver where the sod-covered mound homes stretched out of sight. With a curt nod, the chief kicked his horse into a gallop, and we sped along a rough trail that led between the houses and the riverbank. Beyond the homes were simple gardens, and behind them, horses grazed. Packs of dogs scurried out, barking at us as we raced by.

However, in every village we passed, we saw no adults in their prime or children playing about. The mystery of these ghost towns started to unravel three miles later when an immense crowd of natives materialized at the heart of the largest cluster of mud huts we'd encountered. There must have been ten or twelve thousand people crammed together, men, women, and children alike, all fixated on a spectacle hidden from our view. But the pounding of hooves from Awa's posse snagged their attention, causing the crowd to part like a living sea, allowing our column to snake its way through and stop on the edge of a hard-packed clay circle, maybe a hundred feet across.

At the center of this makeshift arena stood a blackened, fire-scorched stump, and bound to it with strips of green hide was the dark-robed figure of a man whose pallid face made my heart lurch. It was Black Robe—Père Hyacinthe, the Jesuit—he who had stubbornly walked away from our group at the western bank of the Mississippi, alone and determined.

His ankles were loosely shackled to the base of the stump, his hands tied behind his back. He could shuffle a foot or so in either direction, but a group of warriors were methodically piling kindling around him, the wood already stacked knee-high. Their attention was momentarily diverted by our arrival, halting their grim work.

The priest's black cassock was the same worn, tattered garment he had donned three years ago. His sandals, barely holding together, were patched as if by hope alone. Every line of his gaunt figure spoke of relentless toil and sacrifice. His emaciated face radiated an almost painful serenity, as though an inner light shone through the misery etched into his features. With eyes shut tight, his face was lifted in prayer. Despite being in what seemed to be the final, most desperate hour of his life, his suffering body somehow conveyed an unearthly joy beyond mortal words.

Indeed, the sheer absence of fear in him, the almost otherworldly dedication, had already drained the savage energy from his would-be tormentors. They weren't used to seeing someone face the prospect of torture without a shred of bravado or triumph, just the serene disdain of a courage that seemed higher than any emotion they knew. I wasn't the only one caught off guard. Annalla clicked his tongue, and Marcus muttered under his breath.

"The Jesuit!"

Trisha remarked with interest, "Another white man!"

And Awa, just as baffled as the rest of us, shouted a question. A group of ornately decorated chiefs and medicine men broke away from the front ranks of the onlookers, clustering around his horse, pointing at us with eyes nearly popping out of their heads. Evidently, they were just as surprised. It wasn't often these wild plainshorsemen saw three white men at once, or so I reckoned.

"The Great Spirit's ways are hard to fathom," commented Annalla. "He's led us again along Black Robe's path."

"Awa will see in this capture a reason to defy my Orenda," I said, not hiding my pessimism.

"No, no," squeaked Corlaer. "All is not well with the Pawnee. Look how they're gawking and whispering together."

It was true. Awa's face was a mix of baffled rage, hysterical superstition, and incredulous awe. His gaze flitted rapidly from us to Black Robe, who stood with eyes closed and lips murmuring in silent prayer. The medicine men and chiefs who had swarmed toward the war-chief stared at us with unmistakable fear. Awa spat out an expletive and urged his horse closer to us.

The crowd's attention was laser-focused on us now, like a pack of wolves circling prey.

"So, where did you say you came from?" demanded the chieftain, using the garbled trader's dialect to address Annalla.

"From beyond the setting sun," Annalla replied with grave solemnity. "I have journeyed to the Land of Lost Souls, and there, I found this maiden who once loved me on earth. She's returned with me to rejoin my household."

"And this Taivo, this white man?" Awa jabbed a finger at me, suspicion thick in his voice.

"He, too, has traveled with me from the land beyond the sunset."

Awa barked orders in the Pawnee tongue, and one of the medicine-men, a vividly painted elder with a face carved by time, picked up the conversation in Comanche.

"It was foretold by the white man at the stake that you'd come," he began.

"That's probable," Annalla replied calmly, not a flicker of doubt in his eyes.

"He told us," the medicine-man continued, casting a fearful glance at the dark figure bound to a tree stump, "that he served a God who'd descend from the sky. And when we asked if he meant Tirawa, the Old One in the Skies, he said no. But when we asked if this new God would come from the sunset, he said it might be, that He'd arrive in a blaze of glory, with the power to bend all to His will. Is this Taivo at your side the God the first white stranger spoke of?"

Annalla quickly translated the essence of this to me.

"Tell them we come to announce the arrival of that God," I instructed him. "Just as the white man at the stake came to tell the Chahiksichahiks that we would come from the setting sun."

The medicine-man and his entourage, even the fierce Awa, absorbed this revelation with growing awe.

"As a sign," Annalla added, "the Taivo, who permits me to call him brother and who is attended by the great white warrior with the strength of many buffalo, showed Awa, the war-chief, how he could deflect arrows and use them against his enemies."

“Let Awa speak for me!”

The war-chief, feeling a ripple of awe, no longer sullen but visibly agitated, acknowledged the magnitude of what had just transpired. His heart pounded with the realization that he was a central figure in a miracle unlike anything his people had ever witnessed.

“But what about the maiden?” he pressed, the practical part of him surfacing. “Didn’t Tirawa command you to bring her here for the sacrifice?”

“The maiden is sacred,” replied Annalla. “She has already paid the price of life on this earth. She comes from the Land of Lost Souls, as mentioned. Would Tirawa demand the sacrifice of one who has descended directly from his own realm?”

The medicine-man erupted in fierce disagreement, silencing Awa's arguments.

"Make them release Black Robe," I suggested, as Annalla conveyed what had been said to me. A hush fell over the gathered crowd, as profound as a deathly silence, as their gazes shifted from us, bound and helpless, to the figure of the Jesuit strapped to the torture stake.

"No," the Seneca countered with a glimmer of humor, "but first, brother, we need to make them release us."

His eyes locked onto Awa.

"We have suffered the ignorance you forced upon us for many cycles," he announced. "We have been reluctant to spill any more of your people's blood. We came here to aid the Chahiksichahiks, to assure them of Tirawa's favor. But now the time has come for us to know if you will offer us the respect due to Tirawa's messengers. Shall we break our bonds and, in doing so, decimate this multitude, or will you choose to honor us?"

The medicine-man lunged forward, cutting through our bonds. Beads of sweat glistened on his forehead. The tension broke with an almost audible snap, but the shadow of something darker still lingered.

Awa, as fierce and imposing as he was, averted his gaze from us. But I caught the tremor in his sinewy hands gripping the horse's bridle tighter than before.

"It's alright," said Annalla. "Give my white brother, the Messenger, the knife, and he will free the Fore-goer, who has stood stoically at the torture-stake, holding back Tirawa's wrath with his prayers."

The medicine man handed me the knife, his eyes wide with innocent curiosity.

"But does a messenger of Tirawa need a knife to cut simple hide thongs?" he asked, genuinely bewildered.

"No," Annalla replied, "but if Tirawa's power is invoked, the thunder and lightning that shake the world could bring unforeseen consequences. The Chahiksichahiks have been foolish. Let them be satisfied with what has happened. If they are wise, they will win Tirawa's favor. If they persist in their folly, Tirawa will obliterate them right here."

He raised his arm, and the chiefs and medicine men shrank back, faces pale.

"No, no," the medicine man pleaded. "We have seen enough. Release the Black One with the thin face. We misunderstood him. He spoke to us like the Comanche and the Dakota, and we thought he was dismissing our gods, commanding us to worship another. We were ignorant, but we meant no disrespect."

Annalla shrugged.

"That remains to be seen," he said. "The Taivo will consult with Black Robe, and speak through me afterward. It is for him to decide."

I stepped into the circle, my movements deliberate, maintaining my composure. I crossed the kindling stacked for what would have been a grisly pyre without our interruption and the twist of fate that followed. The fire-makers had retreated. Inside the circle, it was just Black Robe and me now. He stood there, eyes closed, a murmured string of Latin escaping his lips like the whisper of leaves in a haunted forest.

For a second, I was taken aback by the traces of suffering etched into that worn, skeletal face, the skin stretched thin over sharp bones, the eyes recessed in shadows, and the deep lines carved into his pale cheeks. In an instant, I glimpsed the tremendous toil he must have endured since our last encounter. Who could fathom the endless miles he had trekked, the relentless hardships he had faced, all without the solace of a single soul of his own kind? This thought ignited a sudden understanding in me, revealing the intense flame that was the lifeblood of his existence, the fervent commitment to a cause that overshadowed every other aspect of his life. I felt an unexpected warmth towards him, momentarily forgetting past grievances, and dismissing the barriers of race and creed.

"Père Hyacinthe," I murmured softly in French. His eyes remained closed, but his lips stopped their whispered Latin prayers.

"I must be dreaming," he muttered to himself, in that gentler tone I remembered from another time, when he let the stern mask slip and a hint of his past self emerged.

"Was that Gaston's voice? Yes, I recall—he surprised me once as I read in the garden at Morbouil! Those dear old days! Their memories visit so infrequently. There's so little time left for all the work that remains. Ah, Jesus, the burden is so heavy..."

He opened his eyes and locked them onto mine.

"You!" he gasped.

"Yes, it's me, Father Henry Ormerod!"

"My enemy! France's enemy!"

"Not your enemy! And never France's, unless she chooses it so. I'm here to save you."

"How could that be?" he asked, bewildered. "Are you alone among these savages?"

"I'm alone with friends you know—and one woman."

"Then you can't help me," he replied firmly. "You'd better leave if you can. These people are the most independent of all the tribes. They fear nothing except their own superstitions."

"And even though you're considered a heretic, I can't wish the same death upon you that they're planning for me."

"You didn't show such pity for me in the past," I said curiously. He sighed.

"The truth is difficult to grasp. I honestly don't know. I've thought about it a lot, but I don't have an answer."

I cut the bindings on his arms, then stooped to free his legs. Everyone around us remained silent. His face reflected a shock that replaced the usual tension it held.

"See this?" I said. "They handed me the knife to set you free."

"Incredible," he murmured. He used his first moment of freedom to stiffly reach for the crucifix hanging from his belt and bring it to his lips.

"How did you manage to subdue them?" he asked, his mood soft and humble, a rare quality for him.

"I believe it's through God's mercy," I replied. "But judge for yourself."

I quickly recounted what had happened since Awa proudly led his men into the circle around the torture stake. The Jesuit's eyes darkened and his mouth set in a hard line.

"What blasphemy is this?" he snapped. "Do you mock divine authority? You're no more divine messengers than these savages!"

"How can you be sure?" I asked.

"How can I—"

He stopped, deep in thought.

"Is it just coincidence," I pressed on, "that when you climbed the Mississippi bluff, I stopped my companions from killing you as they wanted to? And is it coincidence that I saved you from them before, and from the wrath of the Long House? Can you still say it's a mere coincidence that we crossed the Mississippi together, and now both face death, yet find ourselves saved through the tangled web of our separate imprisonments?"

"Think about it, Père Hyacinthe! Where does coincidence end and Providence begin? Are you so certain you know what Heaven intends?"

"Can you really afford to throw away the life that's been given back to you? Do you have the right to sacrifice the lives of four other people? How do you know that today's events weren't meant to give you another shot at spreading your message?"

He paused, head hanging low.

"Go!" I urged, feeling a genuine stirring inside. "Say whatever you want! I could stop you, but I won't take the responsibility of messing with another man's sense of honor. The lives of my comrades are in your hands now."

He looked at me, puzzled, uncertain.

"I don't know," he repeated, his voice filled with doubt. "It feels different. You're a heretic, yet I can't make sense of it. God's wonders are strange—I can't even begin to understand—"

"Who does?" I asked.

He shook his head slowly.

"I used to be sure," he said, almost as if talking to himself. "But now I don't know. I had come to terms with dying. I wasn't afraid of the suffering. I wanted to make a last stand, to move these people. And now you say they respect me, that I'm free, that I can do as I please."

"Yes."

"It's too much for me to decide, Monsieur Ormerod. Maybe I'm getting weak. Well, we'll see. But I think you're right! Maybe I have been given a second chance to win them over for Christ. God's wonders are indeed strange! Impossible to comprehend! And you, a heretic, the companion of a savage! It baffles me."

He suddenly stopped.

"You spoke to me first?" he asked, voice tinged with confusion. "There was no one else?"

"No one."

"Strange," he muttered to himself again. "Gaston, I thought I heard the garden at Morbouil! Ah, Maman, Maman! So many, many years!"

Chapter Twenty-five

To my surprise, Father Black Robe wanted to join us on our continued journey East.

"I've said all I need about what you've told these people about me," he stated, matter-of-factly. "But I fear I might lose favor with God if I continue my mission fueled by the heathen superstitions you've stirred."

I pointed out that he'd probably face even more dangers traveling with us once we crossed the Mississippi.

"On the contrary, you'll face fewer dangers if I'm with you, Monsieur Ormerod," he replied. "I need to return and face the discipline of my superiors for the good of my soul. I've wandered too long on my own, and my pride has swelled too greatly. I've flouted the rules of my order in my heart. It's best I head to Quebec and accept the punishment my sins demand."

"Sins? What sins?" I asked incredulously.

"There are sins of the spirit just as vile as those of the flesh," he responded cryptically. "Anyone who considers themselves worthy of martyrdom is only feeding their pride. Enough on this. I will go with you."

"Why?" I pressed. "It's not like you to show any favor towards my people, Father Hyacinthe."

His grim face creased with a rare smile, hinting at some long-buried kindness.

"You are tenacious like all heretics. Why can't I return good for good, as well as for evil?"

I couldn't get anything more out of him. In the months that followed, he would sometimes sink into bouts of intense fanaticism. But no matter how long they lasted, eventually, he would smile with a childlike humility and silently bestow a gentle kindness around him. I don't pretend to understand the transformation of his character, but the fact remains, he had become a different man from the zealot who had once accused us on the Ohio.

He talked to us only when absolutely necessary; Trisha, he ignored entirely, much to her irritation. But he pulled his weight, and his reputation helped us move on swiftly once we crossed the Mississippi.

Still, we had a long, grueling journey ahead before we reached the Great River. Awa and his medicine man, along with the other leaders, wanted us to stay on in the Pawnee villages, and they opposed our departure as diplomatically as they dared, given that they saw us as demi-gods. But Annalla pacified them by explaining that the potent medicine I was set to give their tribe would only reach its full strength after I had left.

Under the Seneca's guidance, this medicine was prepared with great ceremony and considerable fanfare. Trisha had sewn a deerskin bag, and in front of all the Pawnee dignitaries, I solemnly removed the bag hanging from my neck—one that Guanaea had placed there—and repaired by Marcus. With gravitas, I introduced its open mouth into the throat of the bag Trisha had made. After a suitably tense moment, I removed my bag, hung it back around my neck, sealed the new bag, and entrusted it, now empty, to the chief medicine man, with strict orders never to open it lest the medicine be lost.

The Pawnee were appeased. They believed they were now prepared to confront any neighboring tribes and were certain they would never be short of buffalo meat, horses, or warriors. They were willing to do anything for us. When we finally departed for the East, Awa and five hundred warriors accompanied us, forcing an Osage village to provide us with a canoe for the Mississippi.

We spent many days paddling downward from the mouth of the Ohio, battling the current both on the Father of Waters and after we turned east into the first stream. Indian Summer had begun by the time we reached the mouth of the Wabash, our bodies aching with the strain and suspense of each paddle stroke.

We thought we'd part ways with Black Robe then, but he surprised me once more.

"You're still many weeks away from your homeland, Monsieur Ormerod," Black Robe noted. "And if you keep to the rivers, you'll have to paddle against the current the whole way. Why not just go overland?"

"Because your people and the tribes they control wouldn't be too happy about that," I replied with a chuckle.

"Come with me to Vincennes," he offered. "I'll get you safe passage to Jagara."

"Are you sure—" I started.

"That I can do what I say?" he cut in. "I have some authority in New France. You can trust my promise. I'll even accompany you as far as Jagara. It's on my way to Montreal and Quebec."

I discussed it with the others, assuming Annalla and Corlaer would be skeptical. But they agreed without hesitation.

"Black Robe no longer hates those who don't share his faith," said the Seneca when I asked about the priest's shift in attitude. "He's learned we are honest in our beliefs. He's realized that love serves the truth."

"Ja," Marcus added. "And he remembers the time he was a man before he was a priest."

"He's a nasty old ant," Trisha huffed. "Flaps around like a raven. Ugh! I hate him!"

We paddled up the Ouabache to Vincennes without any trouble from the natives along the river. Though the French garrison at the trading post eyed us with suspicion, they didn't interfere. On the overland trek to Le Detroit, the French outpost on the straits between Huron Lake and Lake Erie, Black Robe guided us safely past the hostile stares of tribe after tribe. Annalla's presence was a grim reminder of their feared enemies, the People of the Longhouse. Whether they were savages, traders, settlers, trappers, or soldiers of the Fleur-de-lis, they all bowed and stepped aside at the sight of Black Robe, his gaunt figure and crippled hand lifted in blessing.

Beneath the tattered folds of his robe, he guided us through the heart of the burgeoning French empire sprouting below the Great Lakes. He saved us from countless months of perilous and roundabout travel. From Le Detroit, he led us to the fortress at Jagara, a bastion constructed by the famed French soldier and statesman of the wilderness, Joncaire, as a defense against the Iroquois.

We said our farewells here, in the forest lining the glacis that sloped gently towards the fortress's stone walls. The distant thunder of mighty falls murmured in our ears. French sentinels in their bright white coats patrolled the fortifications. At our feet began a tenuous trail, the Northern approach to the Western Door of the Long House. Black Robe offered Annalla the traditional Iroquois parting gesture. He clasped Marcus's hand warmly, and upon Trisha, he bestowed a blessing.

"There is a special place in Christ's embrace for you, my daughter," he said in the fluent Seneca dialect she had mastered. Trisha scowled back, a look that might have evoked laughter from anyone with a sense of humor.

"We are not Christians," Annalla declared proudly. "The gods of our people are good enough for us. Have they not brought us together again, beyond the threshold of death!"

The priest sighed deeply and pulled me aside.

"Do you ever pray, Monsieur Ormerod?" he asked.

"I have done so."

"Do not forget one Louis Joseph Marie de Kerguezac. He is dead, Monsieur, though he lives. Please, do not forget him. He needs your prayers, heretic or not, he needs them! And I fear the same for Hyacinthe, of the Order of Jesus—a hard man who has caused much harm under the guise of saintliness."

“Oh God, we truly don’t understand what we’re doing, do we?”

"You’ve been tough before, Father," I said, "but I recognize now that you’ve redeemed yourself in my eyes. Yet I believe no man, including myself, can judge you after what you’ve endured for your faith."

He pondered this, clutching his crucifix.

"Who can say?" he finally replied. "I've been too self-focused all my life. Never trust yourself too much, Monsieur Ormerod. Man is flawed. You’ve known suffering too. That gives you an understanding that suffering is worth it, as long as you don’t take pleasure in it. You, Monsieur, went away to forget a woman nearly four years ago, didn’t you? Have you really forgotten?"

It was my turn to reflect.

"I haven't forgotten," I decided, feeling something stir within me but without resentment. "But the pain has dulled. Let's say I've made peace with the loss."

His face twisted with torment.

"Four years and you're at peace! Monsieur Ormerod, I've tried to forget for twenty years, and the pain still sears my soul! I chose the wrong path, the wrong way!"

He turned and staggered out of the forest, his hands reaching out as he moved blindly towards the fort.

"The wrong way! The wrong way!"

Those were the last words I heard him say. Months later, in New York, I heard that Père Hyacinthe, famously known as the Apostle to the Savages, was serving a disciplinary sentence at the headquarters of the Order of Jesus as a scullery servant. On the afternoon of the second day after leaving Jagara, we were intercepted by a scouting party of Seneca Wolves, the Watchers of the Door, who filled the forest with their joyful cries when they recognized Annalla. They eagerly asked for tales of our travels. But their joy turned to sorrow at the first question as they shared the grim news that Donehogaweh, the Guardian of the Door, was on his deathbed. A gangrened wound had festered around the jagged head of a Miami arrow lodged in his shoulder during his last brutal raid.

We forgot everything else in our frantic rush to reach Deonundagaa before the Royaneh's time ran out. The sun had just dipped below the horizon, painting the western sky with the last strokes of twilight as we broke free from the dark embrace of the forest, bolted across the gardens, and charged into the village. The longhouses flanked us, brimming with people cloaked in mourning. Eyes widened in astonishment as they spotted Corlaer's towering frame and Annalla's familiar silhouette. A loose procession gathered behind us—warriors jostling for a word with our escort, women gossiping in hushed murmurs, and children shrieking in excitement.

We finally arrived at the wide clearing by the council lodge. There, just outside the entrance, reclined Donehogaweh on a pallet of skins, fulfilling his wish to spend his final moments under the open sky. A cluster of Royanehs and chiefs encircled him, their faces masks of stoic resolve, their silent sympathy a heavy presence in the air. Guanaea hovered at his side, her eyes betraying the sorrow she couldn't vocalize, her lips quivering. Her gasp of astonishment was what signaled our arrival to Donehogaweh. He turned his massive head, the gray in his hair catching the last of the light, and his fever-bright eyes locked onto us with disbelief.

"Is it truly you, my sister's son?" he asked, his voice a frail whisper. "Do I see Otetiani with you, the white son of my twilight years, and Corlaer with his prodigious belly? Or do cruel figments plague me once more?"

"We're here, my uncle," Annalla replied, kneeling by the pallet and pulling Trisha down beside him.

"And who is this maiden with you?"

"She is your daughter."

"My daughter? Not..."

Guanaea let out a soft cry and moved closer.

"Ranno?" the dying Royaneh questioned. The chiefs leaned in, their stoic veneer cracked by a spark of shock. Guanaea knelt beside Annalla and Trisha, her eyes boring into the girl's.

"Yes, she is Ranno," Annalla said. "Annalla and his white brothers have journeyed to the Land of Lost Souls, beyond the sunset. They have crossed the barriers of Haniskaonogeh. They have stood upon the altar of Hawenneyu."

They had crossed the mountains at the edge of the world, where everything is cloaked in ice and snow. They had braved Dayedadogowar, the Great Home of the Winds. And in the Land of Lost Souls, they spoke with Ataentsic and Jouskeha, as our people's legends foretold. The Lost Soul of Ranno emerged from a pumpkin shell and danced. We seized her and brought her back to our land.

"She isn't the same Ranno I gave birth to," protested Guanaea, breaking the dead silence that followed, while the piercing eyes of the old Royaneh scrutinized the faces of the pair beside him. Trisha glanced sideways at her somewhat defiantly, but kept silent, waiting for any cue from Annalla. Donehogaweh gave a weak nod.

"Of course she looks different," he said. "Who wouldn't, after death? Will I look the same an hour from now? Yes, she is different, yet she resembles the Ranno who once was. And did you truly find the Land of Lost Souls, Annalla?"

It was Corlaer who responded, his voice resonant in an uncanny way when he spoke in the native dialect instead of English.

"It was exactly as the legends predicted," he said. "The maiden had come straight from the Great Spirit's keeping, entrusted to Jouskeha. Ataentsic was reluctant to let her go, but Jouskeha helped us, and we took her by force, with the Great Spirit's aid."

That was a long speech for the Dutchman. I felt compelled to support him.

"If that wasn't the Land of Lost Souls," I declared, "then the Hodenosaunee legends are a sham."

"Yo-hay!" cried Donehogaweh, and he struggled to sit up. "Welcome back to my lodge, Ranno, although you leave it to—"

He choked and collapsed, dead.

"Woe! Woe!" wailed Guanaea. "The pine tree has fallen! The light is dimmed."

Now the lodge was a pit of darkness and despair.

Annalla grasped her hand, his voice catching in his throat. "Look here," he said, his eyes pleading. "You were like a mother to me. I've brought back the daughter you thought you'd lost. In your loneliness, we'll be your children now."

But Guanaea wasn't soothed. "Who am I to reject the generosity of Hawenneyu?" she cried out, a sorrowful wail. "Who am I to question the deeds of valiant warriors? I'm just a woman, a mother abandoned by her children, a widow whose husband journeyed to the land of shadows before her. Yet I can't bring this new Ranno to my heart. She isn't the child I nursed or the stubborn maiden whose spirit I tried to tame. No, all I can do is mourn. I'm an old woman, outliving my time. I will cover my face, sit by the cold ashes, and weep."

With those words, she drew her robe over her head and stumbled back to the lodge she once shared with Donehogaweh, the old women of her clan surrounding her like a flock of mournful crows. Ganeodiyo, the senior Royaneh of the Senecas, leaned over and closed the eyes of his fallen comrade, then stood tall, solemn.

"Annalla has traveled many moons on a twisted path," he said, his voice a low rumble. "He and his white brothers have filled us with pride. They've done what no warriors before them could. There was a stain upon the women of their tribe, but they've cleansed it. It's good. Our eyes are blinded by the splendor of their achievement. Our ears ring with the cries of their conquered enemies. The face of the maiden they recovered seems strange to us now, but we will grow accustomed to her again. Her feet will find the paths she once knew. Everything will return to how it was."

She will seem as though she never left.

"Well, I'll be damned!"

"Marcus," I said once we were finally alone in the dimly lit guest chamber of the bachelors in the Wolf Clan, "did we do the right thing by lying?"

His eyes glinted with a mischievous spark.

"Lying?"

"Yes, lying," I repeated. "Didn't we just support something fundamentally untrue?"

He pondered for a moment.

"Yeah, maybe we lied a bit," he conceded at last. "But all we did was agree with what Annalla said, and that's not exactly a lie."

"How do you figure?"

"Do you believe Annalla believes what he says?"

"Yes."

"He'd die rather than admit it wasn't true." Marcus spoke with an unusual intensity. "You'd never meet anyone who worships the truth more than Annalla. What he claims he saw and did is true, right?"

"Yes."

"And what you can't believe is this 'Lost Souls' stuff, huh?"

"Precisely."

"But Annalla thinks it's the gospel truth, doesn't he?"

"Yes, Marcus, I've already said that."

"Then what makes it a lie, huh? You think the Lost Souls are nonsense. Annalla thinks it's the gospel. Now, between you and Annalla, who's lying?"

"But–"

"No, no, not so fast. Annalla knew what he was looking for, didn't he? You didn't. Why are you so sure he's the liar and not you? You saw exactly what Annalla said you'd see, didn't you? He was right about that, wasn't he?"

"Yes, but–"

"So it stands," Marcus continued inexorably. "Annalla believes what he says. You don't. If there's a liar here, it's you. It's your lie, not Annalla's. But how can you be sure Annalla is wrong?"

"The girl, Trisha Guanaea–"

"Trisha looks like Ranno. And as Donehogaweh said, if she had been dead, how could she look exactly the same? Impossible!"

"But Guanaea!" I insisted.

"She's a woman, and women are strange creatures. She never cared for Ranno before."

"So what do you believe, Marcus?"

"I believe what Annalla says. It's good for him to believe it. It doesn't hurt anyone, does it? So I believe it too. Yeah, that's better!"

Chapter Twenty-six

The skeletal branches of the forest trees cast long shadows over the meadow, lightly powdered with snow. Only a tiny fire broke the monotony of white, its smoke curling lazily into the overhanging treetops. Across the clearing, the rooftops of the village provided a backdrop to the entire population of Deonundagaa—men, women, and children gathered to witness the proceedings. Beside the fire, the seven surviving Royanehs of the Senecas, with Ganeodiyo at the helm, each accompanied by an assistant, brought vibrant splashes of color to the winter landscape. Through the bare foliage, I could just make out the long procession of the Royanehs from the other four nations: the Mohawks, Dagoeoga, the Shield People; the Onondagas, Hodesannogeta, the Name-Bearers; the Oneidas, Neardeondargowar, the Great Tree People; and the Cayugas, Sonushogwatowar, the Great Pipe People.

Though the Tuscaroras, the sixth nation of the great league, had no official seats in the Hoyarnagowar, they stood as silent witnesses, their chieftains respectfully following the procession. Tradition had dictated the number of names or seats, and no Iroquois would dare disturb the foundation their ancestors had laid.

I've been to many ceremonies in my life. I've watched the Pope celebrate mass in St. Mark's Basilica and experienced the opulent, almost theatrical, rituals of the French Court at Versailles and the Louvre. Yet, I've never seen anything as imposing as the condoling council of the Iroquois. This was the ceremony that honored a great man who had passed and, simultaneously, installed his successor. The air was thick with anticipation for the ritual known as Deyughnyonkwarakta, "At the Wood's Edge."

At a signal from Hoyowenato, the Keeper of the Wampum, the long line of Royanehs moved out from the forest and arranged themselves in a half-circle opposite the Seneca Royanehs, the fire between them. Ganeodiyo, the Senecas' spokesperson, stepped forward, his arms outstretched in a gesture of welcome to their guests.

His voice, honed by years of practice, resonated through the clearing like a thunderous sermon, opening with a sentence in the ancient tongue, rich and mysterious:

"Onenh weghniserade wakatyerenkowa desawennawenrate ne kenteyurhoton!"

"Today, I am deeply moved by your voices emerging from the depths of the forest to join us here."

He continued, the rhythm of the greeting rolling off his tongue:

"You have traveled with heavy hearts, overcoming every obstacle in your path. Along the way, you saw the places where those we once relied upon gathered. My children, how can your mind be at peace? You saw the traces of our ancestors; and the faint smoke still lingers where they once shared the pipe. Can you, then, find peace while you weep along the journey?

"Great thanks, therefore, that you have arrived safely. Now let us smoke the pipe together. For all around us, hostile forces plot against our purpose. Here lie thorny paths, falling trees, and wild beasts in hiding. You could have perished, my children, by these dangers, or been swept away by floods, or met by an axe in the dark outside your home. Every day, these threats diminish us; or insidious diseases could have claimed you, my children."

His voice echoed, each word imbued with emotion like a masterful symphony. He recited the laws set by the forefathers, a solemn litany that named the villages of the three original clans: the Wolf, the Tortoise, and the Bear. Then the fire was extinguished, and one by one, the Royanehs made their way from the meadow to the council house of the village. There, Ganeodiyo ignited a new flame, and they formed a wide circle, settling on the robes meticulously laid out by their aides.

Hoyowennato carefully retrieved the ceremonial pipe from its case; the soapstone bowl, intricately carved with ancient symbols, was packed with tobacco. He handed it to Ganeodiyo, who lit it with a glowing coal from the council fire. Ganeodiyo inhaled deeply, then exhaled smoke to the four directions, to the earth, and to the sky. The pipe was passed to Tododaho, the eldest of the Royanehs, the guardians of the council fire that had blazed eternal at Onondaga, a beacon through the ages. As the pipe made its way around the circle, a palpable reverence hung in the air. When it was returned to Hoyowennato, he placed it gingerly back in its case. Tododaho stood, his presence commanding yet gentle.

"My children, today we gather," he began, his voice carrying the weight of countless ancestors. "The Great Spirit has decreed this day. We come together because of the solemn event that has darkened your lives. The one you all depended on has been returned to the earth. In these moments, we have shared our sorrow.

"Now, we must wipe away these tears, so that you may once again see clearly and find peace in your hearts.

"We also believe there's a blockage in your ears. Let us, then, remove this obstruction, so you may hear our words without difficulty.

"And we sense there is a constriction in your throat. We say, let us clear this, so you may speak freely as we greet each other.

"Furthermore, my children, I must speak of the sorrowful event that has befallen you. Each day you lose your great ones."

They were being carried into the earth, blood soaked into the ground beneath them.

"Now," a voice echoed through the chamber, "we say, we cleanse the blood stains from your seat, in the hopes that this place will be purified where you sit."

Their words lingered, a solemn promise hanging in the air. "And now, to prepare our hearts for the wisdom of our ancestors and to honor their greatness, we sing the hymn 'Yondonghs Aihaigh.'"

Almost a hundred voices burst into the somber melody:

"I come again to greet and thank the League; I come again to greet and thank our kin; I come again to greet and thank the warriors; I come again to greet and thank the women. What my forefathers established, My forefathers, hear them!"

The song resonated, every note soaked in the weight of history. When it ended, Tododaho began to pace up and down the council house, his voice rising in a mournful cry:

"Hail, my grandsires! Listen while your grandchildren cry out in sorrow because the Great League you founded has aged.

"Even now, oh, my ancestors, the Great League you established has grown old!"

You use it as a pillow beneath your heads, there in the earth where you now rest—the Great League that you built. Though you said it would persist far into the future."

The hymn was sung a second time, and then Tododaho began to call the roll of the founders, starting with Tehkarihhoken and ending with Tyuhninhohkawenh. After each name, the Royanehs boomed their responses:

"This was the roll of you, You who joined the work, You who completed the work, The Great League!"

Tododaho took his seat again as a Royaneh from the Cayugas stood to speak for the so-called Younger Nations—the Cayugas, Oneidas, and Tuscaroras.

"Our uncle has passed," he began solemnly, "the one who toiled for us all so we might foresee brighter days ahead—for the warriors, for the women, for the children running about, even for the little ones crawling, and the infants bound to cradle-boards. He labored for all to usher in those brighter days. This we, the Three Brothers, now say.

"And now, we Younger Brothers have more to add. You mourn in deep darkness; I shall clear the sky for you, ensuring not a cloud will mar it. I shall grant the sun to shine upon you, so that you may gaze at its descent in peace.

"And further, we declare, should anyone fall—be it a chief, a Royaneh—another will be promptly appointed to fill his place. This we, the Three Younger Brothers, vow.

"I have finished. Now, reveal the man!"

A tense silence wrapped the council house in its grip. All eyes pivoted towards the door where Annalla stood with Marcus and me. Ganeodiyo and another Seneca Royaneh rose from their seats and walked across the room toward us. At a sign, Annalla stepped forward to meet them.

They took their places, one on each side, gripping him firmly by the elbows, guiding him towards the center of the circle around the council fire. Three times they led him around the circuit of Elders. Then Ganeodiyo spoke.

"Denehogaweh is no more, Elders! Tears have clouded our vision. Our hearts are weighed down with sorrow. We've cried out in our grief. Yet the forefathers gave us rules to follow, and we adhere to them even now. A vacant role must be filled. Abandoned duties must be resumed. The foundations laid by our ancestors must remain firm, so our children can thrive in peace.

"Behold, Elders, in keeping with our traditions, as instructed by the founders, the wise women of the Wolf Clan convened in Council. In their wisdom, they deliberated deeply. Denehogaweh was gone. One of his bloodline must succeed him. Denehogaweh was the Guardian of the Western Door. No enemy breached the Long House under his watch. Who among us could hope to fill his shoes?

"The wise women pondered, Elders. They pondered long and hard. They remembered that Denehogaweh had a nephew, Annalla, Warden of the Door. He was his uncle's support, his right hand, a seasoned warrior, feared by the foes of the Great League, respected by the subjugated nations, a friend to our allies.

"Elders, we present him to you! He is no longer Annalla. He is now Denehogaweh! He is the Guardian of the Western Door. Bestow upon him your favor!"

"Aye! Aighai! Kwa, Kwa!" The Elders applauded. Marcus and I quietly slipped out of the gathering as they formed a procession. We joined Trisha— I cannot call her by the name Ranno as Annalla did—to watch the formal presentation to the assembled Senecas gathered in the open around the gaondote, the war-post. A cheer of approval erupted from the crowd when Annalla, now Denehogaweh, was brought forth by Tododaho and Ganeodiyo.

"The Guardian of the Door!" they cried. "He is favored by Hawenneyu! Kwa!"

"Yay!"

Trisha clapped her hands with delight, a spark of mischief in her eyes. Her glee seemed a stark contrast to the dense forest shadows around us.

"He got his uncle's place!" she cried out. "I was worried that old nag Guanaea would cause him trouble. Maybe I'll sneak a snake into her bed one night."

"Don't be ridiculous," I chided gently. "She is your mother. Her eyes are clouded with grief. Show her some kindness, and maybe she'll come around."

"Love me? I don't really care if she does," Trisha scoffed. "I have Annalla's love, and that's enough."

Marcus tugged at my sleeve. "Come," he whispered, and I followed him to a spot behind a thick ganasote tree. He pointed to a narrow opening in the wall of the forest, the dark maw of the Long House trail.

"This isn't our place anymore," he said softly. "We've said goodbye to Annalla. He has a new life now. He's one of them, an Indian. He has a wife and... a mother-in-law..."

"Who doesn't really count as his mother-in-law," I teased half-heartedly.

"Yeah, maybe not. But that's not important now. We're white men. He's an Indian. We don't do him any good staying here. We'd better leave him alone."

"Yes," I agreed slowly, feeling the weight of his words. "You're right, Marcus. It's unusual how you can be so tactful yet so blunt. But where should we go?"

He gave me a peculiar look. "It's better if you go home."

"Home?"

"Yeah, New York—the governor and all..."

He didn't finish the sentence, sparing me from the reality I dreaded. I felt a hollow emptiness where enthusiasm had once fueled my steps. The eagerness for our homeward journey was gone. But I couldn't argue with Marcus's suggestion. The governor expected a report from me. Anything beyond that, I shrugged off. I felt no longing for the house on Pearl Street, no urge to imagine what waited for me there.

A snowstorm hit us hard near the headwaters of the Mohawk. After we secured snowshoes from a nearby Oneida village, we decided to cut southeast through the forest along the west bank of the Hudson River. Our goal was simple: avoid Fort Orange and its settlement, and cross the river where the ice was thick enough to support us. Corlaer knew this wild territory like the back of his hand and never hesitated to carve a straight path in any direction he fancied.

This detour meant we didn't see another white face until we reached the outer villages near New York. The residents there were clueless about the goings-on in the town, having been isolated by heavy snowdrifts since Christmas—an occasion we'd all but forgotten. We had lost track of time altogether, not even sure of the month. For us, life was defined by the seasons. It was either hot or cold, Winter or Summer, and that was that.

The burghers of the Out-ward gave us wary glances, probably thinking us wastrels in our deerskin shirts and leggings, and belted bearskin robes. Our long hair and beards only added to the wild look. We didn't spot a familiar face until we reached Broadway just above

Green Lane. There, John Allen, my clerk, turned the corner and almost walked right past us, his eyes darting with unease.

"How, now!" I called out. "Is that how you greet your master, John?"

His bundle of papers dropped into the snow as his jaw went slack.

"It's really you, Master Ormerod! We had given you up two years ago—all of us, except Master Burnet."

But if it were up to the magistrates, they would have settled your estate long ago.

For reasons I couldn't explain, I was seized by a maniacal urge to laugh. I clutched my sides and laughed so hard that people on the other side of the street thought me mad and hurried past us.

"I'm glad there's at least one smart man left," I said when I finally caught my breath. "But I never doubted the governor, John."

"He's not the governor anymore, sir."

"What?"

Even Marcus let out a sharp Dutch curse.

"Yes, sir. Just last month, the Lords of Trade sent notice transferring him to Massachusetts. He sailed ten days ago."

"He's gone?"

"Yes, sir."

"But who took his place?"

"Master Montgomery, sir. And oh, Master Ormerod, things are very different now. The malcontents in town have the new governor's ear. There's a lot of talk about municipal reforms and little concern for the fur trade and the alliances with the savages that Master Burnet cared about."

I slapped Marcus's thick shoulder.

"Then there are two of us who'll give Master Montgomery something to think about," I declared. "We'll tell him about the Wilderness Country, eh, Marcus? We'll enlighten him on the French's doings!

We'll show him the empires and kingdoms waiting for the Englishman, if he has the courage of his ancestors!"

"Nein," said Marcus. "You go."

"But you?"

"I go with John here."

"Suit yourself," I said with a nonchalant wave. "Shall I find the governor in the fort, John?"

"Yes, sir." He hesitated. "But surely, Master Ormerod, you'll stop by Pearl Street. Elspeth and..."

"Soon, soon," I said airily. "I'm not much of a homebody, John."

And I swaggered on, poor fool that I was, secretly dreading the memories Pearl Street might stir up. At the fort, an officer recognized me and ushered me into the governor's house with a speed that made the hour I spent cooling my heels in his anteroom all the more frustrating. But all things come to an end, even the whims of petty officials.

A liveried servant opened the inner door, and I found myself ushered into a room that screamed of its occupant's obsession with minute, finicky details. Master Montgomery, a small man with an air of puffed-up importance and features that spoke of vanity and pride, did little to hide his disdain at seeing me dressed so rudely in my motley forest clothes.

"Master Ormerod?" he said with obvious distaste. "Ah, yes, I know who you are. The late governor left some notes about you and the absurd mission he sent you on. Almost four years now, correct? You've been gone far too long, sir."

"One moment," I interjected. "You deem my mission absurd. Do you grasp the significance of the information I bring back? Does it mean nothing to you that I have intelligence on the French positions in the Wilderness Country?"

He silenced me with a dismissive hand wave.

"You're giving undue importance to your adventures, Master Ormerod," he admonished. "Here, we have enough work to occupy us for generations. The failures of my predecessor—I must frankly state—stemmed from his unfortunate inclination towards extravagant ambitions and policies. I assure you, those days are behind us. In New York, we're focused on improving the lives of our loyal, law-abiding citizens and removing obstacles to trade and commerce."

He picked up a document from the pile on the table.

"I have a draft of the new charter I'm issuing to our citizens! Such matters have been neglected for far too long, and it falls upon me to remedy that neglect."

"Do I understand correctly that you have no interest in my report, your Excellency?" I interrupted.

"Some other time, Master Ormerod. At the moment, I am engrossed in matters of grave importance."

"But the French—"

"Tut, tut, sir," he cut me off sharply. "You place too much emphasis on the French."

My predecessor had a habit of blowing the animosity of the French way out of proportion. Treat them fairly, live and let live—that's my motto. I have no issue with the French expanding. There's enough land for everyone on this continent. And as for the nearby natives, we've coddled them more than we should. From now on—

I don't remember how I got out of that room, but somehow I managed to stem the flow of pompous prattle and futile arguments. I brushed past everyone in the fort who tried to stop me and found my way to Pearl Street along the well-worn paths. Anger still boiled in my veins as I reached the red-brick house. I knocked, but no one answered, so I pushed the door open and stepped into the wide hallway. I called out, but the house stood silent, unyielding. Then, from the rear garden, I heard a bubbling chuckle followed by Corlaer's high-pitched laughter. It was a sound that clanged like a secret hammer against my heart. I caught my breath and moved softly through the corridor to the door that led to the garden.

On the steps below me sat stout Scots Elspeth and John Allen, both of them doubled over with laughter despite the falling snow. In the center of the garden, a small, lively kid in breeches, gripping a wooden scalping knife in a mittened hand, circled the towering figure of Corlaer, who managed an impressively believable imitation of terror.

"And now I shall scalp you!" the child shrieked in delight. But Marcus signaled him towards me, and the boy turned with a joyous cry. The knife slipped from his hand, and two little feet scrabbled in the snow as two small arms reached up to me, two brown eyes—eyes that felt hauntingly familiar—gazed into mine.

"You're back!" the high-pitched voice exclaimed. "John said you would be! So did Master Burnet! Do you always have a beard? Will you buy me clothes like the ones you and Marcus wear?"

"Can you teach me to throw a tomahawk and shoot a bow and arrow? Will you take me to live with the Indians? Did you kill many this time? What did you find beyond the sunset?"

I swept him up in my arms, my gray eyes steady despite the mist that clouded my vision.

"I found contentment and love," I said. Elspeth burst into tears.

"Oh, but those are beautiful words," she blubbered. "The master's home and right in his mind again!"

My son's laughter rang out, bubbling and infectious. I peered over his shoulder to see Corlaer waltzing awkwardly, like a clumsy bear, clutching John Allen tightly against his massive belly. And then I sat down beside my boy and laughed—laughed like I hadn't in years, with the pure, unrestrained joy of a happy heart.

THE END.

Printed in Great Britain
by Amazon

59017582R10169